# THE WINNER'S GAME

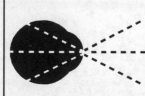

This Large Print Book carries the
Seal of Approval of N.A.V.H.

# THE WINNER'S GAME

## KEVIN ALAN MILNE

**WHEELER PUBLISHING**
*A part of Gale, Cengage Learning*

GALE
CENGAGE Learning·

Farmington Hills, Mich • San Francisco • New York • Waterville, Maine
Meriden, Conn • Mason, Ohio • Chicago

**GALE**
CENGAGE Learning®

**LIBRARY OF CONGRESS CATALOGING-IN-PUBLICATION DATA**

Milne, Kevin Alan.
   The winner's game / by Kevin Alan Milne. — Large print edition.
    pages ; cm — (Wheeler publishing hardcover)
    ISBN 978-1-4104-7094-2 (hardcover) — ISBN 1-4104-7094-6 (hardcover)
   1. Families—Fiction. 2. Teenage girls—Family relationships—Fiction. 3. Heart—Diseases—Patients—Fiction. 4. Marital conflict—Fiction. 5. Life change events—Fiction. 6. Large type books. I. Title.
   PS3613.I5919W46 2014b
   813'.6—dc23                         2014014427

Published in 2014 by arrangement with Center Street, a division of Hachette Book Group, Inc.

*In remembrance of Zoe.*
*Half a heart . . . full of love.*

For where your treasure is,
there will your heart be also.

# Prologue:
## Ann

Nine lousy minutes. That's how long it takes the doctor to deliver the bad news. You'd think something like this would be an all-day affair, with lots of pomp and circumstance and maybe a condolence or two for what lies ahead. Nope, he's all business.

Oh well. It's not like I wasn't expecting it, and I certainly know what all the ramifications will be, because this is the exact outcome I was hoping to avoid.

Now it's unavoidable.

After the doctor briefs us on a few details, my mom rushes out of the room sobbing. When she returns half an hour later, she hands me a brand-new diary.

*A diary?*

I thought maybe some chocolate or a new outfit to cheer me up. But no, a diary and a pen. She says no matter what happens — good or bad — she wants me to remember the next few months. "Make it your memoir," she says. "Document the beauty of each new day. Paint a picture with your words."

*Uh . . . OK.* My younger sister, Bree, is the artist in the family, but given the circumstances, I see why my mom would want me to put my thoughts and feelings on paper.

*For posterity . . . should I have any.*

There's a nurse in the room with us when Mom gives it to me, and she agrees that patients in my situation sometimes find it helpful to write down what they've been through — or what they're still going through — because it can help them come to grips with the possible outcomes. She says psychologists call it "expressive therapy."

*Perfect . . . now I'm my own therapist.*

Just to make sure I'm doing it right, I ask the nurse if I should just start writing from today forward, or if I should look back at the past. In order to really sort everything out in my head, she suggests I start at the very beginning — the point that started everything.

*That's easy . . . it started with the butterflies.*

Actually, the butterflies had come and gone before that, but they were just sort of there, if you know what I mean. Not really doing anything. Then, when I was fifteen, they began to change, like a metamorphosis, getting bigger and more noticeable. I didn't mind the butterflies, though. They motivated me. Forced me to focus. Fired me up to achieve more.

Every time I stepped up on the starting blocks above the pool, I felt their flutters in my stomach. Sometimes they even ventured up into my chest and down into my arms.

My coach told me to ignore the nervousness, but I embraced it — owned it, loved it — because I always swam faster when I was swimming scared.

The year before, as a freshman, I knew I was the fastest girl on the team, but I capped my effort at maybe seventy-five percent, thinking the "cool crowd" would like me more if they weren't always losing to me. That was probably me shying away from the butterflies, rather than leveraging them to my advantage.

Anyway, my freshman strategy was an epic failure, so my sophomore year I took a different approach: Win every time, and don't look back! It didn't earn me any more friends than intentionally losing did, but at least they respected me. *I think.*

The day that changed everything was our district meet. I was slated for six events and had already won the first five, earning three personal records and one new Oregon state record.

The butterflies were on fire!

As I stepped up on the blocks for my final event, the girl next to me was shaking out her arms and legs, loosening up. It was Bianca, the only other girl from my school who qualified for the four-hundred-meter Freestyle final. "Good luck, Ann," she said, which caught me off guard.

I happen to know for a fact that Bianca hated my guts. She was a senior, who didn't take well to losing to underclassmen like me. She wouldn't have even known my name if it wasn't always ahead of hers on the leaderboard. "Thanks. You too."

She laughed and said she was kidding. Then she whispered so only I could hear, "I hope you drown."

The butterflies in my stomach were flying faster now. I focused on them instead of on the mean girl to my left. In a few minutes she could hate me all she wanted, but I'd be the one laughing all the way to the state finals. I shook my arms out, pressed my goggles over my eyes, and took a deep breath.

Right then the loudspeaker guy said, "Swimmers, take your mark."

Swim cap in place? Check. Muscles

tensed? Check. Butterflies swarming? Check. All systems were go.

The buzzer rang . . . and I was off!

In the water, everything felt perfect. This is where I belonged — staring at the bottom of a pool, beyond the criticism of others who don't "get" me. When I popped up from my initial dive, I was already in the lead. After a few strong strokes my lead had grown. The competition was fast, but I was faster. As I came out of the second turn, I got a good look at the rest of the pack — I was nearly a full body length ahead of the next swimmer. I knew right then I could slow down and cruise to an easy victory, but that's not me. I'm a competitor. I'd held back in years past, but not anymore. I pushed harder, churning through the water as fast as I could — a win is good, but a new record is even better. At two hundred meters it was becoming a landslide.

If I listened carefully between breaths, I could hear the clapping and cheering. I had no friends in the crowd — unless you count my family, which I didn't — but I pretended that everyone in the aquatic center was screaming for me.

The butterflies in my stomach had gone largely unnoticed for the past hundred meters, but as I was closing in on the three-hundred-meter mark, they really began to buzz with excitement. They even fluttered up into my chest. Then out of the blue, for the first time ever, one of my friendly butterflies bit me! And it hurt!

That exact moment in time was the very beginning of my nightmare — the singular point that changed everything.

After the butterfly bit my chest, the world was chaos.

My arms slowed down. I was floundering and flailing. Sinking, not swimming.

I sucked water hard, gasping for breath, but the pain was too intense for anything but panic.

The bottom of the pool was clearer than ever, and growing closer.

The deep end that day was deeper than it ever was before.

And darker.

Oh crap, I thought in the final, fuzzy seconds before the darkness engulfed me. Bianca's wish came true! I'm drowning! *Please, God,* I prayed, *don't let her win . . .*

*Fly home, little butterfly, fly.*

# CHAPTER 1
## DELL

Four hundred seventy days ago, right before my eyes, my oldest daughter died. Clinically, anyway. When they pulled her body from the pool, it was limp, like one of the rag dolls she kept on her bed when she was still a little girl. According to the giant timer on the swim-center wall, it took rescuers eighty-nine seconds of CPR to bring her back to life.

Those were the longest eighty-nine seconds in the history of the universe; with each tick of the clock I felt like I'd aged another year. The four-hundred seventy days since, by comparison, have been fractions of an eyeblink. I honestly don't even know why I started keeping track of the lapsed time. Maybe it's because I didn't want to forget the number of extra days we've been graced by her presence.

Or maybe because I've been holding my breath since then, nervously counting the days until the next unforeseen hammer falls.

I remember wanting to cover my son's eyes when the medics began pounding on Ann's chest, but my greater impulse was to rush to her side. I was helpless, though. Impotent. Unable to do anything but watch and cry as they worked on her. Then she sputtered, coughed, and took a ragged breath.

Within minutes I was riding with her in an ambulance, holding her hand and praying to God that whatever was wrong with her wouldn't be serious.

When we finally got word from the doctors, my prayer went unanswered. Not only was it serious, it couldn't have been much worse.

"Congenital cardiomyopathy," a cardiologist explained. "It's a defect she's had her whole life. It's likely that the strain of swimming caused her to have a brief seizure, and then she went into cardiac arrest. She's lucky to be alive."

"What are her chances for a full recovery?" I asked.

"Fair."

*Fair?* I hate that word, because nothing ever is. Fair, I mean.

As my granddad used to say, "Life is many wondrous things . . . but fair isn't one of

16

them." The fact that my fifteen-year-old was in the hospital at all was just the latest evidence supporting this truth. Life is too unpredictable to be fair. It takes from some while giving to others, without rhyme or reason or warning. So don't tell me that my daughter's chances are "fair," because then I'll know for sure they're not.

As if to prove my granddad right, Ann has spent the last four hundred seventy days in and out of the hospital for ongoing procedures, specialized therapies, diagnostic exams, and countless routine checkups. Yet all of the medicines, tissue ablations, and open-heart surgeries have proven fruitless, which is, in this father's opinion, far beyond unfair.

*Life is many wondrous things . . . but fair isn't one of them.* My granddad may have said it, but Ann knows the truth of it better than anyone.

It is nine thirty at night and I'm sitting in the car in the driveway, trying to pull my thoughts together. I know Emily is probably worried by now, but I can't help that. On a normal weekday I would've been home three hours ago, but Emily called before I left work and said I should join her at the hospital for some "new news." New news tends to be bad news, and this was no exception.

Emily and I left the hospital at the same time, almost ninety minutes ago, saying we'd have a chat with Bree and Cade as soon as we got home.

She went straight home.

I took a detour.

I didn't mean to, but as I turned onto Sunset Street and saw the steamy glass windows of the Sherwood YMCA, I had to go peek. I haven't been to a swim center in four hundred seventy days, but this seemed as good a time as any to return. I didn't go inside, though. Looking through the glass was more than enough. The swim team was there, tearing back and forth through their lanes like torpedoes. Ann should have been there too, leading them, but instead she's back at the hospital coping with the worst news imaginable.

My phone buzzed in my pocket while I was standing there. It was Emily, probably wondering what was taking me so long. I didn't answer.

I watched the swimmers until their practice ended, then I slowly paced back to the car. As I drove aimlessly around town for another thirty minutes, my thoughts were sunk with the weight of it all. Ann's sickness, I mean. It's not her fault, of course, but the effects of her health have been staggering. Financially, the burden has been huge, but I don't even care about that — there's no amount of debt I wouldn't go into to keep my child alive. The heavier strain has been on Emily and me, which is why I was reluctant to head straight home.

It's like there's this giant chasm between us that neither is willing to traverse. With each new day the gulf grows wider. We talk about bridging the gap, we pretend to do things that should close the distance, and yet each time we're given more bad news about Ann, we seem to end up farther apart.

I look at my watch. It's nine forty. Emily just peeked out through the front window. She knows I'm here, so there's no sense in delaying any longer. Besides, the kids deserve to know what's going on before they go to bed.

"Have a seat, guys," I say soberly while hanging my coat in the closet.

"Ann didn't come home with you either?" asks Bree. "I thought maybe she was coming in your car."

Emily sniffles and wipes her nose. "Not tonight, Breezy."

I lock eyes with Emily. "Did you tell them anything yet?"

She shakes her head.

"What's wrong with her now?" Cade is eleven and is just wrapping up fifth grade. He tends to say what he thinks, so I'm seldom surprised by his bluntness.

"Have a seat," I say again.

Bree is the first to plop down on the couch. She's only a little more than three years younger than Ann, but *sooo* different. Where Ann has always been fairly mature, Bree sometimes teeters on the childish side. Ann is average height for her age, but Bree has always been several inches taller than her peers. Ann likes long hair, Bree prefers short. Ann is quiet, and Bree . . . isn't. Ann likes to think things through before proceeding, whereas Bree is perfectly fine leaping on a whim and accepting the consequences.

Cade doesn't prefer one sister over the other, but he definitely knows whom he can count on for what — Ann for assistance, Bree for trouble. Ann's just always had those mother-hen, protective instincts, not that Cade necessarily always wants her help. I recall once when he was in kindergarten, when Emily and I were away, he jumped from our second-story window with a Hefty garbage bag as a parachute. Who came running out the back door of the house at just the right moment to break his fall? Ann.

And who stepped in to save him in first grade when he picked a fight with a fourth-grade bully named Rick "The Brick"? Ann. And later that year, when Cade thought it would be fun to play Dodge-Car on the busy road near our house, who was there to drag him by the collar to safety, narrowly missing the delivery truck that nearly ran both of them over? Who else but Ann?

It's always Ann to the rescue, just as it's almost always Bree who comes up with those harebrained ideas that get Cade into trouble.

"Dell, you OK?"

Emily's comment alerts me to the fact that I'm staring blankly at Bree and Cade without saying a word. I nod, take a deep breath, and then carefully explain how the doctors are seeing increased fibrosis in both of Ann's ventricles, while the functionality of her myocardium has continued to deteriorate to the point where cardiac death is becoming a constant threat. "They're keeping her overnight to run some more tests," I finish solemnly, "mostly because the irregular rhythm is back."

"Which means what, exactly?" asks Bree. "In simple words . . . so Dimwit can understand."

"Yeah," remarks Cade, pointing back at

her, "so me and Dimwit can understand."

Emily shakes her head and sighs, then cuts to the chase as tears fill her eyes, causing them to look glassy. "It means her heart isn't healing . . . nor is it likely to. She needs a transplant. The sooner the better."

We've had enough family talks for the kids to know what a transplant means, and it isn't good. "Only as a last resort," we've told them from time to time when the subject came up. "The risks are high, and the outcome not always optimal."

As a wave of dread washes over me, I lean forward in my seat. "I want you guys to know, above all else, that things are going to be OK. In the long run, this will be the best thing for Ann, so we should be happy. And they do transplants like this all the time, so no worries there." *Easy words to say . . . I just hope they're true.* "But what it means is that we're going to need something from you guys for the next several months. Two things, actually." I pause to make sure they are listening. "*Peace* . . . and *quiet.* School gets out in a few weeks, and we can't have you running around like mad March Hares all the time. It's going to be more important than ever that Ann have a stress-free environment until she can have the surgery. Her heart literally might not be able to handle having to deal with some of your . . . well, your occasional shenanigans."

I hate to admit it, but I'm hardly one to talk about having peace and quiet at home. Or shenanigans, for that matter. Before Ann's medical problems, I like to think that I was a pretty decent husband and father — calm, caring, fun to be around, that sort of thing. But nearly eighteen months of dealing with the uncertainty of the situation has taken its toll. Sometimes I blow up at the kids for the littlest things, such as accidentally spilling water on the floor or forgetting to flush the toilet. Once or twice I've heard Emily trying to cover for me, telling them I'm just overly stressed from work, but we both know that's not the only thing eating at me. This chasm between Emily and me, it just has me constantly on edge. Her too. Sometimes I feel like so much of our focus is on Ann that there's not much left for each other. Emotionally, we're tapped out. We're both still going through the motions of being parents, but somehow we've forgotten to be a couple. The result has been an increasingly dysfunctional relationship, including more and more frequent outbursts — snapping, fighting, arguing, complaining — from one or the other of us.

"OK," Cade says resolutely. "We'll take it easy. For Ann."

Emily nods her head in appreciation. "She just needs to relax and be happy — 'chill,' as you kids say — and bide her time until the right heart comes along. Then, hopefully, things will get better." She glances at me briefly, then quickly looks away.

*Does she mean "better for Ann"? Or "better for us"?*

"When will she get it?" asks Bree.

I have to shrug. "Tough to predict. She's on a list, so she has to wait her turn. Could be a month before they find an adequate donor, could be much longer. But the doctors are really hoping it happens by the end of the summer. If she avoids strenuous activity for the next few months, she should be fine. But the longer it takes to find a donor, the greater risk of . . . well, let's just pray they find a donor."

"So that's what we have to look forward to this summer?" Bree whines. "Sitting around here doing nothing, all because Ann can't do anything?" Bree's not a bad kid, but she's at that stage in life where she knows the world turns, she just hasn't figured out that it doesn't revolve around her.

"Well, not quite," I tell her. "An opportunity has presented itself, and we'd like to know what you think. As you know, your great-grandmother's health has taken a turn for the worse. Now that she's in the nursing home full-time, she really needs someone to look after things at her beach house, and we've been asked if we'd like to stay there for the summer. We talked it over with Ann tonight, and she would love a change of scenery. It's kind of a win-win — the ocean would obviously be very relaxing for Ann, Mom would get to be near her grandmother all summer long, plus you guys would have the beach, so you wouldn't have to be cooped up all day. What do you think?"

For Cade, it's a no-brainer. "Awesome!"

Bree's reaction, while less than enthusiastic, is no less predictable. "Uh . . . b-t-dubs, I have friends to think about. You're taking me away from them all summer?"

*B-t-dubs.* That's Bree's long way of saying "b-t-w," which is a short way of saying "by the way." Apparently it's an eighth-grade thing. I tried telling her once that saying "by the way" would be a whole lot easier for people to understand, but she just rolled her eyes.

"Breezy, it's for Ann," Emily replies.

"It's always for Ann," she groans.

"Your friends will still be here when you

get back, Bree," I interject. "And who knows, maybe they can visit over the summer. It's not that far. I'll be coming back and forth anyway — maybe I can bring a couple of them for a weekend."

"What do you mean you're coming back and forth?" asks Cade. "You're not staying there with us?"

My eyes are drawn briefly toward Emily, but she looks away again. "Actually," I reply pensively, "that's the other thing we wanted to talk to you about. I know it's not ideal, but I won't be able to be there the whole time with you guys. I'll go for a day or so at the start, to get you settled in, but then I've got to come back to Portland. I've got a lot going on at work right now, but I'll come visit as often as I can on the weekends."

I hate lying to the kids. The truth is, Emily and I agreed we needed some space. Well . . . I agreed. Emily is mostly just going along.

I look her way again. She wipes at something in her eye, then forces a weary smile and bravely tells the kids, "We'll make do when he's not around. The important thing is that Ann gets away for a little bit. She's always loved the ocean."

"You guys aren't like . . . separating or anything . . . are you? Because that would be totes lame."

"Totes," I recently learned, is the lazy-teen vernacular for "totally." And she's right, separating would be "totes lame." Maybe that's why we're not calling it a separation. It's more just . . . an opportunity for some space.

Sadly, it isn't the first time in the past year that that particular question has been voiced in our home. It usually comes up after one of our arguments, during those awkward moments when we're still not speaking to each other.

"Oh, heaven's no," Emily gushes. "This is just . . . given the circumstances and every-thing . . . and let's not forget it will be a good change of pace for everyone. So even if it's not the perfect situation, at least we'll be together as a family on weekends."

"Absolutely," I chime in, trying to be posi-tive for the sake of the kids. "As many weekends as I can break away." I focus on Bree, then ask, "Why would you ask that, sweetheart?"

She shrugs. "I dunno. Just making sure."

Emily scoots closer to Bree on the couch and puts an arm around her. "It's been a really hard year, Breezy, and your father and I have certainly felt the strain that comes with adversity. But we love each other very much. So, other than Ann's well-being, there's nothing to worry about."

Bree gives a nod that she understands, but I'm not sure that she completely bought it. "Um, OK." She pauses momentarily, and then says, "New topic. Is it OK for Ann to be so far away from here if a heart becomes available?"

I glance at Cade, who looks a little squeamish. Talking about hearts so casually has never been easy for him. The unstated reality of his sister's remark, which he only recently fully grasped, is that a human heart only "becomes available" when its owner no longer requires it. Even as a macho eleven-year-old boy, he still clearly finds the thought unsettling.

"The doctors say it's fine," I explain. "She'll have a pager on her at all times, and if we get a page — *when* we get a page — we'll just need to get to the hospital within a few hours. Cannon Beach is only seventy-five miles away, so we have a little buffer. And in many cases, the donor is on life support, so they wouldn't harvest the heart until we arrive. Worst case, they could arrange an ambulance service to get Ann there sooner if needed. But the doctor says the benefit of spending some relaxing time away at the beach far outweighs any risk of being farther away."

I can't help but notice Cade cringing when I say "harvest," as though we're talking about picking vegetables from a garden.

There is a momentary pause in the conversation, then Emily gently says, "Cade, you look like something's on your mind. Care to share?"

"Just thinking about Ann, I guess. She sometimes gets on my nerves and all that, but . . . I just hope she's gonna be all right." Without blinking, he asks, "She is gonna be all right, isn't she, Mom?"

Emily's eyes start to fill up once more. She looks down briefly and then refocuses on our son. "There are no guarantees in life, Cade, so I can't make any promises. The situation isn't bleak, but neither is it rosy." She stops to collect herself. "Ann understands the possible outcomes, and she's trying hard to process that right now. But I'll tell you what, I have no intentions of losing her. I have to believe there's a heart out there just waiting to be shared by someone who God calls home. When we go to the beach, we all just need to love her and allow her to enjoy it, and give her the peaceful, restful environment that she needs. The rest is in God's hands."

"Mom . . . ," Cade says hesitantly, as

though unsure how to voice what he's feeling. "I hope God has big hands."

# CHAPTER 2
# BREE

My entire life is a solar eclipse. Have you ever seen one, when the moon passes between the earth and the sun, blocking out all of the glorious light? Yeah, that is *so* my life. I'm the sun, Ann is the moon, and she's always getting in my way. It's not that I'm not sympathetic to her very real, very unfortunate situation, but when will it be my turn to shine?

Mom and Dad say I have middle-child syndrome. I looked that up once, and I'm not so sure I do. I think I just have "undernoticed-child syndrome," which is not even anything, 'cuz I just made it up, but it sounds like what I feel sometimes.

If I did happen to develop middle-child syndrome, though, I guess it wouldn't be like a big shock or anything. I mean, everything about me screams "middle"! Even my name is in the middle, and not by coincidence. My parents named us alphabetically from oldest to youngest — Ann, Bree, and Cade. Recently, though, Dad joked that they actually named us after the letter grades we would earn in school. I laughed when he said it, but in retrospect, it isn't very funny. Whatevs. I guess I should just be glad they didn't name me Faith. And b-t-dubs, his name is Dell — with a big fat D — so the joke is on him.

It is early in the afternoon on Sunday, and I'm busily going through the mail . . . with a clothes steamer and a steak knife.

"What are you doing?" Cade is standing in the doorway, staring at me and my tools.

*I knew I should have locked myself in the bathroom!*

"Oh, I'm telling Mom and Dad!" he shouts as he finally puts two and two together. "You're being sneaky."

"I'm not being sneaky. *I'm bored.* But you're too young to understand." I know he hates being painted as young and dumb, but sometimes I just like to get a rise out of him.

"Shut up."

"What? It's true. Bored people sometimes do things that might be mistaken as sneaky, even if they're totally not. Heck, I wouldn't have even bothered getting the mail if I wasn't bored out of my mind for like the millionth day in a row." I pause and smile. "It's because of you, Cade. Babysitting you is boring. You drove me to this."

"Shut up," he says again. "I'm not a baby and you're not my babysitter." He motions to the letter in my hand. "Just open it already."

The letter is from the school district, addressed to the parents of Ann Bennett. It came in the mail with a stack of medical bills that my parents will likely request to defer, since they're already overdue on others.

I slide the knife beneath the envelope's seal and gently peel it open.

Then I read it and groan. "You've got to be kidding! Why does she have to get all of the attention?"

"What does it say?"

I clear my throat so I can read it in the snootiest voice possible, 'cuz that's how it sounds in my head. "Listen to this: *Dear Mr. and Mrs. Bennett. We are pleased to inform you that Ann has been selected as Student of the Year. We realize that she has faced substantial adversity throughout the school year, which only magnifies the significance of her accomplishments. It is no small feat that she has been able to maintain perfect grades during both semesters while working independently from home. We believe her success is a reflection of her dedication and commitment to education . . .* Blah, blah, blah. *We hope you are able to attend a year-end banquet, where she will be honored . . .* Blah, blah, blah." I slap the letter on the counter, just to make sure he knows how upset I am. "Can you believe that? The whole education system is screwed up. She didn't even attend school, and they made her the Student of the Year! I got good grades too, you know! Mostly. Heck, I should get an award just for putting up with her all the time. Right?"

"I guess."

"It's so unfair. Just because she's sick, she get's everything handed to her. *Ugh.* I hate her."

"You do?"

"Yes!" I pause, then back off. "Well, maybe not 'hate.' But not 'like,' that's for sure."

Do I have to like my sister? I mean, I think I love her — not out loud or anything, but inside. Isn't that enough? Do I have to like her too? I bet I'd like her a lot more if her health problems didn't overshadow everything I do!

*My life is a solar eclipse.*

I neatly fold up the paper, shove it back in the envelope, and reseal the flap. Part of me hopes she'll notice it was tampered with so I don't have to pretend to be surprised and happy for her when she announces the good news.

A few hours later, Ann comes home from the hospital wearing brand-new, fluffy, pink designer slippers. My best friend, who is lucky enough to be an only child, has the same exact pair in blue that I've been drooling over. I can't help but howl when I see them on Ann's feet. "Mom, I showed you those slippers at the mall just last week! I said they would make a nice present, but I didn't mean for *her.*" Redirecting my frustration to the recipient of my parents' generosity, I add, "Unbelievable. Every time you go to the doctor, you come home with something new. And what do I get? Stuck babysitting, that's what! *Totes lame!* I hardly even get to see my friends anymore because I'm always stuck at home with Cade!"

"Oh, excuse me for being born with a crappy heart," replies Ann, her face heating up. "Maybe you'll feel better *after I die.*"

"Girls!" snaps Mom. "That's enough. And Ann, you're not going to die. You're going to get a new heart, so don't say that."

Dad is carrying Ann's backpack so she

35

won't have to lift it on her own. No surprise there; she never has to lift a finger. While setting it down on the counter he gives me "the glare." "Remember what I said last night, young lady? *Peace* and *quiet.* No arguing, period. Especially with Ann."

I deliberately roll my eyes. Interestingly, so does Ann. "I don't live in a bubble," she tells him. "If Bree wants to express herself, I don't have a problem with that. I'd rather know how she really feels than have her walking on eggshells."

"*I* have a problem with it," Dad responds. "This family can — *and wants to* — support you while you're going through this. Isn't that right, Bree?"

"Right," I mumble.

"Good. Now, is there something you'd like to say to your sister?"

I don't want to, but finally I say, "Sorry Ann. I . . . um . . . really like your slippers. Maybe someday I'll get a pair like that. You know . . . if I break my neck or something."

Dad immediately points to the stairs. "To your bedroom. *Now.* And stay there until you can be a little nicer."

"What?" I reply, throwing my arms up as I stomp out of the room. "I said sorry . . ."

# CHAPTER 3
## ANN

I don't know why Bree always gets so jealous. Sometimes I just want to scream at her, "You have a healthy body! What more do you want?" But a healthy body isn't the only thing she's got. She's popular, she's talented, she's got a ton of friends, she's got an outgoing personality. I could go on and on. And yet she's all jacked up about some dumb slippers that Mom picked up on discount to give me something to smile about after learning that I need a heart transplant?

Does she not understand that I'm a time bomb waiting to explode, and that I might not ever get a heart? Or that even if they find a decent match, my body could reject it?

I love Bree, but sometimes she gets on my nerves. I wish she'd see that I'm the one who should be jealous of her. She wants my slippers, but I would love to be in her shoes.

Still, I would never wish my problems on Bree. She's got too much potential that would be wasted. People would miss her if she had a heart attack and died. If it happens to me, I doubt anyone will know the difference . . .

I'm sitting by myself in the living room when Cade comes up from behind and pokes his nose over my shoulder. "Whatcha got?"

I hold it up for him to see. "My pager. It's sort of my lifeline. I'm supposed to keep it with me day and night for when they find me a heart."

"Why don't they just call your cell phone?"

"This has a better signal. They can pretty much reach me anywhere, even without a cell tower nearby."

He's fascinated, so I let him hold it. He cradles it gently, like a baby bird. It's all black and about the size of my palm, with a belt clip on one side and a digital display for text on the top. "Pretty cool," he says.

"Actually, not so cool." It's hard to put it in words, but I try my best to explain to him that ever since they gave it to me I have this constant pit in my stomach. I keep looking at it, thinking it could start buzzing at any moment, but then it doesn't, which is nerve-racking. It's like I can't relax with it near me, but I probably couldn't relax without it either, because I'd be too worried about missing my page. Kinda sucks.

"Is that why you're staring at it?" he asks. "Hoping it will go off?"

"No. I was just thinking how — Never mind. You'll think I'm stupid."

"No I won't."

"Yeah, you will. I know you."

Cade sits up as tall as he can. "I won't! Cross my heart and hope to die."

The comment hits me hard, and I don't bother hiding my reaction. He immediately apologizes and says he'll never say that again.

I think about it for a second, then tell him not to be sorry, because I've said that a thousand times too. I just never thought about what it means until right now. It's really kind of morbid.

After a brief silence, I decide to answer his question, just to change the subject. I take back the pager and hold it gingerly in my hand. "I was thinking . . . it's like me," I tell him quietly. "Kind of vanilla. Plain. All it does is sit around waiting for something to happen."

He looks confused. "You're like the pager?"

"Uh-huh. I saw doctors at the hospital walking around with these cool, flashy ones — very sleek and shiny. But they gave me the plain black one. No style, just a little boring."

I'm not trying to be critical of myself . . . just self-aware. It's no secret that I like to play it safe. Apart from swimming, I've always had a hard time putting myself out there, I guess. I'm nothing like my sister in that regard — she's anything but safe.

*Is it a bad thing to be the dependable and predictable one? Or would it be better to be like Bree, carefree and spontaneous?*

I like who I am, but sometimes I wonder. Just once, instead of playing the hostess, it might be nice to be the life of the party.

Cade seems surprised that I just called myself — and the pager — boring. "So change it," he says.

"I can't just give it back to the hospital and ask for another one."

"No. I mean *change* it. Paint it or something. Make it less boring."

"Can I do that?" I admit, I feel dumb posing that question to my little twerp of a brother, but it's really more of a rhetorical question.

"You're asking me? I'm eleven. But if it's your pager . . ." He leaves the thought blowing in the wind, perhaps hoping it will land somewhere fertile and take root.

It does.

I stare at Cade for several seconds, and then at the pager, and then again at Cade. "You know what?" I say eventually. "I am going to change . . . the pager. Stay here." I get up and leave the room without saying another word. In a few minutes I return downstairs with six or seven bottles of nail polish, all different colors. Cade doesn't have socks on, so he quickly tucks his feet beneath himself to hide his toes — I painted them once before with alternating pink and purple, and his friends still tease him about it. For the next twenty minutes I methodically dip and dab until a colorful picture begins to emerge on the pager's black plastic shell.

"Who is it going to be?" Cade asks as a face takes shape on the front of the pager, with pearlescent highlights flowing down the sides and back.

"Just a face," I tell him. "A friend. Someone to look back at me until I get my heart."

In the end, my enamel friend has sparkly orange hair, lavender eyes, hot-pink lips, and French-vanilla teeth. The final touch is

41

a ruby-red heart on the pager's lower-right corner, where the figure's chest would be.

"I think I'll call her Page."

"Pretty cool," he says when I give him a closer look.

"Yeah," I reply, feeling a sense of pride in what I've done. Then a horrifying thought occurs to me: "Dad's going to kill me."

"Nah. He'll only be mad for a minute. He won't yell at you anyway. You're off-limits, at least until after the transplant."

Cade's right. Dad and Mom let me get away with just about anything, because they don't want to upset me in any way. It's kind of nice, but I know it drives Bree and Cade crazy sometimes, because they don't get away with anything.

I lower Page and absently reply, "Yeah . . . until then."

I'm about to get up and head to my room, but a muffled cry from the other end of the house stops me. "Was that . . . ?"

Cade looks worried. He whispers, "I think they're fighting again."

A few seconds later a door slams shut, then it slams shut again. In no time at all, my father comes striding through the living room, tailed by my mom. He's fuming. She's crying.

He's headed for the closet to grab a jacket.

She's maneuvering to the front door to block it.

Neither of them seem to notice us on the couch, so we just sit there, watching the drama unfold. If we had popcorn, this might feel like a movie. And the script would go something like this:

**MOM**
*(crying)*

I can't even talk to you without you blowing up! All I said was it'd be nice if you helped out a little more around the house.

**DAD**

But *the way* you said it! It's like you're constantly accusing me of being lazy! Do you know how hard I work for this family?

**MOM**
*(Tears streaming down her face; she doesn't bother wiping them away.)*

I didn't say you don't work hard!

**DAD**

You insinuated.

**MOM**

This is so stupid! I should be able to ask for a little help without you blowing it out of proportion. I can't do it all myself, Dell.

**DAD**

And I can't have you nagging me every time I sit down for five seconds to rest, just because you feel like something needs to be done that very instant.

**MOM**

Except if I didn't ask you, it'd never get gone. Or I'd end up doing it myself, which is usually what happens.

**DAD**
(pulling on his jacket, huffing loudly)

Are you going to get out of the way? I can't be around you right now.

**MOM**
(somewhat sarcastically)

Right. Just like you can't be around me when we go to the beach, except for (She

44

*drops her voice to mimic his.)* "as many weekends as I can break away." Admit it, you could stay longer if you wanted to.

**DAD**

Is that was this is all about? You pick a fight with me about putting my shoes away because you're mad about the beach house?

**MOM**

No, but you are being really selfish with your time. It's *our daughter,* Dell. You should be around more than just a week-end here and there.

**DAD**

Oh, now I'm being selfish? Really? Did you really think I'd be able to stay all summer at the beach? I have a job, Emily. Is it self-ish to want to stay gainfully employed? My job — and the insurance that comes with it — is the only thing keeping us afloat.

**MOM**
*(whispering)*

You don't even want to come. Admit it . . .

**DAD**
*(shakes his head in disbelief)*

I've got to get out for a little bit. We'll talk about this later.

**MOM**
*(fresh tears welling up)*

Where are you going?

**DAD**
*(glances at us, then at Mom)*

Out.

I hate hearing them talk like that. I wish I could just get up and run out the door myself so I wouldn't have to witness the crumbling of their marriage. But I am held in place by the worst kind of fear there is.
*The fear of the unknown.*
*The fear of not knowing what the future holds for our family.*

# CHAPTER 4
## EMILY

A tunnel. That's how Ann described her near-death experience — like heading down a very dark tunnel, with no end in sight. She said she knew what was happening — that she was dying — and she was looking for a light on the other side. At length, a sliver of light crept into view. At once, she felt complete peace and she knew that all would be well. Then, without warning, she was thrust back into the bitter jaws of mortality, where light was plentiful, but so was pain.

She doesn't talk about the experience anymore, but I think about her "tunnel" all the time. Maybe that's because right now, on the worst days, I view myself in a similar tunnel, looking for the light. There is darkness around me so often, born of worry and fear and frustration at all of the things in my life that seem to be going wrong. All I want is a little light at the end, to know that everything is going to be OK.

*What have I done . . . ?*

I lean against the door for a full minute after Dell leaves, staring at the ground, not saying a word. I know the kids are all watching me — Ann and Cade on the couch, Bree at the top of the stairs — but I can't bring myself to look at them. They must be so disappointed.

Isn't marriage supposed to be about love? Don't we love each other? Why, then, is it so hard? Why am I so weary? And sad? And lonely? And heartbroken?

*And guilty.*

I take a deep breath, feeling my chest swell, then retract. The air fills my soul with a tiny shred of hope that somehow, some way, this will all pass.

*We'll make it. We have to.*

I finally stand erect and lift my gaze to meet my audience. "I'm sorry, kids." My voice is still shaky. "Especially to you, Ann. But please don't worry about your father and me. This is just a little misunderstanding."

"Sure, Mom." I can't tell if Ann is agreeing with my comment or sarcastically expressing doubt about it. I guess it doesn't matter.

I lift my chin and announce, "Tomorrow

will be a better day." Slowly, but deliberately, I begin moving in the direction of my bedroom. As I pass by the couch, I silently mouth the words, "I hope."

The bedroom is warm, but the bed is cold. It's been like this for a while now, and I don't just mean tonight. Gone are the times when we kissed good night, then slept as one, wrapped together, sharing each other's heat. Nowadays, we turn out the lights in silence and retreat immediately to the lonely edges of our mattress, lying awake, neither of us venturing so much as a toe across the unseen middle divide. We're more like boxers in our corners awaiting the bell to fight than lovers wishing for a small sign of tenderness. I know he could reach me if he tried — and I him — but of late, neither of us have been willing.

Tonight, I stretch my arm as far as I can across the cold bed, wanting to touch his broad shoulders . . . but I know the act is a lie. If he were here, I would not be so bold. I would keep to my side, to myself, waiting for him to want me . . . and he never would.

It is almost one in the morning, and Dell has still not returned home.

I can't sleep when he leaves. I worry about him. I want him here with me, even if we're

49

fighting.

Fighting is infinitely better than ignoring!

And resolving our differences . . . well, that's infinitely better than fighting.

I wish I knew what to say or do to get us out of this rut.

I wish I knew how to show him that we're not broken, just bent.

I wish he would come home, walk into the bedroom, take me in his arms, and just . . . love me. Like he used to. I would apologize, I swear it! I would love him back.

At a quarter after one I hear the front door open, then close. Then footsteps across the floor. They stop outside our bedroom. The door opens, and Dell's shadow enters.

The black shape crosses to his side of the bed and undresses in the darkness, then slips beneath the covers.

"You awake?" he whispers.

"Yes."

"Sorry about earlier."

"Me too."

There is a long silence. "So . . . we OK?"

*Are we?* "I guess."

Another pause. "Good night, Emily."

"Good night."

That's it. No kiss. No embrace. Not even any resolution.

*The bed is still cold . . .*

# CHAPTER 5
## CADE

The principal is standing inside the front door when I get to school. "Ahoy there, matey," he says. "Be that Mr. Bennett beneath the eye patch?"

"It be indeed, Principal Smitty."

Principal Smitty is a good guy. I'll miss him next year when I move up to middle school. He's very big on "spirit days" as a fun way to "kiss another school year good-bye," as he likes to say, so every day during the last week of school has its very own theme. Monday was Make-Your-Own-Hat Day. To show my spirit, I wore a giant sombrero made of cardboard and scraps of linoleum I found in the basement, plus duct tape and bright blue glitter from Mom's craft desk. The best part was that it stuck out at least a foot and a half from my head and poked people when I turned. For Tuesday's Pajama Day I swiped one of Bree's pink nightgowns and wore it over a

51

T-shirt and a pair of shorts. I barely got past the front office before the vice principal, an old fart with crooked teeth, pulled me aside and made me take it off. Worse, he made me call my mom (for like the tenth time this year), just in case she'd forgotten what a "special" son she's raising.

Wednesday and Thursday were Backward Day and Mismatched-Socks Day, but in protest over the whole nightgown thing I chose not to participate. This morning, though — the last day of school — the protest is over. How can I not participate in Talk-Like-a-Pirate Day?

This is the best day ever! And I'm a natural! With a little effort, I manage to stay in character all the way until the end of school. When the final bell rings, I'm having so much fun that I decide to see how long I can keep it up at home.

"Avast, woman," I boldly tell my mom when I walk through the front door after getting off the bus. "I be home fer the summer. Have ye snacks to eat?"

"Ahoy, Cap'n Cadey," she laughs. "Welcome home. How was your last day?"

"It be good . . . er, was good. But have ye no cookies or whatnot fer munchin'? I be a hungry pirate."

"Sorry, kiddo. Not today. Your dad is on

his way home right now, and he's bringing a special surprise that I need to get ready for." She turns to go, but stops halfway. "Which reminds me. I need you to find a sleeping bag and an extra pillow. You've been volunteered to give up your bed tonight."

"Somebody else be sleeping in me bed?"

"Yes sir, Captain sir. We've got a stowaway for the night." She winks and then speeds off to her bedroom.

*What the heck is that supposed to mean? A stowaway? In my bed?* "Arrgg," I grumble as I go down to the bonus room in the basement.

Bree's bus hasn't arrived yet from the middle school, but like most days, Ann is sitting on the couch in front of the TV. "Hey Cade," she says as I walk by. "You have a good day?"

I stop in place, eyeing her suspiciously, as any good buccaneer would do. "Aye."

"Huh?"

"*Aye,* said I. It be Talk-Like-a-Pirate Day."

"Oh. Wasn't that just for school?"

Channeling Blackbeard, I growl, "It be fer as long as I want it to be fer!"

"Whatever." She turns back to her daytime drama. When I come out of the storage closet a minute later and toss my favorite sleeping bag on the couch next to her, she looks away from the TV long enough to tell me I shouldn't make a mess because Mom is cleaning the house in preparation for our trip.

It's not too often that I know something that Ann doesn't, so I jump at the chance to share the news. "She's cleaning for a guest, not for our trip."

Now I have her full attention. "Seriously?"

*Oops . . . that didn't sound like a pirate.* "What I meants to say, is, yer old lady dun found a stowaway, and she be sleeping like Goldilocks in me bed 'til morn."

Ann's eyes bulge a bit. "Wow, you're actually really good at that. Annoying, but good. But tell me you're not serious. Someone is staying here? Tonight?"

"Aye. A surprise, said she. And I be booted to the couch like a filthy bilge rat."

"A what rat? Wait. You know what, never mind." She dismisses me and returns to her show.

With nothing better to do, I stay there and watch it too.

When Bree arrives a little later, she lies down on the floor in front of us. "Did you guys hear someone's coming over?"

"Who told you?" Ann asks.

"Mom. Didn't she tell you?"

"No." Once again, Ann looks mad at being left out of the loop.

"Well, did you get off the couch today?"

"I'll have you know," Ann replies calmly, "that I reread *Anne of Green Gables* today. The whole thing. One day. You'd be lucky to get through half that much."

"Yeah," Bree chuckles, "because it would totally put me to sleep."

Ann's face turns a little pink. "Can you just be quiet? I'm watching a show."

Bree jumps to her feet. "This is totes lame. I don't want to start my summer vacation sitting around watching a sappy soap opera. Cade, did you see Dad bought a new garbage can?"

"Yeah."

"Well, I was thinking, before it gets all dirty and stuff . . . you want to see what it's like rolling inside it down the hill at the park?"

"Aye, aye! The big hill, or the little one?"

"The little one is for sissies," she says. Then under her breath she adds, "It would be perfect for Ann."

Ann pretends not to hear.

Ten minutes later we're at the top of a fifty-yard slope. I climb inside the can and hold on tight as Bree gives me a shove. As she lets go, she shouts, "Bon voyage, sucker!" Thirty yards later my head is ready to explode from the spinning.

Ten yards after that I cry out for help.

As I reach the flats at the bottom of the hill and begin to slow, I try — unsuccessfully — to stick my nose out for some fresh air, but it's too late. With the entire world still doing flips in my head, I puke all over myself. *Twice.*

Bree comes running down the hill behind me, laughing so hard that it brings her to tears.

Mom doesn't think it's funny at all. She gasps when I walk through the back door a few minutes later and step into the kitchen, drenched in my own mess. "What happened?"

"Rough seas," I say stoically as I wipe my mouth on my sleeve. "Went down with me ship."

Then my odor reaches her nostrils. "Oh goodness, our guest will be here in ten minutes! Straight to the shower, young man. Double time! And don't come out 'til you smell like a rose." As I make my way down the hallway, she calls out once more. "Put your clothes outside the door, Cade. I'll start a load before anyone catches a whiff of you."

Once I'm good and clean, I wrap a towel

around my waist and stroll into the hallway. I haven't gone two steps from the bathroom when Bree yells, "They're here! They're here!"

"Who's here?" I shout back, picking up speed toward the front door.

When I come around the corner of the entryway, Bree has her face pressed against the window. "Dad and the guest!" she says with such excitement that her hair bounces with each word. "I saw them pull in."

The first thing Mom sees when she joins us from the kitchen is my towel around my waist. "Cade, what are you doing? Go put some clothes on! You can't just waltz around half naked."

At the same time, Ann appears from the basement, stopping one step below the landing. "No doubt. Cover up that scrawny white body before you blind us all."

"I will," I mutter, "After I see who it is."

There's only room at the little window near the door for one person, so Bree gives us a play-by-play of what's happening outside. Well, she tries, but what she says is not very helpful. "OK, the car door is open . . . wait . . . who needs one of those? It kinda looks like . . . no, can't be. Oh, there they come . . . still coming . . . closer . . . Is that . . . ? Yes, it — No . . . is

57

it?" There's a long pause — longer than it should take for someone to walk from the driveway to the front door. Bree finally turns around. "Mom, is that who I think it is?"

"Tell us who, already," demands Ann.

A second later the front door swings wide open. In the doorway, standing behind a four-wheeled walker, is an old woman with funky reddish hair, dark sunglasses that hide half her wrinkly face, and a pink sweater.

"Welcome!" Mom exclaims. "Come in, come in!" She joins the old woman at the door and reaches over the walker to give her a hug.

"Oh, my little Emily! How are you, darlin'?"

"Good, good. I'm just happy you had time to come see us. Can I help you with anything?"

"Well, you can get this durned walkamajig outa my way. I don't really need it. Handy on the plane, though. One look at this puppy and I was the first to board."

Mom moves the walker against the wall, not too far from where I'm standing. "Mom," I whisper, trying to keep from being noticed, "who is that?"

Either I'm terrible at whispering or the old lady has really good hearing aids. Step-

58

ping through the door in my direction, she cackles softly and peels off her shades, revealing two bright blue eyes and more wrinkly skin. "Who else? It's me! Aunt Bev!"

Great-aunt Bev, to be exact — my great-grandmother's sister. That's about all I know about her, other than that she lives year-round in Florida. I don't remember where, exactly, but I know it's within an hour's drive of Disney World, because my parents took us there like three years ago, and we stayed with Aunt Bev and all the other old people in her retirement village rather than getting a hotel for the week. That was back in the good old days before anyone knew Ann had a heart condition.

"Wow," I tell her. "You look really different."

Aunt Bev tussles the back of her hair playfully. "Yes, well, I got a little bored in Cannon Beach, and a beautician there said dusty red is the new gray for old women. It may grow on me yet. If not, I can correct it in Florida."

A lightbulb finally turns on in my head: *Aunt Bev flew out to Oregon to visit her big sister — my great-grandma — in Cannon Beach.* She's been there for like six weeks, mostly just taking care of the house and spending time at the nursing facility looking after her big sister. Now that we're heading to the beach and can help with Great-grandma, she's on her return trip to the palm trees of Florida.

"Out of the way, coming through," says Dad as he steps through the doorway. Each of his arms is weighed down with one of the woman's two large suitcases. He sets them down to close the door, then lifts them again and steps around Bev. "We've got a room all made up for you upstairs. I'll leave these there."

"Bless your heart. Drive all the way out to the beach to pick me up, and then carry my luggage to boot." Turning to my mom she says, "I always said you married well. You love that Delly boy, Em, and don't let him go."

Mom and Dad look at each other awkwardly, then he disappears up the stairs. "I'm trying," Mom says, mostly to herself.

Turning toward me, Bev pinches my arm. "You've grown a bushel and a peck since I last saw you, haven't you, Cade?" Her pinch on my bare skin reminds me that I am still standing there shirtless, holding the towel at my waist.

I glance down at my chest to examine my "pecks." "I guess so," I tell her, feeling more than a little embarrassed. Whatever a bushel is, I'm pretty sure I haven't grown one since my trip to Disney World.

Bev and Mom both burst into laughter. Ann and Bree snicker too. "That's just old farmer-speak," cackles Aunt Bev. "Nowadays, a bushel and a peck just means 'a lot.' "

"It's time for you to get some clothes on, Cade, and cover up those 'pecks,' " Mom says. "Hurry up. Aunt Bev will still be here when you're decent."

# CHAPTER 6
## EMILY

"Would you like to go upstairs too, to settle in?" I ask Bev as Cade bounds up the stairs.

"Heavens no. We've got some catching up to do first."

I motion to Ann and Bree. "Girls, why don't you take Aunt Bev in the other room. I'll fix up something to drink. Are you thirsty, Bev?"

"Yes, but no ice. I can't seem to keep warm these days. Here it's already June, and I'm still wearing a sweater."

On my way into the kitchen, a framed picture on the hutch catches my attention. Though I see that frame every day, it's been a while since I've really paid it much attention. The picture itself is a handmade postcard, a snapshot of a man and a woman holding hands in front of the Eiffel Tower. It has been sitting on the hutch collecting dust for years. I hold it up, smiling, remembering the day the postcard arrived in the mail.

*Those were better times . . .*

For fun, I pull off the frame's velvet backing to expose the other side of the card, which is addressed to me. The French postmark is dated more than nineteen years ago, right before I married Dell. Though I have the words committed to memory, I take a moment to reread the beautifully penned text.

My Dearest Emily,

Greetings from the City of Love and Lights! Your grandfather and I are enjoying our fortieth anniversary even more than we did our twentieth. Life together just keeps getting better and better! Looking forward to being back in time for your special day with Dell. You found a real keeper; hold on to him tight. Twenty years from now, once your marriage has a couple of decades under its belt, I picture you both standing right here in Paris celebrating your life together, while looking ahead to many more years of love. See you soon!

Je t'aime! — Grandma Grace

"I didn't know that was a postcard."

The comment catches me by such surprise that I drop the frame on the carpet. Thankfully, it doesn't break. "Cade? What are you doing?"

"Nothing. I just saw you there and . . . you looked kind of sad."

"I was just thinking of old times."

"Sad times?"

"No, just . . . times." Actually, what I was really thinking about when he snuck up on me was not so much the past but the challenges of the present, along with a future that feels acutely uncertain. The future Grandma Grace predicted feels nothing like the way things have played out.

I could cry just thinking about it.

"Can I see it?" he asks, pointing to the postcard. I hand it to him and he immediately flips it over to examine the front. "That's Grandma Grace, right? And Great-grandpa?"

"That's right."

"She looks so young." He flips it over once more and reads the message. When he's done, he hands it back. "That's pretty neat."

"Yeah, it was 'neat,' " I say, amused by his use of that phrase, which was my grandfather's go-to description for everything. How was vacation, Grandpa? Oh, pretty neat. What did you think of the movie? The neatest movie I've seen all year. How are the kids doing? Oh, you know . . . they're neat kids. Doing all right, I'd say.

"You're smiling. What's so funny?"

"Nothing. Did I ever tell you that that postcard somehow got waylaid in the mail?"

He shakes his head. "You didn't even tell me it was a postcard."

"Right. Well, it did, which meant Grandma and Grandpa beat it home from France. I guess it must've gone on the slow boat. It was perfect timing, though — it arrived right on my wedding day. The mailman delivered it as we were heading out the door to the church, and it was the best wedding present I got." I pause, remembering that day — the excitement and wonder of opening a new chapter in my life, the thrill of stepping into uncharted territory with my best friend, the fear of the unknown. "I was nervous. Every bride is, I think. But that little note from Grandma was just what I needed to calm me down." I pause again, taking the postcard back and glancing once more at the picture of the Eiffel Tower. "We didn't have much of a honeymoon, but I made your dad promise me we'd go to Paris for our twentieth anniversary, just like Grandma and Grandpa suggested." I can feel my nostalgic smile waning.

"That's this year, isn't it?"

I nod. "December thirteenth."

"So? You still going?"

*How do I respond to that?* For starters, I exhale very slowly while contemplating the complexity of . . . everything. The harsh reality is that the twenty-year celebration I once dreamed of is very unlikely. Not only would Ann's health issues need to be considered, but there is also the matter of money. A trip like that would cost thousands of dollars, and as far behind as we are on medical bills, there is just no way. Worse, though, even if there weren't the other obstacles, with the way we've been fighting I have to wonder if my marriage will even make it the six remaining months until December. "We'll see," I say before putting the postcard back in the frame and returning it to the hutch.

When Cade and I join everyone in the living room, the discussion with Aunt Bev is chugging right along; I am genuinely impressed that a woman of her age — eighty-one years young — is intellectually nimble enough to keep even Ann and Bree on their toes.

There is an empty space on the love seat next to Dell. I set the pitcher of lemonade on the coffee table and take a seat on the floor.

"So let me get this straight," says Ann. "Out of the blue, the guy sitting next to you just reached over and took your cookie?"

"Exactly like that," Bev insists. "But not just a cookie. It was one of those fancy biscottis, and I was saving it 'til the in-flight movie."

"What did you do?" asks Bree.

"Oh, for a while I just sat there, completely befuddled. Eventually, though, I got up the nerve to ask who gave him the right to steal my food. He says to me, 'I don't know what you're talking about, lady.' Well, if that didn't frost my cookies — no pun intended. There were still crumbs in his mustache, for goodness' sake, and I saw both wrappers — his and mine — sitting right there on his tray beside the peanuts! So I waited a minute or two, then I pushed the button for the stewardess. When she got there, I asked if I could have another biscotti, because mine had turned up missing, and I also asked for a fresh tea, since mine was spilled on the gentleman beside me." She pauses to cackle, then continues. " 'No it ain't,' the hornswoggler says to me. When he looked down at his shorts to verify, I dumped my whole cup of tea square on his lap! Poor fellow about shot through the overhead compartment. About the time his nether region stopped steaming, the stewardess returned with my tea and biscotti and informed me that I'd been upgraded to first class!" She pauses once more, then asks, "Did you know they have slippers up there for everyone? And steamed towels to freshen up? I hope I can finagle one of those seats on the return flight tomorrow."

"You haven't changed a bit," I tell her. "Same old Auntie Bev."

" 'Old' being the operative word," Bev cautions. Her edgy smile suddenly dulls to a soft grin. "I'm slowing down, Emily. Maybe not my mind, but my body. These old bones are not what they used to be." A sad shadow creeps over her face. "My sister is worse, I'm afraid."

The room is now very quiet. "How bad is she?"

Before Ann's sickness we used to go see Grandma Grace about every other month, and probably more than that during the summer. Lately, though, it's been tough to make time.

"She has her moments. You'll see next week. Sometimes she's there, sometimes she isn't. She's definitely getting weaker, though, which makes me glad I was able to come out when I did. We were still able to talk about old times, laugh a little. It may end up being the last time I get to do that with her. In this life anyway."

"Well, I know she was looking forward to having you around. It's so nice you were able to come for so long."

Bev smiles. "And now it's your turn to get a little Grace-time." She turns to Cade and slaps his leg. "Cade, you be sure to enjoy your great-grandma this summer, while you have the chance. She's a grand old lady."

"I will," he promises.

Knowing Cade, he hasn't given a moment's thought to the fact that his great-grandmother is deteriorating over at the coast. Since he found out we're going there, all he talks about is how much fun it's going to be spending the whole summer playing on the beach. He's convinced that he is going to build the world's largest sand castle, and last night he drew a picture of the kite he's going to make that looks and flies just like a seagull.

"You too, girls," Bev tells Ann and Bree before turning back to me. "I know I've just arrived, but is it too soon to talk business?"

Dell and I share a perplexed look. "What business?" asks Dell.

Bev's purse is sitting on the ground at her

feet. She bends over and retrieves some papers. "I hope it won't be a burden," she says as she rifles through them. "Actually, I know it probably will be a burden, but I hope it's the type of burden that you won't mind." She looks up, her eyes earnest. "I'd like you to fix the place up a bit. It's long overdue for a face-lift, which it will surely need in order to sell it."

For a moment, all is quiet. Finally I find my words. "What are you talking about? Grandma's house?"

"Yes. While you're staying there, would you mind terribly sprucing it up? I think it will sell for more if you get rid of — Well, you know how she loves that ocean theme. But it's a little outdated. More than a little. With some elbow grease and your knack for decorating I'm sure the market value will be quite handsome." Bev winks playfully, as though she's toying with us, leading us carefully down a path. "Grace and I thought you could get more out of it if you put a little into it. But if you want to sell it as is, that's fine too, I suppose."

Dell makes a sound like he's choking on phlegm, then asks, "What do you mean if we sell it? Why are we selling it at all?"

A gigantic smile spreads across Bev's wrinkly old face. "Because, Delly boy, you and your family are loved." She smiles even bigger and shrugs playfully. "Grace and I discussed it, and given all of your bills and whatnot, we want you to sell that house so you can pay things off." She reaches out and hands him the papers. "While I was there, Grace had me meet with an attorney to make some legal preparations for — Well, for when she's no longer here. I did so, and as part of that, Grace already signed the house over to you." She pauses once more, clasping her withered hands together. "It's all paid off and everything, and yours to do with as you please."

All Dell can manage to stammer is, "Oh my gosh . . . Are you serious? . . . Oh my gosh . . ."

I don't even try to speak. With tears streaming down my face I stand up and join Bev on the couch and just squeeze and squeeze.

Just like that, we own a beach house.

And just like that, there is the tiniest sliver of light at the end of my tunnel.

# CHAPTER 7
## CADE

*It's the first full day of summer vacation. Shouldn't I be able to sleep in?*

I guess not, because the squeak of old-woman slippers coming down the stairs just woke me up.

When I open my eyes, Aunt Bev is tiptoeing across the floor in bright-green pajamas and pink leather moccasins. She freezes when she sees that I'm awake. "Sorry," she whispers.

"Fer wakin' me up? Or fer takin' me bed?"

"Oh my," she laughs, "I didn't realize there was a pirate in the family. And a feisty one at that." Bev wags a bony finger at me. "But I be pretty feisty too, young sir, so be ye warned." She laughs again, then asks, "You hungry? Ah, heck, you're a growing boy. You're always hungry."

In the kitchen she goes through the entire pantry looking for the perfect meal. After opening all the drawers and cupboards she chooses dry corn flakes drizzled with chocolate syrup.

"No milk?" I ask. *Weird.*

Aunt Bev gives a disappointed look. "Is that how a pirate would ask? Surely you can do better."

I think for a second and then snarl, "Alas, where be the milk fer yer crunchy grub?"

She claps her aged hands excitedly. "You are too cute for your own good. I bet it'll be good for my sister to have you around. She gets lonely in that facility." Aunt Bev folds her arms and stares at me. "You'll look out for her, won't you, Cade?"

"I guess so."

"Well, if you promise to, I'll tell you a secret."

"What kind of secret?"

"The kind any pirate like you would want to know. A *treasure* secret."

*Sneaky old woman knows just how to reel me in!* "Fine. I'll look out for Great-grandma. Now what's the secret?"

"You promise not to tell anyone I told you?"

"I promise."

"Very well." Aunt Bev bends down close, looking over her shoulder to make sure we're still alone. "In the attic," she whispers, "if you're brave enough to venture up there, you'll find a metal detector — one of the very best money can buy."

"What's it for?" I whisper back.

She looks like she wants to laugh. "Uh . . . to find metal."

A metal detector sounds cool. But . . . "Why do I need to find metal?"

"*Treasure, Cade!* The metal detector will find buried treasure! I know you kids never knew your great-grandfather, but he believed there was treasure buried out behind the house. That's why he bought the metal detector. He'd spend hours and hours out there, combing the beach, just waiting to find riches buried beneath the sand. And according to my sister, he and she found treasure all the time."

As she's speaking, my heart is pounding faster and faster. "You think there's still buried treasure out there?"

"Only one way to find out. But if I had to wager, I'd say your chances of finding something valuable are quite high. Quite high indeed."

"Sweet!" I shout. "I'm gonna be rich!" I've always wanted to be rich . . . and now I will be!

Right then, Aunt Bev and I both hear something. A second later Bree stumbles into the kitchen. "Oh good. I thought maybe you'd already left."

"Soon," Aunt Bev replies. "But I need some help first."

"With what?" I ask.

She checks her watch. "With waking your dad up. He said he'd take me to the airport in thirty minutes."

"I'll do it," says Bree. "I have to go back upstairs anyway. I forgot to take out my retainer."

"I wish you the best of luck, Cap'n Cade," Aunt Bev says once Bree is gone. "A good pirate doesn't give up until his treasure is found."

"Arrgg," I growl. "If there be treasure to find, I'll find it." I pause. "Now, where's the Cap'n Crunch? I'm hungry."

On Monday morning, I really just want to be happy about going to the beach, but my annoying sisters are making it hard. I don't know what got them started, but they're arguing over every silly little thing. Like why a certain pair of socks is found in the other's top drawer. Or whose headband is whose. And something about who looks best in boot-cut Levi's.

*Pants! So stupid.*

Rather than listen to their complaining, I sneak off to a friend's house to shoot hoops for a couple of hours. By the time I come home, Mom has already done my packing for me. "Your suitcase is on your bed," she says. "Bring it upstairs so you're all ready when your father gets home. Oh, and bring Ann's upstairs while you're at it. She shouldn't be lifting heavy things like that."

Ann overhears the comment too. "I'm not an invalid," she replies. "I can get my own suitcase."

"No," Mom tells her, "you can't. Cade, do as you're told, and bring Ann's luggage upstairs."

While rolling her eyes, Ann mumbles, "So lame."

"It's for your own good. Just until you get your new heart. Then everything will be better. I'll let you lift all the suitcases you want."

When I inspect the suitcase that my mom packed for me, it takes me maybe a second to see that she missed all the important stuff I'll need for a summer at the beach. Sure, here are plenty of shirts, socks, and underwear. But what about my slingshot for warding off sharks, or my binoculars to keep an eye out for killer whales? And what respectable pirate would go on a summer trip without a BB gun, buck knife, lighter fluid, and fishing pole? By the time my dad gets home from work, I have all that packed and more.

"Let's go!" I hear him shout as soon as he comes in the door. "I want to beat the traffic!"

Bree is brushing her hair in the entryway mirror when I drag my suitcase up the stairs. When she sees all the extra goodies tied to the outside of my bag, she says, "You know this is not a hunting expedition, right?"

"Mind yer own business, lass."

She gives me a nasty look, then yells over her shoulder, "Mom! Cade's still talking like a pirate!"

"Mom! Bree be a yellow-livered landlubber, and she can't tell me how to talk!"

"Just leave him alone, Bree. It'll wear off. And Cade, don't call your sister names."

I give her my best wicked smile and whisper, "If ye hates me talking like a pirate, I won't ever stop." Then I load my booty in the car.

On the ride to Cannon Beach, Dad makes me and Bree sit together in the very back of the minivan so Ann can sprawl out on the middle bench. I am sure it's going to be miserable sitting next to my sister for so long, but it ends up being pretty . . . um . . . interesting.

There's a lot of things I don't like about Bree, but one thing I can't *not* like is how good she is at art. She's the only person I know who can draw or paint anything. So I'm not at all surprised that she brought a large pad of paper and markers to help pass the time. But after not too long, she leans over and whispers, "Hey, I have an idea." After eleven years as her younger brother, I know what "I have an idea" means. It means she has a plan to do something that we probably shouldn't. In this case, it means she has an idea to do something with her supplies other than doodling sketches. "Check it out," she says.

I watch as Bree takes a wide blue marker and writes a message for the cars behind us to read.

"Honk . . . if . . . ," she says, whispering the words to herself as she spells them out, "you . . . love . . . ice . . . cream!" When she's done writing, she holds it flat against the rear window. Ten seconds later the truck behind us gives two loud beeps. Knowing that our dad will be looking, Bree quickly drops the paper as soon as she hears the horn.

"Why is that jerk honking at us?" he asks almost instantly. "I'm going five miles over the speed limit."

"Because he likes ice cream," replies Bree matter-of-factly.

"Oh. Seriously?"

"Aye, aye, cap'n," I shout.

That seems to pacify him.

After Dad changes lanes, Bree hands me a pen and paper and I write my first message: *Wave if you are nice!* OK, it isn't exactly brilliant, but it does earn a gesture from a large woman in the cab of a semitruck.

"She waved!" I whisper excitedly.

Bree tries to swallow a laugh. "That's not a wave, Dimwit. Unless she only has one finger on that hand."

My sister's next message says, *I like your car! Flash lights if U want 2 trade.* The Mercedes driving behind us quickly speeds past without flashing any lights.

Since Bree has already come up with two good messages, I have to step it up. It takes a few minutes to think of one, but eventually I write, *Sister is 17. Never been kissed. Honk if that is sad!* Within a minute, my message earns five loud beeps from a bunch of teenage boys driving by in a rusty Volkswagen Bug.

"What's the problem now?" asks Dad, thinking he is getting honked at again. "Why are people so rude?"

"It's just some teenage boys being dumb,"

Bree assures him. "Don't worry, Dad, it's not you."

"What are you guys up to back there?" asks Mom.

"We're just being nice to the other cars. It's fine."

"Hey, as long as they're not fighting, I'm happy," Dad tells her.

"I like it when there's no fighting too," states Mom. I can't tell if she is talking about us kids or about her and Dad. From the extra look he gives her, I'd say he is wondering the same thing.

Bree doesn't come right out and say it, but her body language says she thinks my last message was way awesomer than hers. Not to be outdone by her little brother, she takes the pen and paper and starts scribbling again. When she's done, she laughs, then she shows me what she wrote. "When I hold this in the window," she whispers, "you have to look really scared, OK?"

"Aye."

An old couple in a motorhome pulls up behind us in the slow lane. When Bree puts the message against the glass, I do just what she told me. The couple looks really scared. They wave at us and stuff, then they take the very next exit. Once they're gone, me and Bree start laughing, then hide the papers on the floor beneath the seat.

Fifteen minutes later two police cars come screaming up behind us, both of them with their lights flashing and sirens blaring.

"Whoa!" Ann shouts, sounding startled as the sirens yank her from a nap. "What's going on?"

My heart is pounding hard against my chest, which makes me wonder what Ann's heart is doing. I shoot Bree a nervous look. She looks even more worried than me. As Dad pulls over to the side to let the cops pass, I know we're in deep doo-doo when they both follow us to the shoulder.

With cars whizzing by on his left, one officer carefully gets out of his cruiser. His gun is still holstered, but his hand is glued to it.

"Bree? Cade? Anything you'd like to tell me?" hisses Dad as the officer approaches.

"Umm . . . not really," Bree says.

"Nay," I add softly.

Dad rolls down his window and quickly pastes a smile on his face. "Good evening, officer. Is everything all right? I wasn't speeding, was I?"

The policeman scans the inside of the car from front to back, looking at every person individually, but paying particular attention to me and Bree. "Where you folks headed?"

"Cannon Beach."

"Can I see your identification, please?"

Dad hands it to him.

"Are the children in the car yours?" the officer asks as he reviews my father's driver's license.

"Last time I checked," says Dad with a nervous chuckle.

The officer doesn't laugh. He asks my dad to open the hatchback, then he comes around back to talk directly to me and my sister. "Do you guys know why I'm here?" he asks. His voice is as serious as Ann's pulse.

I nod yes, but Bree shakes her head, no. "Was my dad speeding again?" she asks innocently. "Mom says he has a lead foot."

"So he's your father?"

"Last time I checked," Bree says with a little snicker, quoting the same thing Dad had told him a minute earlier.

"Then why," the officer continues, "did we get a frantic nine-one-one call saying some kids had been abducted?"

Bree gives him her "I don't know" look and says, "A different car, maybe?"

Despite my sister's brilliant performance, I know it is not time for games. I dig through the papers on the floor and hold up the one that reads, *Help! We've been kidnapped! Call the police!!*

The officer writes our names and ages in his notepad and goes back to his car. A few minutes later he returns, having confirmed that Dell and Emily Bennett are the parents of exactly three alphabetically named children — Ann, Bree, and Cade. "Everything checks out," he tells my dad. "Looks like you've got your hands full, Mr. Bennett."

Dad is still glaring at us in the rearview mirror. "You have no idea. What would it take to get you to lock them up for a few months?"

Luckily, the policeman isn't in the mood to charge us with anything. Dad, however, charges us with mutiny. "Maybe Cade's the only one talking like a pirate today," he says once we're back on the road, "but I swear, both of you are pirate children. And I don't mean that as a compliment." He keeps his voice fairly even so as not to further upset Ann, but I can tell he is ready to blow a gasket. "*Kidnapped?* Our summer trip is less than an hour old, and you've already had me pulled over for suspected kidnapping." He checks the rearview mirror again to make sure we are paying attention. "Guys, do you even recall why we're going to the beach?"

"Yes," Bree says.

"Cade?"

"Aye, cap'n."

"Good. But if you know why, then I need you to act like it's important to you. When I said we can't afford your shenanigans, this is exactly what I was talking about. This summer is about Ann, not about you two hooligans." He stops talking for a second, but his jaw stays clenched tight. "Tell me truthfully, are you two ready and able to make this summer work, or should I turn around right now?"

"Dell," my mom says calmly, "don't threaten to cancel the trip. That's not necessary."

He takes his eyes off the road and stares at her in disbelief. "Why are you undermining me? I'm trying to make a point here so they're not pulling this kind of crap all summer, and you go and say something like that?"

"It's your tone," she says without looking at him. "It's no wonder the kids raise their voices so much."

Dad focuses once more on the road and mumbles, "Oh, here we go again with the tone thing. I'm always using the wrong tone . . ." After letting the dust settle a little, he returns his attention to the rearview mirror. "Sorry for the interruption, kids. Now then, are you ready to behave yourselves, or should I turn around?"

"I be ready."

"Me too," chirps Bree. "Sorry, Ann. I didn't mean to get, you know, you and your heart all excited with the sirens."

Ann is all smiles by now. "Are you kidding? That was hilarious. What other messages did you put in the window?"

For a split second, panic shows on Bree's face, and I know what she is thinking. "Oh, nothing much," she says. "Just boring stuff."

"Well, let me see."

"Nah. They're stupid. Just dumb stuff asking people to honk and wave."

Ann is no dummy. Bree's resistance is more than enough to make her suspect that we're hiding something. She also knows, on account of her heart, that she can pretty much get my parents to do anything she wants, so she immediately turns to them. "Mom, Bree and Cade won't let me see the other things they wrote."

"Bree?" my mother asks.

"Give 'em to her, guys," Dad says flatly.

"But —"

"No 'buts'!" barks Dad before Bree can finish her rebuttal. He gives my mom a quick sideways glance to see if she is going to scold him for raising his voice.

I hand the full stack of papers to Ann. It

takes her all of about five seconds to get to the one about her. "Who wrote this?" she shrieks. Her face turns instantly red, which means her heart is working overtime. "You two are jerks, you know that?"

"Dimwit wrote that one," says Bree quickly. "Mine were completely harmless."

*Harmless? Yours brought the cops!*

"How do either of you know if I've been kissed or not?"

"Well, have ye?"

"It's none of your business!"

"Ann," my mom says, "please, let's not get all riled up. Just take a deep breath and we'll sort this out."

Ann's face is still burning, but she takes a long breath through her nose before turning back to me and asking, "Cade, why would you write something like that?"

It's a fair question. I take a moment to think how best to answer in Pirateese. "Well, ye ain't ever had a boyfriend, an' ye ain't ever brought a swashbuckler home fer dinner or studying, so I have to think ye ain't ever been kissed."

"Ahhh! Dad, will you *please* make him stop talking like that. It's driving me nuts!"

"Cade," says Dad, using his "this-is-the-last-straw" voice, "enough is enough. Talk-Like-a-Pirate Day is officially over. *Savvy?*"

Ann sneers, gloating at the power she holds over me on account of her weak heart.

"Poop deck," I mumble as I turn again toward the rear window.

"Enough from *everyone,*" says Mom, raising her voice for the first time. "We're only half an hour away. I want complete silence until we get there. Nod if you understand."

"Watch your tone, hun," says my dad casually as my mom's face turns cherry red. "It's no wonder the kids raise their voices so much."

# CHAPTER 8
## BREE

There is still plenty of daylight left when we pull to a stop at the beach house, which sits along a cute little road running parallel to the beach. Dad backs the van into the driveway, right beside Grandma's old car, leaving me an open view of the sandy shoreline that will serve as our backyard for the next three months. Beyond the sand, at the crest of the waves, is Haystack Rock, a monolith jutting up to meet the sinking sun. Even with the windows up I can hear the surf pounding against it.

Before Dad turns off the car, Cade is already climbing over the seat toward the door. I bet the rotten little pirate in him can hardly wait to get out and make a dash for the sea, but Dad has different plans. "Nobody does anything," he warns as he unlocks the car doors with the push of a button, "until everyone is unpacked and settled in." Turning to my mom, he asks, "Did you mention the sleeping arrangements yet, Emily?"

Dad's question barely reaches my ears before Ann blurts out, "Dibs on the downstairs bedroom!"

We've stayed here enough times to know the layout of the place. The master and one guest room are on the main floor, with a much smaller third bedroom upstairs near the door to the attic. The master is obviously the biggest of the three, but the other two rooms have the best views of the beach.

"Then I call upstairs!" I yell a split second later.

As the obvious loser in the bedroom race, Cade throws his hands up in frustration. "Where am I sleeping, then? On the floor."

"No," Mom reassures him, "you'll have a bed." She looks at Dad, then adds, "Most nights, anyway. The master bedroom still has all of Grandma's stuff in it, so we want to leave that alone for the time being. Which means your father and I will be in the other downstairs bedroom. There are two twin beds in there, so when your father is away during the week, you can share that room with me. On weekends, you get the couch. But Ann and Bree, you'll both be upstairs on the bunk bed."

"I have to *share*?" Ann blurts out.

"With *her*?" I ask. "Totes lame."

"Totes *fine,*" Mom corrects. "You'll survive, ladies. You're sisters, for Pete's sake. There's nothing wrong with sharing."

Dad is already walking toward the house. "C'mon, gang," he calls, "let's get settled. Cade, you carry Ann's suitcase, please."

"Again?"

"Just do it, son. Be a pal."

The house looks big from the outside, but I'm always surprised how small it feels on the inside.

"Where the heck am I supposed to play?" asks Cade as we walk through the front door.

Dad wraps an arm around him and whispers, "Please don't be negative. Remember, we're really here for Ann. And your great-grandma. You may have to play outside, but that's what the beach is for, right?"

Cade nods, then runs over to look at the beach through the rear window.

I glance at Ann, who is investigating a halibut mounted like a picture on the wall. It never ceases to amaze me how *fishy* this place is. After decades of living here, Grandma — and Grandpa, too, when he was alive — collected more sea-junk than anyone should be allowed. Above the halibut-art, hanging by its mouth on an oversized hook, is a stuffed puffer fish, blown up to its fullest and wired with a bulb to make a creepy overhead lamp. It fits right in, though, because every room in the place is decked out in a gag-worthy assortment of coastal crap — seagull-print wallpaper in the living room, mini-lighthouses in the kitchen, seashells in both bathrooms, fishing nets in the master bedroom, anchors in the guest room, and starfish in the bunk-bed room upstairs. The half bath upstairs even has a hand-tooled sign on the door that reads, FOR BUOYS AND GULLS. High-traffic areas are floored with sand-colored tiles, while the living room, bedrooms, and stairs are covered by a thick, sea-blue shag carpet.

"It's perfect," declares Mom after we've all taken a quick tour to reacquaint ourselves with the place.

*Perfect? More like a Little Mermaid horror film.* "It smells salty," I point out.

"I like the smell," Cade says. "It covers up your perfume."

"I like it too," remarks Ann before I can fire back at Cade. "It's like we're breathing the ocean with every breath. Mom's right, it's perfect for the summer." She pauses and looks directly at me. "Except for sharing a room."

"Believe me," I sigh, "the feeling is mutual."

Dad is standing in the kitchen, examining the floor in every direction. Now that he technically owns the place, he has a more critical eye than in past visits. "I feel a little . . . *off*. Does anyone else feel seasick?"

"I do," I tell him, raising my hand. "I think it's the carpet."

We all watch as Dad takes a pen from his pocket and sets it down on the tile near his feet. "I wonder," he says softly. When he lets go of the pen, it begins rolling, slowly but surely toward the other side of the kitchen. "Wow, the house is off-kilter."

"You're kidding," says Mom.

"Gravity doesn't lie, but I'm surprised I've never noticed it before. It's probably just the sandy foundation, settled a bit over time. This is why the wise man built his house upon a rock." He stops to think. "That might reduce its value some. We'll have to get it looked at before we sell."

"Well, I don't care," Mom says, undeterred. "It's still perfect. A perfect place for us to create perfect memories with our perfect children this summer."

"And with Cade," I say pointedly.

Mom grins and drapes an arm around Cade's shoulder. "Yes, Breezy," she says with a laugh, "and with Cade."

After we unpack our suitcases, Mom takes a drive to the local market while Dad takes the rest of us for a short walk on the beach. The sun has already dropped to just above the waterline, leaving the entire horizon bathed in a fiery brew of orange and purple.

I can't help but notice that Ann keeps filling her lungs with long, deep breaths as we pace through the sand. After one particularly long breath, she twirls around, lifting her hands high above her head, and exclaims, "I could die today and be perfectly happy."

"Well, don't," I tell her, "because I don't want to have to live alone with you-know-who." With my head, I motion to Cade.

"I was joking. Chill."

"I wasn't," I mutter.

Ann takes another huge breath, letting it out slowly, savoring it. "Don't you feel it? The crash of the waves, the roar, the spray — it just makes me feel so alive."

"That's what we want," my father says as he bends over to draw in the sand with his finger. He makes a heart. "Being here is all about feeling alive." For a second or two he and Ann share a peaceful daddy-daughter stare. "It's about you living, Ann, and getting a new one of these." He stands up and brushes the sand from his finger.

"Then it's also about dying," Cade blurts out. "Because if you're getting a new heart, then someone out there is going to have to have a very bad summer."

Ann's face sinks like an anchor. "Thank you so very much for reminding me of that," she says, her eyes turning suddenly red and welling up with tears. "Way to ruin the moment." She turns immediately and marches back to the house.

"Nice job, Dimwit," I say.

Dad shakes his head. "You've got to learn to keep some thoughts to yourself, Cade."

"But it's true, Dad. I don't want Ann to die, but I don't want *anyone* to die."

He smiles half-heartedly and ruffles Cade's hair. "I know you don't. But can I tell you something? As a parent, I'm selfish. I want Ann to live a long, long time. So if someone has to die this summer — and I wish they didn't — but if that's God's plan, then I pray to God that it isn't your sister." Dad reaches out and gives Cade a little squeeze on the shoulder. "C'mon, son." He turns back to me and motions for me to follow them.

I don't move. "Can I just stay here a little longer?" The words come quietly from my mouth, but are carried to his ears on the steady breeze. "Just until the sun sets?"

At first I'm sure he'll say no, that a teen-age girl shouldn't be alone on the beach. But then maybe he sees something in my expression, because he relaxes. "Don't wander off," he cautions. "And the tide is coming in, so don't get too close to the water. We'll see you in a little bit."

Once he is out of sight, I head straight for the water. Not too close, though — just close enough to get my feet wet. It is freez-ing, after all; the Oregon coast always is. For a while I just stand in place, sinking a little in the sand every time the water around my ankles is sucked back into the ocean. Once my feet are sufficiently numb, I retreat to a place on the beach that hasn't been touched by the water. With a stick, I draw a small shape in the sand — a tiny heart, like the one my dad made with his finger.

Only mine looks more like my sister's heart: imperfect and slightly misshapen.

When it comes to art — and to me, even simple sketches in the sand should be treated as art — I'm a perfectionist. I don't want to draw one like Ann's, with flaws. To fix it, I draw a larger heart around the first one, but the new heart is equally distorted.

*What is wrong with me? This shouldn't be*

*so hard. Maybe my hands are numb too.*

Frustrated, in the fading light I continue tracing hearts around the outside, hoping that the next one will perfect the image. Each new line makes the picture bigger, but not necessarily better. Eventually, the collection of hearts grows to a width of at least twenty feet, but by then it is almost touching the incoming tide. When I see that the water will soon destroy my hard work, I tiptoe across my creation to the original cockeyed heart — *Ann's heart,* in the middle — as if my presence there will protect it.

A few minutes later, pulled by the rising moon, the foaming water again tickles my ankles, and the heart of hearts washes away. "Why can't you just leave her alone?" I ask the ocean. Or God. Or whoever.

The ocean doesn't reply. It just keeps rolling in and out, lapping at the sand. Yet as my feet turn blue with cold, each new wave is a chilling reminder of what I already knew. *Imperfect hearts aren't meant to last.*

"Hey, stranger. We were about to send a rescue crew," jokes Mom when I finally come in from the beach through the back door. She's at the stove stirring a pot of spaghetti. With a little curtsy she says, "What do you think of my apron? It was hanging in the pantry, just begging to be worn."

The apron is designed to look exactly like an overgrown Dungeness crab. The main body is the shell, with beady black eyes looking up at Mom's chin, spiny legs wrapped around her back as ties, and two giant claws joined behind her neck to keep it up. "It's . . . sick," I tell her.

"Is that good or bad these days?"

I chuckle. "Take another look at what you're wearing, and you tell me."

"Well, there's not much cooking left to do, but there's also a lobster-apron in the pantry if you want to try it on."

"Nah, I'm good."

She winks at me and then goes back to stirring noodles.

"Have you seen Ann?"

"She's upstairs resting, I think."

Cade and Dad are engrossed in a game of backgammon as I pass through the living room. "Welcome back," says Dad before I reach the sea-blue stairwell.

"Hey," I say, then continue on.

There are three doors at the top of the stairs. The one to the left is the half bath, the one straight ahead leads to the attic, and the one to the right is "the girls' " bedroom. I twist the handle on the right, then push gently.

Ann is laying flat on her back on the bottom bunk. She has a pen in her hand and is in the middle of writing something on the wood slat above her head. When she hears the door sliding on the carpet, she quickly drops the pen and acts like she wasn't doing something that she probably shouldn't. But when she sees it's just me, she relaxes and gives me a half smile. "Hey."

"Hey," I reply. "So . . . how you doing?"

"Fine."

"Has Cade apologized yet?"

"For what?"

*Seriously?* "Duh. For what he said out there on the beach."

It takes her a moment to think. Then she bobs her head indifferently. "He was telling the truth. I just didn't want to hear it right then." She pauses. "It's just so . . . weird."

"What is?"

"The whole transplant thing. You know, about someone else dying. I try to block it out, because sometimes I'm not even sure I want someone else's heart beating inside me."

I nod as though I understand, though I can't even begin to understand how that must make her feel. "So what were you writing on the bed?"

98

She grins. "I was watching you on the beach after we left." There are two windows in the room; she points to the one on the wall facing the beach. Cade's binoculars are resting on the sill. "You inspired me. Want to see?"

Ann scoots over on her bed to make room. When I see what she's drawn, I have to swallow. On the plywood above us is a misshapen, Sharpie-red heart, with a slightly larger heart traced around it.

"A heart in a heart," she says soberly, "because, like it or not, someone else's heart might end up in me."

"Might?"

*"Will,"* she corrects.

"That's really cool, Ann. Are you going to make it bigger?"

"Yeah, but not tonight. I want to add one new heart for each day we're here, kind of like rings on a tree. The heart will continue to grow each day until I get my new one."

"Cool," I say again, deeply impressed that I've somehow inspired her.

She rolls her head on the pillow to look at me. "I still don't like sharing a room with you."

"Ditto."

"Good," she says with a little chuckle. "Just wanted that to be clear." Ann looks

99

back up at the bed above us. With her finger, she traces around the outer ring of the heart. Then, out of the blue, she asks, "Do you think I'm boring?"

The question catches me off guard. Of course I think she's boring. Doesn't everyone? "Umm . . . why do you ask?"

"Because of what you guys plastered on the car window for the whole world to see. You and Cade both think I'm lame, don't you?"

"Hey, Cade wrote that one about the kissing."

"But you do think I'm lame."

"Not all the time."

"Well, that's a big fat yes," she says, sounding more than a little dejected. "I am, aren't I?"

I keep my mouth shut, assuming that to be a rhetorical question.

Ann lifts a finger and traces the heart once more, slower this time. "Maybe I can change," she says firmly. Then, less sure, she whispers, "Maybe not."

# CHAPTER 9
## ANN

The sun hasn't yet peeked above the coastal range when Dad comes busting into our room asking if we want to go with him and Mom to Home Depot.

I rub my eyes and check the clock on the wall. 7:20 a.m.

"Why so early?"

"I'm heading back to Portland this evening, so I want to get a jump on the day. Your mom needs a few supplies — paint and stuff — so she can start sprucing this place up. Who wants to go with us?"

Bree is above me on the top bunk. She yawns loudly, then rolls over. "Not me."

"Me neither," I tell him, still squinting.

"That's two strikes," says Dad. Cade is standing behind him in the hallway. "How about you, son?"

"Strike three," Cade mumbles. "I'd rather stay here."

"I won't force anyone. But we might be a

101

while, so if you stay, there are a few rules. Ann, Bree, are you listening?" It takes several seconds, but he eventually gets Bree to roll back over and open her eyes. "Rule number one, no touching the ocean. You can go down to the beach, but not down to the water."

Cade lets out a long, disappointed, groan. "Why not?"

"I can answer that in three syllables," he replies. "Un-der-tow. The Oregon coast is powerful, and I'm not sure what time the tide is coming in today. You get caught by a sneaker wave and the undertow here will suck you right out to sea before you know it."

"So we can't ever go swimming?" asks Bree, sounding as disappointed as Cade. "We've played in the water here before."

"I didn't say 'never.' All I'm saying is that I don't want you in the water when your mom or I aren't there to watch. It's too dangerous."

"But Ann is a varsity swimmer," Cade argues.

My heart starts pounding when he says it, because I, for one, have no interest in getting near the ocean. It's cold, and wet, and . . . well I'm not a huge fan of water these days. I haven't mentioned this to anyone, but I'm lucky to get up the nerve to step into the shower, and soaking in the bath is completely out of the question, because what is a bathtub, really, but a miniature swimming pool. The last time I got in a swimming pool, I barely made it out.

Dad shakes his head. "And she, above all, is in no shape to face those currents. Got it?"

I secretly breathe out a huge sigh of relief.

"Good," he continues after we all nod, "then the only other rule is . . . ?" He leaves it hanging there, waiting for one of us to finish the thought.

"No fighting," mutters Bree.

"Bingo! Ann doesn't need chaos, so I expect you two to be on your best behavior while we're gone. Don't do anything that's going to get your sister worked up. Understood?"

Cade answers with a simple, "Yes."

"Bree?"

"Uh-huh."

"Fantastic. We should be back by noon. Feel free to make yourself some breakfast. There's plenty of cereal. Eggs, too, if you're in the mood to cook. If we're not back by twelve thirty, there are sandwich makings in the fridge." He says a final good-bye, and then goes to meet Mom in the car.

"Uggh," groans Bree after he is gone. "Now I can't go back to sleep."

"Tell me about it. Couldn't they have just left a note?"

"I've got to pee," Cade deadpans.

*Ew. Little brothers are disgusting.*

Fifteen minutes later everyone is dressed and downstairs eating scrambled eggs. After breakfast we turn on the television, but to our everlasting dismay, the dumb thing only picks up four channels, and even those are marred by static. The last time we visited Great-grandma's house, back when her health first started going south, she at least had the basic cable channels. Perhaps Aunt Bev had them turned off, since Grandma now lives full-time in the care facility. Out of boredom, Bree and Cade seem willing to put up with the fuzziness, but I'm itching to do something more exciting. I sit there for a while, but eventually I announce I'm going for a walk. "There are some cool shops up the road that I want to check out. I'll be back in a bit."

"You can't go by yourself," Bree protests, playing the part of the responsible one, which I find highly unusual. "What if . . . you know, something happens."

I put my hands on my hips and force a

scowl. "You mean what if my heart stops ticking? It's not like I'm running a marathon."

"But aren't you supposed to just take it easy?"

"Easy, yes, but not do nothing. I'm not on bed rest. And if you're so worried about me, then come along. With or without you, though, I'm not staying inside for the next three months watching reruns of *Tom and Jerry,* especially not through all that static."

Bree's shoulders slump forward. I'm positive she doesn't want to go, but she feels compelled. Turning to Cade, she asks, "What about you, Twerp? If I go, you have to come too."

"Don't call me 'Twerp,' Zit Face."

*Kaboom!* Just like that, Bree explodes, and I don't mean her zit pops. "I have one stupid pimple on my forehead! That doesn't make me zit-faced!"

"Actually, the one on your forehead is almost gone," I note cautiously. "But did you look in the mirror this morning? There's a huge whitehead on your cheek."

She runs over to the mirror near the front door and shrieks.

"It's probably your hormones," I inform her innocuously.

"Eww!" she shrieks again, looking repulsed. "Don't say that. I hate that word."

"Hormones, hormones, hormones, hormones!" Cade shouts. I don't think he even fully understands what hormones are, but it's fun watching her reaction when he says it. "Bree's got zits! And hormones!"

Her face goes from whitehead white to pimple pink in about half a second. "Shut up! I hate both of you!"

"Chill. It's no big deal. Everyone gets zits now and then."

"It's a huge deal. You think I want to go outside today with this thing ready to ooze all over my cheek? What if some boy sees me like this? *Sick.*"

"So you're not coming now?"

Bree takes three steps toward the foot of the blue stairs. "No. I'm definitely staying."

"Fine. Cade, what about you? You want to go for a walk with me, or stay here waiting for Little Miss Zit to pop?"

He turns to the TV for a moment, then to Bree, and then back to me. "What kind of stores?"

"Beach stuff. And I know there's a candy store not too far away."

That does it. "Count me in."

"Bree?" I ask once more. "Final chance. You sure you don't want to come along?"

She's already halfway up the stairs. "Just

go," she calls without looking back.

As I head out of the house, Cade holds his hand up like a traffic cop. "Wait. Are you sure you have your little pager thing?"

*So cute of him to remember! Maybe little brothers aren't all bad.*

I pat the front pocket of my shorts. "Always. Page has become my new best friend, sad as that is."

It feels awesome being outside; just breathing in the fresh air and seeing all the green on the coastal hills. In a way, it kind of feels like last night, out on the beach when the roar of the ocean made me feel alive. As we walk, it occurs to me that perhaps I've sort of shut myself inside at home since all of this heart stuff started.

*Maybe that's why the few friends I used to have distanced themselves? Because I distanced myself first . . .*

Who knows.

What I do know is that feeling the coastal breeze in my face feels really good, and that right now, for this moment, I am happy.

Apparently Cade can see the difference in me too. "What's up with you?"

"What do you mean?"

"I don't know. You're just all smiling and stuff."

"I'm happy. What's wrong with that?"

"Nothing, I guess. But do you have to walk different because of it? You're, like . . . skipping or something. It's weird."

*Nope, I was right. Little brothers are annoying.*

I stop walking and point back to our house. "Just go back right now, Cade, if you're going to nitpick. I happen to like being out here — I feel like I haven't been anywhere in forever, so I can walk however I want."

"Geez," he fires back. "Sorry for being honest."

We continue walking, but the talking stops for a while. The lack of conversation allows me to focus on the surroundings. The street is lined with homes, most of them larger and newer than ours, and probably all rental properties. That's just the way Cannon Beach is — not a ton of year-round residents like my great-grandma, but plenty of homes for vacationers to enjoy the majesty of the Oregon coast. Behind a few of the homes, kites are starting to pop up here and there in the morning breeze.

There's an intersection five or six blocks from our house where our road crosses the busiest street in town. We take a right toward a long row of shops a couple hundred yards to the east. The first store sells nothing but kites and windcatchers; it's fun to look around at all the bright colors and designs, but without Dad's credit card there is nothing I could afford. Dad is pinching pennies to pay my bills, though, so I doubt he'd spend his money here anyway. Next to the kite store are a couple of old antique stores, followed by an art gallery and then a clothing store dedicated almost exclusively to swimsuits.

Finally we reach the candy store. As soon as I walk through the door, my mouth begins watering. My nose, meanwhile, is attacked by a blend of sugary goodness — giant shards of peanut brittle, truffles of every flavor, hand-dipped Oreos, at least fifteen different kinds of candied apples, and the largest assortment of fudge I've ever seen.

Once my senses get past the sweet smells, they move on to an even sweeter sight. A totally hot guy is standing behind the counter.

*Be still, my fragile heart!*

He's wearing a brown apron, plastic gloves, and a paper hat on his head that doesn't fully cover the wavy locks of hair hanging over his ears. Unfortunately, on second glance, he looks kind of jockish. You know, sporty. And sporty guys like sporty girls, but I'm not a sporty girl. Not anymore.

In fact, I'm the opposite.

I'm a girl with an acute medical problem.

I'm a girl who sports could kill.

I'm a girl who can't help noticing a cute boy when she sees one, but who knows darn well he's not worth dreaming about, because he would have no interest in a girl like me. Not that I'm not attractive, because I can be totally cute too, when I want to be. But let's face it, I have flaws . . . inside and out.

"Hey," he says coolly after a few seconds, "what's up?"

He speaks, I panic. He's definitely a sporty, too-cool-for-girls-like-me kind of guy, but his voice is as cute as his hair. His words take hold of me, freezing me in place. The best I can do is give him a confused "are you talking to me?" sort of expression, followed by a feeble, "Uh . . . hi."

*What guy like that would want a girl with defects like mine?*

I purposefully drop my eyes to the floor. Not that I don't want to look at him. Only that I feel kind of uncomfortable with him looking at me. At some level, probably not too deep, I'm afraid of what he might see.

"If you guys are looking for good chocolate," he continues, "you've come to the right spot. We make it right here at the store."

"You make it?" asks Cade.

"Well, not me personally. But the owner and his wife come in at like five every day. The only thing they don't make by hand is the taffy, but they buy that fresh each morning from a place in Seaside." I can feel his gaze following me as I approach the glass display. "Where are you from?"

"The Portland area," I reply softly without looking up.

"Cool. I used to live there too. Until my parents split a couple years ago and I moved here with my mom."

"Oh." I turn my back to examine the display of candied apples on the near wall.

"You just here for the day, or are you staying through the week?"

Since my back is to him, I figure he must be speaking to Cade, so I ignore the question for several seconds, but Cade doesn't say anything either. When I finally turn around again, he is still staring at me!

My only move is to play dumb. "Oh, were you talking to me?"

"Who else?"

"My brother?"

"I could talk to him, I guess," he says with a chuckle as he glances down at Cade. "Is your sister always like this?"

Cade shrugs. "Only when boys are

111

around."

"Cade!" I can feel my cheeks getting hot.

The boy snickers at my reaction, but stays focused on my brother. "Cade, is it? Well, Cade, is there anything that looks good?"

"All of it."

"I know, right? Should I just box up one of everything for you, or is there something specific you'd like?"

Cade orders a single square of peanut-butter fudge and two mint truffles.

"Do you think your sister — What's her name again? — Do you think she's going to want anything?"

"Her name is Ann," Cade tells him, tossing a quick glance my way. I'm sure I'm still multiple shades of pink. "And yeah, she wants something."

*Oh, that rotten little brat!* The smirk on his face — and the way he says it! — makes it sound like the "something" I want has nothing to do with chocolate.

*I could kill him!*

Unfazed, the boy winks at Cade with a thankful nod, then focuses on me again. "So, *Ann.* What can I get you?"

"I'm still deciding," I mutter as I ease back toward the glass display counter.

"Well, take your time. I'll just chat with Cade here until you're ready." He smiles and winks at Cade once more, like the two of them are playing a game. "What grade are you in?"

"Just finished fifth. Now I'm starting middle school."

"Ah, moving up to the big leagues. How about Ann?"

"She'll be a senior."

He grins. "Me too. And how long are you guys in town?"

Cade looks at me for a moment, like he's trying to see how he should respond. "Well, I guess we're staying until my sister gets her new —"

"Schedule!" I shout. "Until I get a new schedule for my senior year."

The boy rightfully looks confused. "Why do you need to wait here for your schedule?"

"Well . . . yeah, I mean . . . I didn't like the first one they gave me, so I asked for a new one . . . and this is where they're mailing it."

There's a hint of doubt in his eyes, but all he says is, "Huh."

"The thing is," I continue, now in full ramble mode, "we own a beach house here and stuff, and so we weren't sure where we were going to be exactly, so we told them to mail my schedule here, which means we're sort of stuck here until it comes, because

113

we don't want it to get lost in the mail or anything. Once it comes, we'll head back to Portland. That could be at the very end of the summer, though . . . maybe."

A wide grin splits his face. "Wow, that's a long time . . . maybe. You know, if you guys want, I can show you around when I'm not working. There's more to do in Cannon Beach than people think."

"Cool," Cade says.

But I shake my head adamantly. "We've got a lot going on. I'm sure we're going to be very busy this summer."

He nods. "I understand. But if you change your mind, you know where to find me. I'm here weekdays from ten to four, and Saturdays from nine to one. Other than that, I'm completely free, and will probably be bored out of my mind."

*Is he serious? Did he seriously invite me — well . . . us — to hang out with him this summer? Does he not understand that I'm not like him? I'm not cool, and sporty, and perfect.*

"We should probably get going," I blurt out. "Can I just have a mint fudge and a milk-chocolate cluster? Oh, and maybe a dipped pretzel stick for my sister."

"Sure, Ann." He starts collecting our items. "I'm Tanner, by the way. Rich."

"Wow," I say sarcastically. "Good for you.

114

You're *rich*. Is that supposed to impress me?"

For a second Tanner is like a deer in the headlights, but then he starts cracking up.

Cade laughs too. "I think that's his last name, Ann."

Now Tanner is beaming again. "You think I'd spend my summer working here if I was loaded? Let me try again. 'Sure, Ann. By the way, I'm Tanner Rich. First name Tanner, last name Rich.' "

"Oh," I reply sheepishly. "Sorry, I just . . . sorry." I pull out my wallet and ask him how much I owe.

"It's on the house. Store policy. First-time visitors get five free samples."

I quickly count our items. "We have six."

"Oh, right. Sorry. The policy is the first six."

"You seriously aren't going to let us pay? Won't you get in trouble?"

He winks. "If you're worried about it, just buy extra the next time you come in the store to make up for it."

"And what if we don't come back?"

"That would be a shame." He hands me the bag of treats. "Don't forget, I'll gladly show you around town if you want."

*He invited me — us — again!*

"And don't forget," I say stupidly, "we

have big plans this summer. We're going to be very busy." On that note, I turn and exit the store without looking back.

On the way home, I'm seething. Gone are the happy, alive feelings from earlier. Once again, Cade can tell that something is up.

"What's the matter?"

"What do you think? I'm *soooo* lame."

"Yeah, so what's new?"

"Oh shut up."

"Sorry. Why are you lame this time?"

I try threatening him with my mad face, but it's no use, because I'm not really mad at him. I'm mad at me, and me alone. In frustration, I withdraw my block of mint fudge from the bag and bite off half of it. After swallowing, I lick my lips before replying. "I guess I just thought . . . here at the beach and stuff . . . and I was like all energized and feeling good . . . but then it's like nope."

"Ah," Cade says, even though he probably has no clue what I'm talking about.

"Still just as boring as ever."

Now he understands. "Totally. No wonder you've never been kissed."

"Oh shut up," I hiss again, then I punch him in the arm for good measure.

"I'm telling Mom!"

"Go ahead. You'll just get in trouble for

116

making me mad." I know it's unfair that I use my parents' sympathy for me against my siblings, but sometimes I just can't help it.

He rubs his shoulder and sighs. "You're right. You really are lame."

When we get home, I head straight upstairs and flop on my bed. Bree wants to know what's wrong, but I ignore her. Then I cry myself to sleep.

When I wake up, I am all alone in the room. From my bed, I glance at the door. It is closed, but I can see myself staring back at me in the full-length mirror that hangs on the back of the door. I used to love mirrors, but nowadays I could really do without them. Not that I don't need them to do my hair and stuff, but I hate how honest mirrors are. This one, in particular, is brutally honest; when I'm changing my clothes, it shows me more than I want to see.

I see the scars, and I hate how they make me feel.

Usually I can make myself forget my flaws, but when I see myself in the mirror, it's impossible to ignore them.

I'm sure if Tanner saw me as I see myself in that mirror, he would be repulsed. If he knew anything about the fact that I'm waiting for a new heart, he would never have offered to hang out with me this summer.

I lay in bed for a few minutes after waking up, still lamenting my lameness at the candy store. Then Bree pops in to check on me. Seeing that I'm awake, she says she's getting in the bathtub. With the room to myself, I get up and cross to that mirror.

*The stupid, awful, brutally honest, full-length, impossible-to-ignore mirror.*

I lock the door, just to make sure Cade doesn't come in unannounced. Then I lift my shirt to my chin, examining my hideous red scar for the millionth time. I trace it from my collarbone to my sternum, feeling the fleshy ripple of skin beneath my finger.

*I hate this mirror! I hate all mirrors.*

But mostly . . . I hate scars.

The funny thing about scars, though, is that not all of them can be seen. I don't just mean because they're beneath clothes, like mine. I mean because they're deeper than that. They're ingrained on the heart, or etched in the soul.

Later in the evening, while we're at a restaurant, I am reminded that my parents probably have scars too — things about themselves that they don't particularly like anymore. At first the dinner is going fine, but then the scars of their relationship start to itch and swell.

The first thing I notice is that Mom isn't smiling. I guess I wasn't paying close enough attention to their conversation, because I was too busy watching a seagull dipping and diving around the kites outside, but whatever Dad said to her, it's not sitting well at all.

And her pouty silence isn't sitting well with him either. My ears perk up when he says, "That's it? You're going to stop talking now?"

"We're in a restaurant, Dell. I don't want to talk about it here."

"What's to talk about? This has been the plan for several weeks now."

"I just thought . . . now that we're here, you might like to stay. At least a few days."

"I'll be here on the weekend, Emily. We both agreed that a little space will do us some good right now."

"You agreed."

"Fine! If you want to pin this on me, go ahead. I don't want to argue with you anymore. If we're not together, at least we can't fight." He looks around the table. "Kids, before you ask . . . no, this doesn't mean we're getting a divorce. We just . . . need some space. And this summer is going to allow that."

Mom checks her watch. "Well, you better hop in the car and get going, then. No time like the present to give you the space you need."

"The space *WE* need, Emily."

That's when Mom starts crying. They aren't big tears, like you might get from a brand-new wound. They're just the misty little drops you'd expect from scratching an old scar. "Just go," she whispers. "We're close enough to walk back. We'll see you on the weekend."

He throws two twenties on the table and leaves without saying good-bye.

"You OK, Mom?" I ask as soon as Dad is gone.

"Yes," she replies softly. "Let's go."

Like I said, Mom and Dad have scars.

Cade and Bree probably have scars too, just from listening to Mom and Dad fight, or from dealing with me for the past year and a half.

And me?

*I'm the queen of scars. Chest, heart, and soul . . .*

# CHAPTER 10
## CADE

It's late. Past my bedtime on a normal night. But Dad left tonight, so Mom's been kinda letting us do our own thing. The girls are both upstairs. Last I checked, Bree was sketching in her art pad, and Ann was writing in her journal-diary thingy. Maybe they're both asleep by now.

I've been alone watching the fuzzy television. Mom's been tucked away in her bedroom, probably reading. Eventually she peeks out and says it's time to go to bed. "You're sleeping in my room tonight, right, Cade? Dad's bed is all made up for you."

I'm old enough that I like sleeping by myself, but not so old or dumb that I would turn down a comfortable twin mattress over Grandma's old couch, even if that mattress is in the same room as my mom. "I guess so."

Actually, I'm not really ready for bed yet, but I can't tell her that. How do I tell her that I'm superworried about her and Dad? How do I explain the bazillion things I was worried about while I was watching that lousy TV for the past two hours?

No, there's too much on my mind to go to sleep, but I can't talk to my mom about it, so I just lie awake in the dark for a long, long time. I wish I could turn my brain off. I keep replaying the things my mom and dad have said to each other lately. All their fights and stuff. I don't like thinking about it, but it's hard not to.

*What's happening to our family?* It's like every bad thing possible is going on at once. We've all been worried about Ann for a really long time; worried that she might not make it. And now I have to worry that my parents might not make it either. If they split up, it will probably feel just as awful as Ann dying. It already feels awful sometimes, like when they're yelling at each other. Or worse, ignoring each other.

Maybe the death of a marriage is just as bad as the death of a person. Maybe it's actually worse, because when someone dies, you still love them, love the memories. But when parents divorce, the love is gone. Not buried, just gone.

I wish there was a surgery or something — medicine, maybe — that could fix marriage problems!

My best friend, Sam, his parents got divorced last year. He gets way more presents now than he used to because his dad likes to send him stuff when he's not around, which is pretty cool, but Sam gets sad a lot too, because he doesn't get to see his dad very often. Right now, my dad is gone too. Not for good, like Sam's dad, but he's not with the family at the beach, which still bites.

I wish he was here. I wish he was sleeping in this bed instead of me. I'd gladly sleep on the couch for the rest of my life if it meant that my parents were happy and not fighting.

When Ann first got sick — back when she almost died — I told my dad it wasn't fair. He agreed and told me that life isn't fair. Well, he's right. And the fact that he and Mom can't just get along and be happy is the most unfair of all. Life isn't fair.

Nothing's fair.

There's a nightstand with a lamp and a phone on it separating my bed from Mom's, kind of like in hotel rooms. Even though I'm not right next to her, I can tell that Mom isn't sleeping either. Every so often she rolls over, or sighs, or makes little whimpering noises. At one point I wonder if the whimpering has turned to crying, but the sound of it is muffled by waves crashing on the beach.

My eyes finally start getting heavy right about the time the bedroom door opens. "Mom? You still awake?"

It's Bree.

"Of course, honey. Come in. What's going on?"

"I can't sleep. Ann has the lights on."

"Why is she still awake?"

"She's writing in her diary."

"Ah. Well, that's important too. You want to cuddle with me for a while?"

Bree's dark form crawls over Mom to the nightstand-side of her bed, making the bedsprings squeak. A minute later she asks the very thing I've been thinking since dinner: "I know Dad said you guys aren't getting a divorce, but . . . ?"

Mom doesn't answer right away. "We want to avoid that at all costs, Bree. Marriage just . . . isn't always easy."

"Why not?"

"It's complicated."

"I'm almost fourteen, Mom. Cade might not understand, but I would."

I'm dying to tell her I heard that, but I'm not sure they realize I'm still awake, so I figure it's better to kept quiet, or Mom might clam up.

"I don't want you to worry, sweetheart. We'll be fine."

That doesn't satisfy Bree. "Is it because of Ann? You guys didn't used to fight so much before she got sick."

A heavy silence fills the darkness for a moment. Then Mom says, "Having her sick has certainly put an added strain on things, but it's not Ann's fault. It's nobody's fault but mine and your father's. I think somewhere along the line we've forgotten how to love."

I can't keep quiet any longer. "You mean you don't love Dad anymore?"

She doesn't seem surprised that I'm awake. "No, Cade. I love your father. And I think he still loves me too. But there is a difference between loving someone, and *loving* someone. Does that make sense?"

"No."

She takes another moment to think. "You know what a noun is, right?"

*Does she think I'm a second-grader?* "Of course. Person, place, or thing."

"Good. And what's a verb?"

"An action word," says Bree.

"Exactly. Well, love is both. A noun — a feeling that you have — and also a verb, the way we show someone we love them. Right

125

now, I think your father and I still feel the noun, but we've lost sight of how to live the verb."

I don't completely understand what she just said, but I get the basic idea. Bree seems to get it too. "So what happens to your noun," she asks, "if you don't start figuring out how to verb? Does the noun eventually go away?"

"I don't know, Bree," comes the sad reply. "I just don't know."

# CHAPTER 11
## EMILY

Yesterday afternoon was like a dream. It was perfect and sublime. Our family was together. We were happy. After Dell and I returned from Home Depot, we spent the rest of the afternoon with the kids doing nothing but beach stuff: walking on the sand as a family, collecting shells, building sand sculptures. We even explored the tide pools near Haystack Rock while the tide was out.

Then we went out to dinner and the tides abruptly changed.

*Everything changed.*

As I wake up this morning, it's as though Dell's angry departure has cast a pall on the whole world, including the weather. A steady rain is pouring off the roof, signifying the dawn of a terrible day.

When the kids are finally up and going, I inform them that we're going to see Great-grandma Grace.

Cade is the first to ask if he can just stay home.

"She misses you guys," I tell him. "You all need to come."

"But I don't want to see someone who we know is dying."

Ann puts her hands on her hips. "We're all dying, Cade. Just some of us sooner than others."

Now I place my hands on my hips too. "Ann Marie Bennett, please don't say things like that."

She shrugs it off. "It's true."

"Yes, but . . . just don't, OK? I don't like to hear it."

When everyone is ready to go, I grab an old key hanging on a hutch in the entryway.

"Are we driving there?" asks Ann.

"We could walk, but we'll be awfully wet."

Bree is suddenly all smiles. "So we get to drive in Grandma Grace's car?"

"It's the only one we've got."

I knew they'd love to putt around in Grandma's car this summer, which is why I insisted on leaving our other car back in Portland. Well, that, and I hoped Dell would stay longer with the van.

As we head outside to pile in, I can't help but admire the thing, but then I've always loved this car. My eyes dart from one feature to the next.

*Deep-burgundy paint. Chrome grill. White-wall tires. Fancy headliner. Flowing curves from bumper to bumper.*

It's a 1949 two-door Plymouth Special Deluxe Coupe, in pristine condition. The custom license plate reads, "49-R." The older girls have been in it a dozen or so times, on special occasions, but Cade has only been in it once or twice, and it's clear he can hardly wait to do it again, because he's the first one inside.

Before starting it up, I remind them that it was the first car my grandparents purchased together, and they'd decided to never get rid of it. "It didn't always look so nice, but Grandpa restored it a couple of years before he passed away."

"Are you sure you know how to drive it?" asks Ann.

I give her a puzzled look. "Didn't I ever tell you?"

"What?"

"You know my mother passed away when I was in high school, right?"

"Yes."

"Well, my father had to travel a lot for work back then, just to make ends meet, so I spent much of my senior year living with my grandparents. This thing was pretty rusty at the time, but they let me drive it to high school. I called it the Walrus.' "

"The what?" asks Cade.

"The Walrus."

"Why?"

"Grandpa said each new driver had given it a different name over the years. It was a tradition, I guess. He and Grandma originally named it Dasher, from the 'Rudolph the Red-nosed Reindeer' song, which was the number-one hit in 1949. My uncle Mike named it Thor when he drove it, and my mom changed the name to Morpheus, the Greek god of dreams."

"All those other names are cool," remarks Bree. "So why did you change it to the Walrus?"

I run my hands along the steering wheel, remembering the feel. I turn the key and the old beast roars to life. Finally I adjust the rearview mirror so Bree can see me. "It's the name of a Beatles song. When John Lennon wrote the lyrics, he did so with the express purpose of confusing anyone who might try to find some deeper meaning in them. They're mostly nonsensical phrases, strung together with a catchy tune." I pause, remembering with angst the dark days of my own youth. "My mother had just passed away. I was a confused teenager trying to make sense of a confusing world, so that song really spoke to me."

"What would you get out of a nonsensical song?" Ann asks, her tone verging on critical.

I let out a little sigh. "That . . . some things are just not meant to be understood, I guess. Try as you might to make sense of them, some things in life, like Lennon's lyrics — or the passing of a mother in her prime — are beyond comprehension. Sometimes you just have to accept what you don't understand." I pause for another moment, and then begin softly singing as I put the car into gear and back up. "I am the eggman, they are the eggmen. I am the walrus, goo goo g'joob . . ."

There is an odd silence in the car as my voice drifts off. Finally Ann asks, "Do you think I can drive the car, Mom?"

Ann got her learner's permit when she was almost sixteen, but it was just a few weeks later that her heart stopped working and she nearly died in the pool. Since then, between all of her medical procedures — and with my own hesitancy to put her in harm's way — she hasn't really been allowed to get behind the wheel.

"Oh, I don't think so," I mumble.

"Why not?"

"Because I'm not sure you're ready."

"I'm as old as you were when you drove it to high school."

"I know, but . . . Ann, you're so close to getting a new heart. You just need to hold tight until then. Then there'll be lots of things you can do."

Ann dismisses my comment with a look of disgust. "I am the walrus," she mutters under her breath.

"What was that, dear?"

"Nothing. You wouldn't understand."

When we get to the care facility where Grandma Grace is staying, the misery of the day picks up steam. I've been telling myself for the past nine months that Grandma is dying of old age. After all, she's lived a long time. But the truth is that nobody ever just dies of being old — something has to give. In her case, it's her brain.

The way it was explained to me, Grandma Grace has an uncommon form of Alzheimer's that is causing her involuntary body functions — such as the lungs breathing and the heart beating — to "forget" how to function properly. Like other Alzheimer's patients, she also has increasingly frequent moments of dementia, but the biggest threat to her health is not that she'll forget who or where she is but that her body will simply forget how to work and suddenly stop ticking.

When we get to her room, she doesn't look anything like she did the last time I saw her. Her hair is all matted from lying in bed, there are tubes in her nose and all sorts of electrical leads running from machines near her bed to somewhere on her chest beneath the thin hospital robe.

At least her eyes light up when she sees us, which means she's in one of her better mental states. *For the moment.*

The way she slurs when she speaks makes it hard to understand what she is saying, though she's not doing a lot of talking. "My dear Em'ly," she drawls, very slowly. "You came."

"Of course we came, Grandma. We've missed you."

She swallows several times before she can say, "You too."

"Do you remember the kids? Ann, Bree, and Cade. They were so excited to come visit you."

Grandma nods.

"Thanks for letting us stay in your home. It's such a nice break for us to be able to come here for the summer like this. It'll be so nice to come see you every day."

Cade's eyes get very wide. "Every day?"

he whispers from the other side of the bed.

I shoot him a warning look.

Grandma smiles — or as close to a smile as her frail lips can manage. "Your house now. My gift to you." She turns her head slowly to Ann. "And you."

"Thank you, Grandma Grace," Ann says politely.

"Yes, thank you, Grandma. You shouldn't have, but it's a huge blessing."

Her old eyes begin drooping. She looks exhausted just from that short conversation. It's hard seeing her like this. For a moment, my mind wanders back to the picture of her and Grandpa in front of the Eiffel Tower, and I can't help feeling sorry for her.

I take a seat in the empty chair to Grandma's right. "You look sleepy, Grandma. Why don't you just get some rest? We'll be back tomorrow."

She nods, then lifts her withered, trembling hand. With a distinct twinkle in her eyes, she says, "Kids, don't get old. Beats the alternative . . . but not by much."

Grandma drifts off quickly after that. As soon as her eyes fall completely shut, the kids are ready to bolt.

"Can we go now?" asks Cade. "This place smells."

I know we just got here, but there's no

telling how long Grandma will sleep, so I give in and we all head home. The only problem is, when we get there, there's not much to do. After all, it's still pouring outside, so the beach is out of the question. And the TV doesn't work. And we forgot to bring our board games from home. We play a few card games that Grandma has in the house, but that's about it.

Sadly, Thursday is pretty much the same. We all go to see how Grandma is doing, which isn't all that great, and then we come home and wait for something — *anything* — exciting to happen.

Instead of something exciting, what we end up with is . . . more rain.

On Friday, when we awake to yet another downpour, it feels like everyone is a little more on edge. By midmorning there is a definite increase in the amount of whining and complaining over things like the size of the house, the sharing of rooms, the rabbit ears on the television, and the annoying blue carpet. By noon, the whining is replaced by overt grumblings directed toward specific individuals, mostly in the form of unkind tones and unfriendly glances. As the day wears on, unkind tones and unfriendly glances mushroom into threatening grunts and torrid glares, and before we know it . . .

*kaboom!* It's as though all three of my pirate-children simultaneously raise their black flags and fire their cannons in an all-out war of words. After that point, they can hardly stand to be in the same room without saying something awful to each other, which is problematic because there are only a few rooms to be in.

Since Dell isn't around, I become the default arbiter of every little flap.

"Mom, she's wearing my shirt! And she's so big, she's gonna stretch it!"

"Did you hear that, Mom? She called me fat!"

"Mom, he changed the channel!"

"But Mom, only stupid people watch that show!"

"Mom, she moved her foot to the spot on the couch that's supposed to be for *my* feet!"

"She poked me!"

"He touched me!"

"She looked at me!"

"Mommmm! She's *breathing my air*!"

It's mind-blowing how quickly things can devolve. That's not to say my kids have never had disagreements before. They're kids, after all. It happens. I expect them to have arguments from time to time, or to occasionally tease each other about this or that. What makes this different, at least to me, is that it has never before felt so personal. At the height of their fighting, my only conclusion is that all three of them *truly* hate each other, and I can't help feeling like I've failed as a mother.

At three o'clock, in the middle of their ongoing dispute, the phone rings. I pick it up in the kitchen, but hardly say a word. "Uh-huh . . . OK . . . How soon?" When I hang up, I take a deep breath, before yelling, "I've had it up to *here* with all three of you!" I'm pointing at my neck. "Lucky for you, your father is on his way. He'll be here in time for dinner. If you still have fights to settle when he gets here, you can take it up with him. Until then, I don't want to hear a peep!" To make sure they keep quiet, I sequester them to different parts of the house — Ann on the couch in the living room doing crossword puzzles, Bree in her bedroom doing her art, and Cade in the guest room to unravel the mystery of the Rubik's Cube.

When Dell finally arrives, there are still plenty of things to be hashed out between the kids. The squeak of the front door draws them from their quarters like sharks to chum, each of them thirsty for blood.

On account of proximity, Ann is there

first. "Dad, do you know what Cade did after lunch?" she gushes. "He burped right in my face! An egg-salad burp! I thought I was going to puke!"

Dell looks up to find Cade swimming across the sea-blue shag. "Cade?" he asks, raising his voice and his eyebrows at the same time.

"It wasn't right in her face, I swear! It was like a foot away!"

"More like an inch, you little brat!"

Ann's telling the truth; it was an inch. I saw it with my own eyes. Rather than defend the indefensible, Cade deftly steers the conversation away from himself. "But Dad, do you know why I burped in the first place? Because she was all like, 'When was the last time you showered? You smell like rotten fish.' And I'm like, 'No, you smell like rotten egg.' I *had* to burp. She had it coming!"

"She *so* had it coming," says Bree, backing up her brother. "Before that, Ann said I was to blame for world hunger."

"Come again?"

"Yeah," Bree continues, raising her voice another octave, "she said if I didn't eat so much, there would be more food for the kids in Africa."

"Ann, your sister is so skinny her ribs are showing. Why would you say that?"

"I didn't mean anything by it. Only that . . . you know, she should watch what she eats. She's a beanpole now, but not for long if she keeps shoveling it in like that."

"You are so mean sometimes!" hollers Bree. "Make that 'all the time'! Dad, that's like the fourth time she's said I overeat. Oh, and Cade called me Pizza Face."

Seething, Dell turns back to Cade, who shrugs innocently. "What? She was picking at her face in the mirror again. Besides, before I said that, she told me I need to see a therapist."

Again, Dell raises his eyebrows. "Care to explain that one, Bree?"

She shrugs too. "He sticks his finger in his belly button and sniffs it. Don't they have therapists for that?"

"They have therapists for overeaters," comments Ann under her breath.

By then Dell is so red that the blue carpet nearby is giving off a purple glow. "Stop it! Everyone, just stop!"

I'm standing in the middle of the living room with my arms crossed. Frankly, I'm glad he's getting to experience the vitriol of his offspring firsthand. "See what I have to deal with when you're not around? They've been at each other's throats all week."

"Well, it better end. And I mean *now.*" He

waits to make sure no one is going to contradict him. "If there's any more behavior like this, there will be severe consequences."

Ann raises her hand. "What sort of consequences?" The way she says it, it's as if she needs more details so she can make an informed decision about how she's going to respond to the threat. Her response completely catches Dell off guard.

"Well . . . *bad ones,*" he replies, somewhat flustered.

She doesn't let up. "We've already been cooped up in a tiny house for days on end with nothing to do, and have spent the last several hours in time-out. What's worse than that?"

Glowering, Dell folds his arms. "How about we cancel the trip and go home?"

*Excuse me?* "Oh, don't even think about it, Dell," I quickly interject. "The summer just barely began."

"You're the one who's been struggling with their constant fighting. I'm just looking for a solution. If they're not going to behave, why should they get to stay here?"

"Because we're here for *your daughter.* Remember? The one who needs a heart transplant! For crying out loud, don't waltz in here and threaten to take away this trip when it might be the last one she has!"

*Did I just say that?*

My hands instantly fly to my mouth to cover it up. Then tears begin streaming down my face. As everyone watches, I just stand there bawling, horrified by what I let slip out.

I want to take it back, but even through the tears I know I can't. With my whole face now buried in my hands, my mind starts questioning what's really behind my emotions. Am I still mad at the kids for fighting? Absolutely. Am I also upset at Dell for the ongoing rift between us? Certainly. But on top of all that, I'm a mother trying to cope with the fear of losing my daughter. I've tried so hard to be brave in the face of Ann's trials, yet it is now painfully clear to not only me but the whole family that the thought of Ann's heart not holding out until her transplant . . . well, it breaks my heart too.

"I'm so sorry," I say through choked gasps, looking straight ahead at Ann. "I shouldn't have said that."

"No," Dell whispers, "you shouldn't have." He isn't crying, but in his own way, he looks broken too.

Ann graciously steps forward and puts her arms around me. "It's OK, Mom. It's OK."

"Nothing about this is OK, sweetie."

"I'm sorry for our fighting. We'll try harder."

"Thanks. But I see your point too. I know you've been cooped up, and I know that's hard. Maybe that's why I'm so frustrated, because I wanted you to have this idyllic summer, and it's turning out to be anything but."

A few seconds pass, then Bree asks, "Does this mean we're not in trouble?"

"Nice try," Dell replies. "There will still be consequences if you guys don't shape up. But Mom's right, it would help if you weren't stuck inside all day getting in each other's way." He pauses. "Tomorrow is a new day, and I hear the weather is going to improve. We've got all weekend to be together as a family, so can we all agree to get along?" He pauses. "This is the only family we've got. If we can't get along with each other, who can we get along with?"

My arms are still wrapped firmly around Ann, not wanting to ever let her go. "I ask myself that same question every day," I whisper.

# CHAPTER 12
## DELL

"Well, that wasn't exactly the reception I was hoping for after being away from you all week," I say, trying to lighten the mood as I peel off my shoes and set them next to the door.

"It was only three days, Dell," replies Emily instantly.

*Why does she have to correct me like that?*

"Right. Well, now that hopefully we've got all of the fights settled, who's hungry? That pizza buffet place up the road didn't look too crowded when I drove past."

"Sweet," remarks Cade. "I'm starving."

"Me too," says Bree.

Emily, however, is frowning. "Do none of you smell dinner cooking? I've been slaving away all afternoon to prepare a nice meal."

"Oh, whoops. Sorry, kids. Looks like Mom already has plans. We'll have to eat here tonight so it doesn't go to waste."

Her face turns a little pink, but she doesn't

say anything else. She just turns to go finish her preparations.

The conversation over dinner centers mostly on bringing me up to speed on how boring everything was while I was back home in Portland. Everybody except Emily has examples of how awful it was. I also grill Ann on how she is feeling, going down my usual checklist of worries. Are you getting enough rest? Do you feel tired? Any pains in your chest?

As always, she says she's fine. I hope that's the truth.

When the conversation wanes, I remember something I left in the car. "Who wants to play a game tonight?" I ask. On Monday, when we first arrived, I noticed that there weren't many board games in the house. When the kids were younger, whenever we went to the beach, we would play lots of games, especially when it rained, so after work today I went back to the house and picked up a few of the family favorites. Immediately after dinner I grab them from the car and ask Cade which one he'd like to play.

"The Game of Life," he replies instantly. "I rock at it."

"Emily," I call from the living room, "the kids and I are going to play Life. You want to join?"

"I'd like to," comes her response, "but I've got to clean up from dinner."

"OK. We'll just wait until you're ready."

It takes her another fifteen minutes before she finally leaves the kitchen, wearing the crab apron and a matching scowl.

"About time," I mumble.

Emily turns pink again. "You know what? I think I'm just going to go read. You guys go ahead and play without me."

"We've been waiting here, just for you, and now you're not even going to play? That's perfect."

"I'm sorry, Dell. But I'm not in the mood to play anymore. You go ahead and enjoy Life without me." Her pink is turning red, more like the lobster. She leaves without saying another word.

"Ah crap," I mutter, "it's going to be another one of those nights."

"Can we just play?" asks Bree.

I let out a long breath. "Yes, Breezy, you go first."

The game goes along fine for the first little while. But as it progresses, Ann starts looking more and more uncomfortable each time she spins the dial to learn her new fate in the game. We're maybe halfway around the game board — and she's in the lead —

145

when she stands up and announces that she is quitting.

I'm just as confused as Cade and Bree by her behavior. "What's going on, Ann? I thought you liked this game."

"Yeah, when I was their age," she replies, motioning to her brother and sister.

"What's changed?"

"I have." She appears to be on the verge of tears.

"I don't get it."

In a mad flash of emotions, Ann bends down and plucks her game piece off the board. "You see this, Dad? My little car has *five* people in it! I have a husband and three kids in this stupid game. On my very first turn I went to college, and on my next turn I got married. Now I've got a career and I'm worried about buying a bigger house."

"Oh, I see," I say gently. "I'm so sorry, Ann. I didn't even think of that."

"You know what this game needs? How about a card that destroys your dreams? Where is the cancer card or the miscarriage card or the divorce card? And where is an avert-disaster space? There should be a space that if you land on it, you're suddenly free and clear of life's most unfair circumstances. I don't want the six-figure income or the mansion, I just want the get-out-of-death-free card!" She pauses, narrowing her focus on me. "I hate The Game of Life. I'm going to bed."

"I understand," I say softly as she walks off. "You're right. It's not fair."

After that, the evening sort of fizzles. Bree eventually heads upstairs too, and the pair of them read books until they fall asleep. Cade and I stay up late watching television. It isn't optimal, but when Cade stands next to the TV and holds the antenna just right, we're able to follow along with Survivor.

At eleven o'clock, with Cade yawning every five seconds, I concede that I've been stalling.

Be a man, Dell. You can't avoid her forever . . .

Cade makes his bed on the couch, and I finally make my way to the bedroom. "Good night," I say, ruffling his hair. I wish talking to my wife was as easy as talking to my son.

I slip inside and close the door behind me. For a few minutes, the room is silent. She's on the bed, reading. I know she knows I'm there, but she's actively ignoring me. "So," I venture, "are you going to tell me why you're mad? What'd I do this time?"

She pretends to still be interested in her book. Doesn't even bother looking up. "I'm not mad."

"Of course you are. You're sulking. This is how you act when I've done something wrong."

"Well, you should know what you did. Why don't you think about it . . ."

I let a little time pass to see if she's going to give me any clue. She doesn't. "So you're not going to tell me?"

Another silence. Then she finally looks up from her book and stares me down. "Do you know how long it took me to make dinner? Three hours! I spent all afternoon working on it, so it would be just right. I wanted to start cleaning up Grandma's room today, but I didn't have time because I wanted to have a nice meal for you when you arrived."

"And I appreciated it."

"No you didn't! That's the thing, you didn't even say thank you! If you'd had your way, we would have wasted our money on some pizza joint. I made Chicken Divan, Dell — *your favorite dish* — and not only did you not bother to thank me, but you didn't even comment on how it tasted. Then afterward you go off with the kids to play the game, and nobody even bothers to help clean up the kitchen. You all sat in there on your rears waiting for me to come, when we could have started the game much sooner if you'd just thought to help me out a little."

"You should've said you wanted help."

"I shouldn't have to! I *always* want help. We're supposed to be a team, remember?"

"Fine. I'm sorry. I should have thanked you. And helped you. And whatever else it is that you think I should have done."

"Don't get smart with me. It's very unattractive."

"Don't worry, right now I'm not trying to attract anything."

I know that last comment was hurtful . . . but it was meant to hurt.

It doesn't surprise me at all when she starts to cry. I let her cry it out for several minutes without saying anything. Finally she wipes her eyes and says, "The night you left, Bree was so worried about us that she came down in the middle of the night to ask if I still loved you."

"And? What did you tell her?"

"What do you think?"

I know that's a loaded question, so I don't respond.

"What about you, Dell? What if she'd asked you if you still loved me?"

"I do love you," I say flatly. "Even if you don't love me, I still love you."

"No you don't."

149

"How can you say that? If I say I do, then I do."

"Words alone are hollow. It dawned on me when I was talking to Bree that we don't love each other anymore. We used to love each other. I mean really love each other, fiercely. And I think we still *want* to love each other. Maybe we both still feel that sense of commitment and obligation for the other, but you don't actively love me anymore, Dell, and I'm probably guilty of the same thing. We're hoping for the noun of love, but not applying the verb."

"Honestly, I don't even know what that means."

"You would if you loved me."

"I do love you!"

"Then show it, Dell. That's all I've ever wanted."

"Yeah, well, it goes both ways," I say angrily. "You get what you give, I guess." I hesitate briefly, wondering what I can say now. *Nothing. Stop before the hole gets deeper.* "This conversation is getting us nowhere. We should stop now, before one of us says something we really regret."

# CHAPTER 13
## CADE

When Dad showed up yesterday, he said the weather was going to get better.

He was wrong.

It's still as rainy as last week, and I'm really getting tired of it. I want to be flying kites and building sand castles and feeding seagulls; instead I'm stuck inside doing nothing but adjusting rabbit ears above the television.

I wonder if it's rainy like this back in Portland? I bet not. My friends are probably having the best summer ever, while I'm stuck here with nothing to do.

After lunch Mom and Dad make us go visit Grandma Grace again. I haven't been around a lot of old people, so maybe my opinion is wrong, but I don't think she's doing so hot. She looks so weak, like the smallest movement might break her. It's really a bummer, because she's always been really cool to us kids. Now she's just sort of there, if you know what I mean. Like in limbo, waiting for something else to happen.

It's kind of sad — Grandma Grace would probably like to die, but Ann doesn't want to and doesn't deserve to. I don't understand why Grandma should get to live so long but my sister could just drop dead tomorrow, without warning.

*I don't want my sister to die. I don't want anyone to die, but especially not my sister.*

Anyway, when we get to the place where Grandma is at, I have to plug my nose. I really don't like the smell. I'm convinced it's the old people who smell, but Dad says it's the smell of all their medicines. Maybe he's right, because I spot a nurse going from room to room with plastic cups loaded with humongous pills for everyone.

*How the heck do their old throats swallow those things?*

"Speaking of medicine," says Dad, "Ann, you're looking kind of pale today. Are you keeping up on your meds?"

She rolls her eyes. Ann hates her pills, but she has to take them every day or she gets really weak. "Not because I like to, but yes."

When we go into Grandma Grace's room, it's nice to see that she still recognizes everyone. Mom wasn't so sure she would.

But today her speech is really jumbled, like she's chewing on marbles. On several occasions she says things that we can't make any sense of.

The worst is when Mom tells her we're going to start organizing the things in her bedroom so we can give the walls a fresh coat of paint. Grandma gets a distant look in her eyes, then says something that sounds to me like, "Down throat way the score chards."

"What'd she say?" I whisper.

"Down through the way to score charts," chirps Bree.

*Huh?*

"Right," snickers Ann. "That clarifies things."

Mom leans in closer. "Grandma, I didn't catch what you said. Something about scorecards?"

Every wrinkle on Great-grandma's face pulls together into a massive frown. "The *nude books,*" she whispers slowly. Or at least that's what it sounds like. "I won the nude books."

The way Dad and Mom look at each other, I suddenly have a feeling they are going to sort through Grandma's stuff in private before they let us in the room to help.

Sure enough, when we get back to the beach house, they tell us we'll be called to help once everything is "safe."

The good news is that we don't have to help right away with the work. The bad news is that we now have more time to kill on our own, and the weather still stinks.

"I know," I tell my sisters while we're trying to figure out what to do, "how about we play Twenty Questions?"

"How about not," replies Bree. "You don't know the difference between a vegetable and a mineral."

"What about the games Dad brought?"

"No thanks."

"There are cards. We could play Hearts."

Ann looks up. "I don't think so, Cade."

"Why not?"

"Really? You want me to play a game where the loser is the one who collects the most hearts?"

OK, so she has a point. "Uno, then?"

"No."

"Charades?"

"No."

"Mancala?"

"Double no."

I'm running out of ideas fast. "Hide and Seek?"

My sisters glance at each other. "Yes!" says

Ann. "Great idea. I'll be it first."

"Cool," I tell her. "Count to a hundred."

"I'll count to *three* hundred, just to make sure you have time to get really well hidden." Ann closes her eyes and begins slowly counting.

Bree picks up her art pad and tiptoes to the top of the stairs. I follow her up. When she gets to her bedroom, she whispers, "I'll hide in here. You have to hide somewhere else."

I nod. *Why would I hide with her when I already have the perfect spot in mind?* I tiptoe a few steps farther and twist the handle to the attic door.

It is darker than I thought it would be, even with the light coming in from the hallway. There are six steps leading up to a loft area beneath the roof. For a second or two after pulling the door closed behind me, I am in complete darkness, but then my eyes begin to adjust. There is a light switch on the wall, but I know if I turn it on, Ann will find me in a snap.

Like a wraith, I move up the stairs without making a sound. The higher I go, the more I can see in the dark. The attic platform is right below the sloping roof, so while it is nearly head-high in the middle, toward the sides there is only a couple feet of clearance. Using all my senses, I creep farther into the black, climbing over and around a lifetime of boxes and clutter, most of which I have a hard time identifying with the tiny sliver of light coming in through an air vent. Halfway to the back of the platform I find what feels like a string of Christmas lights; my next step confirms it when I step on a bulb — I freeze, praying that Ann didn't hear it. As I make my way closer to the rear wall, I also come across what I guess to be a set of golf clubs, a Christmas tree stand, an open box of hats, a bag of sweaters, and either a broken globe or a very smooth basketball.

Finally I drop down behind a large box at the very back. Then I wait.

And wait.

After like ten minutes, Ann yells, "Three hundred! Ready or not, here I come!"

Then I wait.

And wait.

And keep on waiting.

*What the heck? Is she really this bad at Hide and Seek?*

After another fifteen minutes, I realize that I'm probably the only one playing the game. No one is coming. I snuck into the attic to hide, and they are perfectly happy letting me stay here by myself forever. In frustration, I stand up to full height and kick at the box in front of me, but the spot where I stand is too short for a nearly sixth-grader like myself. I cry out in pain when my scalp digs into a series of roof staples.

Twenty seconds later, the attic door swings open and the overhead light flickers to life. "Found you!" says Ann.

"You weren't even looking," I mutter, squinting while my eyes adjust to the light. I'm still rubbing my head, feeling for blood.

"You were just really well hidden."

"Liar."

"Seriously. But I knew you'd give yourself away sooner or later."

"I poked my head on nails or something."

"Ouch. You OK?"

"I'll be fine. I just need to —" My eyes latch on to something a few feet away. "Oh my gosh! I found it! I totally forgot!"

"Found what?"

"Great-grandpa's metal detector! Aunt Bev told me it was here. She said there was treasure buried out back." I step over a weathered brown box and pick it up. "I can't believe we've been here a week and I just remembered this now."

"Does it work?"

The handle-end has a silver switch on the side, which I assume is the power. I flip it on, and then hold the scanner-end upside down against the roof staples. It instantly starts going nuts. *BZZZZZZZ!*

"Sweet!"

*Finally, no matter what else happens this summer, I have found something to do. I am going to find a buried treasure!*

I practically run downstairs to go find my fortune in the rain, only to be stopped by my parents just as I'm opening the back door.

"C'mon, kids!" Dad shouts from Grandma's bedroom. "Everyone come help. The coast is clear. There's nothing bad in here."

"No nude books?" replies Ann with a giggle.

I poke my head through the master bedroom door and beg them to let me go outside with my new toy so I can find the wealth that must surely be waiting for me.

*I'm going to be rich!*

"After the work is done," Mom says.

"How about I share my treasure with you if you let me go?"

Dad laughs. "How about you give me *everything* you dig out of the dirt unless you dig in and help us here first?"

It's not even worth arguing; with both parents taking the same side, there is no getting out of it now. I set down the metal detector and head to the closet to help Bree box up clothes. "What if Grandma Grace needs these when she gets out of the hospital?" I ask.

Everyone goes quiet for a few seconds, like I said something wrong.

"We're not getting rid of them," Mom explains. "Just boxing them up for now so they're out of the way while we paint. Don't worry, Grandma's things are safe. If she comes back home, everything will be right where she left it."

"So you're not selling this place?" asks Ann.

"Not right away, no. It wouldn't be right. We don't want to do anything until we see how things go with Grandma."

Bree yanks a blouse from its hanger. "But . . . she's probably not coming home . . . is she?"

Mom is kneeling beside a box of papers she pulled from underneath the bed. She leans back to rest on her heels. "No, sweetie. Probably not. As sad as that is to think about, just keep in mind that the sickness she has . . . well, it's painful. It's hard on her physically and mentally. So we may be sad to see her go, but it will probably be a blessing for her. Plus, she's lived a good long life, so I'm sure she feels like it's time."

Bree nods that she understands.

I nod too.

But Ann? She looks mad. "So it's OK for her to die because she lived a long time?"

"That's not what I meant," Mom says, backpedaling.

"It's what you said. 'She's lived a good long life.' Well, what if you haven't lived a long life? Does that mean it's not OK to die?"

Mom sits back on her heels again, and then drops all the way to a sitting position on the floor. "Ann," she whispers in a voice that says she might start crying, "please don't twist this around. I truly didn't mean it that way. In fact, we shouldn't measure lives by their length. There's nothing that says eighty years is better than fifty years is better than fifteen. It's *how* we live that counts. Yes, Grandma Grace has lived a long time, but it was how she lived each day that made her life special. Made it *'good.'* " She hesitates, then says, "I'm sorry. I should have been more careful with my words."

"So you'll be OK if I die young?" It's an awful question, and the room goes deathly quiet.

"Like hell we will," replies Dad before Mom can respond. "And that's not going to happen, Ann. You're going to be fine. You hear me?"

Ann is still waiting for Mom to say something.

Now the tears begin to trickle down Mom's face. "If you were to die young, I'd be so proud of the life you've lived. And I would come to accept that your time was done, that you did what you came here to do. But would I be OK? No, Ann. Losing you would be the worst day of my life. You know that, right? And though lives can't be properly measured in years, I promise, I would do *anything* for you to be able to live a long, long life." She stops to wipe her sleeve on her face. "Have I ever told you about the train engineer who realized the tracks were broken?"

"No."

Mom tries to smile, but she's not very successful. "I don't remember where I read this, but there was once a man — a train engineer — who was stationed at a fork in the tracks. The electric switch was broken, so he needed to be there to make sure the trains stayed to the right, because the tracks to the left were under repair. If a train went to the left, it would immediately run off the tracks and crash. So the engineer was waiting, and he hears a train whistle blow. The noon train was coming around the bend at

161

full speed. As he should, he pulls on the lever to manually switch the exchange to the right, toward a narrow train bridge. However, as he pulled the lever, he looked up and saw that his own little boy was crossing the bridge to bring him his lunch. At the rate the train was coming, it couldn't stop in time, nor could his son get off the bridge in time to avoid being hit, so he knew if he kept holding on to the lever and sent the train to the right, his son would die. If he let go of the lever and sent the train to the left, all of the people on the train would die."

"I don't like this story." Ann's voice is numb. Looking a little whiter than normal, she sits down on the chair next to Grandma's queen-size bed. "Did this really happen?"

Mom shrugs. "I don't know . . . but I think so."

"What did the engineer do?"

My mother is quiet for a second, then says, "He held on to the lever." After another moment, she explains, "The story was told as a metaphor for God's love. The engineer willingly gave his son so that others could live." She pauses again, looking down at her lap. When she looks up, there are more tears running down her cheeks. "Ann, maybe this

162

makes me a terrible person, but I don't think I'd think twice about it. If it were you, Bree, or Cade out there on that bridge, I think I'd let go of the lever and send the train to the left." She sniffles once, then stands up and picks up the box in front of her.

There's a whole lot of quiet in the room after that. It's all I can do to get the image of a little boy being struck by a train out of my head. What finally does the trick is Ann's snicker and then goofy laugh and then, "I found the nude books!"

Almost instantly, Dad blurts out, "Close your eyes!"

Ann is all smiles and keeps her eyes wide open. She reaches into the box she's been working on and pulls out a handful of small, spiral-bound notepads. As the family gathers around, she flips through several of them quickly. "I think I just figured out what Grandma Grace was trying to say." She opens one of the pads to the first page and shows it to everyone.

In handwritten pen, at the very top, it reads, *1986 — Round #1.* Below that, the page is split into two columns. Grace's name is at the top of the left column, while Alfred's — Great-grandpa — is on the right. Below their names is a page full of small tally marks. Lastly, at the very bottom, is a sum of the tallies: *Grace = 74. Al = 61.*

" 'Don't throw away the scorecards,' " Ann says slowly, translating Grandma's earlier instructions. " 'I want the notebooks.' "

*Down throat way the score chards. I want the nude books.*

There is no doubt that we've found the notebooks, and they definitely look like scorecards. Now there's only one question: *What the heck are they for?*

After a couple of hours of gutting Grandma's room, Dad finally lets me head out back with the metal detector. The steady rain has slowed to a bearable drizzle, so I lug my device to the edge of the beach and power it up.

The red indicator lights up instantly . . . and fizzles out thirty seconds later.

I turn it on again to the same result.

Five tries later, I carry the thing back inside.

"Done so soon?" asks Mom.

"The battery is dead."

"Probably from sitting in the attic so long. Did you see a power cord while you were up there?"

"No, but I'll go look." Sure enough, the

cord is in the attic. I plug it in, and in an hour I'm ready to give it another try. Before heading outside, I stop to examine a picture of Great-grandpa hanging on the wall. I never met the man, but I've seen enough pictures of him that he's familiar. In this photo, he's holding up a salmon by the gills, and there's a fire in his eyes that makes me think he really enjoyed life. Or at least enjoyed fishing. I bet he was an adventurer, like me, and that he and I would get along quite well. So well, in fact, that he'd be proud that I'm continuing the search for his buried treasure. "Don't worry," I tell him. "If your treasure is out there, Cap'n Cade will find it."

I didn't realize Bree was standing behind me, watching and listening. "You're not going to find anything," she says. "There's no buried treasure out there. If there was, it would have been discovered years ago."

"Aunt Bev says I will, if I try hard enough."

"Well, you won't, so don't get your hopes up."

"Will too."

"I bet you fifty bucks you don't find anything valuable."

"Deal."

Just then Mom comes walking by and sees

me with the metal detector. "The rain is picking up again. You sure you want to go out in this weather?"

I smirk at Bree. "Yep. I have a bet to win."

As I step from the kitchen to the back deck, I remember what Aunt Bev told me about hunting for the treasure: *Your great-grandfather believed there was treasure buried out behind the house . . . he'd spend hours and hours out there . . . A good pirate doesn't give up until his treasure is found . . .*

" 'Behind the house,' " I tell myself, not really wanting to go too far away in the rain. "Maybe the treasure isn't on the beach at all, but right here in the yard."

With the flip of the switch I power up and begin tracking back and forth across the lawn, swinging the device in low, smooth motions. In the first thirty minutes I get six blips on the scanner, and each time I dig in that spot I end up finding something: a dime, two pennies, and three bottle caps.

A little while later, once the rain has slowed to a mist, I spot Bree sitting on the back porch under the cover of the roof, sipping a cola. "Any luck?" she asks.

"Twelve cents."

She returns my smirk from earlier. "See. I told you there's no treasure."

"Don't be so sure. I'm just getting

started."

"Search all you want. You're still going to owe me fifty bucks." She smirks again, then stands up to leave.

Right then my buzzer starts going off like never before. I'm standing in the bark dust, just off the edge of the lawn, near the fence that divides our house from the next. "I found something else!"

Curious, Bree wanders down from the deck to check it out. "What is it?"

"I have to dig first. You want to help?"

I give her the hand trowel and I use my hands, and together we brush aside the mulch and begin digging through the dirt. Within a minute we've got a hole a foot wide by a foot deep, but we haven't found anything. I sift through our dirt pile to see if we've missed something, but still nothing. Just to be sure, I scan the pile with the metal detector, but no alarms go off.

"Scan the hole," suggests Bree. "Maybe it's still down deeper."

Sure enough, when I scan the bottom of the hole . . . *BZZZZZ!*

When we start digging again, we take great care to make sure we aren't missing anything. Carefully, we take a scoop of dirt, sift it in our hands, then sift it once more as we deposit it on our growing pile beside the hole. At about sixteen inches deep we finally strike gold. Well . . . probably not gold. But something.

"What is it?" asks Bree again.

"I don't know. Dig a little more."

Bree jabs the point of the trowel under something hard and pries it loose. When she gives it another firm pop, a white-flecked object, smeared with dirt, comes flying out of the hole at Bree's face, hitting her right on the mouth. "Oooh!" she screams, spitting like mad. "What is it?"

I pick it up to give it a closer look. "I think it's a skull."

She spits at least five more times and then wipes at her lips like crazy. "That is so gross!"

It's impossible not to laugh. "Yeah, you just kissed a dead cat!"

She wipes once more, going all the way up her sleeve. "I thought your thingamajig is only supposed to find metal."

"It is." I take the tiny shovel and begin poking around in the hole again, in the area where the skull was. It doesn't take long before I uncover a leather collar with a stamped metal tag attached. *"Mr. Skittles,"* I say aloud, reading the name on the inscription. "That should make you feel better."

"Why?"

"At least your first kiss was a boy."

She punches me as hard as she can in the arm, but I don't care. From now on, no matter how she teases me, I will be able to tell people that a dead cat named Mr. Skittles kissed Bree on the lips, and that's easily worth a bruised arm.

"This is so stupid," she hisses. "I'm going inside."

"Great," I reply with another laugh. "I'll be in as soon as I find a treasure."

For the next hour, I venture farther out on the beach, again swinging the metal detector low across the sand. After a while my arms feel like they're going to fall off, but I continue on, because I can't let Bree win.

*Because I don't have fifty dollars to pay her!*

As it starts getting dark, I begin slowly back toward the house. I don't want to give up just yet, but I know finding treasure in the dark would be hard, even with a metal detector. As I approach the property line, the sun is so low that my shadow in front of me is twice my size.

That's when it happens.

Maybe ten feet from where the edge of the beach meets our lawn, the device starts buzzing again. This is the loudest buzz yet!

Worried that I might uncover another

169

dead something-or-other, I dig carefully, lifting out each handful of sand with care, then letting the grains strain through my fingers until there is nothing left. After twenty scoopfuls, my fingernails scrape along a flat metal surface of something nearly as big as my hand. It isn't big enough to be a treasure chest, but this is definitely the biggest thing I've found so far. *At least it's not some stupid bottle cap!*

Eagerly, I trace around the edges of the whatever-it-is, like an archaeologist uncovering bones. At last, the object takes shape. I dust away the thin layer of sand covering the inscription, salivating over what it might be, and then, just like that . . . the thrill is gone. *"Altoids,"* I mumble, reading the top of a rusty tin box. *"Curiously strong mints.* Gosh dang it! Bree was right. There's no treasure out here."

I'm about to toss the stupid thing back in its hole and bury it, when something rattles inside the tin. Though I don't expect to find more than a rock or a shell, I blow off the remaining grains of sand, open the lid . . . and gasp.

# Chapter 14
## Emily

The girls are upstairs entertaining themselves. Cade is playing techno-pirate on the beach with Grandpa's thingamajig. That leaves Dell and me, alone, finishing up the work in Grandma's room.

Which means it's awfully quiet in here.

We share lots of awkward glances, and occasionally he asks me where to put something, but that's about it. *Why is it like this?* Lately it feels impossible to just have a simple conversation without him reading something into every little thing I say. I'm sure he feels the same about me. It used to be so easy to talk to him, but now it's easier just to go about our business with as few words as possible, because the more we say, the more our words are scrutinized, and the more likely it is that we end up feeling hurt.

Sometimes silence between spouses is a blessing. Sometimes it's a curse. And sometimes it's interrupted by the bloodcurdling scream of a child . . .

"Mom! Dad! Hurry!"

Dell and I look at each other for a split second, then race for the bedroom door. Cade never calls for help unless he's hurt, and even then not always.

"Everybody! Come quick!"

"What's going on?" I ask, panicking, as I turn the corner to the living room. "Are you OK?"

Dell is right beside me. Bree comes bounding down the stairs, with Ann trailing closely.

Cade ignores my question. "Ha! Bree, you owe me fifty bucks!"

"Shut. Up. There's no way you found something out there."

"Oh yeah? Check it out!" In his palm is an old Altoids can.

"That's not treasure," she says. "It's junk."

"Hey, one man's junk . . ." remarks Dell.

"No, *for real*! Open it up!" Cade hands it to me to do the honors. Skeptically, I lift open the rusty lid. The first thing I see is a ring. Not a real ring but a plastic one, like you'd get from a bubblegum machine. On top of the ring, affixed with some sort of hot-melt or glue, is a blue candy heart with the inscription *MISS YOU*.

Beneath the ring, folded in fourths, is a

piece of paper, which I gently remove. I read the first few lines silently, and then gasp as a chill courses through me. "Oh my gosh . . ."

"What does it say?" asks Ann.

It's rude, I know, but I instinctively shush her — and everyone else — so I can read without interruption. Mesmerized by the handwritten words, I continue on. By the time I reach the end, there are warm tears streaming down my face. When I look up, the whole family is staring at me, but the only face I can focus on right now is Cade's. "You found this on the beach? Where?"

"Right out back, just past the lawn. It was buried like a foot and a half down."

"But it's still not a treasure," says Bree adamantly. "Right?"

I glance at her, then at Cade, and then I fold it up and return it to the can. "That's not for me to say," I tell her, choking slightly on the words. "But I bet Grandma Grace might be able to tell us."

"But what does it say?" asks Dell.

I smile at him as best I can. "Come with me to see Grandma. I'll tell you there."

He seems instantly put off. "Why don't you just tell me now?"

"Because it wouldn't be right if Grandma were the last of us to know what this says."

He turns to Cade. "Will you tell me? You read it, right?"

Cade shrugs. "The handwriting is cursive; I only got little bits."

"Just come with me, Dell. Everyone can come. It'll be worth it, I promise."

As we're driving to the nursing home, I keep checking my watch. Visiting hours are almost over. My bigger fear, though, is not that they won't let us in to see her but that Grandma won't recognize us. What if she's in the middle of one of her spells and we're just a motley bunch of strangers to her?

*Not now, God. Please, not tonight. Let her be her, just long enough to hear this . . .*

It looks like she's asleep when we enter her room, but her eyes flutter open at the sound of our whispers. "There you are," she says while taking a large breath through the tube in her nose. "My fam'ly." Her voice is soft and slow, but the words deliberate, which means she's still having a good day.

"We're back again, Grandma," I tell her. "Two visits in one day. Aren't you the lucky one?" As soon as we've given hugs all around, I take a seat at the edge of her bed and hold up the Altoids can. "Have you ever seen this before?"

Grandma's ocean-blue eyes seem to

double in size. She nods eagerly, then asks, "L-l-letter?"

"Yes, there's a letter. Would you like me to read it?"

Grandma Grace's expectant eyes fill with moisture as she nods once more.

I open the lid, unfold the letter, and clear my throat, then read as clear and sure as I can, wanting her to savor every last word:

"July seventeenth, 2000. My sweet Grace. I trust and pray that you will again find our buried treasure. Don't forget: 'For where your treasure is, there will your heart be also . . .'

"It is late at night, and though I am weary, I am unable to find rest. We both know what is soon to come. How many days remain for me in this world only God can say, but this much I know of myself: Even after I am gone, I will always be with you.

"I have prayed for you every night, that you will be kept safe and well when I am gone. Please do not shed too many tears at my passing, for I am never far away. You are, and always have been, my greatest treasure. All my love, Alfred Birch.

"P.S. Consider this my final move in the Winner's Game. I already long for the day when we can play it again!

"P.P.S. If you found this note and you are not Grace Birch, I beg you to return it to the beach where you discovered it. This treasure is not lost . . . it's just waiting for my Grace to find it."

The tiny pools of water that were previously in Grandma's eyes have migrated to the cracks and crevices of her cheeks. A loving smile adorns her aged lips. She seems completely at peace. "R-r-ring?" she asks.

*How could I forget!* "Yes, I'm so sorry. There is a ring." I hold up the plastic ring with its blue candy heart.

She squints, but can't make out the words.

I gently reach out and touch her hand. "It says, 'Miss You.' "

She nods again, then lifts her eyes to the ceiling and repeats the phrase to someone she can only see in her mind. "M-miss you." Another tear escapes her wrinkled eyelids and plummets down her face. With a hint of a smile, she drops her gaze to meet mine.

"Grandma, I hope you don't mind me asking, but what is the Winner's Game? Is that what all your scorecards were for?"

She nods. "In g-gurnels," she whispers, sounding suddenly exhausted.

"Come again?"

She takes a deep breath and tries her darnedest to re-form the word. "Grrr-nels." A look of frustration flashes across her face. Followed immediately by something else. Something awful. Fear, I think. And incredible pain. A second later she winces, then cries out, then gives a little moan and closes her eyes.

In the same instant, one of the monitors near her bed begins flashing wildly while a low-grade alarm screams out for help. We barely have time to register that something is wrong when two nurses come running into the room. Everyone backs away from the bed so the nurses can work on her.

Half a minute later another nurse runs in with an external defibrillator. I hear the word "arrhythmia" used three times before they finish adhering electrical leads to her chest and rib cage.

"Close your eyes, Cade," I shout across the room as Grandma's naked torso jumps on the bed. He doesn't obey. His eyes, like all of ours, are fixed. I wish I could reach across the room and shield his view. I wish I could shield my own view! I wish to God I could *un-see* what is happening, but my grandmother's life is teetering precariously between this one and the next, and I have to know which way it is going to fall.

Ten seconds later, the buzzer stops sounding and the nurses take half a step back.

"Is she . . . gone?" asks Ann.

Before the nurses reply, the ECG monitor provides the answer when it returns to its normal rhythm. I watch as the line on the chart bounces between peaks and valleys, measuring the revived beats of a weary heart.

"She's stable," the senior nurse says. "Lucky, but stable. An ambulance is on the way to get her to the hospital. After an episode like this, she'll need to be monitored there for a while."

As I continue staring at the ECG, I can't help but wonder if, in addition to measuring Grandma's heart, the machine is also magically graphing our lives — high and low, high and low, like a roller coaster ride. Is that what life is supposed to be — a roller coaster? Always up or down, but never steady? Our family has had a lot of lows lately. When do we bounce to the next high?

Part of me wishes there were never any lows, but that's just me being selfish. And unrealistic. Maybe jumping from high to low isn't all that bad, because as soon as you're stuck in a spot where the line goes flat, the thrill of the ride is over.

Thankfully, Grandma's ride is not yet done.

After the kids are all in bed, and Dell is asleep, I wander up to the attic on a hunch. Grandma Grace seemed so set on telling me something before her heart stopped, that I think I owe it to her to look. For nearly an hour I sift through boxes upon boxes of old junk, some of it dating back to when I was still a little girl. But just before midnight I crack open a particularly heavy box that Grace has marked, *Important!* It is filled with carefully stacked books, all of them different colors and sizes. I flip a few of them open to find that they are written in Grace's distinctive handwriting.

Amused and delighted at what I've found — the second treasure of the day — I take one of Grandma's "gurnels" downstairs on the couch and read until dawn.

# CHAPTER 15
## ANN

Do you hate me, diary? You should. I'm an awful person! Great-grandma crashed today while we were visiting her. Just like that, everything went south. One second she's talking to us about a letter from her husband, and the next second she's in cardiac arrest.

That could be me. Probably will be, in fact.

That's what makes me so awful! I love Grandma to death, and I'll definitely miss her when she's gone, but as I watched them working on her, trying to bring her back, part of me didn't want her to make it.

Pretty twisted, huh?

I wanted to see her die! Not that I wanted her to be gone. I just wanted to see for myself what it's like, you know? Dying. I wanted to know if that last moment was painful for her, or if she would look re-lieved.

I've been in her situation before — lying half dead, with people trying to bring you back. I don't remember much other than drifting down a dark, peaceful tunnel. I had no idea where I was going, but I knew I wasn't coming back. Of course, then I did come back, which was much more painful than leaving, that's for sure.

So go ahead and hate me, diary. I would if I were you. But can you blame me for being interested? I just wanted to see death from the other side of the body, so as to better prepare for what's coming . . .

On Sunday afternoon, once we're home from the hospital in Seaside where they've moved Grandma, the weather finally turns perfect. Mom and Dad want some time alone to talk, so Bree and I take Cade out to the beach, where he can dink around some more with Grandpa's metal detector.

To me, the beach is heaven on earth. When I die, I'm going to ask God if I can just take my little harp to Cannon Beach and spend eternity strumming hallelujahs on a comfy beach chair. *Seriously.*

When I'm dead, though, I hope my scars will be erased so I can wear a nice V-neck tankini — pearly white, of course — while I'm lounging on God's heavenly sand. As it stands now, I'm not too fond of being seen in a bathing suit, because the purple line on my chest practically glows in the sun. Rather than suffer through people's stares, I wear a tank top with a neckline that even a nun would feel comfortable in.

For two solid hours Cade traipses back and forth over the beach, covering an area half the size of a football field. Periodically the alarm goes off, signaling hidden "treasures" beneath the surface. Each time, he eagerly marks the spot with his toe, tosses the metal detector aside, digs furiously, sifts through the sand, and eventually unearths . . . a bottle cap. Or a screw. Or some other worthless piece of metal that someone left behind.

No more notes from Grandpa to Grandma.

No treasures whatsoever.

While I'm busy watching Cade uncover junk, Bree mostly just watches the teenage boys playing Frisbee. Two of them, both bare-chested, seem to be showing off for her.

*Don't they realize she just finished middle school?*

Oh well. When Bree wants to be noticed,

she gets noticed. She's always been that way. All popular kids are, I suppose.

When Cade's battery finally dies, he brings his bucket of junk to where I'm sitting.

"What did you find?"

"Not much. Eight bottle caps, a broken piece of a lighter, a screw, and a fishing lure."

"No money, huh?"

"I wish."

"Well, don't give up. It's a big beach."

"Maybe tomorrow. The thing's dead already, so I have to charge it again."

Seeing that the boys are getting a little too flirty, I yell and tell Bree that it's time to go.

She drags her feet, but follows us back to the house.

After dinner, Dad packs up and heads for Portland. Thankfully, this time his send-off is uneventful, unlike last week at the restaurant. There are no long good-byes, just hugs and see-you-laters with the kids. He and Mom each give an awkward wave — nothing verging on affectionate, but at least there are no angry words.

On Monday, Tuesday, and Wednesday the Oregon rain settles in again, meaning more time stuck indoors.

Meaning more fighting. I try to stay away

from Bree and Cade as much as I can, because I really have no desire to argue with them over stupid things like who chews food the loudest or whose turn it is to fix the bunny ears so we can watch a show. Frankly, I'd rather be by myself. When I'm alone, in peace and quiet, I find it much easier to imagine what my life would be like if I didn't have such a crappy heart. Maybe if I were healthy, I'd run a marathon. Maybe I'd even win! Perhaps I'd make it to the Olympics in the two-hundred-meter Butterfly. Who knows, maybe if I didn't have this stupid heart condition, I'd have been willing to flirt a little with that cute boy at the candy shop.

*Tanner. Oh, the possibilities!*

Thursday brings sunshine, but I discover this much too early in the morning, thanks to my mom. "*Cock-a-doodle-doo,* slumber jacks! It's time to greet the dawn!"

My body says that it isn't time to get up yet. My mouth groggily says, "What?"

"Hurry up out of bed," chirps Mom again. "C'mon, girls, up and at 'em."

"It's six thirty," Bree moans. "And summer. Why are you waking us up?"

"I know, I'm sorry. But if we don't get going soon, we may be late. After all, the early bird gets the cameo."

I lift my head and pull at a tangle of hair. "What?"

"The early bird gets the cameo," she repeats.

"It gets the worm."

Cade is standing in the doorway. "A cameo is a worm?"

"No, it's a — What do you mean, 'Gets the cameo'? Cameo for what?"

Now Mom is all smiles. "It's a secret until you're downstairs ready to go. I'm not going to force you out of bed, but if you want to start enjoying this summer, I suggest you shake a leg. This early bird is heading for Astoria in fifteen minutes, with or without you."

At a quarter to seven everyone is in the living room, ready to go, except for me. I need an extra minute to find my learner's permit, which I hold up for all to see as I come down the stairs. "Twenty-one months I've had this," I say, making sure Mom gets a good look at it. "In that time I've driven exactly seven times." I lower the laminated card. "Can I *please* try driving today?"

"Oh, honey," Mom replies, as though it's the silliest idea in the world. "You know I can't let you do that."

"Why not?"

"Well, for one thing you don't even know

how to drive that old car."

"I can learn. If you can do it I can do it."

"I know, but . . . your health, Ann."

"Aren't I healthy enough to drive?"

"Yes, I suppose. You're physically capable, but . . . what if you get into an accident? Beginner drivers aren't known to be safe. Let's just wait until after your transplant. What's so wrong with that?"

"I thought you'd say that." I dig into my purse once more and retrieve my diary. "I wrote this down yesterday: *We shouldn't measure lives by their length. There's nothing that says eighty years is better than fifty years is better than fifteen. It's how we live that counts.*" Looking up, I ask simply, "Sound familiar?"

My mother doesn't respond.

"Mom, I want to start living. I'm not frail. I'm not bedridden. I simply need a new heart, and I'm either going to get one or I'm not. But until I do, I'm tired of doing nothing while I wait around to find out if I'm going to live or die."

She takes several long breaths, studying me intently the whole time. Finally she gives a pouty frown but holds out the key to the car. "I can't believe you quoted me."

"Seriously? I get to drive?"

"Only if you promise to listen to everything I say."

"I will! I totally will."

"And we'll have to go extraslow, so I can't promise that we'll make it in time for the cameo."

Bree is dying to speak. "You still haven't told us what kind of cameo you're talking about. What's it for?"

I've never seen such a giant smile grow on my mother's face. "A *movie*," she says with a bit of flair, complete with epic hand motions. "A real-life Hollywood film! I read in yesterday's paper that they need more extras today for some big scenes."

I feel an instant rush of butterflies. "Shut. Up."

"Yeah, don't joke," warns Bree. "Because being in a movie would be *beyond* totes cool."

Mom grabs a folded newspaper from the coffee table and points to a small article, circled in pen, which verifies her claim. "We've got thirty minutes to get there, so if Ann is driving, we'd better not waste any more time standing here."

As quick as we can, Bree and Cade race out into the sun and climb in the backseat of the Walrus. Mom and I each take our places up front, with me behind the wheel!

"Remind me again why there are no seat

belts," says Bree.

"When this car came out, I don't think they'd been invented yet," Mom replies in all seriousness. "But don't worry, the Walrus is made of solid steel. If anyone hits us, they'll wish they hadn't. That's the only reason I'm letting Ann drive at all."

"Well, at least it's an automatic," I say as I familiarize myself with the buttons and gadgets up front.

"Afraid not, dear," Mom snickers. "They used to put the shifter up there to keep it out of the way. 'Three on the column,' they called it, because it's only got three gears and because the shifter is on the steering column. It takes a little getting used to." Mom gives brief instructions on the gear pattern, as well as how to use a clutch. For practice, I shift through the gears several times with the engine off, and then finally turn it on.

The car lunges forward and immediately dies.

"Foot on the clutch, dear. Always when stopped, foot on the clutch. And the brake."

Behind me, Cade whispers, "I really think we're gonna need seat belts."

"Hey, I'm doing my best." I turn the key again, and this time the Walrus stays on. With the car in reverse I ease off the clutch.

To everyone's surprise — especially mine — the thing backs up without incident. Going from first gear to second while moving is a little rough, but by the time we've gone the six blocks to the main intersection, I'm really getting the hang of it.

The right turn onto the main street looks like it should be a cinch, but every time I think I should go, a car comes buzzing by. "Now or never, Ann," Mom finally says.

On her command I pop the clutch and punch it, sending everyone lurching, but somehow the maneuver lands us safely in the eastbound lane. "There." I sigh mightily. "Easy."

"How's your heart?" Bree asks, "Because mine is on fire."

"Don't ask."

As we approach the next block, a pedestrian near the strip mall catches Cade's eye. "Hey, Ann," he says, pointing. "Isn't that what's his name?"

I nervously look to my left, and then refocus on the road ahead. One quick glance in the mirror confirms that my cheeks are taking on the burgundy tone of the Walrus's beautiful exterior.

"Uh-oh," says Mom as she catches a glimpse of the young man walking on the sidewalk.

"It's nobody," I say awkwardly before she can ask. "Just some kid from the candy store."

"A rich kid," remarks Cade.

"No, that's his last name. Remember?"

Bree is still craning her neck, gawking at him as we drive away. "You actually met *a boy*? And you got his name? All without me?"

"I didn't *'get'* his name. He just came right out and told us his name was Tanner. End of story."

"I didn't get a great view," Bree continues. "Is he cute?"

"Let's just drop it, OK? Yes, I met a boy. I've met lots in my life. No biggie. Now, stop distracting me while I'm driving, or you'll get us all killed."

Bree giggles but doesn't say anything else.

After a long silence, Cade asks Mom if she knows what the movie is about.

She turns in her seat so she can see them in the back. "Didn't you read the whole ad? It's about some kids who get caught up in a modern-day pirate adventure. It should be right up your alley, Cade."

*A pirate movie? Oh great . . . here comes Pirate Boy . . .*

"Arrgg," bellows my brother, right on cue. "That be perfect for Cap'n Cade!"

Mom laughs, but Bree is quick to pounce. "Not cool. The pirate thing was cute for like one minute, and then it was totes obnoxious."

"No more obnoxious than 'totes,' " I say casually.

"Avast," Cade tells Bree indignantly. "Ye called me 'cute.' "

"I said you were obnoxious."

"Aye. Obnoxious be more piratey."

" 'Piratey' isn't a word," I point out. "Just be quiet, OK, Cade? We don't want you to be a pirate. Not today."

"Arrgg," he repeats under his breath. "Just 'cuz ye be boring, don't mean we should all be boring."

"I'm *not* boring!" *Well . . . at least I don't want to be boring.*

"Focus on the road, dear," Mom warns. "Don't mind him."

"You kinda are," Bree echoes gingerly. "But it's OK. That's just who you are."

Mom's brow is now furrowed angrily. "Whoa there. There's no need to get nasty. Let's just have fun and be nice today. Can we do that?"

"It's hard," replies Bree, undeterred. "Between Pirate King and Boring Queen, my life is not easy."

*Oh right, like her life is so hard.*

"Bree, that's exactly what I'm talking about, and it's uncalled for." She pauses to make sure Cade is listening too. "Believe me, your father and I want so much for this to be a good summer for you, but you're not making it easy with comments like that. For obvious reasons, there needs to be a greater sense of peace between the three of you. With Grandma to attend to, I can't always be with you to break up fights this summer. But if this is how you act with me around, I can only imagine the things you say to each other when you're alone."

Her words hang in the air like a balloon, which I quickly pop with a few more sharp words. "It's those two! They're so immature."

"Oh, figures you'd point the finger at us, Miss Perfect," snaps Bree. "You should take a look in the mirror once in a while. Cade and I would get along just fine if you weren't always bossing us around."

"No we wouldn't," Cade counters. "You're both dumb, and I wouldn't get along with either of you."

"STOP IT!" Mom's voice has become shrill. "Oh my goodness. You can't treat each other like that. It's got to stop."

I'm gripping the steering wheel so tight that my knuckles are turning white. "We're just tired," I mutter, "because *someone* got us up too early."

"Oh, so it's *my* fault? Well then, let's turn this ship around right now so you can go take a nap. We don't need to be in this movie anyway."

In almost perfect unison all three of us shout, "No!"

"We'll be good," I promise.

"*Please,* let's keep going," begs Bree, suddenly sounding like the sweetest thing ever. "Being in a movie sounds so awesome."

After thinking for a moment, Mom offers a proposition. "Tell you what. We'll keep driving to Astoria, but only if the ugliness stops right now. Let's only let kind words pass our lips. One more outburst and we turn right around."

Naturally, everyone agrees.

I can tell the Walrus has loads of power, but with me behind the wheel it never realizes its full potential. By the time we arrive at the designated location in downtown Astoria, the parking lot is nearly full. Before we're able to find an open space, a man waves us down.

He approaches my window. "Nice ride."

"Thanks. It's my great-grandma's."

"Well, Great-granny's got some great style." He gives the car a good long look before asking if we're there to be extras in the movie. When I tell him we are, he breaks the unfortunate news that we are too late. "We've already got everyone we need. Some folks showed up as early as five this morning just to get a spot in line, so I've been turning people away for the last thirty minutes."

"That's not fair," says Mom coolly. It kind of strikes me as funny, because she and Dad are always the ones reminding us how things aren't supposed to be fair. "We're here on time."

"It's OK," I tell her. "We tried."

But it isn't OK to Mom. She leans over me so she can talk to the man through my window. "You mean they can't find room for three more kids?"

"I think it's more than that, ma'am. Extras cost money, and we've already got plenty for the scenes today. It's just the way these things go."

"So you work for the movie company, then?"

"I do. I report to the first assistant director, who's off prepping the extras right now."

"And does the first assistant director have a name?"

"Uh . . . yeah. It's Jody."

Mom smiles sweetly and waves. "Thank

you." Then she sits straight up in her seat and lowers her voice so the man can't hear. "You kids stay put. I'll be back in a jiffy." She gives a reassuring wink, then climbs out. Before her door closes, I hear her say, "Can you point me in Jody's direction?" Without waiting for the man's answer, she starts marching toward a series of large tents along the far edge of the parking lot.

"Uh, ma'am," he calls, chasing after her. "You can't just . . . I mean, there's no way. The spots are full."

She brushes him off and keeps walking.

Five minutes later Mom comes back into view, only now she is walking beside a dark-haired woman carrying a clipboard. The man from before is nowhere to be seen. The woman strides right up to my door and crouches low enough that I'm eye to eye with her. "Hey there. I hear you kids want to be in a movie."

"Of course. But the guy said they're full."

The woman, who I assume is Jody, cocks her head very sympathetically. "Well, there's always an exception. Your mom and I had a little talk, and I think we can find a way to get you in. If you'd like to park the car, I'll personally take you over to Wardrobe and get you rolling. OK?"

Something about this doesn't feel right to

me, but in my excitement I ignore the feeling. Whatever Mom said to them, it worked!

Jody takes us directly to a makeup tent, where professionals apply a quick layer of powder to cut down on the sun's glare, then she leads us two blocks north to an old, historic county jail in the heart of the city. There's a lot more gear there than I expected — cameras on special tracks, lights hanging from temporary scaffolding, microphones on special booms, and power cords running every which way on the ground — but there are far fewer people than I would have guessed, especially given all the extras we saw back at the staging area.

When I ask where everyone else is, Jody explains, "The scene you guys are in is where one of the villains breaks out of jail. His family will come speeding up to the jailhouse, he'll jump in their jeep and then speed off. We just need a few pedestrians in the background when that happens. Most of the other extras are heading to a beach down south of here for a much bigger scene where an old pirate ship sets off on its final voyage at sea."

Her last sentence causes Cade's eyes to bulge. Literally.

"Wait . . . a . . . minute," he stammers. "I knew this movie had something to do with pirates, but there's an actual pirate ship? And they're filming it *today*?"

"Of course."

"Uh-oh," quips Bree.

"And I'm not in it?"

"Well . . . no," Jody says, sounding unsure. "This was the scene I thought would be best for you guys."

"Here we go again," I whisper.

Curling his lips, Cade impolitely snarls, "Avast! This be the wrong scene for the likes of Cap'n Cade!"

Jody chuckles at his performance. It takes her another second or two to catch on that he's totally serious. "But in the other scene you guys would just be faces in the crowd, way back in the distance. Here, we'll actually get to see who you are on the big screen."

"You shouldn't have mentioned pirates," Bree states. "He's a bit loco over them, if you know what I mean." She's twirling a finger around the side of her head in the universal gesture for "crazy." Then she covers one side of her mouth and carefully whispers her words, as if to protect Cade from what she's going to say, even though it's obvious that she wants him to hear every bit of it. "B-t-dubs, the whole family hates it when he turns into 'Captain Cade.' We're

197

hoping he grows out of it."

Mom takes a giant step forward and gently grabs Bree's arm near the elbow. "That's enough, young lady. Let's just drop it."

"It's the truth, though," she continues. "Who goes around talking like a pirate?"

Cade's hands are at his side, but they're clenched, prepared to strike. "Watch yer tongue, lass, or I'll gut you like a fish!"

"He's *really* good," Jody comments, sounding genuinely impressed.

"Please don't tell him that." I sigh. "He's liable to go on like this for hours. Maybe even days."

Now Mom steps right into the middle of us, making sure Cade has no path to Bree or me. "Cade, *stop.*" Her voice is still motherly, but she definitely means business. "Ann and Bree, zip it. Got it?" She turns back to my brother. "Cade, this is the scene you've been assigned to. You're lucky to be in it at all, so don't ruin it. Just let the pirate thing go." She holds his gaze until he finally looks away.

In frustration, he quietly spits out what is becoming his favorite pirate-swear. "Poop deck!"

Mom frowns ominously, but the assistant director laughs it off. "The kid's got spunk.

I like that."

Jody has a few things to wrap up ahead of the shoot, but before leaving she introduces us to another of her assistants, who is giving detailed scene instructions to the other extras. We spend the next half hour with five other pedestrians — a jogger, a businessman, a mother with a baby stroller, and a middle-aged couple — sorting out where to stand and how to behave when the so-called "bad guy," played by a man named Jake, comes busting out of jail. Cade is assigned to be the son of the middle-aged couple. His only prop is a very real looking ice-cream cone made of plastic, which he is instructed to lick as he strolls along the sidewalk near the jailhouse. Mom, Bree, and me are a bit farther ahead of Cade along the sidewalk, much closer to where the action will happen. We're coached to walk "gracefully, as though out for a Sunday stroll without a care in the world" and then to scream when the getaway car comes screeching to a stop on the street just ahead of us. The rest of the extras are on the other side of the scene, walking toward us at various intervals.

By the time we've got it down, word spreads that the director is nowhere to be found. When he finally shows up — almost thirty minutes late — he looks frazzled. Without wasting any time he barks out a few orders and crosses the street to a chair on the opposite sidewalk. He grabs a megaphone to get everyone's attention. "Listen up! Quiet on the set! We're running way behind today, and we're renting this street by the hour, so I need this to go smooth, like a baby's butt. Raise your hand if you don't understand?" He doesn't wait for anyone to respond. "Good. I'm told the cameras and mics are hot, so let's do this, people. This is the easiest sequence in the whole movie. If we need more than one take, I'll be extremely disappointed. More than two, and there'll be some explaining to do, because I've got to get out to the other shoot on the beach. Word is that the wind is picking up and the pirate ship is ready to sail."

Upon hearing the word "pirate," Mom, Bree, and I all look at each other and then turn around in unison to stare at Cade. Mom even raises a finger in warning.

I'm pretty sure he sees us, but he hardly notices us, if that makes sense. I can practically see his mind working, trying to figure out how to get the director to take him to the beach to be a pirate in the other scene.

In the middle of my thoughts, I faintly

hear the word, "Action!"

As rehearsed, we begin moving toward the center of the scene. A few seconds later, the front door of the tiny jail swings outward, and a tall Italian-looking guy with straight dark hair comes running out, just as a gray jeep comes screeching up the street. I know I'm supposed to be looking ahead, but an unexpected movement behind me draws my attention to the rear.

I turn just in time to see Cade bolting from his fake parents.

Compelled by his inner pirate, he runs at full speed toward the escapee, screaming like a banshee. Without slowing, he rushes right past me. There's nothing any of us can do but gasp and watch. Holding his plastic ice-cream cone as a sword, he bears down on the actor. Distracted by Cade's fearsome approach, the poor actor stops dead in his tracks on the sidewalk, right next to the getaway car. "I'll run ye through like a pig!" Cade screams. "And send ye to the depths of Davy Jones' Locker!" He presses the ice-cream cone to the man's stomach and furrows his brow menacingly.

If I'm being honest, my brother's acting is brilliant. Should the cast and crew start clapping, I wouldn't be at all surprised. But instead of clapping, there is a terrible silence for several awkward moments. Then the actor grimaces, looks around in bewilderment, and asks, "Uhh . . . did they add that to the script?"

More silence follows.

I look to my right to see the director approaching from the other side of the street. When he reaches Cade, he just stands there, looming, for several breaths. I can't read him very well. He's either very impressed by my brother's impromptu performance or he's having an aneurism. One of his arms is tucked beneath the other; the free hand is covering his mouth. With his mouth thus covered, the words he eventually speaks come out even more garbled than Grandma Grace's. "Gid ab my sut."

"What?" Cade asks, lowering his ice-cream weapon.

The director slowly drops both hands to his side, then bends to Cade's level and points down the street in the direction of the bay. *"Get . . . off . . . my . . . set!"* Without another word he turns and paces back to his chair.

Before I know it, Mom is taking Cade by the arm. "Let's go," she hisses.

"Wait!" shouts Bree. "Do we have to go too?"

"Shut up!" I hiss quietly, hoping not to

draw attention.

Then the megaphone blares again. "Anyone who is here with that kid is hereby excused. Quickly, please. Thank you."

Mom is dragging Cade by the shirtsleeve. When Pirate Boy looks over his shoulder, Bree's face is bright red. If her eyes were guns, I'm sure Cade would be dead, because they are zeroed in on him with lethal precision. "I hate you," she mouths.

I'm upset too, but I know we can't just stand there doing nothing. Everyone is staring at us, waiting for us to leave. I grab Bree's hand and tug her along behind Mom and Cade.

Several blocks away, just before we reach the Walrus, Jody comes running up from behind, breathing hard. "Talk about a show-stopping performance," she says between gasps. "Nice job, kid." She lifts a hand to give Cade a high five.

"Really?" says Mom curtly. "Did you not see what he did back there?"

Jody is still all smiles. "Look, I'm really sorry you got the boot like that, guys, but you've got to admit, that was hilarious." Nobody seems relieved by her comments. "Believe it or not, the director is actually a pretty nice guy. On any other day he'd probably have been rolling on the ground laughing, maybe even worked Cade's ad-lib into the scene."

"What makes today so special?" I ask.

"He was meeting all morning with the producers discussing the budget. That's why he was late on the set. Right now the production costs are running high, so he's a little stressed. Unfortunately, he took it out on you guys."

"It's still unbelievably embarrassing," Mom says to Jody, even though she's looking right at Cade. "Girls, aren't you embarrassed?"

"No," snaps Bree. Everything about her exudes venom — her voice, her glare, the expression on her face, even the way her muscles tense when she looks at our brother. "I'm just *mad*. At Pea Brain. For ruining our one chance to be in a movie!"

"He's not the only pea brain," I whisper, looking at Bree.

"Well, look, I really am sorry about this," Jody tells everyone. Turning just to me, she says, "Most of all for you. But keep your chin up. I'm sure everything is going to be OK." She pats me on the shoulder and then trots off.

*Wait. What did she just say?*

I could scream. Before I get the chance, Mom tells everyone to get in the car.

"C'mon. I want to get home." Her cheeks are flushed; she looks guilty.

Bree and Cade pile in, but I remain firmly in place. "You played the heart card, didn't you, Mom? To get us in the movie."

"I only said that you've been sick, and that you were really looking forward to it. They were happy to make room for us once they knew the situation."

*Uh-huh. Likely story.*

I cross my arms. "Did you tell them I might die?"

Mom is completely silent.

*Guilty as charged.* "You did! Oh my gosh! That's so hypocritical! You're always telling me how everything is going to be fine, but you go tell complete strangers that I'm some freak who needs a new heart so they'll take pity on me?"

"It wasn't like that. You're blowing it out of proportion. All I did was tell them the facts."

"So we could get in the movie."

"Yes! Isn't that what we came here for?"

All I can do is shake my head. "Don't you get it? I don't want pity. Not from you, not from the family, and certainly not from strangers on a movie set. I'm tired of being the girl who always gets coddled. And I don't want to be the girl with 'the heart.' I

205

just want to be *the girl.*" I toss the car key at my mom. "You better drive. Poor, pitiful Ann is not in the mood."

# CHAPTER 16
## CADE

Last year, on the Fourth of July, I remember watching them light the first fuse at the fireworks show we went to at the park by our house. It was really dark, so even from a distance I could see the fuse burning. I knew it was going to blow, I just didn't know when. Everyone must've known it was time, because the crowd got all quiet. Finally a dark shadow shot off into the sky, then a few seconds later the world exploded in orange and red.

The ride home from Astoria is kind of like that. For several blocks, there is nothing but silence in the car. I know the fuses have been lit . . . it's just a matter of waiting for someone to blow up.

I'm not surprised that Bree's fuse ends up being the shortest, or that her mortar is pointed right at me. "I hate you *so much*! Why do you always have to ruin everything, Cade?"

The way she says it, I don't doubt that she truly hates me. But being hated like that sets me off too. "Not more than I hate you. You're the meanest, ugliest person in the whole world!"

"And you're the stupidest!"

I guess Ann doesn't want to miss out on the fireworks either, because she quickly pops off. "Have you checked the mirror lately, Bree? I bet you'd find someone stupider than him looking back at you. If you hadn't opened your big mouth, you and I could've still been in the movie." To make sure I understand that she's not taking sides, Ann also says, "But you're right, he is *really* stupid."

"I happen to love what I see in the mirror, O Boring One!" Bree screams. "It's called *'beauty.'* But you wouldn't know about that."

"Then I guess you didn't see the new zit on your nose, huh? It's been getting bigger all day."

"Yeah, it's really huge," I tell her. "I bet if you squeezed it, it would squirt on the car window."

"I hate you both!"

Ann isn't as loud as Bree, but just as mean. "And I hate both of you more than either of you could ever imagine. I wish I was an only child."

"Well, I wish . . . !" Bree is panting. She looks really mad. Like a rabid dog backed into a corner. She's staring right at Ann. "I wish you were *dead.*" After saying it, she crosses her arms and turns away from us.

Mom's got a really tight grip on the steering wheel, but she doesn't make a peep. She's mad, though. I can tell that. Honestly, I wish she'd just say something. I know from watching her and Dad that whenever she stops talking, it means she is going to have an even worse explosion later.

*Not like fireworks, more like dynamite.*

As we get closer to Cannon Beach, Mom surprises us by pulling off the highway at a state-park lookout spot just north of town. The place is pretty cool, actually. Mom and Dad brought us here once before to look at the cliffs. It has an awesome view of the ocean because it's sort of a peninsula. From the right spot, you can see all the way down to Haystack Rock a couple miles away.

"What are we doing?" I ask.

"Get out," orders Mom without looking at anyone.

For a second, I wonder if maybe Mom is so fed up with us that she wants to push us over the edge onto the jagged rocks below.

*Nah, she'd never . . .*

I quickly dismiss the idea and climb out to find that Mom is busy collecting rocks near the fence at the edge of the cliff. From the looks of it, she already has five or six of them in her hands, all roughly the same size. "Here," she says, handing one to each of us. "We're going to have a little contest. I want to see who can throw the farthest."

"Why?" asks Bree.

"Because. It's *fun.*" The way she says it, it doesn't sound fun.

"I like contests," says Ann, "because I like winning." She weighs the rock in her hand, and then casually tosses it in the air. When she catches it, the look in her eye says that she really doesn't want to lose to me or Bree. Not now. Not ever. In one quick motion she cocks her arm, and then lets the thing fly. It sails over some shrubs, then over the edge of the cliff, and eventually plunks down in the wet sand at the edge of the surf. "Beat that."

Bree's eyes are suddenly on fire and her face is red. She chucks her rock as far as she can, but it lands short of Ann's.

"Weak," Ann tells her, grinning.

"Are you referring to your heart? Or your brain?"

Now Ann's face turns red, too, but she doesn't reply.

"I'm gonna beat you both," I tell them before I throw my rock. I may be younger than them, but I'm the only one who plays baseball. The edge of the water is less than the distance from outfield to home plate, and I've made that throw a hundred times. I give it my all, and just like I planned, my rock splashes down in the water behind the first wave, at least twenty feet beyond Ann's.

"No way!" she yells angrily.

"You suck," says Bree, talking to me.

"That was only round one," says Mom as she shuffles along the fence and gives us each a new rock.

We quickly launch them again. Ann has enough strength to match my first throw, but my second one is better than hers by several feet. Bree's reaches the water too, but is last again.

"One more time," says Mom.

"Don't try too hard," whispers Bree while Ann is winding up. "Remember, your heart can't take it."

After hearing Bree's comment, Ann hesitates at the last second, messing up the motion of her throw. Her rock doesn't even reach the ocean.

Ann drops her hands to her side, knowing she will lose the round. "You're such a jerk."

Bree smirks. "I know you are, but what am I?"

"Did you really just say that? We used to say that in like second grade. Grow up, Bree."

While the two of them are going at it, I take a run at the edge of the fence and throw as hard as I possibly can. My rock reaches the same distance as my last throw, which I assume will be enough to beat Bree's.

My sister, however, is more determined than I gave her credit for. She sprints toward the cliff with a rock in hand, whips her arm as she reaches the fence, and then stops to watch the thing fly. Somehow — from either a gust of wind or sheer dumb luck — her final throw beats mine by a couple feet. "Ha!" she screams, pumping her fists in the air. "The ultimate champion!"

*I lost? To her?*

"One more round!" I shout.

Bree shakes her head. "No way, I already won."

Mom looks back and forth between us, then nods. "One more. But this one will be a little different, and it will definitely be for bragging rights." She hands us each a rock and then takes a giant step back. "Now that we know you can all throw really hard, I want you to take a few steps back, then turn so you can see each other."

I'm a little confused, but I follow her instructions. So do my sisters. After backing up, we're all standing in a triangle, maybe twenty feet apart.

"Now," Mom continues, "I want you to take that rock and throw it as hard as you can at one of your siblings. Whoever hits their target and draws the most blood is the winner." She licks her lips like she can hardly wait for us to start killing each other.

Ann is as confused as me. "Huh?"

"You heard me. Take the rock, throw it at Bree — or Cade, if you prefer — and see how much damage you can do. Extra points if you can hit someone in the face."

"We can't do that," says Bree. "Somebody could get hurt."

Mom just shrugs. "So? Fifteen minutes ago you wanted at least one of them dead."

"That was different."

"Really?" She turns to Ann. "What about you, Ace? Care for a little retribution?"

"What if I put out one of their eyes? Is that what you want?"

"Don't *you* want that?"

Ann scrunches her face in disgust. "You're crazy."

"Weak," says Mom, repeating what Ann said earlier about one of Bree's throws. "Cade? How about you? This is your chance. You gonna take a shot at the sisters you hate so much?"

I stare for a moment at the rock in my hand, wondering what it would feel like to hurl the thing at them. "Maybe, but . . . I have really good aim . . . and I don't want to hurt them."

"Then why," she asks, sounding exasperated, "do you spend so much time and energy chucking verbal rocks at each other? The way you treat one another is toxic, and that's putting it mildly. News flash, guys: *Words hurt,* no matter what they say about sticks and stones. You don't want to hurt each other physically, but, heaven forbid, one of you so much as smiles the wrong way at someone, and it turns into a bloodbath." She glances around the triangle, pausing to lock eyes with each of us. "Stop throwing stones." Mom unclenches her fingers and lets several rocks drop from her hand. She gives us all a final disappointed look and then walks back to the Walrus.

I drop my rock and follow her.

# CHAPTER 17
## EMILY

"Everyone, park it in the living room," I tell the kids when we get home, before they can go their separate ways. They're still not speaking to each other, so this may not be the best time to try this, but it may be the only shot I get.

"Is this going to be another lecture?" drones Bree. "We already got your message loud and clear. 'Don't throw stones.' "

"It's not a lecture," I assure her. "More like story time."

Ann is already halfway up the stairs. As she stomps back down, she mutters, "This better be good."

I have everybody take a seat on the couch, then I sit down in the lone chair near the puffer-fish lamp. "I've been thinking a lot about our family this past week. Well, not just this week — for a while actually, but last week one of you did something that gave me extra reason to pause, and I'd like to discuss it with you."

Bree has a guilty look on her face. "Was it me?"

"It usually is," pipes Ann.

"Oh, like you're so perfect."

While the girls trade glares, my gaze slowly drifts toward Cade, where it remains until he starts to squirm.

"What'd I do wrong this time?" he asks.

Trying to lighten the mood, I snicker. "Do you remember what you did a few days ago when we went to visit Grandma Grace?"

"Uh . . . I shot a rubber band at Bree?"

"You did?" Bree and I ask at the same time.

He shrugs. "I missed."

"No, there was something else you did, when we were going through the large double doors to Grandma's wing."

He shrugs again. "I don't know."

"You held the door open for one of the nurses there who was walking through with a tray of pills."

"I did?"

"Yes. Did you know that nurse?"

"No."

"Never seen her before?"

"Nope."

"Then why did you help her?"

He shrugs a third time. "Just . . . because.

To be nice, I guess."

*Thank you, Cade.* "Excellent. So do you all see why that bothered me?"

Everyone is staring back at me with blank faces. Nobody responds.

"What Cade did truly concerned me, and while I was reading a book last night, I figured out why." I turn once more to Cade. "When was the last time you held a door for your sisters?"

"Like, never."

"Like, precisely. What bothered me about you holding the door for that woman was not that you helped her — which was very sweet — but that we almost never show such courtesies within the walls of our own home. The more I thought about it, the more I realized that we, as a family, treat complete strangers better than we do each other. Why is that? Why are we so hostile to those we're supposed to love, yet kind and courteous to people we don't even know?"

Again, nobody has an answer, so I continue. "During our first week here, I heard all sorts of hurtful things between you kids. I know part of that is just that it's summer time, and you guys were cooped up a little more than expected, but it really bothered me hearing the things you said to each other. 'She touched me.' 'He put his foot too close to me.' 'She eats too much.' 'He's a stupid brat.' And my personal favorite: 'She's breathing my air.' " I let the words hang out there for a moment, then ask, "Would any of you say those things to a complete stranger?"

Again, silence.

"Would any of you even say those things to your friends or acquaintances at school?"

"Probably not," admits Bree.

"No, probably not. And yet those aren't the worst things that have been said around here lately. Cade, would you care to repeat what you said in the car about your sisters?"

"Not really."

"Indulge me."

"But I was mad. I didn't mean it."

"But you said it. And what was it, exactly, that you said? You remember, don't you?

Cade drops his eyes to the floor and nods. "I said I hate them."

"And Ann," I continue, "what was one of the mean things you said this morning? Any one will do."

Her response comes as a whisper. "I wished I was an only child."

I purse my lips. *The best is yet to come.* "How about you, Bree? What awful thing did you say to Ann that you would never tell a random person on the street?"

It takes several seconds, but finally Bree whispers, "I wished she was dead. But I didn't mean it! She made me mad and it just came out!"

I put my hands up to calm her down. "Bree, I know how you feel. None of us is perfect. We all lash out from time to time and say things that are hurtful or that we don't really mean." I pause momentarily, suddenly thinking of Dell and the things we've said to each other over the years, and especially during the last twelve months. *I wish he were here to hear this.* "And I think it's *because* we love each other that we end up saying or doing things that are unkind, as a way to get the attention of those we care most deeply for. Or to retaliate against them for some perceived injustice. When strangers wrong us, we tend to give them the benefit of the doubt. We tell ourselves that it was a simple accident, or that it's no big deal, and we let it slide. But when someone in our family does something that we don't like? Watch out."

"Why are you bringing this up?" asks Ann. "You already gave us your little stone-throwing lesson."

"Because I want to fix it. I want the way we treat each other outwardly to match the way we feel about each other in our hearts.

This may sound odd, but I want us to love each other like family but be kind like strangers."

Bree looks the most perplexed. "How?"

"Can I wait to answer that? I want to read something first, which I think will explain it better than I could." I hold up the thick, leather-bound volume that I finished reading late last night. There is no title on the cover, only a few faded gold letters on the bottom-right corner. "Do any of you know what this is?"

Several heads shake.

"Is it a diary?" asks Ann.

I give her a wink. "To be more precise, it's a *'gurnel'* — one of many old journals that Grandma kept. I found a whole box of them in the attic on Saturday night." I turn to a page marked by a yellow Sticky. "I'll just read a handful of passages to give you a flavor, and to show that not everything I imagined about my grandparents was true. I thought they had the perfect marriage . . . and maybe they did. But it wasn't without its ups and downs." I clear my throat and begin reading:

"Our youngest child graduated from high school last month, and already my fears about Alfred and me are being realized. It seems he is pulling away from me, or perhaps he'd already pulled away a while ago, but I was too preoccupied to notice. Our children have been the center of our world for the past twenty-five years, and now they are gone, leaving a sizable gap in our relationship. It's perhaps akin to a black hole — I can't see it, but I feel the effects of the void sucking us in. Without the kids around, we don't know how to behave; don't know how to interact; don't know how to love."

I turn to another marked page.

"When did I lose my best friend? Was it while I was running the kids to baseball practice and Girl Scouts? Was it while I was helping them with their homework, or prepping them for tests, or yelling at them to do their chores? Did I somehow forget that I had a best friend while I was cleaning the house and cooking the meals and folding the laundry? I don't know where or when or how, but it's becoming increasingly clear that Al and I are no longer best friends. He likes to read, I like to knit. He likes to watch golf, I like to garden. He likes to eat out, I like to cook in. And it's not even so much that we don't like the same things; I think it's more a case of finding different things to fill our time so we don't have to spend so much time together, because when we're together, we fight. I hate quarreling, and so does he, so we both stay in our corners as much as possible to avoid trading punches in the ring."

I look up to check that they are still listening, then turn another page.

"The last week has been a living hell. Nothing I do seems to be right in Al's eyes. It culminated last night with an argument, which began when he made a comment about how loudly I was sipping my tea. My tea! It was hot!! After that we each rattled off at least a dozen things that annoyed us about the other. Then we began itemizing all of the unkind things the other had done to us for as far back as we could remember. It's shocking, really, how well we each recall all the instances of hurt. Though there's been no official scorecard, it's safe to say we've both been keeping score."

"Is that what that box of scorecards was for?" asks Ann. "Did they start keeping an actual score of being mean to each other?"

"I'll get to that." I skip ahead to the middle of the book.

"Al's been spending more and more time at work. It's hard to talk to him. When I try, we invariably end up in an argument. He seems so unhappy; I know I'm unhappy. And still the tally of hurt feelings grows."

I jump down toward the bottom of that same page.

"Last night, when I put supper on the table, I accidentally spilled some of Al's water. It didn't get him wet, but it did make him mad, as though I'd done it on purpose. He seemed very put out that he should have to wipe it up with a napkin, and he even scolded me for not being more careful. Then this morning a very interesting thing happened. We went out to breakfast, and the waitress inadvertently spilled an entire cup of orange juice on Al's lap. Orange juice! An entire cup!! But how did he react? He bent over backward to let her know that it was OK, that accidents happen. He even laughed about it, even though his pants were soaked. When we left, he gave her an extralarge tip so she'd know he didn't hold it against her. I was furious! He's sup-

223

posed to love me, but when I accidentally dribble a little water, he blows up, and then a complete stranger stains his trousers and he gives her a pass! I can't help but wonder if that makes me the bigger stranger in his life . . ."

"Wow," remarks Bree while I turn to the next Sticky. "I'm surprised they stuck together."

"Me too," says Ann soberly.

"Me three," I agree. "Does their fighting remind you of anyone?"

"You and Dad?" chirps Cade.

With a sigh, I nod. "Yes, unfortunately. But you guys too, right? Just because you are kids, are your words any less hurtful to each other?" I pause, but nobody speaks. "Listen to what she writes next; this is getting to the heart of what I wanted to discuss with you. She says,

"It is very late at night. Al is asleep beside me; I am unable to rest. Yesterday was our anniversary, but no gifts were exchanged. No cards, no flowers, no special meal. Certainly no kisses or 'I love you's' — we haven't had those in a while now. After dinner I retired to my room to knit in silence, while Al played Solitaire in the living room. As I knitted, I cried. This isn't the life I dreamed of, nor the marriage I deserve. I was so angry. And tired of us blaming each other for every little thing. So fed up with the constant jabbing and poking and backbiting. So done with it all. I've been approaching this point for a long time, but last night it came to a head. I knew I either needed to do something to repair the damage between us — to find my old best friend — or I needed out. I've been stewing on an idea for several months, having no clue if it will work, but I made up my mind right then that I am going to try. To make sure he knew how serious I am, I packed a suitcase and carried it out to where he was playing his game.

" 'Who's winning?' I asked.

" 'It's Solitaire, Grace. There can only be one winner.'

" 'What a lonely game.'

"He saw the suitcase and asked what it was for.

"When I told him I was leaving, he seemed as stunned as I hoped he would be. 'But we're married. You can't just up and walk out. We love each other.'

" 'Do we? Do we actually love each other? Or do we just remember how we used to love each other?'

" 'What are you saying?'

" 'I'm saying I don't think we love each other the way we used to. Life got in the way, and somehow we forgot how to. But I think we can remember.'

" 'How?' he asked.

" 'I challenge you to a game,' I told him. 'Not like Solitaire, where there is only one winner. We're both competitive, Al. We both like to win — which is maybe why we fight so much. But I want to compete with you in a different way. Mentally, we've been keeping score of each other's faults and mistakes for too long. I want to start keeping score differently.'

"I had a small spiral notepad in my hand, which I tossed on the table, completely scrambling his card game. When he asked what it was for, I told him. 'This is our scorecard. I want to track the number of ways that we can find to be nice to each other — to love each other. I'm tired of pretending that we love each other without either of us really showing it. So if you want me to stay, tell me you'll play.'

"He invited me to sit, and for the next hour we discussed possible rules for our 'game.' We agreed to award ourselves points for saying or doing kind things for the other. At the end of each week, once we've totaled the scores, we'll go on a date as our reward — the winner gets to choose the restaurant. We also agreed that whoever wins the most weeks of our game for the next year will decide how and where we celebrate our anniversary. Next year is our fortieth, and I told him that if we're still married, we need to go somewhere big. He said he's always wanted to visit Fiji, but I said I want to go to Paris.

"Oh, how I pray that this will work. I miss my old friend. Tonight, while we were talking about the game, I saw glimpses of the Al I used to know. I do love him, somewhere deep down — now I just need to show him."

I slowly close the book and look up at all of their faces. "I want you kids to give it a try. I want you to play Grandma and Grandpa's game."

"Like with each other?" asks Bree skeptically.

"Would that mean I have to be nice to my sisters?" asks Cade.

"You would *get* to be nice to them, Cade. And if you're nicer to them than they are to you, then you win."

Bree raises her hand. "What would we win?"

"I don't know. First I have to run to the store to get notebooks for keeping score. I'll do that now, then once I'm back, we'll settle on the rest of the details, including prizes."

Ann scoots forward in her seat, her eyes drilling into me. I can almost guess what she's thinking. "Mom, are you and Dad going to play?"

I try to smile. "I don't know," I reply softly. "I'm not sure he'll go for it. I think maybe if you guys give it a shot, and he sees you getting along, it might help persuade him to give it a try."

She nods. "So if we really try hard at this, we can help you and Dad stop fighting?"

I nod in return.

Her eyes are still fixed on me. "Do you really think it could work? I mean, it seems like it worked for Grandma Grace, but will it work for our family too?"

*Good question.* "If we want it to," I tell her, trying to sound sure, even though I'm not. "If we put our whole hearts into it, like Grandma and Grandpa did, there can be no losers. That's why they called it the Winner's Game."

# CHAPTER 18
## BREE

As soon as Mom is done telling us about the Winner's Game, Ann goes upstairs, making it clear she wants to be alone — or at least away from me. No surprise there. This morning was brutal, and I know she's still mad at me over the things I said.

I honestly don't know what to make of the game Mom proposed. Part of me sees how it could be nice, I guess, if we all got along a little more than we do. But more importantly . . .

*What if I lost?! Ugh . . . imagine how Ann would rub it in my face if she won! And losing to Cade would be even worse.*

No, losing is not an option. As long as we have to play, I might as well win, just like I did in the rock-throwing competition!

But before the game starts there are other things I need to do. "So Mom . . . while you're at the store, can me and Cade go for a walk?"

Cade gives me a puzzled look, but quickly wipes it away. The kid makes me so mad sometimes, but at least he's smart enough to know when I have a plan. He wisely plays along. "Uh . . . yeah," he says. "A walk would sure be nice."

"Of course. Just be sure to stick together. And don't go too far. I won't be more than an hour."

Mom seems relieved that we're finally getting along, though we really aren't. I just need him. As proof that we're still both miffed about what happened earlier at the movie set, we don't say a word to each other while we're walking. But ten minutes later we're standing near a candy store, twenty feet from the door, and I am forced to speak to him. "Is this where he works?"

"Who?"

*"The guy."*

"Yeah, why?"

"Peek in the window. I want to know if he's there."

"That's why you wanted me to come? So I can look in the window for you?"

"Just do it, Cade. I need to know if he's there or not before we go in. And if he's alone. Do it, and I'll buy you a piece of chocolate."

"Two pieces," he demands.

I cross my arms for a counteroffer. "Then none."

"Fine," he mumbles. "One."

"Deal," I laugh. "But I'd have gone for two or three if you'd negotiated better."

He shrugs it off. "Whatever. One piece of chocolate is still good pay for an easy mission like this." As stealthily as he can, he creeps along the front of the store, just below the bottom lip of the large windows, to the cover of a large interior display of saltwater taffy. Once there, he slowly raises his head and peers through the glass, scanning the store from left to right.

When his gaze reaches the middle of the window, he freezes, then drops to the ground.

"What is it?"

"Nothing," he whispers back. "Just . . . nothing." Still on the ground, he crawls on all fours back to where I'm crouching at the corner of the building.

"So?"

"He's there."

"You're sure?"

"Pretty darn."

"Did he see you?"

He kind of looks away and shrugs. "Maybe."

I take a deep breath. *Why am I so nervous?*

*Oh right . . . 'cuz he's a boy.* I know Ann thinks I'm just this outgoing person who can talk to anyone and have all the friends I want without even trying, but she's wrong. It's hard putting yourself out there. It's hard trying to make people think that you're confident, when on the inside your stomach is filled with butterflies. Heck, I bet she's never even had butterflies like me. She would, though, if she'd just put herself out there!

"What are you going to do?"

"*Duh.* I'm going to see if he's cute."

"Why?"

"Are you brain dead? Ann met a boy and didn't say anything about it — *to anyone.* It makes me think she's hiding something. Like maybe she thinks he's cute or something. I couldn't see him that well this morning when we drove by, so I want to get a closer look."

"Why does it matter what Tanner looks like?"

*Duh . . . 'cuz we're going to be here all summer, and maybe he'll think I'm cute!* Of course I can't tell that to my brother. He'll blab, like he always does. "Well, what if he's totally ugly but she doesn't recognize it and they fall in love and get married and have totally ugly children? As her sister, it's my

232

duty to make sure that doesn't happen."

He rolls his eyes like he doesn't believe me. "Whatever. Let's just go in. I want my piece of candy."

I quickly smooth out the front of my shirt, tuck a strand of hair behind my ear, take another deep breath, and plaster a smile full of fake confidence on my face. "Fine. But you go first."

"Fine, I will. I'm starving."

"You came back," I hear the boy say when Cade enters. "I was thinking you were just going to spy on me and run."

One more breath, then I step inside, making sure to flip my hair as I pass through the doorway.

A confused look crosses Tanner's face. He glances quickly back at Cade. "Where's your sister?"

"Ann's at home."

"I'm Cade's *other* sister," I manage to say between heart palpitations. *He's SO cute!* When his eyes settle on me, I can't help but giggle.

"Oh," says Tanner, sounding slightly disappointed. "Is she coming?"

*Disappointed? That Ann isn't here? Doesn't he know how boring she is?* I cross my fingers behind my back. "I think she just wanted to watch TV."

233

*A little lie can't hurt. Right?*

"Oh. Well, did she say hi or anything?"

"No. She didn't even mention you." OK, that's at least a partial truth. "Who are you?"

"Bummer," he says to himself and then shrugs it off. "Umm . . . I'm Tanner. Can I get anything for you guys?"

Cade picks out a piece of chocolate in about two seconds. I circle the store for five minutes, occasionally asking Tanner what he thinks about this one or that one. Eventually I make a decision and we leave. Not that I want to, but it would be weird to linger longer.

"What was that all about?" Cade asks as soon as we're outside. "Why did you tell him Ann didn't want to come?"

"Didn't she say he was just some kid from a candy shop? She obviously isn't interested in him."

"Yeah, but . . . I thought you said you thought she thought he was cute?"

"Did I? Well, he's not, so it's safe."

"You're not worried about ugly children?"

"Huh?"

"If he's not good-looking, they might fall in love and have ugly children. That's what you said."

"Right . . . well . . . I don't think we need to worry about it. He's not really her type."

He stops walking. "You could tell that just from talking to him?"

"Oh yeah, totes. I'm very good at recognizing these things."

"So whose type is he?"

I smile and then, picturing him in my head, reply, *"Mine."* A split second later I come to my senses. Stopping in place, I glare at Cade like the nemesis that he is. "And if you repeat that to anyone — *and I mean anyone* — you'll wish you hadn't. Got it, Pirate Boy?"

"You're mean."

"Which is why you'll keep your mouth shut about where we went."

When we get home, Cade makes a beeline for the upstairs bedroom. I follow him to my room, where Ann is lying on her bed with a pen in hand.

Cade looks back and forth between us, probably trying to decide whether or not to tell her about Tanner. I give him my best warning look and pray.

Ann shimmies to the edge of her bed and sits up. "You guys look like you've been up to something."

"Nope," I say quickly. "Just . . . hanging out."

She eyes me suspiciously, then turns to my brother. "Cade? Did you guys do something wrong?"

"Not me," he says.

"Me neither."

Ann's head dances back and forth a couple times between the two of us, and then she lies back down. "Whatever. I don't care anyway. I'm done caring."

The comment catches me off guard. "What is that supposed to mean?"

Ann lifts a finger to the bunk above her and traces around one of the ink hearts. For a second she remains quiet, but then she says, "I just . . . I was looking at these hearts. There are seven of them now. At first, I wanted to draw one for every day until I get my new heart. But the more I think about it, I realize I could very well be counting the days until I die."

"Don't say that," Cade says immediately. "Your heart is fine, Ann. It's going to last until you get a new one."

"Whatever. I don't care anyway."

"I'm telling Mom you said that," I warn her.

She turns just enough to look at me. "Mom's not home yet. Besides, what would you tell her? That I have a defective heart? Go ahead, knock yourself out. She understands the possible outcomes more than anyone."

236

"So all this time you just pretended to be brave, and now you're giving up?"

"No, I'm just facing reality. I'm tired of not really living. I don't want to die, and I'm certainly not giving up, but I'm just resigning myself to the fact that my life could very well be short — shorter than most anyway — and so I need to make the most of the time I've got." She pauses. "Besides, it's not like any of us is going to live forever. Heck, for all we know, this might be our very last conversation. A meteor could crash into our house right now and we'd all be toast."

"That's called giving up," I fire back, "and I'm telling Mom."

Ann turns away and chuckles dryly. "Hey, what do you care? You already wished I was dead."

My heart is suddenly pounding like crazy. Is Ann's heart condition contagious, because maybe I've got it too? *Does she really believe I wish she was dead?*

The truth is I'd probably die if she were. Doesn't she know that? Doesn't she understand that I was mad when I said that? That's what we Bennetts do when we're mad; we say mean things to each other, hoping it will make us feel better, even though it never does. Doesn't she understand that?

Hasn't she seen Mom and Dad fight? After all, that's what they do. But I mean . . . she's still my sister.

Not knowing what else to do or say, I turn and rush out of the room. "Mom! Are you home yet? Ann says she's going to die . . . !"

# CHAPTER 19
## CADE

Ann is staring again at the hearts she drew. "Everyone's going to die," she whispers softly to herself. "One way or another."

For a full minute I just stand there, not knowing what to do.

*Should I leave? Maybe I should say something. But what?*

Finally she gets up and walks out of the room, saying only, "If Mom gets back from the store before I'm back, tell her I won't be long."

A moment later I hear the back door open and shut. I quickly run to the bedroom window to see Ann walking by herself toward the beach. She has her arms wrapped around herself, like she's giving herself a hug. Someone must've taken my binoculars, because they're sitting right in her window. I pick them up and continue watching. She heads straight for the ocean. Not quickly, though. Slowly, like she doesn't really want to go. When she reaches the wet sand, she stops at the edge of the water, just beyond the spot where the waves fizzle out. It's the closest I've seen her to the ocean since we've been here. Even from this distance I can see that her body is rigid, like she's a statue. The only movement is her hair, blowing in the wind. She is still holding herself. And staring at the water.

*I wish I knew what she was thinking.*

*I wish I knew why she said all that stuff about dying.*

*I wish Bree hadn't wished Ann was dead.*

After standing there frozen for like five minutes, Ann finally starts walking up the beach toward town, so I head downstairs, where Bree is watching the fuzzy TV, still waiting for Mom to arrive so she can be the first to tell her what Ann said.

Sure enough, when Mom walks through the front door with a bag of notebooks and pens, Bree blurts out, "Ann says she's going to die!"

Mom's eyes get humongous. "Like . . . *now?*"

"No, but she's talking like she's giving up. Like she doesn't care if she lives or dies anymore. She even said a meteor might hit our house and wipe us all out."

"Where is she?"

"Out on the beach," I tell her. "She said she'll be right back." I glance at Bree. "I don't think she meant she's dying right now. More like . . . everyone is going to die."

Mom nods, and seems to relax. "I've had this discussion with her, and I'm sure I'll have it again. I don't want her to be afraid of death, and it's natural for her to think about it, given the situation. But you guys can help by not bringing it up." She focuses on Bree. "And saying things like, 'I wish you were dead' are about the worst things you can say to her right now."

Bree throws up her hands. "I didn't mean it!"

The sound of footsteps behind us pulls my head in that direction. Ann is standing in the doorway between the kitchen and the living room. "Good to know," she says. "Since I'm still alive." It kinda seems like she is smiling now, but not quite. But she definitely looks happier than when she left.

For a moment, everyone is looking around to see who's going to speak next. Finally Mom says, "Well, now that we're all here, let's make lunch and then you can start the game."

I love games.
*Duh . . . who doesn't?*

I especially love beating my sisters at games, even though that hardly ever happens, which is why I can't wait for lunch to be over. I mean, it's not like I'm looking forward to being nice to them or anything, but I can't wait to *win.* My whole life they've always been bigger, smarter, faster, or plain old better than me at stuff, but in this game we're all equal.

Whatever it takes, I *will* win.

While we're fixing lunch in the kitchen, Mom helps us set the rules. It's pretty simple: Just like in Grandma's version, everyone will be given their own individual notebook for tallying the things we do to show kindness to someone else. Figuring out prizes is a bit tricky, because everyone wants different things — and there's only so much money Mom is willing to spend, and it's not much — but eventually me and Bree and Ann agree that the winner each week will get first choice of seats on car rides for the following week, and whoever wins the whole summer will get a hundred dollars to spend however we want.

Before we finalize things, Bree has a question. "What if someone says or does something mean? Can we take one of their points away?"

Mom looks around. "You're the ones playing the game, so you can decide. What do you all think?"

After several more minutes of debate, we all conclude that the game will only be fair if we are able to take away points for unkindness. To do this, we'll use the second page of our notebooks as a scorecard for others' *negative* points, which will be subtracted from that person's total at the end of each week.

The final question, also from Bree, is, "Can we start now . . . because I'm totally going to rock at this."

Mom checks her watch. "Let's just eat first," she suggests. "As soon as the last person is done, we'll start."

Ten minutes later, with a mouthful of noodles, Ann asks me why I'm staring at her.

*How can she not know?* "I'm waiting for you to take your last bite."

"Oh, right. That."

Bree is already rinsing her dishes in the sink. She can't hear us over the sound of the water. "That what?"

"The game," I shout back. "The one I'm gonna win."

"Like heck you are," she fires back with a grin. "I have a plan. You might as well not

243

even try, because I'm gonna kick all your butts."

Mom is still sitting at the table. "Don't say 'butts,' Breezy."

Bree rolls her eyes.

"You're both playing for second place." Ann is chewing on another big bite of spaghetti, so her words come out all squishy and garbled. "I have a plan too."

"I'm glad to hear you're all so keen on winning," says Mom. "You guys about ready to start?"

Ann swallows her last bite. "Ready or not."

First we have to clear the table, but then Mom hands out the notebooks and pens. "OK. On your mark . . . get set . . . The Bennett children Winner's Game has officially begun!"

"Ann, you're the best sister ever," I blurt out as fast as I can, then quickly strike a check mark in my notebook.

"Thank you, Cade," she replies politely.

"You're also really pretty," Bree tells Ann, though it is obvious she doesn't mean it.

"Thank you."

"Bree, you're the best sister too," I gush. *Check mark!* "And you're . . . um, pretty, I guess." *Another check mark!*

Bree gives me her "you're an idiot" look. "You 'guess'? That's not very nice." She flips to the second page of her spiral pad and announces, "That's one point for me, and one point *against* you. Wait, two points against you, because you also told Ann she was the best sister ever, so you must've lied to me. Ha! You're losing points faster than you're gaining them, little brother!"

"Well, taking points away from me is mean, so I'm taking two points away from you for taking two points away from me!" I quickly mark two negative points next to Bree's name on the second page of my notebook. "Now we're even."

"Heck no!" hisses Bree. "If it's mean for me, it's mean for you too, so another two points against you, plus one more for raising your voice." She turns to Ann before I can reply. "Now, to gain back the points that Tweedle-Dumb took away . . . Ann, you have great hair, I really like your outfit today, and I don't like to admit it, but you're really smart."

Ann smiles. "Thank you, thank you, and thank you."

I need some quick points too. "Ann, I'm glad you got your braces off last year. You look much better without them."

"Thanks, Cade, that means a lot to me."

*"And,"* I continue before Bree can say anything else, "you're a great swimmer. I

always liked watching your meets, back before . . . well, you know. And I'll be really happy once you get a new heart, because you're really nice and stuff and I don't want anything to happen to you."

"Awww, thanks, Bud."

I mark a few more points for myself, figuring that's probably enough to get me back to zero. "Oh, and Bree, that's three more points against you for taking my three points, and minus another one for yelling, and one more for calling me dumb."

"I said *Tweedle*-Dumb," she growls. "And the way you're acting now, you're proving my point."

"Fine," I tell her. "Minus another one."

Bree and I go back and forth for several more minutes, each of us taking away more points from the other in a never-ending circle of meanness. Once in a while we stop to give Ann a compliment, but we are both bleeding "kindness points" quickly. The math is getting fuzzy, because I don't know exactly how many points Bree has taken from my total, but based on the number of marks next to her name in my notebook, I'm guessing we're both nearing fifty points *in the hole.*

That's about the time when Ann stands up, seeming super-happy at the way the first five minutes of the Winner's Game is going. "I love it when a plan comes together," she says.

Bree and I both shut up instantly.

"What do you mean?" asks Bree.

"Nothing."

"So what if we're a little behind," I say. "It's not like you have any points, Ann."

"Oh really?" She flips open her notepad and quickly flashes a long list of tally marks.

"You didn't say a single nice thing to either of us!" explodes Bree. "What are you giving yourself points for?"

Batting her eyelashes, she says, "*For kindness.* Every time you said something nice to me, I said 'thank you' back. I was being polite, which is one of the nicest, kindest things you can do." She takes a long, proud breath, then quips, "We've barely even started, and I already know who's going to win this week. And it's not either of you."

Bree and I look at each other, and then at Mom. "Can she get points for saying 'thank you'?" asks Bree.

"Well . . . she was being very sweet about it."

"Fine," Bree mutters. "But I'm marking a negative point against her for gloating."

"OK, Sis," replies Ann in a sugary-sweet voice. "If that'll make you feel better, I'll sacrifice a point. But I don't want to take one away from you in return . . . because it just wouldn't be nice." She smiles happily, then says, "By the way, you guys are both so cute when you fight. I know that's really nice of me to say, but consider it a freebie."

"Well, this isn't going like I'd hoped," admits Mom. "Cade, Bree, don't count yourselves out, though. You have the whole rest of the week ahead of you. Just pace yourselves and you can get back in this thing."

I nod, but somehow I get the feeling Mom is wrong, and that she knows she's wrong.

Throughout the rest of the day Bree and I keep at it, going back and forth looking for things that the other person says or does that we don't like.

To be honest, it's actually very tiring keeping up with her constant mean looks — and even meaner words — but I do my best, right up until I go to bed.

Over breakfast the next morning I mark a point against her for slurping her cereal too loud, which I am positive she is doing on purpose just to annoy me.

After breakfast she takes one point away from me for accidentally splashing water on her while I'm rinsing my bowl.

Then I take a point from her for interrupting me when I'm talking to Mom.

She takes one from me for taking too long in the bathroom.

I subtract another from her for not saying "Excuse me" when she burps.

She subtracts one from me for farting.

And on and on . . .

By the end of the second day, Bree calls it quits. "It's not working, Mom," I hear her say in Mom's room. "Look at me and Cade," she continues. "I think we're fighting even more than we did before. And I'm so far behind Ann that there's no way I can win this stupid thing."

"Well, what is Ann doing differently than you two? She's been totally cheerful since the game started, and she has more reasons than the rest of us not to be."

"I don't know."

"Well, let's find out. I'm not ready to give up just yet." A few seconds later Mom comes out of her bedroom dressed in pajamas and calls up the stairs. "Ann! Can you come down here for a second?"

Ann appears in the stairwell a minute later. "What's up, O kind mother of mine?" she asks with a smile and that same sugary-sweet voice.

Mom smiles, shaking her head. "What's gotten into you?"

"Nothing. What's up?"

"I just want to see your scorecard."

"Why?"

"I want to see how many points you've taken away from Cade and Bree."

Ann smiles again and hands her the notebook. Mom turns to the second page, glances up at her almost immediately, and then a little grin splits her face. "Very interesting."

"What is?" I ask.

She doesn't answer me directly. Instead she says, "Cade and Bree, give me your notebooks and have a seat." She opens them one at a time and tears out the second page, then crumples up the papers and throws them on the floor. Then she motions to Ann. "Care to tell us why you didn't give your brother or sister any negative points?"

Bree and I share a guilty look before Ann speaks. "I was planning on it, but then I saw how quickly Cade and Bree were losing points, and I saw an opportunity. It was simple math. I figured if I didn't respond to their unkindness with more unkindness, then they can't take points away from me, and I'll always stay in the lead. So far so good." She still has that goofy grin on her face.

Mom probes further by asking, "Can you

explain why you're so happy all of a sudden? A couple days ago you were pretty sour."

She shrugs. "Why shouldn't I be? Bree and Cade keep giving me all of these great compliments. Even if they don't mean it, it's kind of a nice change from the usual."

Mom hands the notebooks back to me and Bree. "New rule," she says. "From now on, you cannot take points away from anyone. You can give yourself all the points you've legitimately earned for being nice, but you cannot retaliate by taking points when someone is mean. In fact, if someone is mean to you, *not* retaliating should be a point in your favor, because that's a very hard, very loving thing to do."

"Well, there goes my advantage," says Ann, sounding a little bummed.

"But I think you know it's the best thing for everyone," says Mom.

With a nod she says, "I know. Besides, I'm still going to win."

A crooked smile develops on Bree's face as she folds her arms. "Maybe this week, Ann, because I'm really in the hole right now. But I can make you a promise that for the rest of the summer, I'm going to be hard to beat. The hundred dollars will be really nice, but the best part will be seeing you lose." She glances at me and adds, "And you."

"And I love you too, Sis," replies Ann, still smiling sweetly.

# CHAPTER 20
## BREE

Ann dozes off soon after we turn out the lights, but I toss and turn in bed for over an hour. My brain is spinning on all sorts of things — dead cats, the Winner's Game, Ann's heart, and especially the things she said about dying. Her opinion on death has been a little hard to swallow, but eventually I come to accept that maybe she is right. Not only is Ann herself a heartbeat away from her last breath, but any one of our lives could be snuffed out — just like Mr. Skittles' — in the blink of an eye.

*That really sucks.*

Even though the room is completely quiet, if I listen closely, I can almost imagine the sound of Ann's defective heart echoing through the bed beneath me. Beating for now, but waiting, like a robber, to steal everything she has.

The last thing to cross my mind before I drift off is Ann's comment from a couple days ago.

*Everyone's going to die. One way or another . . .*

Even though I know Ann has pretty much won this first week of the Winner's Game, I figure getting a little practice in for next week can't hurt, so I spend Friday morning wandering around with Cade and the metal detector near Haystack Rock.

*After all, what can be nicer than a sister who seems interested in what her little brother is doing? This should be worth a point for every minute I pretend to be enjoying it.* My expectations are low that we'll find anything valuable, but who knows, right? That's the thrill of it, I guess. Each time the buzzer sounds, Cade can hardly contain himself. He digs like crazy, only to find some tiny piece of junk, but then he says that each failure just means he's one step closer to finding the mother lode.

Ann joins us on the beach after we've been out there maybe an hour, but all she wants to do is sit there on her beach towel.

*Sweet! No points for her!*

I stop and look her way from time to time, to make sure she's OK, and each time, she is in the same position, staring out at the ocean.

After another half hour I look up and Ann's towel is empty. I scan the beach and spot her near the edge of the water, where she can almost get her feet wet, but not quite.

"Ann!" I shout. "What are you doing?"

The wind is blowing in her direction or she probably wouldn't hear me. She turns slowly. "I'm going inside," she calls back. "Are you staying?"

I nod. "Just until Cade is done."

"Just make sure you both stay out of the water," she calls back. "It isn't safe."

Shortly after noon Cade's battery dies, so we head back home. Mom is in Grandma's room reading more of her journals. She says she's going to be a while, but asks if I'll go check on Ann.

When I go up to our room, Ann is writing something on the bottom of her bed. "More hearts?" I ask.

She shakes her head, but her eyes remain focused on the pen strokes. "Planning."

"Does Mom know — ?"

She lifts a finger to shush me. "Just a sec. I'm almost done." Half a minute ticks by before she lowers the pen. "What were you saying?"

"I was just wondering if Mom knows you're writing on the bed."

"Yeah, she saw it a few days ago when she was picking up laundry. She said she doesn't care. Dad, on the other hand, would care a lot, so let's not tell him."

I nod. "What are you 'planning'?"

She smiles. "Come see for yourself."

It's been a few days since I've looked at her bunk bed artwork. I kneel down next to her to find not only more hearts inside other hearts, but also tiny words in the spaces between the hearts. "What does it say?"

"Look closer. You've got two eyes."

I crawl up on the bed and read aloud: *"Color my hair . . . Do something unpredictable . . . Swim in the ocean . . . Fall in love . . . Eat sushi . . . Feed a sea lion."* I do a double take at the last one. *"Feed a sea lion?"*

"Yep. Yesterday, while I was walking on the beach, I saw a guy tossing fish guts to two sea lions in the surf. All three of them seemed like they were having so much fun. The sea lions acted almost like they were his pets. Every time he threw something to them, they'd bark for more." She stares at her own words on the wood. "I want to do these things this summer, while I still can."

"Cool."

"I know. I'm going to do them all, and once I'm done, I'll add more things to the list."

"You sure you're gonna fall in love?"

"Hey, don't burst my bubble. If I want to fall in love, I can."

"But not with Tanner, though . . . right?"

"I don't know. Maybe. It could be anyone. I just think I deserve to fall in love, and so I'm going to."

*I don't see how, but whatever.* "So when are you going to start?"

"Falling in love?"

"Any of these things."

With a long sigh, Ann flops back on her pillow and stares up. Then she lifts a finger and presses it against the plywood. Slowly, she traces the outermost heart, like it's written in Braille. "Soon," she replies nervously. After a few more seconds she scoots to the edge of the mattress and stands up.

"How soon?"

"Like now."

"Like, *now* now?"

"Right now."

"Where are you going?"

"Out."

"Out where?"

"Somewhere."

"Can I come?"

"Sorry. Not this time."

"Why? What are you going to do?"

She looks at me for a long time, like she

isn't so sure herself. Then, with a little smile, she makes up her mind. "I'll start with something unpredictable . . . then see what happens next."

I cross my arms and tilt my head. "Are you telling Mom you're going?"

"I have Page in my pocket. I'm fine. Besides, I'll be back long before she finishes reading Grandma's journals."

"What about your cell phone, in case we need to call you?"

She shrugs. "It needs a charge. Besides, you know how spotty the reception is here. But don't worry. I'm totally fine."

"I don't know, Ann. Maybe you should just let her know."

Ann frowns. "We both know if I ask permission she'll say no. Or she'll make me take you or Cade along to babysit me. But right now, I just need to live a little." She points to the words on the underside of the bed. "My bucket list is calling." She pauses. "Tell you what, I'll spot you fifty points for next week's round of the Winner's Game if you just let me go without telling Mom."

*Fifty points! Sucker . . .*

"Deal," I say without hesitation. "Enjoy being unpredictable."

# CHAPTER 21
## ANN

There's plenty of stuff I could be looking at on my walk into town — kites flying above houses, seagulls on the breeze, white fluffy clouds blowing in off the ocean — but I can't take my eyes off the couple walking ahead of me. What are they, like twelve? They don't look old enough to watch a PG movie by themselves, let alone date, and yet they're holding hands like they've been doing so for years. As we continue walking, they're laughing like they haven't got a care in the world.

Seeing them makes me a little jealous. Not of them, per se, but of carefree people in general. How would it be to be like that? How would it be to be impulsive, to not hold back, to just put yourself out there with people and not be scared of the conse-quences? How would it feel to have no regrets at the end of the day and to live like there's no tomorrow?

Bree's like that. I bet she's held hands with guys before. Maybe even kissed one or two of them. Of course she's never had to worry that there might not be a tomorrow. Maybe she wouldn't be so spontaneous if she was constantly battling worries that her heart might burst.

Then again, maybe she'd be *more* spontaneous, because she'd be afraid of missing out on something.

As I approach the row of shops where the candy store is, I slow way down to buy myself a little more time to think this through.

*What if I walk in there and make a fool of myself? What if he doesn't even remember me? What if he's decided he'd actually rather not hang out?*

I check my watch. If I remember correctly, his shift should end in about fifteen minutes.

*I'm completely neurotic!*

This is stupid. Why do I even care what he thinks? What would Bree do? I bet she'd just take a deep breath and walk right in there and start talking to him. Maybe she wouldn't even need a deep breath to calm herself down. Is she so much better than me? For crying out loud, I'm almost an adult. I should be able to show a little interest in a guy without having palpitations, right?

*So why is my heart doing flips in my chest?*

I take a deep breath . . . and force my feet to proceed.

There's a bell hanging on the inside of the door when I walk into the candy shop. I wish there wasn't, so I could try to slip in undetected. But there's no backing out now. The bell has announced my arrival. I'm at my destination. And Tanner is . . . nowhere to be seen.

"Hello there," says an older man behind the counter. "Welcome to my store."

"Oh, I . . . hi."

"Got your mind set on something sweet?"

"Uh-huh." *I assume he's sweet anyway . . . he seemed so last week when I met him.*

"You look like a chocolate girl to me. Am I right?"

"Yeah. I guess."

"Well, you're welcome to sample anything in the store if it'll help you decide."

Just then a familiar face appears through a door behind the counter.

*I'll have one of those, if you don't mind . . .*

"Ann?"

"Hey Tanner."

"I'm surprised to see you."

"Why?"

261

He shrugs. "I don't know. Your sister kinda made it seem like . . . I don't know . . . that you didn't really want to see me or something."

*Wait. Bree came here? Behind my back? To meet Tanner? Oh, that conniving little . . . !* "Really? I didn't even know she came. That's weird."

"So . . . are you here to buy something?"

If I had a smile that was cute or charming, I would use it now. But I honestly don't even know what a smile like that would look like, so I just grin sheepishly. "Actually, I was coming to see if . . . you know . . . you wanted to hang out. You said something before about maybe showing me around town?"

Tanner seems a little surprised . . . but in a good way. He checks his watch. "I'm off work in about ten minutes. Can you wait?"

The man behind the cash register chuckles. "Oh, for crying out loud, Tanner, never keep a lady waiting. Your last ten minutes is on me. You kids go have some fun."

As Tanner leads the way through the door, I feel my heart racing again. But this is different from normal. It doesn't scare me. I have no worries about what might or might not happen as a result of the pounding inside my chest. For the first time in a long time, the strained beating of my heart feels strangely . . . *happy.*

# CHAPTER 22
# EMILY

Reading about Grace's life has given me ample cause to evaluate mine. I used to think she walked on water, but looking at my grandmother through her own eyes, I realize that she had her own challenges and imperfections, just as we all do. That knowledge doesn't necessarily make my challenges any easier to face, but at least I know it's not just me.

I remember the year I graduated from high school. Without my own mother there to support me, Grandma filled in as best she could. For her efforts, I made her a special Mother of the Year award. Thinking about it makes me laugh — not because it's funny but because right now I'm so far from earning such an award from my kids. What would they even write on the award? *"Thanks, Mom, for asking us to throw rocks at each other"?*

*Yeah, not exactly award-winning mothering.*

Of course, our Winner's Game experiment probably removes me from award consideration too. I mean, what kind of mother offers her children money to be nice to each other? But the thing is . . . it seems to be working! All the game needed was one tiny little change, and now relationships already seem to be mending between the kids.

With the way Bree and Cade were fighting when we first started, I was certain our little experiment — and ultimately our family — was doomed. In hindsight, it's clear that the problem was that they were looking for the negative, looking for ways to punish the other for mistakes. Now that there is no motivation to look for the negative, they are staying more focused on the positive.

If I step back, I suppose it's the same way with Dell and me in our relationship. We're constantly keeping score of all the perceived injustices between us, which I'm sure hinders us from seeing all the good in our marriage.

*I can only pray that Dell will play the game with me . . .*

But for now, I'm tickled to see that one tiny little change in our game has brought a glimmer of hope. The game itself may yet fail, but I can see, hear, and feel the difference in the way my children interact, and it's a beautiful change for the better.

Yesterday, for example, Cade pushed Bree's hot buttons several times. I think he was just trying to see how she would react, given the rule change. In the morning he pointed out that her breath stank, but rather than yelling at him or making some rude comment about his intelligence, she actually thanked him for bringing it to her attention. Then she gave herself a point for restraining her emotions and marched straight to the bathroom and brushed her teeth! And in the afternoon, when he told her he'd just seen a six-year-old-girl trot by on the beach wearing the same ugly swimsuit as hers, she laughed it off and said that that little girl must have good taste.

When she was alone, I asked her why she didn't lash out at his comments. Her answer made a lot of sense: "If he's being mean, and I'm nice back, I win! It's not easy, because deep down I still want to punch him, but smiling instead will help me get that hundred dollars."

I'm not saying everything is suddenly perfect between them — after all, they are still rival siblings — but the tone and intent of their interactions has taken a noticeable turn for the better. Without the burden of focusing on everyone's little shortcomings, they all seem more inclined to look for and embrace the positive.

*Dear God . . . just let it last.*

I'm nearing the end of another page in Grandma's journal, when Bree knocks on my bedroom door, then waltzes in.

"What'cha up to?"

I finish reading the next sentence before answering. "Just reading. You?"

"I painted a picture of you and Dad. Want to see?" Without waiting for my reply she produces a small watercolor from behind her back. I have to look at it from several different angles before I see the forms of a man and a woman embracing.

"I can't tell where I end and he begins."

Bree smiles knowingly. "That's kinda the idea."

*Aww . . . she really can be sweet when she wants to be.*

I check my watch. It's later than I thought. "Was Ann upstairs with you? I haven't seen her in a while."

Something flashes across her face, but I can't read it. "No. I . . . um . . . I haven't seen her in a while either."

I still don't want to stop reading, but I know I should. At least until I'm sure Ann is safe. Bree hands me her painting as I approach. "Can I keep it?"

"As long as you promise to show Dad."

"Promise."

After setting the painting on the night-stand in the next room, I find Cade on the deck with his slingshot, shooting popped popcorn into the air at a frenzied mob of seagulls. Where does he come up with these ideas? The other day I saw him out back with a fishing pole fixed up with a Buffalo Chicken Wing tied to the end of the line. He cast the line to a nearby seagull, and when the thing swallowed the piece of chicken whole, he began reeling it in. The gull, of course, had the chicken bone in its belly, so it was kind of stuck. It immediately took off flying, and eventually snapped the string, but for a few seconds, Cade had his very own living kite. "Hey, Sport, what's with the poncho?"

"It's for the —"

"Oh poop," I groan as one of the seagulls swoops overhead and drops a white streak on my Polo windbreaker.

Cade is grinning from ear to ear. "Exactly."

I retreat a few steps to the cover of the roof and begin carefully peeling off the jacket. "Hey, I was just looking for Ann. Have you seen her?"

He lowers his slingshot. "Like three or four hours ago. I saw her heading out the front door."

"Did she tell you where she was going?"

He shrugs — not like he doesn't know something, more like he's not sure he should say.

"What did she say, Cade?"

"Uh . . . all she said was . . . uh . . . not to tell you that she was going."

"Those were her exact words?"

"Uh-huh."

I don't wait to hear anything more. "Bree!" I yell through the doorway. "Ann took off!"

Cade quickly dumps the remaining popcorn over the side of the deck, to the delight of at least fifty diving birds, then tears off his poncho, and we hurry inside. Once we're all together in the living room, I pelt him with more questions. *When exactly did she leave? Did she say when she'd be back? Any idea where she was going? Why would she not want me to know?*

Before her medical problems, I wouldn't have thought twice about Ann going out for a little while on her own. But given her current condition, and knowing that if the pager suddenly rings and she isn't close to home, she could miss out altogether on a transplant, I need to be extrakeen on always knowing her whereabouts.

When Cade guesses that Ann might have walked to town to "see that boy at the candy shop," Bree zings him with her best scowl. "You better not have told her!"

"Told who what?" I ask.

Cade seems to be covering for Ann, but he is more than happy to rat out Bree. "Bree took me with her so she could meet Tanner. Without Ann knowing."

In moments like this, placing my hands on my hips and frowning is almost instinctual. "Bree Grace Bennett, why on earth would you go behind your sister's back like that?"

"Uh-oh," warns Cade. "Full name."

For a second or two, Bree has that deer-in-the-headlights look, then she throws her hands up in the air. "You're missing the point here! Ann snuck out of the house to do *'something unpredictable'*! So don't turn this around on me." As soon as she says it, she realizes she may have said too much.

"What do you mean 'to do something unpredictable'? Is there something you aren't telling me too?"

"Maybe?" she whispers.

"Spit it out, Bree."

In the next thirty seconds, Bree quickly

explains how Ann "paid" her fifty points in the Winner's Game to keep her secret that she was heading off to fulfill her summer bucket list.

"Fifty?" asks Cade dejectedly. "Oh man, I only got twenty for keeping my mouth shut."

Once I'm clear on the details about Ann, I circle back to the point about Tanner. "Now explain to me why you went to meet this boy without your sister."

In response, she throws her hands up in the air again, like I'm nuts for even asking. "Seriously? That's what you're worried about? Ann snuck out of the house to do 'something unpredictable'! For all we know she could be hitchhiking down to Hollywood, or stealing a car and going for a joyride. Heck, have you even checked to see if the Walrus is still in the driveway?"

" 'Unpredictable' for Ann does not mean stealing a car."

Bree doesn't back down. "True, but what about her heart? She could be out there right now *dying,* while we're in here worried about some dumb boy? C'mon, Mom, we should go look for her!"

It's so hard being mad at one child when I'm worried about the other. I drop my hands from my hips. "You're right, we should go find her. But I expect a full explanation later, young lady."

It only takes a minute to reach the candy shop by car. I hop out and rush inside, leaving the Walrus idling. "She's not there," I tell the kids when I return a minute later. "Neither is Tanner, but the man behind the counter says he left with 'a young lady' hours ago."

Bree is next to me on the front seat. "Was it Ann?"

"I assume so." As I'm pulling out into the street, I add, "Oh, that girl is in so much trouble."

"Why?" asks Cade from the backseat. "She didn't do nothing wrong."

" '*Anything* wrong,' Cade, and she most certainly did. Since when is it OK to sneak out of the house?"

"Maybe she didn't sneak. Maybe she just walked right out."

"Well, she didn't ask permission. And she obviously knew it was wrong, or she wouldn't have asked you to cover for her."

"Am I gonna have to ask permission to go for a walk when I'm seventeen?"

"If you have a serious heart condition and you're going to pal around alone with a girl, most definitely." I can feel myself growing increasingly irritable with every word.

"I just don't think she's done anything wrong."

"Cade William Bennett! Stop arguing with me!"

"Uh-oh," remarks Bree. "Full name."

"I'm just saying . . . ," he mumbles.

"Zip it, young man."

Just to be sure Ann isn't nearby, I drive slowly along the little strip mall, checking every window to see if she's there. At the next intersection, we turn a corner and start individually checking every store that looks promising. After we've canvassed the area thoroughly, we turn around and take side streets slowly back to the house, hoping every face along the way is Ann's.

None of them are.

When we make it home thirty minutes later, there are two figures — a boy and a girl — sitting on the front step of the porch, deep in conversation.

Ann waves as we pull to a stop in the driveway. "Where have you guys been?" she asks as we pile out of the car.

I'm fuming inside, but I try not to lose my cool in front of Tanner. "I was just about to ask you the same thing."

Ann gleefully holds up a white paper bag. "Sushi! Oh my gosh, at first I thought I was going to puke. But after that it was kind of good."

Tanner stands up as we approach. "Hi. I'm Tanner."

"So I've heard," I say, finding it hard not to clench my teeth. "It's nice to meet you."

"Hey Cade," Tanner says, holding up a smaller paper bag. "I brought you something."

"*Eww.* No way. I hate fish."

"It's not sushi, dude. Trust me, you'll like it."

Reluctantly, Cade takes the offering. Inside is an assortment of goodies from the candy store.

"They're rejects," Tanner explains. "Broken pieces we can't sell. But they still taste good. I thought you and Bree would like them."

As if on cue, Bree waves daintily at him, her cheeks blushing profusely.

*Oh great — two teenage girls, one teenage boy. As if we need any more drama this summer . . .*

"So I have to share?" asks Cade.

"Of course you have to share," I tell him before Tanner can respond. "Thank you, Tanner. That's very nice of you."

He nods, then checks his watch. "Well, I should probably get going. My mom doesn't know where I'm at."

*Sounds familiar.*

Then the most awkward thing happens, or at least I find it awkward. Without so much as a hesitation, Tanner turns to Ann, opens his arms wide, and gives her a hug! Right there in front of me! Didn't they just barely meet? How did they progress to hugging so quickly? When I was a teenager, it took more than a single afternoon together to reach hugging status, and I would have *never* done so with someone's mom watching!

"Thanks," he says. "I had fun."

"Me too." Ann is practically glowing. "Thanks for the sushi."

Behind them, Bree is glowering.

"So are we on for tomorrow?" asks Tanner.

Ann shifts her gaze to me and smiles. "Mom, can I hang out with Tanner tomorrow?"

"Define 'hanging out.' "

"You know, just chill at the beach and stuff."

"And maybe surfing," says Tanner. "She said it sounds fun."

"Surfing? Ann, you know I can't let you do that. What if you — ?"

"Freeze? You're right, the water is really cold and I don't have a wet suit. Plus, I'm probably not a strong enough swimmer. Maybe I can just watch him surf?"

I am utterly stunned by my daughter's comments. Why would Ann suggest that she's a weak swimmer, when she's already proven to be one of the best in the entire state of Oregon? After an extended silence, I finally say, "We'll talk about it. I'm not sure what we have going on tomorrow, since your father will be here. He may already have something in mind."

"Oh right," Ann drones. "Dad is coming tonight. You know what, Tanner? Maybe we should just wait until Monday to do something."

"No prob. I'll come straight over after work. See you then." With that the young man turns to go. Before he gets very far, I ask if he needs a ride home, to which he chuckles and says, "Nah, I only live a few blocks away. Isn't that so cool? I don't even have to have a car, and I can still come see Ann all the time."

Forgive me if my nod and tone are somewhat unenthusiastic. "Yeah. So cool." Once Tanner is out of earshot, I let out an exasperated breath and then shoo everyone inside. "On the couches. I only have three questions — one for each of you — but that should be enough."

As instructed, the kids file into the tiny living room and plop down on the sofa. They are seated side by side, with Cade in the middle.

"All right. Let's start with the easiest question first. Cade . . ."

"Uh-huh," he says weakly.

"What do you know about this Tanner kid?"

He sits up, pleasantly surprised. "That's an easy question."

"And the answer is . . . ?"

"Not much," he replies with an honest shrug.

"Well, just tell me what you do know, even if it's only a little."

"OK. Ummm . . . he's seventeen. His parents are divorced. He used to live in Portland, but now he lives here with his mom. Uh . . . his name is Tanner. And . . . he works at the candy store." He pauses, pursing his lips as he tries to think of anything else. "Oh, and he lives just a couple blocks away. And he surfs." He pauses once more, glancing nervously at Bree. "And . . . Bree thinks he's her type. At least that's what she said right after she met him."

"You little brat!" explodes Bree.

"Well, you did say it. Right after you said

he wasn't Ann's type because they would have ugly children."

"What?!" screeches Ann.

Bree clenches her fist. "I ought to . . . !"

"Bree Grace Bennett! Don't you dare."

"But he's such a brat!"

"Runs in the family," remarks Ann.

Before things get any more out of control, I hold my hand up to quiet them. "Enough, all of you. We're just answering questions. No need to get upset." I take a deep breath to calm myself down. "Thank you, Cade. That was very informative. Bree, you're next."

"Great," she mutters.

"Don't worry, yours is easy too. Did you, or did you not, take your little brother to the candy store with the express intent of undermining your sister's chances of getting to know Tanner?" I lean back in my chair, waiting for her response.

"What's so easy about that?" she asks glumly.

"It's a simple yes-or-no question. Did you . . . or did you not?"

Bree takes a moment to think, and then crosses her arms and says, simply, "Yes."

"Yes what?"

"You said it's a simple yes-or-no question, so I'm telling you simply, *yes.*"

"Yes what?" I press.

"Yes, I did or did not do what you said."

"Did or didn't?"

With arms still folded defiantly, Bree again replies with a determined, "Yes."

I could scream, but I just shake my head instead. Under my breath, I angrily mumble, "Takes after her father . . ." I clear my throat, then continue. "Very well. I appreciate your honesty." I immediately turn my focus to the other end of the couch. "Ann?"

"Yes," she says solemnly.

"Your turn. One question."

"You promise . . . just one?"

"Just one. But it's not an easy one." We lock eyes for several seconds. I almost hate to ask this. I wish I knew the answer without having to pry it out of her. It would be so much easier if I could just read her like a book and learn everything I need to know. "Why did you lead Tanner to think you're not a good swimmer?"

Ann stares at me for several seconds, and then diverts her attention to the floor. "Because."

"That's not an answer."

There is a very long silence, then Ann finally admits, "Because . . . he's really cool. And I think he likes me."

"Good! You're very likable. But to really like you, he needs to know you, and that's not likely to happen with lies. You're an incredible swimmer, Ann, among other amazing talents. You should be proud and let him get to know the real you."

I hardly realize that Ann has started crying until she stands up and places a hand over her heart, like she's about to give the pledge of allegiance. "Yes, I'm an incredible swimmer," she says, gagging on the words. "But one who can't swim. Just like I'm a runner who can't run, and a straight-A student who hardly went to school last year." She hesitates, trying hard to compose herself. "What I really am, though, is a time bomb. I'm a heart attack waiting to happen. I'm a future that no boy would want, because my future is so uncertain." The tears are flowing freely now, running down her cheeks and spilling onto the sea-blue shag. "So for now — *to him* — I don't mind lying a little bit. I don't want his pity. I don't want him to see me as the girl who might die next month, or the girl on some dumb waiting list. I just want him to know *me* — Ann Bennett, the girl from Portland who is so carefree that she tried sushi on a whim just because it sounded cool. Just let me be *that girl,* OK, Mom?" She wipes away her tears and waits to see how I'll respond.

But I don't know how to respond. I honestly have no clue what to say right now. When did parenting get so complicated? When did my cute, cuddly babies grow into teenagers? How is it that my beautiful little girl is standing in front of me, on the cusp of womanhood, looking to me for guidance about how to balance the youthful desires of romance with the unkind realities of a dysfunctional heart? What do I say to that?

*And for crying out loud, somebody please explain to me how kids have become so bold as to hug in front of their parents on the very first "date"!*

I'm still speechless.

When I don't respond, Ann wipes her tears once more, then whispers, "I need to go lie down before I send my stupid heart into failure."

I check my watch as she disappears upstairs.

Where is Dell? He should be here by now. *I can't do this parenting thing on my own . . .*

# Chapter 23
# Dell

I always thought it would be rewarding to be a lawyer. Not financially rewarding but emotionally, in a help-your-fellow-man sort of way. Before law school I had this grand vision in my head that I was going to become a public defender. Representing the downtrodden in our legal system sounded noble, I suppose. I wanted to help people in difficult circumstances; I wanted to make sure every average Joe had equal access to quality legal advice; I wanted to make sure nobody slipped through the cracks. In my vision of the future, I'd end each day with a smile on my face because I felt so good about what I was doing, even if the pay wasn't all that great.

After my first year of law school, however, I met Emily. We got married before the start of my third year, and suddenly everything changed. My old vision of helping others was traded for a new one, wherein I was a successful provider for my beautiful bride. Emily told me to follow my heart, but instead I sold out and followed the cash; when a giant computer-chip maker in Portland's silicon forest handed me an offer to join their legal team, I couldn't — or didn't — say no.

In the nineteen-plus years since then, I've never even sniffed a courtroom, except that one time when I got selected for jury duty, but that doesn't count.

In retrospect, I should have stuck to my guns. After all, money isn't everything — a fact I've learned particularly well since Ann's health problems started, seeing as her medical bills have sucked away all of our savings.

Even if I didn't go into public defense, I could have at least chosen a field where I had a little more flexibility with my hours. As it stands now, I am expected to work until the work is done . . . and the work is never done.

All of which explains why I'm sitting at my desk at six o'clock on a Friday night, when I should already be with my family in Cannon Beach.

"Big plans this weekend, Dell?" asks my boss as he swings by my office.

"Not really. Just . . . lots of work."

"Well, things should slow down a bit once we reach quarter-end."

*How many times have I heard that? Enough to know it's not true.* I nod anyway.

"Say, how are things going with your daughter? I haven't heard much lately on that front."

"She's hanging in there."

He points at me with his finger, like it's a pistol, then makes a clicking sound with his mouth. "Well, you hang in there too. And hey, I know you're a little behind on the Samsung contract for next week, but don't stay here too late tonight. Get home and spend some time with your family before they're all in bed. There's always Sunday for catch-up, right?"

*Sunday?* "Of course. Have a good weekend."

After he leaves, I stare blankly at my computer screen until it starts getting blurry. Then I dig into the contract again, hoping I can make enough headway on it now so I don't have to spend my entire weekend on it.

At eight thirty, I'm nowhere close to being done.

At nine thirty, still sitting at my office desk, I know it's hopeless.

I've thought of calling Emily several times,

but I didn't want to talk to her unless I had good news. I know if I call to tell her I can't make it this weekend, she's going to assume that I don't want to be there with her.

*Then again . . . do I?*

What am I thinking? Of course I do. I just don't want to be there when she's in one of her moods where she picks apart every little thing I say, which is pretty much all the time lately.

*She's probably already furious that I haven't shown up or called.*

I stare at the phone next to my computer for several minutes, trying to sort out exactly how I'm going to tell her. Finally, I decide there is no good way — she's going to flip, no matter what I say — so I pick it up and dial the house.

After four rings she answers. "Hello?"

Before I respond, I hear what sounds like another click on the line. "Did someone else pick up?"

"I think it's just me, Dell." I can already hear the judgment in her voice. "Why are you calling this phone instead of my cell?"

"I don't know, I just did." I pause to collect myself. "So how are things?"

"Fine. Where are you?"

"Still in Portland."

"Why? What time will you be here?"

"Emily, I . . . I don't think I'm coming this weekend."

She doesn't speak for the longest time. When she does, her voice is teetering. "You don't call me all week, and when you do, it's to tell me you aren't coming? Why?"

"I'm behind at work."

"So? You're always behind at work."

"Yeah, but this time there's a major customer that wants to review their new supply terms on Monday morning, and I'm not even close. And before you ask what I've been doing all week, let me assure you that I've been working my tail off. There's just a lot going on right now. It sucks, but it is what it is."

"So that's it?"

"That's what?"

"The only reason you're not coming."

"Em . . ." I want to say more, but the words jam in my throat.

"What? Tell me what you're thinking."

When I sigh, I make sure it's loud, so she can hear it through the phone. "There's no way I can come this weekend. If I could, I would. But at the same time, we both know how it's been lately between us. I don't want to come all the way out there just to argue with you."

"Then don't."

"I'm not."

"I mean don't argue. Come, but don't argue with me."

"I already said, I *can't* come. As far as arguing goes, it's hard not to when you constantly want to pick fights."

"That's not true."

"It is, and you know it. You're either picking a fight or you're nagging me about this or that. And frankly, I've had it."

"Oh, now you've had it? What is that supposed to mean?"

"It doesn't mean anything, other than that I'm not coming this weekend. I'm staying here, catching up on work, and not fighting with you."

The line goes silent again. The next sound is that of my wife crying. *I knew this conversation would lead to tears.*

"What . . . what should I tell the kids?" she whimpers.

"Tell them I'm sorry and I'll be there next weekend."

"We can't keep going on like this, Dell."

"What do you mean?"

"We can't just keep pretending that something is going to change. Yes, Ann has a heart problem, but right now my heart is broken too! And we're not doing anything to fix it."

"We're surviving. That's the best we can do right now."

"No it's not! We're not surviving . . . I'm not even sure there is a 'we' left anymore. I feel like I'm alone in this. And so are you. So if this is really the best we can do . . . then . . ."

I have to take a moment to process what she just said. If my ears heard right, I think I'm going to be sick. "So what, Emily, are you saying 'it's over'?"

"I'm not saying that at all. I'm just saying . . . I don't know. I think maybe it's good that you're not coming tonight, so you can figure things out. Maybe we both need a little more time away from each other to decide how important this marriage is to us and if we're willing to do what it takes to get things back on track."

"How do we even do that?"

"Just give our marriage some thought, Dell. Before we try to fix anything, you've got to know if I'm worth it to you. I'll see you when you've figured that out."

Emily clicks off without saying good-bye.

I hold the phone to my ear a second longer, only to hear a second click.

*Someone else was listening . . .*

# Chapter 24
## Ann

I should be sleeping. I wish I was! Bree is snoring away on the bunk above me, blissfully unaware of what I heard when I went downstairs earlier to get a drink.

*I should never have picked up the phone. After I did, I should never have listened . . .*

Now I might not sleep at all tonight. I bet Mom won't either. She's probably bawling her eyes out this very second. Maybe Cade's down there awake too, quietly listening to our mother consoling herself.

I'm sad about the whole situation with my parents, but right now I'm also kind of upset with them. I don't think they understand how lucky they are simply to have fallen in love. What a miracle to find someone you love and who loves you back!

*Note to self: if you somehow make it to adulthood and find the man of your dreams and have beautiful kids, don't blow it being mad at each other for stupid little things.*

Sometimes my parents make me so mad I could scream! If Bree weren't sleeping, maybe I would. *Then again, that little sneak went and tried to get all flirty with Tanner behind my back. Maybe she deserves to be woken up . . .*

Hearing the way my parents talk to each other makes me wonder how it used to be between them, back when they first met. Did Mom think Dad was cute the way that I think Tanner is cute? Did she feel electricity when he hugged her? Did she spend at least half of every minute thinking about him?

I kind of hope not, because that might mean the way I feel about Tanner is not enough.

After I've been lying restless for what seems like forever, eventually tiredness sets in. With my eyes beginning to droop, my anger at my parents gives way to happy memories from earlier in the day.

In my mind, I see Tanner and me at the sushi place, picking colorful items off a conveyor. Then we're walking around town. *He knows so many cool things about this place!* I hear him explaining how William Clark and Sacagawea visited this beach during the Lewis and Clark Expedition. And how Cannon Beach is named after an old cannon that washed ashore in 1846 from a US Navy schooner that sank while trying to cross the Columbia River bar. Then I see us visiting the site where the cannon remains to this very day. All the while, as we walk from place to place in my mind, I remember how good it feels to not feel sorry for myself. At no time when I was with him did I have the thought that some other kid out there has to die in order for me to live. There was no wondering how old I'll be when I die. For those few hours with Tanner, I was just a normal girl, and it was magical.

As the memories continue, I feel myself drifting off. With my final thought, I pray that the memories will continue while I sleep, so that I can say without question that Tanner Rich is the man of my dreams . . .

Without Dad around, Saturday flies by. Mom is in a rotten mood; she spends most of her time reading Grandma's old journals, which have held her attention for the better part of a week. Since Bree already knows I'm going to win the first week of the Winner's Game, her overt acts of kindness toward Cade and me have slowed somewhat, leaving her more time to fiddle with her art supplies, but I know that as soon as the next round starts, she'll be right back at it — she's really taking this seriously; if I'm not careful, she might just sneak out a win.

*Nah . . . I'm not going to let that happen. If she thinks she can be nice, I can be nicer!*

For his part, Cade wants to spend all day on the beach with his metal detector, believing he's going to find something to make him rich. I keep reminding him that he already found something more valuable than money when he dug up Grandpa's letter to Grandma, but he's bound and determined to keep looking. Actually, I don't mind so much, because while he's on the beach with his gadget, I get to lie out in the sun daydreaming of Tanner.

On Sunday, just before dinner, Mom calls us to the kitchen table to share the point totals from our notebooks. It takes a few minutes to correctly tally them, but when all is said and done, there is no surprise that I've won by a landslide. For my effort, I get the first choice of seats in the car next week, and a big fat "1" next to my name on a Weekly Winner's chart that Mom hangs on the side of the fridge.

"Now, everyone flip to the next page in your notebook," Mom tells us, "and we'll start the scoring all over again for the week ahead. You've all got a blank slate — tabula rasa — so it's anyone's game."

"Actually," remarks Bree, "it's my game. This week, I won't lose."

"We'll see about that," says Cade.

I nod and smile. "Yes, we will."

As soon as Mom gives the official "Go," the second week of the Winner's Game starts out just like the first did, with Bree and Cade rattling off as many inauthentic compliments as they can think of — mostly to me, but also to each other — only by now they've learned to say "thank you" to the compliments so they can give themselves a point for being polite, which is how I took such a big lead last week.

After five minutes I call a time-out. "Everybody just hold up a second. Bree, what's your score right now?"

My sister counts up the marks in her notebook and says, "Eighteen."

"Cade, how about you?"

He does the same and says, quite proudly, "Twenty-two."

"And I'm at sixteen."

"So you're losing," Bree points out, with no small amount of satisfaction.

"Am I? I've hardly even tried, and I'm only down two points."

She cocks her head to the side. "So what's

your point?"

"That this isn't really working right now. When we're all just saying a bunch of stuff we don't mean so we can give ourselves a point, and then the other person takes a point for saying 'thank you,' it's a wash. Nobody gets ahead. Not really."

Mom has been listening closely to the conversation. She steps forward and puts a hand on my shoulder. "Ann makes a good point. I know it's great practice to say nice things to each other, but if your only intent is to do it so you can rack up quick points, isn't that missing the purpose?"

Bree shrugs. "You made up the game, not us."

"Actually, Grandma did," Mom says, correcting her. "But her intent was to motivate Grandpa and herself to be genuinely kinder to each other, not to pay lip service for the sake of a win."

Frowning, Cade says, "Don't tell me, you want to change the rules again."

"No," Mom says with a chuckle. "But can I make a suggestion? Rather than simply saying nice things for the sake of saying them, perhaps you'd be wise to try doing things for your siblings that will actually make them happy. As Ann pointed out, at the rate you're going, nobody is really going to win. Maybe you need to be a little sneakier about your good deeds — and I know you all know a thing or two about being sneaky. Do things for your brother or sisters when they aren't looking, or when they least suspect it, so you can earn points without them knowing. I'm not saying you have to, I'm just saying . . . think about it."

Cade looks concerned. "If we're doing things in private, how will anyone know if we really earned all the points we mark down? Like maybe Bree will mark points she didn't really earn and nobody will be able to prove she didn't, so she'll cheat and win."

"I'm not a cheater," counters Bree. "I don't need to cheat to beat you."

"Nobody's calling anyone a cheater," says Mom. "A big part of being kind and loving is trust. In order for this to work, you have to trust that you're all playing fair. And remember, if you're all thinking of everyone else, earning points will be a cinch."

"I'll still be the one with the hundred dollars," I mumble.

Mom shoots me a look. "Just give it a try, kids. Be on the lookout for things to really make each other happy. That doesn't mean you can't say nice things too, but random compliments shouldn't be the extent of your kindness, especially if you don't mean them. Be creative with it. Have fun. That's when it will really become a game. Or perhaps that's when the game will become *real.*" She pauses, taking a moment to look at each of us. "You know what? There is one request I'd like to make. When your father gets here later this week, that's when you need to be extrasneaky. Don't hide the fact that you're being nice to each other and doing kind things, just don't let him see your score-cards. Make that part of your game, OK? Keep being nice, just don't let him know what you're up to. I want it to be a little bit of a surprise when he finds out."

"Why?" I ask.

She shrugs. "Because if he finds out too soon, I might not be able to convince him to play too." She pauses again, no doubt thinking about her phone conversation with Dad on Friday night. "And I *really* need him to play."

Overnight, Mom's suggestion that we be a little more covert in our kindness must've really taken root in someone, because on Monday morning, after taking a shower, I return to my room to find that my bed is made up perfectly and there is a piece of chocolate on the pillow! Then, when I go to pick out an outfit, I discover that someone has folded every single article of clothing in my drawers!

To earn a point for myself, I quickly head for the closet and pick up Bree's dirty laundry from the floor, then take it downstairs and throw it in the wash.

As I pull out my notebook to mark my score, I decide it's actually worth more like three points — one for picking up, one for carrying the load downstairs, and one for putting it in the wash.

Later in the morning I spot Cade tiptoeing out of the attic with something behind his back. "Uh-oh, what are you up to?"

"Nothin'," he replies, with the guiltiest look ever. "It's none of your beeswax."

"Then why are you hiding something behind your back?"

"I'm not." He inches along the wall, making sure to keep his back hidden from my view. Once he's past me, he darts down the stairs and out of sight. An hour later, when I return to my room, there is an old four-by-six picture on my bed of Great-grandpa holding a baby. There's also a note, written in Cade's crummy handwriting, which reads, *I found this in the attic. Thought you'd like to have it.*

On the back of the picture, in blue ink, it reads, *Ann & G-Pa Al, 1996.*

He died three years later, just a couple months before Bree was born.

Though we're all having fun sneaking around throughout the day earning secret kindness points, when the doorbell rings at three o'clock, winning the game is suddenly the farthest thing from my mind. I know I'm all smiles when I answer the door, but I don't care.

Tanner is smiling too. "Hey, you still got time for me today?"

"Are you kidding? I've been waiting all weekend." I don't mean to sound so eager, but I can't help it.

He comes inside to say hi to everyone and then asks if I want to go for a walk on the beach.

As we're heading for the back door, we pass by Bree, who I can tell is totally jealous, which is a little troubling, because she's too young for him anyway. Why can't she just let me enjoy this for right now without sticking her nose in it? She'll have her turn. But me? *This could be my only chance to have a genuine relationship with a really cute guy!*

As we walk, Tanner shares more fun facts about Cannon Beach. I always knew, for instance, that the giant rock out there is called Haystack Rock. What I didn't know is that the smaller, pointy rocks near its southern edge are called The Needles . . . as in, needles in the haystack.

At one point Tanner wants to jog in the wet sand. I know I shouldn't . . . but I do it anyway.

*Oh my gosh, I'm so out of shape!* As we're jogging, I feel a sharp prick in my chest after about thirty seconds, so I tell him I just want to walk. I'm pretty sure he sees me flinch, because he asks if everything is OK. I lie and say I'm fine.

At least now I know what my limits are: *Spending time with Tanner? Good. Jogging? Bad.*

Tanner comes over again on Tuesday, but this time it's kind of drizzly, so we stay inside and play games. Mom likes that a lot more, because she can keep an eye on us. Cade likes having Tanner there too, but Bree still seems jealous.

*Oh my gosh . . . !* Does she think he's going to fall madly in love with her? Who knows what goes on in that girl's mind sometimes.

On Wednesday, Tanner wants to go for a bike ride, but I tell him I'm not a big fan of bikes. I happen to love riding bikes, but it's the only thing I can think of to get out of it. It's a worthy lie, though, because instead of biking he takes me horseback riding on the beach!

Mom says it's too risky for me, but when am I going to have another chance? Besides, it's not like I have to do anything but sit in the saddle and steer.

The best part is when Tanner helps me climb on the horse. Even if it is brief, his hands are on my waist to lift me, sending butterflies through my stomach. The good kind of butterflies, not the ones that bite.

The next day when Tanner comes over, I'm in the mood for another walk on the beach.

"Fine," says Mom, "but just to warn you, I might send Cade and Bree to spy on you, so be good."

Sure enough, I catch the two of them sneaking along about fifty yards back. Tanner sees them too. "Too bad they're there," he says coolly.

"Why?"

"I dunno . . . I just thought . . . maybe if you wanted, we could hold hands. But they'd probably tell your mom."

"They would definitely tell her," I reply, feeling my cheeks getting hot. I quickly glance over my shoulder once more. Bree is watching us like a hawk. *Perfect.* I swallow hard, then tell him, "But I don't care what they say."

"Really?"

"Really."

Another rush of butterflies swarm as he takes my hand in his!

When I check over my shoulder, Cade is pointing at us. Bree, however, looks mad. She turns at once and stomps away.

When we get back to the house, Mom is standing on the deck with her hands on her hips. I figure Tanner might try to let go of my hand when we see her there, but he keeps on holding.

The first thing Mom says is, "Uh-oh . . . this looks like trouble." I'm expecting her to be mad, but she seems more conflicted than anything. It's like she's happy for me and yet incredibly worried for my well-being. The second thing she says is, "Maybe Tanner should come over for dinner on Sunday and see what your father says about this."

Dad is supposed to arrive sometime in the next hour, so after Tanner leaves, we all start preparing for his arrival. We haven't heard from him all week, and Mom seems a little on edge.

Is that what love does over time? Twenty years ago, did my mom feel butterflies when my dad held her hand? Did they laugh and talk like they'd known each other forever, even though they'd only just met? Then what happened? They kissed, got married, had kids, and suddenly forgot that they loved each other? Forgot how it felt when it first started?

I don't ever want that. If I live long enough to get married, I'll love that person fiercely, every single day. It may be someone else's heart that I have to use, but I'll love him with the whole of it . . .

# CHAPTER 25
## EMILY

Last Friday when I spoke to Dell on the phone, I told him he needs to figure out how important our marriage is to him. It's Friday night again . . . and he's not here. Again.

*I guess I know his answer.*

It hurts just to think about it, so I'm trying not to. To avoid having a complete meltdown in front of the kids, I keep coming up with mental distractions.

At six o' clock I scrub the bathtub.

At six thirty I make a batch of cookies.

At seven I start on a crossword puzzle.

At seven fifteen I read the clue to 33 Down — *Spousal severance.* The answer is a six-letter word beginning with *D.*

When the answer — "divorce" — comes too quickly, I know it's time to find another distraction. "Kids, I'm going to see Grandma! Does anyone want to come?"

Bree and Ann are quick to decline my

invitation, on account of already having seen her once today. I can see in Cade's eyes that he doesn't want to go either, but maybe he recognizes by my expression that I could really use the company. "Fine," he mumbles. "If no one else will."

It hasn't been a great week for Great-grandma. Yesterday she was so drugged that she could hardly open her eyes, and the day before that she was fully alert, yet couldn't remember who we were. When we arrive, the attending nurse explains that it's been another rough day. After dinner Grandma lost track of where she was and kept telling the staff she's in the wrong place and needs to be moved back to the farm. I can only guess that she is remembering her earlier life out in Pendleton.

When we enter her room, Grandma's eyes are open, but she looks worn out. "Hi there, Grandma," I say softly. "How are you?"

There is no recognition in her eyes. Maybe a little curiosity, and definitely some fear, but no recognition. When she speaks, her mouth struggles to form the sounds. "I . . . I d-don . . ." And then she starts crying. Not bawling. There isn't even any sound. Just a tear or two meandering down through her wrinkles. "I d-don . . . know you."

"It's Emily. Your granddaughter."

"Do you know th' f-f-arm? I wan' to go."

Now a tear drops down my face too. "It's OK, Grace. Just rest. You're safe here."

Within a minute, Grandma Grace closes her eyes.

We sit there in silence at her bedside for fifteen or twenty minutes, during which time she opens her eyes several times, looks around wildly, and then closes them again. Once I'm sure that she's actually asleep, I reach up and caress her hands. Then my tears really start to flow. Seeing Grandma like this is hard; she's always been my anchor in life, and now her boat is drifting away. I want so much to get her advice. I long to hear her say, like she has a thousand times before, "It'll be all right, Emily, just you wait and see."

I know she can't hear me, but I desperately need a sounding board, so I give Cade a few dollars and send him to find a vending machine so I can have a few minutes alone with her. "You know you've always been my hero, Grandma, right? I've always looked up to you in every way. You were there when my mother passed, and you took me under your wing and tended me like I was your own. You spent so much time caring for me that I never thought to consider that you were suffering too, over losing your daughter." I rub her hand some more, then wipe at a pesky tear. "You and Grandpa were my angels back then. I wanted to grow up and be just like you. I wanted the marriage, the family, the perfect life you had. And now . . . ? Now I might lose it all. That's what I've dreamed of all these years, just having the kind of love that you shared with Grandpa — the kind that would go on forever and ever. For a while, I thought I had that. For years I was absolutely sure that I was on the same path as you. I thought it would be so easy . . . but then life got in the way."

A few seconds tick by in silence. In the vacancy, I continue fiddling with Grandma's coarse fingernails and bony knuckles. Then I feel her flinch, and she clasps my hands. It catches me by surprise, but I don't pull away. I squeeze back, and when I do, Grandma's eyes suddenly open, just a sliver. "Don't give up, Em," she whispers, plain as day. "It'll be all right." As soon as she says it, Grandma's eyes fall closed again.

I'm crying profusely, but smiling. She didn't say much, but for tonight, it is enough.

"Thank you, Grandma," I say just before Cade returns with a half-eaten Snickers bar.

As we exit the room, Cade asks the one

question that's been constantly on my mind since we left the house. "Do you think Dad is there yet?"

"I hope so, Cade," I reply honestly. "I really hope so."

Five minutes later, when we pull up to the house, Cade is the first to assess the situation when he casually says, "Nope."

I know just what he means, and it splinters the pieces of my breaking heart.

*Dell still isn't there.*

# CHAPTER 26
## ANN

When I'm working on homework or something, I frequently tune people out. I just get in that zone, you know, where the rest of the world evaporates. Painting the living room walls is nothing like homework, except that the entire family is in the zone — or zoned out — which is probably why none of us hears the front door open or close when Dad arrives on Saturday morning. All of a sudden he is just sort of there, with his hands in his pockets, watching us work.

At first I don't even realize he's behind me. The thing that makes me turn around is when Mom stops rolling her roller and stares, unblinking, past my shoulder. "You came," she says, choking on the words.

Immediately, everyone stops what they're doing. Bree and I back up two steps so we aren't right between them.

Cade drops his angled brush down in the bucket near his feet.

"Did you think I wouldn't?"

"I thought you'd be here last night. Or at least call."

His hands remain in his pockets, but he motions to the bedroom. "Should we go talk in private?"

"No," I blurt out, surprising even myself. "I want to hear too." I glance quickly back and forth between my parents. "I was . . . on the phone last week, the last time you talked. I heard everything."

"I see," says Dad, not seeming too surprised at my eavesdropping.

"So if what you're going to say to Mom is bad news, then I want to know too, because whatever happens with you and Mom affects all of us. Besides, these walls are paper-thin, so we'll probably hear the whole conversation anyway."

He looks at me with apologetic eyes. "Very well, in front of everyone, then." He glances at Bree and Cade, then he focuses again on Mom. "Here's the deal. I got out of work early last night, thinking I'd come straight over in time for supper. But when I got in the car, I just felt like I needed more time to think. So I went home. I'd have called, but I didn't know what I'd say." He takes a deep breath. "It was a very long night, Emily, but I figured it out."

"Figured what out?" she asks.

"You said not to come until I figured out how important our marriage is to me, and what you're worth to me."

"And?"

"And . . . I'm here. Whatever has happened to drive a wedge between us, I want to figure out a way to remove it. I don't know how, or how long it will take, but I want to try."

"Me too," she whispers. "Except . . . I might have an idea of where to begin."

In my mind, a hug or a kiss might be a nice place to start, but I'm sure she's referring to the Winner's Game.

Dad pulls one hand out of his pocket and holds up a piece of paper. "Maybe we start here."

"What is that?"

With a growing smile, he says, "A vacation request form for the next two weeks. My boss signed it last night. It'll use up every day I have left for the rest of the year, but I think, given the circumstances, it's a good investment of my time."

"Thank you, Dell." Mom is trying to hide her emotions, but there is an unmistakable wisp of a smile playing at her lips. "That means a lot to me."

Dad nods, then addresses the rest of us.

"So, what's new, guys? What did I miss? Cade, did you find any more treasure yet?"

"Nope. Ann found a boyfriend, though."

While I let out a small yelp, my dad nearly chokes. Mom laughs. Bree frowns.

"He's not my boyfriend! Yes, he's a boy, but . . . we're just friends."

Cade's not done throwing me under the bus. "Then why did you hold his hand?"

"Whoa, hold on a second," says Dad, waving his hands. "Ann, I'm gone two weeks and now you're off holding hands with strangers?"

"He's not a stranger to me. We hang out every day."

"What! You can't start relationships with guys this summer. Given your situation, it's irresponsible. You know that."

"Well, I did."

"But you can't, and that's all there is to it." He looks over at my mom. "Emily? How could you let this happen?"

Naturally, that comment doesn't sit well with her. It takes about half a second for her mood to turn south. "So it's my fault? What was I supposed to do, Dell, lock her in the closet? She's seventeen years old."

"Oh, so you approve of this?"

"Of course not! I tried to dissuade her too. She wouldn't listen."

311

"That's true," I say, hoping to take some of the heat off Mom. "She did. And I wouldn't."

Dad shakes his head in frustration. "I can't believe this. I expected that you'd at least keep her safe while I was away working. Was that too much to ask?"

"Don't go there, Dell."

"Well weren't you the adult around here? How could you let our teenage daughter set the rules?"

"There's no rule against me having friends," I point out.

Dad rolls his eyes, almost as well as Bree. "You don't hold hands with friends."

*I knew we'd eventually have this argument . . . just didn't want it to be the moment he walked in the door.* "There are no rules against boyfriends either! I'm just trying to have a normal life here, and having a friend like Tanner is not abnormal. What's the big deal?"

"You are waiting for a *transplant*! That's a big deal! You're so close, and this is just one more distraction that could get in the way of that, or put you at greater risk."

In frustration, I throw my hands in the air. "How, Dad? Explain it to me. How is having a boyfriend going to put me at risk?"

He shakes his head again, then pauses to

breathe. "This is your first relationship. Do you know what happens with every first relationship? Sooner or later, they fall apart. Trust me, Ann, I was a teenager once too. It'll be lots of fun for a while, and then something will happen and he'll break your heart. And sweetie . . . you don't need another broken heart right now."

"And she's not even telling him the truth, Dad," Bree chimes in. "He doesn't know about you-know-what." She points at her own chest.

*Oh, that rotten little jealous weasel!* "Shut up, Bree!"

Dad's shoulders sink. "Seriously, Ann? You didn't even tell him the most important thing about you?"

"That's not the most important thing about me."

"Until we find a donor it most certainly is!" Dad looks exasperated. "Emily, how could you let her do this? She has to at least tell him the truth, right?"

"Again, don't go there, Dell. Don't pin this on me. I told her the same thing you're telling her now, but she wouldn't listen. She's stubborn . . . *like her father.*"

Dad's jaw is clenched tight. "Well, if I'd been here, and she wouldn't tell him, I'd have told him myself."

Mom crosses her arms. "Great. You'll have your chance tomorrow night, because he's coming for dinner."

"You're not telling him, Dad! It'll ruin everything."

But he doesn't back down. "Either you tell him or I will." He says it with an unmistakable finality, signaling the end of the discussion.

I can feel my eyes welling up with moisture, then a big drop plummets onto my cheek. As I cross the room to the stairs, I belt out the one thing that I know will sting, even if I don't mean it: "I wish you'd just stayed in Portland! We'd all be better off!"

# CHAPTER 27
# DELL

It's twenty minutes after five o'clock on Sunday evening, and there are about a million things I'd rather be doing right now than standing in front a mirror, changing my shirt . . . *again.* It's the fourth such wardrobe change in thirty minutes.

Emily has been relatively quiet since I arrived yesterday. At first she seemed genuinely happy to see me, but then the whole Tanner topic came up, and the moment sort of unraveled.

*I still can't believe she let Ann start a relationship with some punk at the local candy shop!*

At any rate, Emily seems to find my wardrobe changes amusing, since she's usually the one who can't decide what to wear. *Oh well, at least she's not frowning in my presence, so maybe things are looking up.*

"You know he's not coming to see *you,* right?"

"Just want to make sure he knows who's the boss, that's all."

"And a Seahawks jersey will tell him that?" When I flex my biceps in the mirror, she laughs openly. It's good to hear her laugh, even if she's laughing *at* me rather than with me. "That's it, Dell. Show him those guns of yours tonight. That'll send him running for cover."

I honestly don't mind the ribbing. I know perfectly well that I'm making a big deal about having a teenage boy in the house for dinner. But I'm the only one in the family who knows exactly what that boy's intentions are with my daughter. After all, I too was a seventeen-year-old boy once. "Oh I will. And if I had real guns, I'd flash those too. What kind of father would I be if this kid leaves here tonight thinking I'm just some pushover?" I look at myself in the mirror again and scowl menacingly. "How's this?"

"If you're going for Dirty Harry, you nailed it."

"Excellent. I think I'm ready." I flex once more for good measure.

"I better warn Ann what she's in for," she mutters on her way upstairs.

A few minutes later, the doorbell rings, and I make sure I'm the one to answer. As I wipe my palms on my jeans and prepare to open the front door, my mind wanders back to the day that Ann was born. We thought we were having a boy, so when she showed up without a Y chromosome, my whole outlook on fatherhood abruptly changed. Rather than thinking of myself as the preparer of a future man, I was suddenly the protector *from* future men. For seventeen years I've been gearing up to dissuade would-be suitors, and now the moment is finally here for me to fulfill my charge as a father.

I squint once more like Dirty Harry, then pull on the doorknob. "Hello."

"Hey, what's up? I'm Tanner. Is Ann here?"

*"What's up?" Who says that?* I offer him a barely audible sound in the affirmative, then motion for him to come in.

"You a Seahawks fan?" he asks, pointing at the jersey.

Instinctively, I flex my chest, hoping to fill the jersey out a little more. Then I nod and give a carefully articulated grunt.

I can see in Ann's eyes that she is fully embarrassed by my performance, but that's OK. I'm sure she'll thank me someday, years from now when she has the luxury of checking her pulse just for the fun of it. For

317

now, though, she shakes her head and steps forward to greet Tanner with a hug.

*A hug! Right in front of me!*

After the hug, Emily and Cade both greet him with a wave. Bree is at the back of the pack, and she either has something in her eye or she's batting her eyes at him.

*Oh great . . . now I have TWO teenage daughters to protect from this young man.*

Ann must have seen it too, because she steps in before Bree can get two words in edgewise. "Sorry for the big welcome, Tanner. You're our first dinner guest here this summer, so everyone's kind of excited."

"Not everyone," I mumble softly enough that Tanner can't hear.

"Nah, it's cool. You have an awesome family."

"Well, I think my mom has dinner all ready. Do you want to follow me to the kitchen?"

The single-file parade to the kitchen table makes me think of a funeral procession. At first the thought amuses me, like maybe the presence of this pestering teenage boy will be the death of me. But then I realize that the person at the front of the line — the hearse, as it were — is Ann, and suddenly it isn't so funny.

Emily catches me stalling at the tail of the

line and holds back to speak to me. "C'mon, Dell. Give him a chance. He's really not so bad."

"That's just a ruse. Trust me."

"Oh, relax. This is just one little dinner."

Trying to smile, I explain, "I just don't like the thought of our little girl growing up, and one little dinner could be the gateway to adulthood."

Her mood turns instantly serious. "She should be so lucky."

I don't have a good comeback, so I give a little grunt, turn on a tough scowl, and follow her into the kitchen.

For most of the meal I just sit there listening to and watching the various interactions with Tanner at the dinner table. Everyone has questions for him, but they all ask them in such different ways, and likely for very different purposes. Emily's questions are short and sweet, but always seem intended as lead-ins to say something flattering about Ann. Cade is just glad to have another guy in the house, so when he speaks up, it is usually to further establish the fact that they share a common bond: They aren't girls. Then there is Bree, whose every syllable has but one obvious objective: to make Tanner notice *her* instead of Ann.

During dessert Tanner turns the tables by

asking a question of his own. *Of me.*

"Mr. Bennett, what do you like about being a lawyer?"

*Think Dirty Harry thoughts!* "Well . . . I suppose I just really get a rush seeing criminals get what they deserve. Do you know how many punks your age I've helped put behind bars for . . . oh, I don't know . . . curfew violations, public displays of affection, things of that nature?"

"You're a corporate lawyer, Dad," chimes in Ann, "not a criminal prosecutor. And those aren't criminal offenses anyway."

"OK, fine. But I do have friends who are district attorneys. *Two of them.* And they can both do background checks on *anybody* I want. Plus I've got a cousin who's a police officer." I purposefully narrow my focus on Tanner. "A gun-carrying, law-enforcing police officer." I hesitate long enough for that to sink in, then add, "Just saying."

"You're embarrassing yourself," Ann tells me flatly.

"And us," echoes Bree.

I readily admit that I would *love* for Tanner to be petrified, but despite my unveiled threats, the kid seems as calm as can be, just sitting there smiling like he's enjoying the show. "Mr. Bennett, I get the impression that you're maybe a little nervous about me being here tonight. Hey, I totally get it."

*Teenage chump say what?* "You do?"

"Yeah. I talked to my dad last night on the phone, and he warned me this could happen. See, you're a father of a teenage daughter. Well, two of them actually, and you probably just want to keep them safe, so teenage boys are bound to make you nervous. My dad says that's just normal protective-dad stuff."

I'm completely speechless.

"If I were in your shoes, I'd be overprotective too."

"Overpro— ? You would?"

"Of course. And based on what my dad said, I took the liberty of collecting some character references for you, hopefully to put you at ease." He slips a hand in his rear pocket and produces a neatly folded paper, which he slides across the table. "I hope with these you'll feel OK about me going on a date with your daughter."

Just like that, my jaw drops right to the table. From the corner of my eye, I see Ann's mouth hanging open too, but in a good way.

I quickly unfold the paper and scan through several names and titles: a pastor, a scoutmaster, a teacher, and yes . . . a police officer.

While my mind and sight are stuck on the paper in my hands, from across the table I hear Bree ask, "Which daughter?"

"Bree!" Emily chides.

"What?" Bree replies, playing innocent. "I'm old enough to date."

"You turn fourteen in August," I remind her. "You've got a couple years of dreaming yet before that happens."

All eyes return to Tanner, who is smiling graciously. "I think you're great, Bree, but I actually meant Ann." He turns to his immediate right. "I planned to ask you in private, but since it came up . . . would you like to go on a date with me? Like, not just hanging out. A real date. On Wednesday. My mom says I can borrow her car." He quickly turns back to me. "Which she says I have to have parked back in the driveway by ten thirty."

The flame of Bree's excitement is immediately doused.

Ann, however, is floating on cloud nine. "I would love to! Dad? Mom? I can go, right?"

Emily and I look at each other for a second, sharing an entire conversation in a glance.

"Is that a yes?" Ann asks eagerly.

"Well, I'll have to make sure these references check out . . ."

"Dell," warns Emily, chastising me with my own name.

"Fine," I tell Ann reluctantly. "But you know the rules, Ann. Tell him, and you can go."

Her face turns ashen white, then bright red in record time.

"Oh, this should be good," states Bree sarcastically. "Hey Tanner, don't forget about me after you hear what Ann has to tell you."

Before Bree even finishes her sentence, Emily shoots up out of her chair and points to the hallway. "Bree Grace Bennett! Straight to your room. And don't even think about coming back down! I'll be up to talk to you later."

"You can consider me part of that conversation too, young lady," I growl, shaking my head. "Unbelievable."

There is a long, uncomfortable silence after Bree leaves, with everyone sort of looking around wondering who is going to say what next.

Ann eventually breaks the ice. "Tanner . . . there's, um . . . something I guess I need to talk to you about."

"I gathered that. Did I do something

wrong?" For the first time all evening he seems totally out of his element.

*Excellent!*

She shakes her head. "No. Nobody did. But . . . we just need to talk, that's all." Ann holds his gaze for a moment longer, then looks across the table at Emily and me. "I want to talk to him alone. I can do that, right?"

Emily and I speak to each other again with our eyes and then nod.

When Ann turns back to Tanner, she reaches down and takes his hand in hers, which makes me cringe. "Come on," she tells him as she pulls him to his feet. "Let's go outside."

# CHAPTER 28
## ANN

The summer sun is still high in the sky
when I lead Tanner to the back deck and
cross the small patch of grass to the beach.
When we reach the sand, I let go of his
hand, because what I am about to share is
definitely going to make my palms sweat,
and holding sweating hands right now
would only be a distraction.

My tangled nerves don't go unnoticed.
"What's going on?" he asks. "You're acting
different all of a sudden."

*No kidding.* "I am different," I tell him flat
out. "That's kind of what I wanted to talk
to you about." His look of confusion doesn't
come as a surprise. "Can we walk?" Without
waiting for an answer I slip off my flip-flops
and toss them onto the grass behind me.

He nods and removes his shoes as well.

Side by side we high-step through the
loose, dry sand. Once we reach the cooler,
wetter stuff near the water, I set a course

for the tide pools on the south side of Haystack Rock. We are halfway there when he finally asks what this is all about.

"My dad's crazy," I say, not really answering the question. Or maybe that's the perfect answer. "I think most lawyers probably are, but he takes it to an extreme sometimes. You were right about what you said about him being overprotective. He's very afraid of me getting hurt. But with him — with me — it's not just the normal overprotectiveness that your dad mentioned. My dad is sort of *over*-overprotective, which is why there's something I need to tell you, so you know what you're getting into when you hang out with me."

Tanner stops walking, making me think I've already said too much — or the wrong thing, or . . . who knows. There is nervousness in his eyes. And doubt.

*Maybe he's just realized he'd be better off asking out the younger of the Bennett girls.*

We stand there, quietly staring at each other, sinking into the wet sand. Finally he clears his throat. "My mom says bad news doesn't get better with time."

*At least he knows it's bad news.* "My mom always says not to beat around the bush, but this is a very big bush, and maybe the only way to get around it is to beat it a little."

Frowning, he says, "Just tell me already."

"Fine. For the record, though, I'll totally understand if you change your mind about our date."

"Why would I do that?"

It's all I can do to answer, but eventually the words come out. "Because I lied to you." I wait to see how he's going to react, but Tanner's face is granite. "I made you think I'm this carefree, do-whatever-I-want kind of girl, but I'm not like that at all. In fact . . . I *can't* be that kind of girl. I have limits, you might say. Some self-imposed, others simply as a precaution. Do you remember you said you wanted to teach me to surf, and I thought that would be totally cool, and I told you I'd always wanted to try surfing?"

"Yeah. That was a lie?"

"No, that's all true. It does sound cool, and I would love to try it sometime. But the truth is . . . I can't. Not right now."

"Why not?"

"Because I can't swim."

"But you said . . ."

"Oh, I can swim. I'm a fantastic swimmer. I just can't swim right now. I was a competitive swimmer a couple years back,

327

but then . . . everything changed."

"What happened?"

I take a deep breath. There are tears just waiting to let loose, but I won't let them fall because crying right now would prove that I still feel sorry for myself, and that's not what I want him to see. "My toes are cold," I whisper and then ask if we can go back to the warm sand. Without waiting for Tanner to respond, I make a beeline for higher ground, hoping he'll follow. Once I find a nice spot, I carefully smooth out the sand with my foot and then sit down facing the ocean.

Tanner quietly takes a seat next to me.

I have to take another deep breath or I might faint. The coastal breeze fills my lungs to capacity as I focus on the horizon. When I stop to listen, the volume of the world somehow turns up a notch, which is exactly what I need right now. I take solace in the chorus of waves and wind and gulls, all singing and crying just for me. "It's beautiful, isn't it?"

"The best."

"I can't imagine anything more inspiring. Lately, when I look out past the waves, I find myself wondering how far I can see. From here it looks like the water goes on forever, but I know there's an end out there.

Somewhere." I pause, then whisper, "Everything has an end." Inside, I can feel my emotions rising quickly now, like the tide, but I press on. "And I know that on the other side, there's this whole great big world out there, full of sights and sounds I've only dreamed of, and there's probably some girl over there, just like me, staring back this way right now wondering what's going on over here, wishing she could see what it's like. But our worlds are just too far apart." I take another long look, from north to south, soaking in the majesty. I'm stalling, and I know it, but that's infinitely better than leaping straight to the part of the conversation where I tell him everything, and then, out of fear of being with a time bomb, he cancels our date and walks away.

Tanner is very quiet. Just when I start to worry maybe he's already lost interest, he says, "Ann, whatever it is you need to say . . . just say it. It can't be that bad."

I actually laugh at the comment! Not only can it be that bad, it couldn't be worse. With my finger, I draw a heart in the sand between us. While slowly tracing my drawing, I finally get to the point. "The last time I went swimming was during a swim meet. I was winning. I had a seizure, right in the water." I trace the heart again. "Drowning really sucks."

"Whoa."

It's so hard to speak . . . I have to pause so I can swallow. "It was all fuzzy, but I remember not being able to help myself, because I had no control of my body. I sank to the bottom of the pool. I thought for sure I was dead. In fact I did die, in the technical sense, but they resuscitated me and took me to the hospital."

"Oh my gosh. Was everything OK?"

Still tracing the heart, making it ever bigger, I shake my head. "They ran tests on me . . . and found something bad. A hole, actually. Not a big one, but big enough. I guess holes in your heart don't have to be big to be a big problem." I can't look at him. Won't. Instead, I listen for the telltale signals that I expect to hear — a gasp of horror, a dramatic sigh, or a pathetic "I'm sorry" — anything to show that he pities my feeble existence. I stay motionless for several seconds, but he remains mute. I poke the sand right in the middle of my sketch to make a hole. "They tried to fix it," I finally tell him. "But it didn't work."

"What does that mean?"

Now I carve an X through the heart with my finger. "It means I need a new one. I'm on a list. My parents brought me here this summer just to sort of get away from things while we wait. The doctors say I need to get a new one in the next few months or things could really get ugly."

"You mean . . . ?"

I know what he's asking, and that particular question, coming from him, is the one that my defenses can't resist. Tears begin running down my face — some are tears for everything that might never be, but others are simply from embarrassment that I feel so stinking sorry for myself. I nod, but again refuse to look at him. This is the moment where I'm sure he'll find some graceful way to bow out of any presumed interest he might have had in me. Who knows, maybe he'll even stop by the house on the way back and take Bree up on her offer. After all, my little sister is whole, while I am defined by a hole.

A moment later, Tanner grabs my hand. "On the bright side," he says sweetly, "you're on a list."

Something about the way he says it makes me laugh, even through my tears. "Yeah. Great."

"Nah, I'm serious." He motions toward the horizon. "Just look out there, Ann. Right now there's this incredible ocean between you and the world beyond, but that doesn't mean you won't eventually get to meet the girl who's over there looking back. Once you reach the top of the list, you're on top of the world."

I want to giggle at his earnestness, but when the sound mixes with crying, it comes out as a wimpy snort. "That was deep."

With a wink, Tanner waves a hand very seriously at the ocean. "Like the deepest trench of the deep blue sea," he says in a ridiculously deep voice.

Now I laugh for real. Something about his humor helps quell my tears. "More like deep quicksand, and I think you're in over your head. Since when are you so poetic?"

The deep voice continues. "Only when trying to impress a really cool girl." He pauses briefly, then goes half an octave lower. "Is it working?"

My laughing abruptly stops. He said it in a funny voice, but I can tell he's also being semiserious. "Did you hear anything I told you, Tanner? I need a new heart. *Soon.* And you still want to impress me?"

His normal voice returns. "You're not impressed?"

I shrug. "I'm just . . . yes. I'm impressed that you haven't walked away yet."

"Walk a— ? Why would I do that?"

"Gee, I don't know. A heart defect is a

pretty good reason. Don't you get it? Right now, this very minute, I could have a heart attack and die. Doesn't that scare you?"

"Does it scare you?"

"Yes!"

He checks his watch once, then looks away, and then he checks it again. "Well, that minute is over and you're still here."

"Huh?"

"You didn't die that very minute."

"But I could have. If not that minute, then the next one or the next, or maybe tomorrow or the day after that."

"Or maybe never, because you're on a list."

I don't have a comeback to that one. "So after hearing this about me, are you sure you still want to go out on that date?"

"Why wouldn't I?"

I smile up at him, admiring his wavy hair and warm smile. A rush of something courses through me. All at once I'm excited and confused and deeply, deeply impressed. Before getting up, I wipe away the crossed-out heart in the sand and quickly replace it with a new one, bigger than the original and without a hole in the middle. "I don't know," I whisper, "But I'm glad."

*Glad? Did I just say I'm "glad"?* Oh my gosh, "glad" doesn't begin to describe how

I feel right now. I'm so happy I could kiss him — in fact I would, but I'm afraid my parents might be watching. Instead, with a giant smile on my face, I take him by the hand — sweaty palm and all — and we head back to the house, where Tanner confirms to my parents that I've told him the truth, the whole truth, and nothing but the truth, so help him God.

Before Tanner leaves, my dad pulls him aside for a final "man to man" chat. It's supposed to be private, but I can hear every word from the other side of the room.

"I just want to make sure we're clear," Dad says. "I'm not too keen on Ann having you around, but seeing her happy like this is . . . a nice change."

"OK. That's good."

"Yes . . . for now."

"For now?"

Dad nods. "What I'm trying to say is, *don't blow it.* Don't hurt her. If you're thinking you can just have a little fun for a while, then break her heart later, just get out now."

"Dad!" I yell across the room.

He holds up a hand. "Just a sec. I'm almost done."

"Don't worry," says Tanner. "That's not going to happen."

"You promise?"

"Yes."

"All right, then, I'm holding you to it. I am a lawyer, remember, and what you and I just entered into is a verbal agreement. Don't let me down."

That's all I can stand. I quickly cross the room and pull Tanner to safety. "That's enough legal-talk, Dad. You're on vacation, remember?" I turn to Tanner. "Sorry about . . . *that.*" I motion with my head to my dad, who once again has that stupid scowl on his face. I think he's trying to look mean, but it's not working. "Anyway, thanks for tonight. I know you have to get going, but I'm really looking forward to Wednesday."

"Me too," he says. "See you then."

It's a little stalker-ish, I know, but I watch him through the front window until he is completely out of sight. Then I rush upstairs to write every little detail in my journal. Most of the days from the past couple of years I'd just as soon forget, but this one I want to remember forever!

Dear Diary,

Do you know that feeling you get when you're falling, and your stomach launches into your throat, and you panic and feel like you might die? I've always hated that feeling. And yet right now I'm falling — fast — but I don't really mind. I don't know when I'll hit the ground, but for right now I'm just enjoying the fall. There have been plenty of times when I doubted I would ever say this, but now I want to shout it from the rooftops: I THINK I'M FALLING IN LOVE!

# CHAPTER 29
## CADE

"*Psst.* Ann. Mom wants us downstairs."

My sister is lying on her bed, writing in her journal. She looks up and smiles with that same dumb smile she had on the day she first met Tanner. "I'm busy."

"No, she says come now. Dad just jumped in the shower."

"At eight o'clock at night?"

"Yep. He said he needed to wind down after dealing with your boyfriend."

Normally she would yell at me for saying "boyfriend," but instead she repeats the word, like she's trying it on for size. " 'Boyfriend.' He's not, but I like the sound of it."

"Just come downstairs. Mom's waiting."

"Fine."

She follows me to the living room, where Bree and Mom are waiting.

"Got your notebook?" asks Mom.

"Do I need it?" asks Ann.

"I want to tally scores while your father is in the shower."

Ann rolls her eyes, marches back upstairs, and is back down pretty quick. "Do we even need to count?" she asks when she reaches the bottom step. She's flipping her notebook open to her current sheet. "I think we all know who won again."

"Not you," says Bree. "You were too busy with *Tanner* to do much of anything else."

"Yeah," Ann says lightly. "I was . . . and you weren't. Sorry, Sis."

Bree's face turns red, but she doesn't say anything. She just takes a deep breath, and opens her scorecard. "That's one more point for me," she mumbles, "for not punching your lights out."

"Girls," says Mom, raising her voice slightly. "Take it easy. Up until tonight you've all had a really great week. Have you noticed? You've gotten along better this week than I can ever remember. Don't spoil it now."

Ann is still smiling, but now her smile doesn't look quite so nasty. "Mom's right. I'm sorry, Bree. That was mean of me."

I let out a loud sigh to get everyone's attention. "Can we just find out the score already?"

Bree snickers. "Why are you so anxious?

338

You have the least chance of all of winning."

"Oh yeah?" I ask, holding up my notebook. "I've got eighty-nine points. How many do you have?"

Bree's eyes scramble to recount her marks. Finally she blurts out, "No way. You cheated!"

"Did not."

"Did too! I only have fifty-three. There's no way you beat me by that much."

"Oh really? How many chocolate chips did you find on your pillow this week?"

"Like twenty."

"See!"

"You can't — Mom, can he take a point for every single chocolate chip? I didn't even want them!"

"It's the thought that counts," says Ann. "I thought it was sweet. Cade, thank you for all of those. You deserve every point you took."

I glance at Bree; her face is red again. She's staring at Ann. "So let me guess . . . you're fine with him having those points because you beat him anyway. Am I right?"

Ann shakes her head once and says, "I wish. He beat me by a mile. You beat me too, by the way. I only had forty-nine points. I guess I really was caught up with Tanner this week." She pauses. "But next week, I promise, I'm bringing my A-game, so watch out."

Bree seems to relax. "I really beat you?"

"Really. But you still lost to Cade, so it doesn't really matter."

"Oh, it matters," she says. "It proves you're beatable." She turns and looks directly at me. "Now I just have to get you to enter an honest score, and I've got this game in the bag."

I don't care what she says, I earned my points fair and square. "Oh yeah? Well I —"

*"Shhhh!"* Mom has her finger over her mouth.

"What?" I ask.

Then Dad calls from the bathroom. "Emily, can you grab me a fresh towel from the laundry room? We're all out in here."

"OK, scorecards away," Mom whispers. "He's almost out of the shower. Cade, good job this week. Keep it up, everyone."

Ann and Bree head off to their room upstairs. Mom goes to the linen closet to find a towel. When she comes back through, I stop her just long enough to ask, "Do you think Dad will play the Winner's Game?"

"Pray for it, Cade," she says sincerely. "That's what I'm doing."

Later, with the lights out in the living room,

I slide out of my sleeping bag and kneel beside the couch. "Dear God," I whisper in the darkness, "Mom told me to pray, so that's what I'm doing. I guess I just wanted to say that . . . my dad's not a loser. So if the Winner's Game is for winners, then please let him want to give it a try." I pause, unsure what else God might be interested in hearing. Eventually I finish with a simple, "That's it, I guess. Amen."

# Chapter 30
## Dell

I generally dread Mondays, because it seems like that's the day for everything to go wrong. And though the workweek is just getting started, I always feel like I'm already behind on everything.

On this Monday, however, I'm determined that things will be different. I'm on vacation, which means I don't have to face the corporate ignoramuses who usually occupy my Monday mornings when I should be getting a head start on my contracts. Then again, maybe I'm no better off than normal, because I have to face a certain teenage girl who is walking on air from the moment she crawls out of bed. Her permagrin when she comes down for breakfast confirms that she is still reliving — and reveling in — last night's success with a certain teenage boy.

I'm not exactly happy about the situation, because I know how this is going to end, but it's nice seeing her feel good about something. She needs something to feel good about right now; I just wish it wasn't a hormonal young man.

I try talking to her while we're eating, but her head is somewhere else. Just to test whether she is aware of anything beyond the thoughts in her head, I casually tell her she looks like a cow. Not to be rude or anything, just to test her reaction.

"I love cows," she replies dreamily while staring out the window at the ocean.

After breakfast she puts her arm around me and says, "Your bovine daughter wants to take the Walrus for a spin so she can practice driving."

I know I should say no. I want to. I'm about to. And then I look into her Guernsey-eyes, and I can't bring myself to do anything that might spoil her current state of happiness. But I only agree to it because the Walrus is a tank on wheels. Any other car, and I swear I would not give in. *I swear.*

Emily stays at home to go through stuff in the attic, but Bree and Cade tag along for the ride to Seaside, about ten miles up the road, hoping they might convince me to stop and play at the giant arcade there. Video games are out of the question, but I do splurge on a bag of fresh saltwater taffy for the ride home, most of which is already gone by the time we re-enter Cannon Beach and rumble through the center of town.

About eight blocks from the house, out of the blue, Bree gasps as loudly as anyone can gasp. With a mouthful of taffy she exclaims, "Is that — ?" As we all turn to see where she is pointing, she screams, "It is! It's Tanner!"

Only Tanner isn't alone.

Worse, the short, blond-haired girl hanging on his arm is not just pretty, she's a knockout.

*There. Now it feels like a Monday morning.*

With Ann's eyes fixed on the couple, the car heaves to the right, nearly hitting the curb.

"Just keep driving," I tell her emphatically as I grab the wheel to help straighten us out. "No sense in crashing over this."

I keep a sharp eye on Tanner as Ann regains control. Near as I can tell, Tanner doesn't see us. He's in his own little world, talking and laughing with the girl like he doesn't have a care in the world.

*I knew this would happen! Oh, that rotten little son of a gun . . .*

Rather than easing carefully into the driveway, Ann doesn't slow down until she absolutely has to, despite all my efforts to pump the imaginary air brake at my feet.

The hard stop sends everyone sliding forward in their seats. Ann takes half a second to turn off the engine, but leaves the key in the ignition as she throws open her door and runs into the house. As she passes in front of the Walrus, I catch a glimpse of her face . . . dripping wet.

"Great," Cade mumbles from the backseat, "there goes the summer."

"There goes more than that," bemoans Bree.

"Let's try to think of Ann," I tell them. For several moments, we all sit there quietly; none of us are quite sure what to make of what just happened. After a bit, I venture to ask Bree what she's thinking, because the look on her face says it's something serious.

"I think this sucks," she blurts out. "Did you see her? She's barely taller than me!" She huffs loudly, then adds, *So stupid.*

Cade laughs in her face. "Ha! You wish you were the one holding his arm!"

With a scowl that could kill, she replies, "Be quiet, Twerp. You don't know anything."

"I know you like Tanner."

"Just *shut up!* Dad, can you make him shut up? Actually, better yet, let me out. I want to go for a walk on the beach."

"Sure, Bree. Just . . . stick to the beach, OK?"

She doesn't respond, but I let her out anyway. Without bothering to go inside, Bree marches around the near side of the house and makes a straight line through the tall grass to the beach and then disappears from sight.

"It's gonna be a bad day today, isn't it, Dad," Cade says after a minute.

"Probably so." I sigh. "It's Monday."

# CHAPTER 31
## BREE

*I hate it when my little brother is right.*

He said I wished it was me hanging on Tanner's arm instead of that blond girl, and well . . . I did. When we first saw them, all I could think was that if I was just a year or two older, maybe Tanner would have noticed me instead of Ann, and since I don't have any of her medical problems, maybe it would have worked out.

*I hate being the little sister just as much as I hate it when my little brother is right!*

I don't know why I wanted to go for a walk — I guess just to blow off some steam. It seems to be working, because the farther north I go, the more I start thinking about Ann and what she must be feeling right now. I bet she's crying her eyes out, which is honestly too bad. As much as I think I'd be a better fit for Tanner — if he'd just give me a chance! — she definitely doesn't deserve what he did to her.

After twenty or thirty minutes of marching in the sand, my legs are getting tired,
but I'm not ready to go back yet, so I find a
nice spot on a giant piece of driftwood to
rest. Not too far away, a young family — a
mom and dad and two little girls, maybe
seven and three years old — is building a
beach fire, preparing to cook lunch over the
open flames. The littlest girl seems fascinated by everything her older sister is doing. When big sister skips in the sand, little
sister does the same. When big sister exam-
ines the empty shell of a dead crab, little
sister squats down and grabs it from her to
get a closer look. And when big sister picks
up a stick and tosses it on the budding fire,
so does the little one, earning both of them
a stern warning from their father.

"But I'm big enough to help with the fire,"
the big one says, her voice carrying on the
wind.

"Maybe," her dad replies, "But your job is
to set a good example for Missy, and right
now that means staying clear of the fire until
we're ready for hot dogs."

The older sister is quiet for a minute, then
she says, "Daddy, I'm tired of being the big
sister. When Missy's around, I can't have
any fun. And I don't like her copying me all
the time."

The dad laughs, blows at the base of the fire, and then he wraps an arm around his oldest daughter and speaks quietly just to her.

I think I know what he's saying to her, even though I can't hear. It's what Dad said to me when I used to complain about Cade.

"The only reason she copies you is because she looks up to you. She wants to be just like you. That's why it's so important for you to help out and be a good example."

I can tell the girl is thinking it over. Finally, kind of like she still doesn't want to, she turns to her younger sister, takes her by the hand, and says, "C'mon, Missy, I'll show you how to build a sand castle while Daddy makes the fire."

I don't know why, but as I see the pair of them waddle off toward wetter sand, my eyes start to tear up. I remember vividly when Ann taught me how to make a sand castle. Just like I remember her giving me pointers on riding a bicycle, spelling my name, curling my hair, painting my nails, and a million other things she helped me with.

It's not the same now, but I remember wanting to be just like her. I, too, would follow her around like a puppy, copying everything she did and frequently taking her things because they seemed cooler than my own toys. And Ann, like this other big sister walking away from me on the beach, tolerated it. Sometimes that meant not getting to do what she wanted to do, because she was looking out for my best interest.

As the girls start building their sand castle, the older one keeps looking up, watching her father stoking the blaze. I can see in her eyes that she wants to be there too, doing big-girl stuff like putting sticks on the fire, but she dutifully stays with her younger sister.

A hint of guilt washes over me. How many times over the years did Ann miss out on things she'd rather have been doing because she was doing her duty as the big sister?

"Well, not anymore," I whisper. "Ann deserves to play with a little fire right now."

*Before her flame burns out . . .*

As the beach house comes into view, an idea pops in my head that could turn the whole game in my favor. Two ideas, actually. One for Ann and one for Cade. "That's it!" I say out loud.

*I am totally going to win the Winner's Game!*

Eager to get started on my plan, I pick up the pace. When I reach the house, Dad and Cade are on the back porch grilling hamburgers.

Dad sends Cade inside and asks me to have a seat at the picnic table.

"Am I in trouble?" I ask.

"No. I just want to talk. This whole Tanner thing . . . I kind of want to take your pulse a bit. You seemed a little upset that he didn't . . . you know, consider you instead of that other girl."

"That's not true," I reply defensively, even though it totally is.

"You sure? Because it kind of seems like you've had a little crush on Tanner too."

"Why does everyone keep saying that?" *Because it's true, but that's beside the point.*

"So it didn't hurt when Tanner asked Ann out? It's natural to feel a little jealous. After all, you're getting to that age, hormonally speaking, when —"

"Stop!"

He holds up his hands to show that he's backing off. "OK, peace. I get it. That's a touchy subject. But can I just point out one thing?"

I cross my arms and wait for him to continue.

"I know I'm a little overprotective, but it's because I love you girls. I don't want either of you to get hurt. So when I see that this kid already has another girl hanging on him, after making Ann believe he was interested in her, I just hope you see what that says about him. And I hope you have enough common sense that you're not still hoping you're the next one on his list."

Now I can feel my face burning, and it's not because I'm sitting too close to the grill. "I do have good sense, Dad. But I was thinking, maybe he doesn't really like that other girl, and maybe if I just talk to him, he'll see that —"

"Whoa. Time-out. You're still thirteen, Bree, until the end of August. Don't forget that. He's going to be a senior, and you haven't even started high school yet." He pauses. "But besides all of that, he's shown that he's not trustworthy."

"You don't know that."

"So you do still have a crush on him?"

I look away briefly, then roll my eyes. "I didn't say that. And b-t-dubs, I've been around Tanner enough to know what he's really like. And I know *who* he likes."

Dad throws up his hands in frustration. "Perfect."

"Wait, I'm just saying that maybe I could talk to him and see —"

"The answer is no. No way, no how. Don't you see that you can't trust this guy any farther than — ?"

Mom pokes her head out through the

back door. "*Psst*. Dell. Sorry to interrupt, but a certain teenage boy is at the front door asking to speak to Ann."

He shoots me another frustrated look. "Well, look at that. Speak of the devil and he comes a-knockin'." Turning back to Mom, he asks, "What did you tell him?"

"I thought maybe you'd want to handle this one, so I told him to wait right there."

"Does Ann know he's here?"

"Uh-huh. She's crying again."

He exhales. "Fine. I'll take care of it."

I follow Mom and Dad into the living room. Mom and I remain back just a bit as Dad continues to the front door.

"Hi," says Tanner. "Is Ann here?"

"She is."

"Can she like . . . come down? I wanted to tell her what to wear on our date."

"You think you're still going out with her?"

Tanner looks confused. "Why wouldn't I?"

"Oh, I think you know," Dad replies as diplomatically as he can.

"Sorry?"

"Doubt that."

"Huh?"

Dad steps closer to the door, blocking our view. But we can still hear. "Listen, I'll make this very simple. Last night you and I had what I thought was a pretty clear verbal agreement that you would not do anything to upset Ann unnecessarily. Not only did you upset her, you broke her heart, and her heart can't take that. So yes, Ann is here, but she doesn't want to see you. Please, just leave her alone. Bree too, for that matter, in case you had any ideas. Consider this home officially off-limits."

"But I don't —"

"Good-bye, Tanner." Dad closes the door before Tanner can get another word out.

I can feel the heat from my face again. "That was really harsh."

"That didn't come anywhere near harsh, sweetie. Trust me, I was holding back."

Mom is watching through the window.

"Is he leaving?" I ask her.

She nods. I join Mom and watch as Tanner walks up the road in a bit of a stupor. Periodically he stops, turns around, and looks at the house, and then continues walking.

"Good riddance," Dad mumbles as he heads back out to tend the burgers.

"It breaks my heart too," Mom says, almost to herself.

"What does?" I ask.

She shrugs. "I just wanted Ann to have a little slice of happiness. I wish there was something I could do."

"Yeah," I whisper as Tanner turns a corner in the distance and disappears. "Me too."

# CHAPTER 32
## EMILY

When leisure time was free for the taking, reading was one of my passions. I would devour at least two new novels every week, often reading late into the night to find out what became of the characters' lives and loves and dreams. Then my own daughter drowned before my eyes, was brought back to life, and was sentenced to the handicap of an incurable heart and the constant fear of death. For a while after that, I was too numb to read anything. Then I began immersing myself in medical journals and the like, wanting to know more about Ann's condition, all the while looking for any little tidbit of knowledge that might help the doctors treat her.

Nothing that I found ever helped.

More recently, with a transplant looming and a marriage in doubt, I've been hesitant to read much of anything anymore. I know it might be a good distraction from reality, but I've felt like maybe I should face my own reality before I lose myself in someone else's fantasy.

Then I found Grandma's journals in the attic last week, and suddenly my love of reading has never been stronger.

As I close the volume I'm in the middle of, my thoughts express themselves in a long, deep sigh.

"You OK?"

Dell's comment startles me. It's late, and I didn't realize he was still awake. I hope my reading didn't keep him up. "I'm fine," I whisper. "Sorry if I woke you up."

"It's not you, it's me. I've got too much stuff churning around in my head."

"About Ann and Tanner?"

"Yeah, that too, I suppose. But mostly . . ."

Since Dell showed up yesterday morning professing to want to fix things, we haven't made any progress in that direction. Between scolding Ann for getting involved with a boy, blaming me for allowing it, and then dealing with the aftermath when everything went just as bad with Tanner as he said it would, he hasn't had much time to focus on us.

*Please, God, let that be what's keeping him awake . . . and help us to find a way to fix things.*

"Mostly . . . ?"

He leans up on one arm in bed so he can see past the nightstand that separates our beds. "You know . . . property values. How much do you think we'll be able to get out of this place?"

I could scream . . . or cry. Maybe both. "That's what's keeping you up?"

Dell chuckles dryly. "I'm kidding."

"You're awful."

"I am, you're right. Just trying to keep this lighthearted."

I sit up in bed so I can see him squarely. "Please don't joke, Dell. The state of things right now between us is hardly funny."

He sits up too, propping himself against the headboard. "I know. I'm sorry. I just . . . I don't know where to begin."

*But I do . . . I hope.*

I glance at the closed book on my lap. "How about we start with something simple?"

"Such as?"

"A question. If I ask you a question, will you give me an honest answer? I want the unvarnished truth."

He nods. "I can do that." With his eyes locked on mine, he waits to hear what's coming next.

"It's pretty simple actually. A follow-up to

our phone conversation."

"I'm all ears."

"OK. Dell . . . do you love me?"

"That's it?"

"For starters."

"Yes," he replies soberly. I can hear the sincerity in his voice, and I know that he means it.

"Good. Me too."

"You love you too?"

"No jokes, remember."

"Sorry. I'll be good. Do you have another question?"

I exhale and nod at the same time. "This one's more difficult. How do you love me?"

He takes a second to think, then says, "Just the normal way, I suppose. I'm attracted to you, of course. And I appreciate all of the things you do for this family. I love the way you're always taking care of us and helping the kids. And even though we haven't had a lot to smile about recently, I do love your smile. Oh, and your dry sense of humor — when you show it — cracks me up."

"Those are reasons *why* you love me, or what you love about me. I asked *how* you love me."

"How?"

"How."

He needs more time to think. "Well . . . I go to work every day, to provide for you."

"And I appreciate it. So if you didn't love me anymore — say the worst happens and we get divorced — would you stop going to work for the rest of your life?"

"No."

"Then that's not something you do just because you love me. So I'll ask again, how do you *love* me? What do you do to show me your love?"

"Well, I . . ."

I don't want to interrupt him, but as the silence grows, it's probably for the best. "Let me help you. I think part of our problem is that you say you love me, and I say the same thing back, but that's often where it ends. We love each other, but don't *love* each other."

His shoulders slump slightly against the headboard. "That's what you were talking about last week. The noun and the verb, right?"

I nod.

"So what do we do?"

I take another breath. This is the point where he either plays along . . . or he doesn't. "Do you remember our first year of marriage, when we played Scrabble all the time at night?"

"Yes, how can I forget? You're the queen of triple-word scores. You'd beat me like nine times out of ten."

"So why did you keep playing?"

With a little shirk he says, "Because I hated losing. And the fact that I lost so frequently made my victories all the sweeter."

"You're competitive, Dell. We both are. It's one of the things I've always loved about you. Which is why . . ."

He raises his eyebrows expectantly. "Don't leave me hanging."

I'm about to say something else, but another question comes to mind. "Do you want to win?"

"Win what?"

I smile. "Well, take your pick. Do you want to win in our marriage? Do you want *us* to win? Do you want to win me over?" I pause, looking right at him. "Do you want to win *me*?"

"You're the prize?" he says with a wry smile. I haven't seen that smile in a long time. I've missed it.

"Uh-huh."

"Then yes, I want to win all those things you said. I certainly don't want to lose you."

"Good, because I want to win too, which is why I want to challenge you to a game."

"Of Scrabble?"

"No. Not Scrabble."

"What sort of game?"

I hold up the journal I've been reading: "The Winner's Game."

I can tell before he speaks that he's skeptical. "Didn't your granddad's letter mention something about that? The one Cade found in the Altoids can?"

"Yes."

"Emily, look, I'm serious about making things better between us. I want to work on it. But . . . a game? I was thinking we needed full-on counseling."

"And maybe we do, but I think, first, this is a good place to start. It's more than just a game, Dell. It's motivation . . . to help us love like the verb. Maybe it's crazy, but after reading my grandmother's journal, I think this could really work for us, if we give it a try."

His eyes are still skeptical. "You're serious, aren't you?"

I nod, then stand up and motion for him to join me. "C'mon, I want to show you something." I cross to the bedroom door, then lead him into the kitchen where the kids' weekly score sheet is taped to the side of the refrigerator. Ann and Cade both have one point below their names. Pointing to it,

362

I ask him if he knows what it is.

He shrugs. "A chore chart?"

"A chore — ? Seriously?"

"I don't know, maybe those marks are the number of jobs each kid has done."

His comment makes me chuckle. "Our kids are lazy, but not that lazy." I pause, getting more serious. "Do you remember the 'nude books' we found in Grandma's room? The box full of notebook scorecards? Well, this is part of our children's scoring system. They've been playing the Winner's Game for two weeks already."

"Seriously?"

"Uh-huh. And you know what? I've seen real changes in them. Nothing earth-shattering — I mean they're still kids. But the petty fighting has gone way down, and they're getting much better at biting their tongues when someone does something they don't like. And believe it or not, they're actually looking for subtle little ways to do nice things for each other."

Finally he seems quasi-interested. "Like what?"

"Well, like yesterday morning, after I told Cade to put away his sleeping bag, I came through the living room and saw Ann putting it away for him while he was still in the bathroom. Then she went and gave herself a point. And Cade asked me at least four times last week if I had any spare pieces of chocolate, because he wanted to put them on his sisters' pillows. Eventually I ran out, so he scrounged around until he found chunks of baker's chocolate in the pantry. I think he gave himself a point for every individual piece of chocolate he delivered — bitter or otherwise — but at least he felt good doing it."

Dell laughs lightly. "And Bree? Has she been playing along too?"

"Sort of," I tell him, bobbing my head from side to side. "I'm not sure what her strategy is. As you can see, she hasn't won a week yet. But she assures me that she has a plan. Of course, she was slightly more temperamental to begin with, but even with her I've noticed a marked change in how she treats Ann and Cade. She may not be winning, at least in terms of points, but she is trying, and that's really the purpose."

He studies the score sheet on the refrigerator for a few seconds, then looks up. "So if we were to play, what would we be playing for?"

"Same as my grandparents. Whoever has the most points at the end of the week gets to choose what we do on our weekly date."

"But we don't have a weekly date."

364

"Well, that's just another perk of the game. If we play, we get a weekly date."

"Is that it?"

"No, there's a big prize too. Whoever wins the most weeks out of the year gets to choose how and where we celebrate our anniversary."

"And you'd choose . . . ?"

*Does he even have to ask?* "Paris. If we play, we're going to Paris in December, just like we've always planned."

He pretends to frown. "I've never really wanted to go there. So *if* we play . . . and I'm not saying I will, but *if,* and if I won — which I would — then we'd go deep-sea fishing in Cabo San Lucas. What I wouldn't give to reel in a two-hundred-pound marlin."

*But . . . you promised me Paris . . .*

"Fine," I tell him, not hiding my disappointment. "If you win — which you won't — you can choose Cabo. But come December, don't be too disappointed when we're looking out our window at the Eiffel Tower."

He chuckles and shakes his head. "Then Cabo it is."

"So you'll play?" I can feel myself biting my lip as I wait for his answer.

"Do you really think it will work?"

"I'll give you the same answer I gave the

kids. I read what happened with my grand-parents, and I honestly believe it can work for us too . . . but only if we really try. If we really want to win, then there's no way we can lose."

His playful smile suddenly becomes more sincere. "Then I'll play." He pauses, then asks, "So are there any rules that I should be aware of?"

I consider giving him a hug to thank him for playing at all, but that would be too bold, given how things have been lately. Instead I smile. "C'mon. Let's go back to bed and I'll give you all the details. The biggest thing to remember, though, as the kids quickly discovered, is that it's better to give than to take . . ."

When I wake up in the morning Dell's bed is empty. I check my watch.

*Seven thirty.*

With a robe on, I slip out of the room and am immediately assaulted by the smell of something burning. Grease, if I had to guess, and it's left a thick layer of smoke permeating the whole downstairs. I wave my way through it toward the kitchen, where I find Dell standing over the sink with a frying pan, pouring hot grease down the drain.

"Stop!" I scream. "What on earth are you doing?"

He keeps on pouring. "Cleaning up."

"Dell, stop! You can't pour that down there. What's wrong with you?"

I can feel my agitation settling in, right under the skin. This isn't the first time I've told him not to pour grease down the drain. *Why doesn't he learn? Does he just not listen to me? I swear, sometimes he's worse than the kids. This is just pure laziness . . . too lazy to dispose of it correctly.*

Now he stops and turns around, his expression sinking. "What's wrong with me?"

"Yes! You know that'll just clog the pipes. I've told you this over and over again. It doesn't take much to do it the right way."

"The right way?" he asks defensively. "Or your way?"

"I can't help it if my way is the right way."

"It always is," he mumbles. Something — I can't tell what — flashes across his face when he says it. He takes a deep breath, then he puts the pan down on a hot pad and folds his arms. I'm expecting him to find something else vindictive to say, since I know I'm already loading my next round of words into the chamber. Instead, he lowers his head and mumbles a barely audible,

"I'm sorry, Emily."

"You're . . . what?" I'm so confused. This isn't how our fights go. It hasn't escalated far enough yet. Nobody is yelling, though I'm very close. And where is the door-slamming or the name-calling?

"I'm sorry," he repeats. "You're right. You've told me a dozen times to let it cool in another container. I just . . . wanted to clean up the mess and get rid of the smell before you woke up."

Now I'm *really* confused.

*Who is this imposter, and what's happened to the real Dell Bennett?*

"Why?" I ask, almost reluctant to know the answer.

He shrugs. "I wanted to cook you breakfast in bed, but I burned the bacon."

I am frozen. I can feel my lip starting to quiver — mostly from guilt. And a tear is tugging at the corner of my eye. "Why?" I ask again.

Dell allows a sheepish smile to brighten his face. "Because I really want to go deep-sea fishing in December." He pauses. "I figured breakfast in bed would be a good way to give me an early lead."

*The game! Oh my gosh . . . he remembered! Even after a long night's sleep, he remembered. And I . . . forgot.*

The tear breaks free. "I'm so sorry, Dell. Take a point for trying. Heck, take ten. You deserve it."

"You forgot, didn't you? When you saw the smoke, your instincts took over, and you forgot we were playing."

"This game is going to be harder than I thought."

"Yeah."

"You bit your tongue, didn't you? When I was yelling at you. You wanted to lash out, but you held back."

He nods.

"Then take a point for that too," I tell him. "Plus one for apologizing. That couldn't have been easy."

Now his mouth stretches into a grin. "No, it wasn't. But to be honest, it was not as bad as I thought. Certainly a lot easier than hours of fighting and being mad, and I'm pretty sure that's the direction we were headed." He quietly pulls his notebook from his pocket and makes a few marks on the first page.

I can't stop myself. I walk across the room and wrap my arms around him in a giant hug. "Thank you, Dell. Thank you so much." I love being this close to him. It makes me feel . . . *whole.*

The rest of the day isn't perfect, but it's

much better than usual. We're both trying hard to be nicer to each other, and it shows. Especially Dell — he really is competitive, making it clear that he wants to win. Whenever I'm on the verge of picking a fight with him for something innocuous, all he says is "Cabo," and suddenly the tension is gone.

By the time we crawl into bed at night, I can tell he's really starting to get into the swing of things, because he pays me a compliment for no reason at all: "You smell really nice tonight. Is that a new perfume?"

"Nice of you to notice," I reply dryly. "I've been wearing this same perfume since Christmas. You put it in my stocking."

"Did I?" He sounds embarrassed, but he laughs it off. "I guess I'm not surprised that I'm not more familiar with it. We haven't been all that close since then."

"No."

"I'm sorry about that, by the way."

"I know. Me too."

"But it's going to get better, right?"

"Yeah. I hope so."

The darkness goes quiet for a minute. Then he reiterates something that validates my hope. "I *am* going to beat you at this game, Emily. I just want you to know that." His voice is kind, but earnest. "I don't want to fight with you anymore, so whatever it takes, I'm going to win. I'm going to win *you*."

"I don't know about that. I'm very good at games."

"At Scrabble, yes. But dear, this is not Scrabble."

For a moment, I can't speak. *He called me "dear"!* "We'll see about that," I tell him finally. "Because I'm pretty set on winning too. Fishing for our anniversary just doesn't sound like fun to me. Not when we could be in the City of Love."

He hesitates for a moment before speaking. When he does, there is worry in his voice. "If we go away on a big anniversary . . . what will we do with Ann?"

*Good question.* In my zeal for an improved marriage, I haven't considered such details. The unfortunate truth about his question, which I'm sure we're both thinking, but neither of us will say, is that if Ann doesn't get her new heart soon, it may be a moot point. There's a chance she might not still be around in December. What will we do then? How could our family exist without her? How could we leave Bree and Cade alone without their big sister, just so we can go off on some grand trip?

I can feel the mood in the room has changed. It's gotten suddenly cooler. And darker. "We'll figure something out," I whisper.

He sighs. "How do you think she's doing?"

"Physically, or emotionally?"

"All of the above."

Now I sigh too. I'm sure she's upstairs at this very moment wondering what in the world she could have done differently with Tanner. It breaks my heart every time I see her. She's trying so hard to put on a brave face, but I know inside it must be killing her. I just wish I knew what caused him to turn on her so quickly. Did he think of this as a summer fling? But how could he after what she told him? He just didn't seem like that kind of boy. But then, I only met him a few times, and he'd have been on his best behavior.

I wish I could do something to help her — just rewind the clock somehow and have it go perfectly next time. Or perhaps I just need to go find that boy and shake some sense into him.

"She's . . . hanging in there," I tell Dell with as much optimism as I can muster, which isn't much. "You were right all along, Dell. She shouldn't have gotten involved with him. She didn't need this heartache right now."

A breeze from outside lifts the curtains away from the window for a few seconds, adding some light to the room. In the moonlight I can see that Dell is lying on his back on his twin bed. His hands are behind his head.

*I wish he wasn't so far away . . .*

The room goes dark again, and I see the dark form of his body roll over toward the other wall. "Good night, Em," he whispers.

"G'night."

Despite the melancholy that put us to bed, in the morning I can tell that Dell still intends to win our little game, because he does something that I thought he might never do again, and what I wished he'd have done last night. *He kisses me!* Not only that, but he calls all the kids into the kitchen to watch.

"I need you all to be witnesses," he explains before revealing his plan. "Because I'm about to earn a ton of points." Then he wraps me up and plants a bunch of rapid-fire kisses on my lips. He ends with one long one, then proudly shouts, "Ha! Were you all counting? Twenty kisses! That's got to be the fastest twenty points any of us has earned."

"Tied for fastest," I tell him playfully.

"Because I just earned twenty points too."

"How?"

"I was kissing back." *Now this game is going exactly as I had hoped!*

"Oh, your mother is sneaky, kids." He grabs me again before I can slip away — not that I'm really trying to — and plants twenty kisses on my cheek. "There. Those twenty points are all mine. If I have to kiss my way to victory in this game, I will." He pauses. "And don't tell me your cheek was kissing me back."

"If that's how you want to play, I certainly won't stop you."

Our eyes linger on each other for an extralong moment. It's the kind of affectionate stare we used to share before life got all complicated. When he's done admiring me, he turns to Cade. "What do you think? Care to try this strategy on your sisters? Kissing is easy points."

"Uh . . . not on your life."

Ann pretends to take offense. "What? You're too good to kiss me?"

"No, I just . . ."

She hunches over and points at her cheek. "Well, c'mon then. You're the one who made a big deal about me never having been kissed. Man up, Cade, and give me one right there."

Embarrassed, Cade takes two large steps backward. I'm about to tell him how cute he is when he's blushing, but then he opens his rotten, eleven-year-old mouth. "Sorry, Ann, your last hope for getting a kiss was Tanner, and you blew it."

Just like that, all of the air is sucked out of the room.

Ann stands up straight, looking like she's been stabbed.

For the past few days we've all tried so hard to avoid using the T-word, and Ann has done a decent job pretending like the sting of seeing Tanner with another girl didn't pierce her to the core. The look on her face, however, suggests the charade is over.

"Winner's Game or not," she hisses, "that was *cruel.* I won't say I hate you, Cade, but right now . . . I won't say I don't." She spins on her heels and rushes out of the room.

"Dude," Bree says slowly, "you totally crushed her."

"I . . . I didn't mean to. It just came out."

"You owe her an apology," Dell says. "A big one."

"I know. I will."

"Let her cool off first," I tell them both. "She'll need a while before she's ready to talk."

Cade responds with a nod.

Dell gives Cade a long, disappointed look. "In the meantime, your mother and I have some errands to run." As he's speaking, he looks at me affectionately, almost making me forget that our daughter just ran off in tears. "We'll probably be gone beyond lunchtime, so just fix yourself something to eat. And keep an eye on Ann. Cade, she's your responsibility until she has a smile on her face."

"Fine," Cade mumbles.

"Oh, and I have a little surprise. To earn another point in this game, I made reservations for a nice dinner at the Stephanie Inn — one of your mom's favorite places."

I can feel my heart jump with excitement. "You did?"

"Uh-huh. I thought the kids would enjoy it too, so we'll all go." He turns back to Cade and Bree. "It's down the beach a ways, but I thought we could walk there. We'll probably need to leave by about five, so you two make sure Ann knows, so she's ready to go."

# CHAPTER 33
## CADE

"You can't just leave by yourself," I tell Bree after my parents are gone. She's heading out the back door in her flip-flops.

"Sure I can. Just watch me." She opens the door and walks onto the deck without slowing down.

I run out after her. "But what about Ann?"

"She's your problem until Mom and Dad get back. I'm not staying inside all day when I don't have to." I continue watching for a minute longer as she tiptoes across the lawn, onto the sand, and starts walking north up the beach.

"Great," I mumble as I go back inside. "Now I'm stuck." It's my own fault, though. If I hadn't opened my big mouth about Tanner, Ann wouldn't be upstairs crying, and I wouldn't be here babysitting her. I do feel bad about it. I mean . . . I wasn't trying to be a jerk.

After a while I go up to Ann's room to

377

talk to her about what I said, but she's locked me out. All she says to me through the door is, "Go away, Cade, I'm not in the mood to talk."

So I try again a little later.

And then again.

"Fine," I tell her on the fourth attempt, "but don't say I didn't try. Oh yeah, and I left your meds outside the door. Mom says you haven't taken them in a couple days. Just because you're mad at Tanner doesn't mean you can stop taking your medicine. And Dad says you need to be ready to walk to the Stephanie Inn for dinner by five. You can't wear shorts, but pants and flip-flops are OK. And in case you're wondering, I really am sorry about what I said."

At two o'clock Bree finally returns.

My parents don't get home until after four o'clock. I consider telling them about Bree, but I decide not to so I can give myself a point for not tattling. Ann still hasn't come out of her room. In fact, she doesn't come down until Dad calls for her a few minutes before five o'clock.

"How are you feeling?" asks Mom when she sees her coming down the stairs.

"I'm fine." She doesn't look fine.

"See, she's fine," says Bree, sounding impatient. "Can we get going now?"

"Lead the way," Dad tells her. "You and Cade."

As we walk toward the Stephanie Inn, Mom and Ann stay a few steps behind the rest of us.

"Is it just my imagination," Mom asks Ann, "or have I seen you grimacing in pain a couple times this week? Is there something you're not telling us?"

"It's nothing."

"Earlier today, when Cade said . . . what he said, was it more than just his words that hurt? I could have sworn you winced."

"I had a little gas or heartburn or something."

"In your chest?"

"Yeah, but . . . it's not serious. It went away. Besides, the doctors said I might have pains."

"Yeah, as your condition gets worse! Ann, you need to keep us in the loop on these things. Maybe you're doing too much."

"I'm not doing *anything,* other than reading books on the beach, watching TV, and going for walks."

"And horse rides."

"Fine, yes, horse rides too. But if that's too much, then —"

I turn around to see why she's stopped talking. Ann is watching an old man and woman coming toward us, both of them grinning suspiciously. The man is holding a long-stemmed red rose. The rest of my family sees the couple too, and we all sort of slow down together to see what is going on.

When he is just a few feet away, the man holds out the rose to Ann. "I believe this belongs to you," he says, and then he and the woman continue walking.

"Wait," calls Ann. "What's this for?"

The man turns around and winks, but keeps walking.

Everyone huddles around Ann excitedly. "Why did he give you that?" I ask.

"Probably just an old creeper," remarks Bree. "Likes to flatter girls."

Dad looks worried. He still has an eye on the old couple as they walk away.

Mom is the first to notice a small string tied to the stem, just below the petals. The string has a tiny piece of paper attached to it, like a tag, no bigger than my pinky fingernail. "What's that?"

Ann flips the paper over. "It says, *N.*" She passes it around so everyone can see for themselves.

"This is superweird," says Bree when it is handed to her. "What kind of person just hands a rose to a complete stranger?"

No sooner does she say it than a boy,

about eight years old, leaves his parents and comes running over with his hands behind his back. "S'cuse me," he says, then produces another long-stemmed rose from behind his back. He hands it to Ann and then takes off running.

"It has another thingy on it," I tell my sister immediately.

Ann is still staring at the boy. When he reaches his parents, they all wave at us, then start walking up the beach.

"It's an *O,*" says Bree. *"N.O."*

I can hardly contain myself. "No!"

"Great, you can spell," Bree deadpans. "But what does it mean?"

Ann's eyes are darting back and forth between the rose and the boy who delivered it. "This is kind of freaking me out."

"Any chest pains?" asks Mom.

Ann rolls her eyes.

For the next minute we stand right where we are, watching people walking by, wondering if the next stranger might be carrying another rose. Eventually Dad says we need to keep going, but we've barely gone twenty steps when a barefoot jogger comes out of nowhere, turning toward us with a rose in her hand. Without saying a word, and barely breaking her stride, she hands the flower to Ann, who is now more confused than ever.

Whatever is going on, it is definitely not by chance.

"It's a *T*," she tells everyone after inspecting the tiny paper. " *'Not.'* "

"Not what?" asks Dad.

"Not normal," says Bree.

Mom snickers. "Just what I was thinking."

For the next twenty minutes, the pattern continues. Every couple of minutes a new stranger appears carrying a rose with a tiny tag tied to it. There is no obvious rhyme or reason to the people — some are old, some young, some by themselves, some in groups, some in swimsuits, some fully clothed. The only thing they all have in common is that they all have roses, and they all give them to Ann without saying anything. There are lots of smiles, though, and giggling from the younger ones.

" *'Not what u thin,'* " says Ann slowly, reading all of the tags in order.

"Maybe someone thinks you're fat," says Bree. " 'Not thin.' "

Ann ignores the comment. "I'm pretty sure there's still at least one more rose to come."

As we continue farther south, past Haystack Rock, I watch closely up and down the beach. By this time we are all pretty sure that Tanner is hiding somewhere in the crowd. Sure enough, when a cluster of people ahead of us splits up, there is one person left standing there.

And he's carrying a rose in one hand.

And grinning from ear to ear.

Dad was all smiles a moment earlier, but now he looks mad. "I said stay away from my daughters," he growls as we all stop walking.

Tanner doesn't seem to hear him. He is walking toward us, still smiling. When he is within arm's reach of Ann, he finally stops and hands her the rose.

She quickly inspects the tag. *"K,"* she says aloud. *" 'Not what u think.' "*

Before she can say anything else, Tanner jumps in to explain. "It's not what you think, Ann. The girl I was with is Laura, my sister. She lives with my dad in Portland."

Shocked, Ann looks around at everyone. Mom is smiling happily, obviously loving the attention Ann is getting. Dad seems . . . humbled. Bree is harder to read, because she is biting her lip.

"I'm really sorry," says Tanner. "If I'd known that you saw me and her walking, I could've explained."

My father jumps on that comment. "Well, why were you arm in arm with your sister in the first place?"

Tanner's face turns instantly pink. "It's a little embarrassing. We were just walking to the store and I was telling her about . . . well, about Ann. And she asked if we'd held hands, and I'm like —" He stops for a second, still staring nervously at my dad. "Anyway, she said she thinks it's cool when girls hold on to guys' arms. It's like more romantic or something. She was just showing me how. That must've been when you drove by."

There is an awkward silence, which Dad finally kills with an even more awkward, "Oops."

"Oops is right," says Mom. "Sorry for shooing you away so quickly, Tanner. But kudos to you for . . ." She motions to Ann and the roses. "For this. It's very sweet."

Tanner looks really relieved. "Well, you said the house was off-limits, so I figured catching you on the beach was the only real option I had."

Ann shifts slightly, squinting in the sun. "But how did you know we saw you arm in arm? And how did you know we would be here on the beach right now?"

"Yeah," chimes Bree. "Are you, like, stalking us?" Under her breath she mutters, "Creepy."

Tanner looks quickly at my mom, then

back to Ann. "A little bird told me," he says. "And good thing, too. I was pretty bummed. The worst part was not knowing what I did wrong."

"Which bird?" asks Dad.

Tanner smiles sheepishly. "I can't reveal my sources."

"Well, it's perfect," Ann says like she's in the middle of a dream.

"And cheesy," Bree says under her breath.

Ann shuts her up with a quick glare.

Tanner is shuffling his feet in the sand. "So am I forgiven?"

Rather than simply telling him yes, Ann steps forward and gives him a huge hug.

"Gross," I say loud enough for them to hear.

"So forgiven," Ann whispers while they're still hugging. When Dad makes a little *ahem* sound, she lets go and steps back.

"Then I have two more things," Tanner tells her.

I hadn't noticed before, but Tanner had one hand behind his back the whole time he was standing there, even while Ann was hugging him. When he brings his other hand around front, he is holding a piece of paper and small box. First he hands the paper to Dad. "This is for you, sir."

At first Dad looks concerned, but once he

starts reading, his mouth turns into a smile. "A blatant appeal to the lawyer in me," he says when he's done.

"Read it out loud, Dell," Mom tells him. "We all want to hear."

Dad clears his throat. *"Mr. Bennett, I'm sorry for all of the confusion. The last time we spoke, you said I broke a verbal agreement. Would you mind if we formalized that agreement in writing?"* Still smiling, he looks up at Ann, then continues. "There's a subtitle that reads, *Application to date your daughter: Under contractual agreement, I, the undersigned applicant, do hereby swear to do nothing that would undermine the trust of Dell and Emily Bennett. For the right and privilege of dating their daughter, Ann Bennett, I do solemnly promise to be courteous and kind to her at all times, to treat her with respect, and to ensure her safety. I do also promise that she will be brought home on time. Furthermore, and above all, I do agree that I will not break Ann's heart. Signed, Tanner Rich."* He pauses, slowly eyeing Tanner. "Young man, I'll be happy to countersign this when we get back to the house. You have my permission to take Ann on a date."

Tanner is grinning. "Awesome. Then, Ann, this is for you."

When she opens up the small box, there is

386

a note inside: *Ann Bennett, please do me the honor of going on at least one date with me. Time? Tomorrow night at six pm. Dinner? Yes. Other activity? It's a surprise!*

Below the note is a tightly folded pair of plastic dish gloves. "Uhh . . . ?" she says when she holds them up.

"They're for our date," he says, smiling.

"Rubber gloves?" asks Dad. "Maybe I should rethink signing this."

"Trust me, sir, there's nothing to worry about. It's not anything weird. Just . . . *unique.* She'll appreciate the gloves."

"Well, thank you," Ann says. "I think. I look forward to . . . whatever it is we're doing." She turns to Mom. "And thank you for talking to Tanner."

"Well, if it was me, I'm not saying. My lips are officially locked." She turns an imaginary key near her mouth.

"That's what Ann really wants," I snicker. *"Lip locking!"*

Ann goes rigid. "Can I punch him, Mom? *Please?"*

Everyone laughs except Tanner, who is blushing.

"Cade," Dad says, "consider yourself warned. One more comment like that and I'll let her at you."

"I can outrun her easily."

"But you can't hide forever, little man," she says, holding up a clenched fist.

"Ah, sibling love," says Mom. "And on that note, I think it's about time for our dinner reservation. I bet we can squeeze in one more. Tanner, you care to join us?"

"I'd love to," he replies, "but my mom and Laura are already cooking something. I think they'll be mad if I skip. Thanks anyways, though." He looks at Ann. "So, tomorrow night?"

"I'll be waiting."

As Tanner walks away, Ann takes several big sniffs of the roses, breathing in the aroma.

"You act like you've never smelled flowers before," says Bree as we continue walking toward the inn.

Ann takes another long breath. "These don't smell like ordinary roses," she says. "They smell more like . . . *happiness.*"

I expect the comment to earn a complaint from Bree, but instead she just smiles back and then skips ahead.

I stay with Ann at the back of the group. As we walk, she takes another long breath of the fragrance.

*Amazing. To think that thirteen flowers can heal someone so quickly.*

What a difference a few hours makes.

Earlier, she was crying her eyes out, and now she's on top of the world.

It suddenly feels like the perfect day. Ahead of us, our parents are walking side by side and talking — *not yelling.* Bree and I are getting along. The sun is setting nicely. The surf is pounding on the beach. And Ann has thirteen roses.

As though she just read my mind, Ann says, "This is the perfect day, Cade — your earlier comments notwithstanding. This is why we came to the beach this summer." She pauses, and for the first time ever, she looks completely at peace. "I could literally die right now and be happy." She sighs and then corrects herself. "No, wait. Tomorrow night would be better. One fantastic date, and then I'm good to go . . ."

# Chapter 34
## Ann

First dates are important to every girl, but I tend to think this one is more important to me than most are to most other girls. Does that sound overly self-important? I hope not. I just mean . . . I don't think most girls go out on their first date wondering if it might be their last. For me, that's a real possibility, which is why I don't mind spending four hours before it starts picking out clothes, doing my hair, and putting on makeup. As long as I have the opportunity to live a little, I might as well make the most of it.

I know Dad is trying to play it cool when Tanner arrives for our date, but he starts getting antsy as we head for the door. I can tell because he begins pelting Tanner with a bunch of questions he already asked at least once before.

"So you'll be home by ten?"

"Probably more like nine thirty."

"And, you're a safe driver?"

"Uh-huh."

"No tickets or accidents?"

"Not yet."

"And you won't let her lose her purse, right? It has her pager in it."

"Of course. I'll double-check everywhere we go."

"And you're definitely staying local, right?"

"Just to Astoria."

"I thought you said Seaside before? Now you're going all the way to Astoria? That's another ten or fifteen miles."

Thankfully, Mom steps in. "It's been Astoria all along, dear. Just let them go." She wraps an arm around his waist. "They'll be fine." I like seeing her arms around him. I haven't seen them so touchy and nice to each other for a long time. I hope they keep it up.

Tanner doesn't own a car, but his mom let him borrow her Accord for the night. As we drive up the coastal highway, I keep fishing for clues about where we're going — and especially why we need the rubber gloves — but he doesn't bite.

"You'll see," he keeps saying. "I want it to be a surprise."

Our first stop is a restaurant on the promenade in Seaside, about halfway between Cannon Beach and Astoria. It's a small restaurant, but it isn't too crowded, which I love because we can talk without having to compete with a lot of noise.

After ordering our food, Tanner produces an envelope from his jeans pocket. It looks like a letter, but he says it's a "get to know you" activity that his sister put together. Inside the envelope are a bunch of random questions. The idea is to take turns drawing a question to ask the other person.

After he explains it, I propose that we turn it into a game. "The first person to not answer their question loses."

"OK, but you're so going to lose," he warns. "I'm very competitive."

"Good to know. But I think you've met your match."

A waitress comes to fill our cups with water and asks if everything is OK. I tell her it couldn't be better, which is exactly how I feel about being out on a date with the guy sitting across from me.

When the woman is gone, Tanner opens the envelope and holds it open for me to take a paper. " *'Who is the most important superhero, and why?'* " I ask, reading the question to him. "That's so easy."

"Easy? Measuring the relative value of

humankind's greatest allies is hardly 'easy.' "
He's clearly joking, but he acts all serious
anyway, as though he's contemplating
something hugely important. Finally he
says, "It's got to be Wonder Woman."

"Oh, please. Why her? And if you say
because she has the best outfit, you officially
lose."

"Why not her? First, she's got an invisible
plane. Think of how that has helped develop
stealth technologies. And then her headband thing that doubles as a boomerang
weapon — that's cutting-edge fashion. But
mostly, consider what she has done for
advancing women's rights. Who else, among
all the superheroes, has been the kind of
strong role model for young female minds?
Yeah, it's got to be Wonder Woman." He
grins, obviously pleased with his answer.
Then he draws a question to ask me. "OK,
your turn. *'What's the very first impression
you had of the person sitting across from
you?'* "

"Seriously? You got a superhero question,
and I have something personal like that?"
*Totally not fair.*

He folds up the paper and sets it down. "I
didn't write it, I just picked it. Are you not
going to answer?"

"What, and lose?" I feel some butterflies

flitting about, but not enough to give up. "No, I'll answer. I, um . . . saw you behind the counter at the candy store, and I remember thinking you looked like a boy I once met at the hospital during one of my stays. And then you started talking and I thought — Don't laugh, OK? — I thought, 'Wow, he sounds a lot smarter than he looks.' "

Tanner nearly spits out his water. "Laugh? I think you just slammed me."

"No, it was a compliment. You look like one of those cool guys, you know, who are athletic and good-looking and fun to be around, but not very smart. Or at least not studious. But when you spoke, I could tell there was more to you than I first thought."

He relaxes and smiles. "Aww, thanks. I think." Tanner slides the envelope back across the table.

I can't believe it when I read the next slip of paper. "What the heck? It's another easy one: *'Which is better, and why — dog or cat?'* "

*So lame.*

When he smiles at me again, it sends a shiver down my spine. What a great smile! Even if it is a little crooked, it's also confident, but not arrogant. And warm and inviting without being cheesy.

*So adorable!*

"I'll go with cats," he says at length. "I'm probably more of a dog person, but cats have nine lives, and who wouldn't want that?"

The way he is looking at me, he's probably thinking about the frailty of my life, and how having nine lives would be a drastic improvement. It's a sweet thought, but I don't agree with his assessment. "I don't know, cats are so serious all the time, and all they do is sit around, completely self-absorbed. Dogs have fun and are kind and want to spend every moment with the people they love. Plus they are true friends, sometimes to a fault. Emotionally, and even socially, I think I'd rather have one dog life than nine cat lives."

"Really?"

I nod. "Positive. I've been a bit of cat for the past few years. I'm ready to be a dog."

The waitress walking by must've overheard that last bit, because she gives me an odd look.

Tanner sees it too and busts up laughing.

*Awkward!*

He takes a sip of water and draws another question from the envelope. "Oh boy," he says very slowly after reading it. "You're not going to like this."

"You can't be serious. How come I keep

getting the bad ones?"

"Just dumb luck, I guess." There is a twinkle in his eye that I can't quite read.

"Here goes. *'What was the name of your last boyfriend, and what did you like most and least about him?'* " The twinkle in his eye grows.

"Wait a minute!" I snatch the paper from his hand and read it out loud. *" 'Sunrise or sunset, and why?' " He's been making up his own questions the whole time!* "Oh, you're a trickster, Tanner Rich."

"And you're awesome, Ann Bennett."

My heart does a backflip, and it doesn't even hurt! I LOVE hearing him say that. Just like I love the sound of his laughter. I even love the fact that he is interested enough in me to make up personal questions. "So this means I win, right? Cheaters always lose."

"That's fair. But you're still welcome to answer the questions. If you want."

"Actually, those are both easy questions. I've never had a boyfriend, and I definitely choose sunrises over sunsets."

"Why sunrises?"

I suddenly wish I hadn't volunteered to answer the question. Not that it's any big secret, only that I don't want to be all gloom-and-doom when we're having such a good time. "Just because. Sunsets are an end, you know . . . and I'm more in favor of new beginnings. Every day I wake up and there's a new day ahead of me . . . it's a good day."

His smile puts me at ease. "Cool. I like sunrises too."

I nod and smile back.

A few minutes later, dinner arrives. Maybe it's the company I'm with that makes it taste so good, but I think this meal will go down as the best fish and chips I've ever had.

When we leave the restaurant, he runs around the car to open the door for me before I can do it myself. "Aww," I say as I climb in. "Do you open the door for all your dates?"

"What dates?"

I honestly can't tell if he is being serious. "You know, past girlfriends, or whatever."

"I live in Cannon Beach, Ann," he says very directly. "Most girls are here for a week or less. And my school is so small . . . I've never thought to date any of the locals. This is my first legitimate date." He pauses. "How am I doing so far?"

*His first date!*

My mouth is probably hanging wide open, but I can't help it. "Good," I stammer. "I'm having a great time."

"Me too," he says, flashing his crooked smile.

*Adorable!*

As we pull out of the parking lot, I ask him what's next on the agenda. My box of rubber gloves is at my feet on the floor, and I am dying to know what they're for.

He tells me to guess, but I have no good ideas. "For a minute there I was worried maybe we were going to pay for dinner by washing the dishes at the restaurant."

That earns a nice chuckle. "I'm not rich," he says, "but I'm not cheap. Guess again."

"Hmm. How about . . . bowling?"

"With rubber gloves?"

"It could be fun."

"Next time, then."

"OK, are we digging in the sand somewhere?"

"Nope."

"Clamming?"

"That's digging in the sand."

"Just checking. Maybe we're . . . robbing a bank, and you don't want us to leave fingerprints."

"You guessed it. Tanner and Ann, high school bandits."

"Fine. Give me a hint."

All he'll say is that it will be a night to remember.

Ten minutes later we pull into a mostly empty parking lot, not far from where I got kicked off the movie set with Mom, Bree, and Cade. The place looks different without all the rigging and lights and cameras.

Tanner opens the car door for me again, and then we walk several blocks toward the bay. When we reach the end of the street, we're overlooking a marina. "OK, put on your gloves," he says. "And take my arm."

He has a pair of gloves for himself too, tucked into his back pocket, so we both put them on.

"Is this because your sister says locking arms is romantic?" I ask with a giggle as I take hold of his biceps with my rubberized hand.

"Well . . . maybe," he replies, blushing. "But also, I told your dad I'd keep you safe, and we're going down some stairs." With that he leads me down a steep metal ramp over the water, then down eight even steeper steps. At the bottom is a locked gate. "My friend's dad has a boat moored here. He gave me the code." He punches in a series of numbers, and the security gate clicks open. We are on safe footing on the flat of the dock, but I don't let go of his arm, nor do I get any sense that he wants me to.

"Now will you tell me what the gloves are for?"

"You'll *see,*" he teases. "And I'm not *lyin'.*" He stops, snickers, and announces, "That's a pun!"

"What's so punny about that?"

"You'll *see,*" he says again, "And I'm not *lyin'.*"

"I still don't get it. 'See'? 'Lying'?" I pause to think, then say it once more, faster. " 'See lyin'? 'Sea lion'! Oh my gosh, are there sea lions here?"

Just as I ask the question, I start to hear their distinctive barking near the end of the pier.

"A whole herd of them. The fishermen hate it, but they've taken up home here. The city is trying to figure out how to get rid of them without hurting them. In the late afternoon they come right up on the docks, down there at the end, and soak up the sun."

I hold up the hand that isn't locked around Tanner's arm. "So what are the gloves for? I'm not petting them."

"I hope not. They'd probably bite. But they do like a free meal now and then, which is probably why they came here in the first place."

"You mean we're . . . ?"

"Feeding the sea lions."

Now I drop his arm and face him. "That's on my bucket list for the summer."

"Really? I had no idea." There is that darn twinkle again, just like over dinner when he was "lyin.' "

"Who told you?"

"What? I do this all the time. Who doesn't love feeding the sea lions?"

"Seriously, Tanner. Who told?"

He shrugs. "The little bird may have mentioned it. But it sounded like so much fun, I wanted to do it too. I had my friend leave a bucket of herring on his boat. C'mon. It's just up there, closer to the sea lions."

Tanner fetches the bucket, and together we approach the herd, slowly, until a few of them start getting restless. "You first," he whispers. "Just grab a fish and toss it right over there. Slow motions, though. You don't want to spook them."

"Do they know it's fish?"

He suppresses a laugh, but he is obviously amused. "They're sea lions, Ann. They know a fish when they see it."

"I meant, how do they know we're not throwing something else at them? I could be tossing a grenade, for all they know."

"They know that when people come down here, they'll probably get a bite or two. Plus,

I'm sure by the way they're acting that they can smell what's in the bucket. Just nice and easy, toss one over."

Though the thought of holding a slimy dead fish is unsettling, even while wearing a rubber glove, I can feel adrenaline running through my veins, nudging me to do it. Very deftly, I reach into the bucket, grab the first fish I touch, and toss it in a high arc toward the group of anxious beasts. Like a trained circus animal, one of them shimmies forward on its flippers and catches the fish midflight. "Yes!" I shout, throwing my hands up in excitement as though I've just scored a goal.

Then it happens.

The sharp pain in my chest. Same as yesterday when Cade made that comment about me blowing it with Tanner, only . . . not the same as yesterday. This is worse. It starts in my chest, then runs down my arm.

There are no friendly butterflies, only the sting of a bee.

I want to scream, but it hurts too bad. All I can do is double over. As I do so, I faintly hear Tanner asking what's wrong.

"Nothing," I lie. Then everything goes black.

*This is just like the swim meet! Oh, please, God, don't let me fall off the dock and drown . . .*

When I first open my eyes, everything is foggy. There is a boat. And another one. The dock. The herd. The sunset.

A spot on the side of my head is pounding, but at least the chest pain is gone.

I crane my neck a little farther and find what I'm looking for: *Tanner!* As the cobwebs continue to clear, I ask him what happened.

"You tell me." His voice is hoarse. And worried. No, not just worried . . . he's kind of freaking out. "You threw the fish, bent over, and then . . . I tried to catch you, but I was too slow. Oh my gosh, I'm so sorry."

"That's why my head hurts." I wince in pain when I touch the spot with my hand.

"The bucket broke your fall."

I look around once more to get my bearings. I'm definitely still on the dock, but sitting rather than standing. Something smells. I look down and see that my shirt is completely soaked. I look down a little father and realize that all of the fish that were in the bucket are now lying around and under me on the wood. In half a second I'm on my feet, scrambling for safety.

Tanner bends down, grabs a couple fish, and tosses them to the sea lions. "There, now we can both say we fed them." When he says it's time to go home, I tell him flat out that I don't want to.

"But you passed out."

"So."

"So? Ann, *you passed out*! Doesn't that worry you?"

"Not really."

"Does that happen a lot?"

I don't respond.

"Has it ever happened?"

"Once. The last time I swam."

"Oh, you mean the time you nearly died? Like I said, we're going home. *Now.*"

"It's no big deal. I just got a little woozy. Seriously, don't let this ruin our date."

"It's home or the hospital, your call."

"Home," I mumble.

He snickers, flashing that adorable crooked smile, and leads me toward the stairs. "Even if you hadn't passed out, you have fish scales all over you. You really want to stay out smelling like that?"

I know he's right.

I wish he wasn't.

I don't want the date to be over, but by virtue of the circumstances, it kind of already is . . .

# CHAPTER 35
## BREE

I'm not really much of a snooper. Spying on people just isn't my thing. If I want to know what someone is up to, I prefer just asking them. But this is different. I mean, I was just drawing a picture in my room, minding my own business, when I heard a car pull up. So I went to the nearest window to see who it was, and Cade's binoculars were sitting right there, so I picked them up.

I guess I should have shut the door so nobody could see or hear me, because while I'm staring through the binoculars, I happen to mumble, "Oh crap," just as my dad is walking up the stairs to check on me.

"Uh, what did you just say, young lady?" he asks as he steps into the room. "You know I don't like that word." I quickly try to hide the binoculars and wipe the guilty look off my face, but it's too late. "And what, exactly, are you up to?"

"I was just . . . I mean . . . Ann's home. Parked outside."

He checks his watch, then calls downstairs. "Hey, Emily, can you come up here for a second?"

While we're waiting for Mom, I keep trying to steal peeks out the window to see if anything else has happened.

Twenty seconds later, Mom reaches the bedroom door, trailed by Cade. "What's wrong?"

Dad folds his arms. "One of our daughters is spying on another of our daughters. And she swore."

"I said 'crap'!" I snap defensively. "That's not swearing. Dad, you say it all the time."

"Only when I'm mad."

"Well . . . *I'm mad.*"

Mom steps closer to me and looks out the window at the car. "Bree, there's no need to be mad. Or jealous. Just let Ann enjoy herself."

I fold my arms defiantly. "Look closer, Mom. I think they're fighting."

My mother puts the binoculars to her eyes and leans in close to the window. "Boy, she doesn't look too happy, does she? I hope her blood pressure is OK."

Dad puts his forehead against the glass too. "Should we go out and say something to them?"

"No!" gushes Mom. "Leave them be. Maybe they'll kiss and make up."

"Gross," Cade mumbles.

"Oh, they're getting out of the car," says Mom. "How cute! He's making her get back in so he can open her door."

"But she doesn't seem too happy about it," I note. "Look at the scowl on her face. Even without the binoculars, I can see — *Duck*! She saw us!"

Instinctively, the whole family crouches down below the level of the windowsill. A few seconds later the front door opens and Ann calls up the stairs. "Hello! I know you're all up there spying on me. You can come down now."

"Phew," says Cade. "That wasn't long enough for a kiss on the doorstep."

Dad smiles and pats Cade on the back. "Exactly what I was thinking."

When we come downstairs, Ann is waiting for us in the entryway, still frowning.

"Uh-oh," says Mom delicately. "I smell trouble."

Ann's frown deepens. "It's fish, actually."

The scent hits all of our noses right about the same time. "So the date really stunk, eh?" says Dad, trying to keep things light.

"No. It was great. I just . . . spilled fish on me."

Mom cocks her head to the side, smiling. "What were you doing with fish?"

"Oh, like you don't know. We fed them to sea lions."

"How would I know that?"

"Because it's on my bucket list, on my bed. It's OK, though, I'm glad you told him. It was really fun. Well, most of it was fun."

"You wrote on your bed?" asks Dad.

"You wanted to feed sea lions?" asks Mom.

Ann isn't buying it. "Whatever. I know you told him."

"You really stink," I tell her. "You should go change your clothes."

Dad agrees with a nod. "Good idea. Ann, you go up and change, then we want to hear all about your fish story."

Ann turns to her left. "Tanner, are you staying or going?"

"Staying. At least until you tell them."

"Fine," she huffs, then marches up the stairs to her room. Five minutes later she returns in sweats. "You didn't say anything, did you?" she asks Tanner as she sits down next to him on the couch.

"Nope."

Dad crosses one leg over the other. "So

408

what's going on?"

"It's nothing. We shouldn't even be talking about it. In fact I wouldn't if Tanner wasn't forcing me to."

A small smile tugs at the corner of Tanner's mouth.

"So here's the deal," continues Ann. "Not a *big* deal, though. Tanner took me to feed sea lions in Astoria, which was way cool. There's this dock there with a big herd of them, and Tanner had a bucket of fish to —"

"Herring," Tanner clarifies.

"Right. Herring. And so I threw one of the fish to them, and the thing caught it in midair — totally awesome — but then I sort of . . . *stumbled,* and fell on the bucket of fish, and they got all over me. I was lying in them, actually. On the dock. So then . . . I was wet and smelled like fish, so we came home early."

"That's it?" asks Mom.

"Yep."

Tanner crosses his arms and clears his throat. He obviously thinks there is more to tell.

"Spit it out, Ann," Dad tells her.

My sister rolls her eyes with a long sigh. "Fine. There was maybe a little bit more than that. See . . . I sort of, like . . . passed out a little bit after I threw the fish. That's why I fell. Actually, I hit my head pretty good on the bucket when I went down, so I have a bump up here, but it's really no biggie." She rubs the left side of her head, just above the ear.

"Oh my gosh!" says Mom.

"You should have called us," Dad adds. "How long were you out?"

"It was like two seconds! *So* not a big deal. This is why I didn't want to tell you, because I knew you'd blow it way out of proportion."

Mom stands up and starts pacing. "Ann, we're your parents, so we have the right to be concerned. And this is your life we're talking about. We're not blowing anything out of proportion. We just want you to be safe."

"Well, I am safe," she shoots back. "See?" Ann points at herself and smiles. "People pass out all the time, Mom. This has *nothing* to do with my heart."

"You're sure?"

"Positive. I was just all excited about feeding the sea lions and I jumped and shouted and . . . I don't know. I think the smell of the fish got to me. I got a little woozy and then . . . *plop*. Right on the bucket."

Mom and Dad share a concerned look.

"That's it? No sharp pains?"

"None."

*No way . . . she's lying right to their faces! Am I the only one in this family who can tell when Ann is lying?*

"Any other symptoms?"

"Nope. Just a lot of fishy smells, and it made me dizzy." Dad and Mom still don't seem fully convinced, so Ann throws in a heartfelt, *"Honest."*

"Fine," Dad says at length. "If that's all there is to it. But you'd tell us if there was more to tell, right, Ann?"

"Of course, Dad."

*Liar.*

He walks over and gives her a half hug, with one arm around her shoulder. "Good. Because any day now you're going to land at the top of that list, and that pager of yours is going to go off, and then we won't have to worry about stuff like this all the time."

"Can't wait," she tells him.

Dad lets go of her and extends a hand to Tanner. "Thank you for bringing her straight home. That was very responsible of you."

Tanner shrugs it off. "It seemed like the right thing to do. Besides, it was either that or risk not getting to go out with her again."

He pauses. "Assuming you'll let us . . . ?"

Dad nods. "Let's just take a day or two to make sure she doesn't have any other episodes like this, but then I'm sure we can probably find a way to make that happen."

Mom and Dad thank him again, as does Ann, and then he lets himself out.

Even with the window open, the upstairs bedroom is too hot to sleep. Ann is on the bunk below me, but I'm sure she's awake too, thinking about her failed date. I don't get it. Why does this kind of stuff always happen to her? Why is everything always so messed up for her? Would I rather that Tanner liked me? Yes, that's no secret. But as long as she's on a date with him, can't it at least go well?

Is it something about her? Bad luck, perhaps? Or is life really so unfair that a teenage girl who's had a miserable couple of years can't have one good date with the one boy who has ever paid attention to her?

Right now, I'm sure she's asking herself similar questions.

After lying there in silence for a long time, I want some answers.

"So?"

"So what?"

"Are you going to tell me about it?"

She doesn't respond immediately.

"What do you want to know?"

"Well . . . I guess mostly I want to know why you were fighting in the car."

She's quiet again, for a long time. Then I hear her roll onto her side. "When we got home, I told him not to mention the whole passing-out thing to Mom and Dad, but he said he signed a contract to keep me safe, so he had to. I kept trying to convince him that I'm fine, but he said if they ever found out that something happened and we didn't tell them about it, they'd never let us go out again."

"That's true."

"I know. And it was very sweet of him. I just didn't want to deal with them freaking out."

"Is that why you lied?"

"When did I lie?"

"About passing out. You said it was from smelling the fish. I've seen you wincing a lot lately. It was from your heart, wasn't it?"

The bed shakes when she flops back onto her back. "Do you know what would happen if I told them the truth about my heart pains? Their kneejerk reaction would be to send us all back to Portland to be closer to my doctors. And what good would that do? Are the doctors going to operate again? No.

Are there more medications they can give me to slow down my heart's condition? No. And most importantly, would I be able to go on another date with Tanner if I were all the way in Portland? Definitely not! Don't you see? I had to lie. For all of us."

"Does Tanner know why you really fainted?"

In a whisper, she replies, "No." After a few seconds she asks, "Any more questions? Or did you get the rest answered while you were spying on me?"

"I wasn't — That was an accident. I heard you pull up, and I looked out to see who it was. I didn't think it would be you, because it was so early."

"Yeah, well . . . it was. But you didn't have to keep watching."

"Sorry," I whisper.

"It's . . . fine. There wasn't much to see anyway."

"I saw him hug you in the car."

"Like I said, not much to see."

"Was it at least a nice hug?"

"Well . . . yeah. I guess. But I sort of spoiled it."

"How can you spoil a hug with a cute boy?"

She lets out a long sigh. "After the hug, I opened my big mouth and said, 'That's all?'

I guess I was kind of hoping for something more. I know that's a little forward, but Cade is right — time is running out. Much longer and it might be too late."

I have to laugh. "Oh my gosh! What did he say?"

"He was all embarrassed. He said, 'I want to . . . you know, kiss you, Ann. But not tonight.' " Her voice is low, mimicking Tanner's. "I asked him if he was afraid that kissing me might kill me."

"And?"

"He said that years from now, when we look back on today, he doesn't want to associate our first kiss with the smell of herring. He said he wants it to be just like *me*."

"Like what?"

She takes a deep breath, then whispers, "I'm pretty sure the word he used to describe me was 'perfect.' "

*Perfect? Ann? It is SO not fair that I'm not a few years older . . .*

"Good night, Ann."

"Good night, Bree."

# CHAPTER 36
## EMILY

When the telephone rings on Sunday morning, the news is good. Grandma Grace is being released from the hospital and they are transporting her back from Seaside to the nursing facility in Cannon Beach. We meet her there at ten o'clock, unsure of what her mental state will be, but hoping for the best.

As I enter the room, the first thing I notice is the expression on Grandma's face. It's a tired smile, but peaceful.

The second thing I notice is that she has noticed me. "There you are," comes her familiar greeting, drawn out in slow, deliberate syllables. "My fam'ly." Her speech isn't perfect, but better than most days. More important than the pronunciation, her simple words make it abundantly clear that she is "there." We really can't ask for more than that.

She is still very weak, so we can't stay long

— thirty minutes, tops. During the course of our visit, we all take turns telling her about our Winner's Game.

"You play with Dell?" she asks excitedly. "Oh good."

When it's Ann's turn to speak, she points at the old Altoids tin that is still on the table next to Grandma's bed and asks if it was a regular part of the original Winner's Game with Great-grandpa. I already know the answer, since I recently read about it in one of her journals, so to save Grandma the effort, I help fill in the details. "Burying treasures for each other started years after they began the game. She'd bought him the metal detector after they retired to Cannon Beach, but he rarely found anything of value. So one year for Valentine's Day she planted something in the sand out behind the house — a love note in an Altoids can, along with a candy heart. He found it a few days later. In response, Grandpa made a treasure map for her, and sent her out with the metal detector to do some searching of her own. She returned with a love note too, along with a different candy heart, glued to a plastic ring, just like the one Cade found. After that, it became their own little tradition to bury love notes and candy hearts in the sand near the house for the other one to find.

"Took turns," Grandma adds with some effort, but with a giant smile. "Him, then me. Back and forth."

"According to what she wrote, this became their most prized reminders that the love they shared was a treasure."

Grandma nods. Now there is a happy little tear in her eye. "Yes," she says resolutely. Then she reaches out and takes my hand, and her eyes begin to water even more. "I miss him, Em'ly."

"I know you do, Grandma. I miss him too."

"I'll see him soon," she whispers.

"Not too soon, I hope."

"Soon," she says again. It doesn't sound like she's giving up, more like she's just certain that her time is drawing near and that she isn't afraid of what's to come.

On the drive home from the nursing facility, I ask for an update on the kids' scores for the third week of their game.

While Ann and Bree pull out their miniature notepads, Cade quickly throws some compliments their way to help bolster his score. "Bree, have I told you today how much I love you? And your hair looks kinda nice — not so poufy, like it normally does."

"Gee, thanks," she replies. "Right back at you."

"And Ann, I love you too. You're smart and funny and pretty and . . . smart."

"Smart twice, eh?" she says, chuckling. "I must be *really* smart. Thanks, Cade."

Cade quickly jots down some marks on his score sheet, then tallies everything up.

"Everyone ready to share?" I ask.

"I am," Cade blurts out. "Ninety, on the dot." Glancing at his sisters on either side of him, he adds, "Beat that."

"OK," says Ann. "I think I will. I'm at one hundred and two."

A look of disappointment crosses Cade's face, but I reassure him that he's still within striking distance, with the rest of the day still to go.

"Bree?" asks Dell. "How about you?"

Bree was all smiles before Ann and Cade read their scores. Now, though, she looks despondent. I'm pretty sure she's on the verge of tears. "Do I have to share?"

Dell is driving, so he can't see her expression. "I think it's only fair," he tells her. "So that Ann and Cade know what they have to do to beat you. Aren't you the one who was so adamant you were going to win this week?"

"Yeah, but . . . I messed up." Now a tear

does escape, cascading down her face until it drops onto her lap.

"It's OK, Bree," I assure her. "You've done wonderfully. You've gotten along with Ann and Cade so well this week, and that's the whole point. Just tell us your score; maybe you're still close enough that you can work extrahard today to catch them."

"Thirty-three," she whispers through more tears. Then she flips to another page in her notebook and rips it out. "Here, Cade," she says, reaching across Ann to hand it to him. "This is for you. Number thirty-four."

Cade reads the message on the paper several times, but looks confused by it. "What is this? A poem?"

"A clue," she says, choking up. "You'll need the metal detector."

"Oh, Bree," I say, reaching behind Dell's seat to touch her knee. "That is the sweetest thing ever. Cade, tell us what it says."

He reads it silently once more, then finally shares it aloud: *"Pirate Boy near haystack's slope, near the needles you must grope, in the sand, for there you'll find, a piece of metal left behind."* His eyes light up now that he understands what it is. "You mean you buried a treasure for me?"

She nods. And sniffles. And wipes her

nose, which is now running in time with her tears.

Dell adjusts the rearview mirror so he can see her too. "Sweetie, that's very thoughtful. Why did you say you messed up?"

"*Because.* After we started the game over — when we stopped counting the negative things — I was really glad that we fought less, but I wanted to do more than just make up compliments all the time, like Cade, or be very polite and say 'thank you' to everyone like Ann. Then we started sneaking around doing little things here and there, like all the chocolates on my pillow and making beds for each other, and that was great too, but I still didn't feel like I was giving Cade or Ann things that would make them really happy, you know? Like, *really* happy. So I thought of some things, and it took a lot of work; it's made me really happy to do them, but . . . maybe a lot of little things is better than a couple big things, because I'm still the loser in the game."

"You're not the loser," I tell her. "Remember, we all win if we're all happier."

"Then why am I crying?"

"It's OK to cry, Bree," Dell tells her. "I've felt that way before too, when things didn't work out the way I planned. It hurts. But that doesn't take away from the things you

421

did for your brother and sister. And what you did for Cade is probably the nicest thing anyone did for anybody all summer."

"No it's not," Bree whimpers. "I did something even bigger for Ann."

Everyone is very quiet for several seconds. Finally Ann asks, "Bree, what 'big thing' did you do for me?"

Looking away, she replies, "I don't want to say."

At first I'm not sure why, but suddenly Ann starts crying too. Then she unbuckles her seat belt so she can more easily wrap her sister up in a hug, which Bree doesn't resist. "It was you," she says, weeping openly now. "You wanted Tanner to notice you . . . but you went to him *for me.* You told him, didn't you, that we saw him with his sister? You told him about my bucket list, and the sea lions. You even told him when we were going to be on the beach, so he could deliver the roses."

"Somebody had to," Bree says sadly. "Before it was too late."

Ann finally lets her go. "And how many points did you take for that, Bree?"

With a shrug, Bree says, "Three. One for clearing things up with Tanner, one for the roses, and one for your date." She sniffles once more. "I was going to give myself another one if you got your first kiss, but that didn't work out. That's why I kept watching you when you got home. I wanted to see if I would get another point, but all you got was a hug."

Ann grabs her once more and squeezes as hard as she can. "What you did is worth at least a thousand points, little sister. I love you so much." When she releases her this time, Ann takes Bree's notebook from her hand and writes *"1,000"* in bold figures along the bottom. Then she turns to Cade. "Good luck catching up to her this week, Cade."

"I know," he mumbles. "She deserves to win." Then Cade takes Bree's notebook too and adds another thousand points for whatever treasure she'd left for him out in the sand.

Bree is all smiles and tears now. So is Ann. So is everybody.

It is an absolutely perfect moment.

Unfortunately, I'm old enough to know that perfect moments can only last so long.

*Life is so unfair . . .*

# CHAPTER 37
## ANN

It is already starting to get hot outside by the time we get home. The beach is filling up with tourists, but it is still a perfect day to be out there in the sun, so everyone puts on their swimsuits and finds a clean towel — and Cade grabs the metal detector — and we head out back. Dad stakes out a nice spot on the dry sand, about fifty yards back from the ocean.

With both parents there, we are given permission to wade in the water, which Cade and Bree are both eager to do, even though it's freezing. They look like they're having a good time splashing around in the waves, but I can't bring myself to join them. Improving my tan from the safety of my towel feels like a much better use of my time, since getting near the water runs the risk of reliving my last open-water experience, which is something I'm not prepared to do.

Once Cade is fully numb, he wants to go find his treasure. For that, I'm eager to participate. Bree hovers close, but doesn't do or say anything to spoil the surprise. Cade's hands are full with the metal detector, so he asks me to keep track of the clue.

*"Pirate Boy near haystack's slope,"* I read as we walk toward Haystack Rock. *"Near the needles you must grope."* I point just ahead of us. "Those little rocks to the left — those are The Needles. Tanner told me that." Once we're in the vicinity of the rocks, I finish reading the clue. "*In the sand, for there you'll find, a piece of metal left behind.* OK, Pirate Boy, turn that thing on and let's find the treasure."

The tide is out far enough that we can go all the way out to The Needles without having to worry about the waves, but I know that won't last long, so I try to hurry him along. Eventually the water will rise beyond my comfort level, and possibly even cover up whatever Bree buried, depending on where she buried it. We choose to start right at the base of the rocks and work our way inland.

For the first twenty minutes, on the wettest part of the beach, we find nothing. Once we start to get farther away from the rocks and tide pools, the detector beeps several times, but all Cade finds are a couple of bottle caps.

Each time he uncovers one of them, Bree giggles or snickers. By our third false alarm she mumbles, "Getting closer."

A few minutes later Mom and Dad come to check on our progress.

Cade proudly shows them the bottle caps he's found. "More for your collection," jokes Mom. "I hope Bree isn't sending you on a wild-goose chase."

"It's here," Bree reassures us. "It won't be long now."

From the corner of my eye I see Dad casually reach out and take Mom's hand in his. "Well, we're going to head up the beach for a while," he says. "Just for a walk. Ann, you're in charge. And you two, no getting wet until we get back."

Cade goes back to work immediately, swinging the metal detector in his normal back-and-forth motion, making sure not to miss any spots in front of him. Within just a few minutes of my parents' departure the alarm goes off, and this time it's much louder than with the bottle caps. Bree is biting her lip, which is a good sign.

Cade and I both kneel in the sand and start digging furiously. At eighteen inches down I find the buried item: a tin Christmas container with a poinsettia-shaped lid.

"I found it in the attic," says Bree before we have it fully unearthed. "I didn't think Grandma Grace would mind."

"No, she won't," I tell her. "She'll love that you put it to good use. When did you bury it?"

"Last night. I snuck out after everyone was asleep."

"That's awesome," says Cade.

Bree is beaming.

When Cade finally lifts the tin out of the sand, he shakes it twice, trying to measure its weight. "What's in here? Air?"

"Just about," Bree giggles. "Open it up."

Cade holds on to the bottom as I use both hands to lift off the lid. Inside is another tiny piece of paper from Bree's spiral notebook.

Nice work, Pirate, almost there! (The treasure isn't buried here.) Go due north for thirty paces, then head west until you face the base of the giant rock of hay, for there your treasure lies today!

"The base of Haystack Rock," I blurt out.

Cade is already two steps ahead. "Hurry up!"

At thirty paces we all pivot toward the

ocean and march straight ahead to Haystack Rock. The inbound tide has already made significant progress; waves are lapping against the rock by the time we get there.

"Do you want to give us a hint where to look?" Cade asks Bree.

"Nope. You've got to use your metal-finder thingy." She glances briefly at the ocean. "You might need to hurry, though. Pretty soon the water will be too high. Or you can just wait until tomorrow."

"No way. I want to find it today."

*Me too . . . but there's no way I'm getting any closer to that water.* "Well, you're on your own, then," I say as I begin backing away from the remnants of a wave that is chasing my feet on the wet sand. "Come show me when you find it."

Not wasting any time, Cade goes right to work, waving his wand along the base of the rock. Periodically, Bree warns him of a big wave rolling in, and then they both go running. It doesn't take long before the only chance Cade has to search is while one wave is going out and before the next one comes in. During one such lull, the detector's alarm sounds with such fury that I can hear it from where I'm sitting. Bree gives a little hoot, all but confirming that he's found it.

Cade is careful to keep an eye on the spot

as another wave chases them back up the beach. As soon as it retreats, he sets down the metal detector and makes a run for it. He jumps down and starts digging, but he's not fast enough.

"Another wave is coming!" Bree shouts.

"I've almost got it! Just a second!"

A few seconds later she yells again, "Cade! Get back!"

Right before the wave hits him, Cade grabs on to a small outcropping on Haystack Rock. The freezing water pours over his skinny bare back, but he holds tight.

After it passes him, Cade stands up in the thigh-deep water, still holding on to the rock. He gives a little victory shout, followed by a quick yelp.

I follow his gaze inland to see that the previous wave is now speeding back out to sea, like it's being sucked through a straw. There is no stopping it . . . and Cade is in its path.

"A sneaker wave," I gasp, recalling the label my Dad gave them. *They sneak up on you . . . and take you back with them.*

As the momentum of the water pushes seaward, Cade loses his grip.

My first worry is that he'll be slammed against the rock, but then I see him moving away from it in the surf. For a lightweight,

Cade is a pretty decent swimmer, but against the fury of the currents he is driftwood, getting tugged and tossed in the foam.

A swarm of butterflies take flight in my stomach.

From somewhere beyond my focus I hear Bree screaming for help.

*There's no one to help him . . . there's no one . . .*

I keep watching as he is sucked under again, gasping and flailing.

*He's drowning . . . Oh, please, God . . . not Cade! Don't take my little brother like this!*

When he goes under again, I pull my eyes toward the horizon, wondering about that girl on the other side of the ocean who I'd very much like to meet someday. But I know I'll never get the chance. For a split second I recall how awful it was to feel my lungs filling with water, how impossibly terrifying it was to be unable to fight it, and to know with certainty that I was going to die.

*That's what Cade is going through . . . Oh God, can't you help him?*

In that moment, I am reminded of something Cade told my mother when he found out I needed a transplant. She'd told him that whatever happens, it's in God's hands, to which he replied, "I hope God has big hands."

*He does have big hands, Cade! He has us! We can be God's hands.*

Just then, I catch a glimpse of a hand, then a head, pop up out of the water thirty yards out. It's brief, but it's enough to reveal his location.

In half a heartbeat, I am running toward the ocean. Not jogging but sprinting at full speed toward the water. There is no time to worry about the consequences now. I know my body cannot handle this kind of exertion, but if I don't give it everything I've got, the consequences for Cade are sure.

In record time I reach the water, but I don't slow down, even as the first frigid wave hits me.

Bree is screaming louder now, for both of us. She's giving directions, but I can't make them out because my ears are full of saltwater. My eyes are burning from salt too, but they are locked on a point forty yards out. As I'm swimming, the butterflies fly faster.

*He's got to be here! Push harder! This is why you're a swimmer, Ann. This is why you're the big sister.*

The ocean is fierce, but so am I. I move through the waves like I am part of it. My strokes are as sure and strong as they ever were, as though I've been training for this meet every day of my life.

When I reach the spot where I last saw him, I dive under, feeling around for anything. When I come up, Bree is still screaming something. I pause to look, and see that she is pointing north. I turn just in time to see Cade's face go under again, twenty yards up.

In what feels like no time at all, I am there, diving again beneath the surface. I hold my breath as long as I can, groping blindly in every direction. At the last possible moment, I feel a clump of hair, attached to a head. Then I have him by the neck and I'm pulling him up. I get him to the surface and continue to pull toward shore.

Dragging him with me, against the undercurrents, is killing me. *Literally.* The butterflies in my stomach move up into my chest, and suddenly they are swarming bees.

One of them bites me, then another and another, but I press on. I feel Cade trying to kick, but I know it is my power alone that will save us. There is no lifeguard on this beach. There is nobody but me.

Eventually we're aided by a wave that sends us sprawling into the shallows. As the water recedes, we are once again on wet sand. Bree and a stranger are right there to help pull us farther up onto the beach, beyond the ocean's deadly reach.

Cade is safe, but still very shaken — and shaking. As he tries to get up on his knees, he vomits a bunch of saltwater. I can tell it hurts — probably even burns — but the color is returning to his face.

I can't catch my breath, so I have to lie down on my back. I'm clutching my chest, but ignoring the pain. I turn my head so I can still see my brother. "You OK?" I ask, gasping.

He nods wearily. "I'm so sorry."

I take a deep breath, still starving for air. "Don't be . . . It felt nice . . . to swim." My chest heaves in and out several times. Once I've got a little more air in me, I finish my thought. "One more item . . . off my bucket list."

# CHAPTER 38
## CADE

I hate the taste of salt. I also hate the taste of puke. But I love the taste of air, so I'll put up with the other awful tastes for now. I feel weak, but weak is a lot better than dead. Thanks to my sister, I'm alive!

*Oh man, I'm so lucky . . . to have a big sister.*

From behind me I hear Dad calling out. When I turn around, he and Mom are running up the beach about fifty yards away. When they get there, the man who helped us onto the beach tells them what he saw.

Bree is crying.

The burn of salt in my throat makes me cough a lot, but I don't mind. *I'm alive!*

Ann is holding on to her chest kind of funny, and she can't seem to catch her breath.

*Oh man, I hope she's OK.*

"My daughter has a serious heart condition," Dad says. "She needs an ambulance."

Dad has a cell phone on him, so he calls

nine-one-one. The nearest ambulance service is in Seaside; they tell him they'll be
here in fifteen minutes. Dad gives the ad-
dress of our beach house, and then he
scoops up Ann in one motion and carries
her all the way inside.

The rest of us follow, not bothering to pick
up our towels on the beach.

In the house, while my parents tend to
Ann on the couch, Bree puts on a T-shirt
and shoes.

"What are you up to?" Mom asks her.

"I have to tell Tanner."

"That can wait."

"No! I have to. This is my fault and . . .
and he would want to see her before they
take her away."

I know what she really means: *He would
want to see her in case she dies.*

*"Please,"* says Bree, begging.

"Well, you can't go alone."

"I'll go!" I shout, just wanting to do
anything to help.

Mom thinks about it for a moment, then
agrees.

I throw on a dry shirt, grab my sneakers
by the door, and then Bree and I tear off
down the street toward the center of town.
In a matter of minutes we're at the candy
store. Tanner is behind the counter with an

older man, who must be the owner.

"Ann needs you!" Bree says right away.

The man and Tanner seem startled at first. Then Tanner realizes that this isn't an ordinary visit. "What's wrong?"

"She saved me from drowning," I blurt out, "and now her heart is hurting. They called an ambulance!"

In one giant step Tanner flies around the corner of the candy display. "Where is she?"

"At the house," Bree says, panting.

Without waiting to find out more, Tanner is gone.

Bree and I are both out of breath, but we chase after him. Out on the sidewalk, we can hear the sound of a siren heading through the middle of town.

"Tanner! Wait!" Bree calls before he can get too far.

He slows down so we can catch up.

Bree forces out her words between gasps for air. "I need you . . . to do something."

"Anything."

"My sister needs . . . her first kiss," she says. "Don't let her die . . . without that."

Tanner tries to smile. "I'll see what I can do." He takes off running again.

"Promise me!" she shouts.

"I will," he yells back as he bolts across the busiest intersection. I can tell that the ambulance is very close, probably just around the corner, and approaching fast.

All of the cars on the cross street are pulling to the side of the road to let the ambulance through. Bree has a longer stride than me, so she's maybe ten yards ahead. When she reaches the intersection, she follows Tanner's lead and goes straight through.

*No! Stop!* "Bree! Look out!"

The next few seconds are the longest of my life — even longer than nearly drowning.

When Bree rushes into the road, she doesn't see that not all of the cars got out of the way of the ambulance. But I can see perfectly, and I know immediately what is about to happen.

It's not fair that I can't stop it.

It's not fair that the driver of the red car doesn't get out of the way when he hears the sirens.

It's not fair that he speeds up to get through the intersection before the other cars, and that he doesn't see Bree until it's too late.

It's not fair that I have to see it happen.

Life is not fair.

I don't know why, but as I shout at Bree, my focus is on her feet, and my eyes somehow stay glued to her shoes. Unfortunately, her shoes don't stay glued to her feet. On impact, one shoe flips up over the back of the car, and the other is whipped at least forty feet away, in Tanner's direction, on the opposite side of the intersection.

With the horror in front of me, I freeze. I don't know what else to do. I can't move my feet. I'm the closest person to the accident, but I'm stuck at the edge of the sidewalk.

*I want to puke again, like I did back on the beach.*

From the sideline, I watch as Tanner turns and runs back to the scene. He is the first one to reach Bree.

The ambulance slows to a stop; its siren is still blaring as a paramedic jumps out of the passenger side. He kneels beside Bree, on the opposite side of Tanner, then signals something to the driver and the siren cuts off.

I stay for a minute as they begin working on her. Then my feet thaw and I take off running for home, leaving Tanner and Bree there in the middle of the road with the paramedics.

As I'm running, I want to die, because I know I'm to blame. If I had just waited to dig up Bree's treasure when the tide was out, none of this would have happened. Or if I'd listened to Bree and waited for the big wave to pass, she'd be fine right now. Instead, I got greedy, got sucked out to sea, nearly drowned. Now both of my sisters are in trouble, because of me.

What do I do if Ann is already dead when I get home?

What if Bree is dead too? How do I explain to my family what happened to her? *How do I tell them this is all my fault?*

I slow for the last few steps leading up to the porch, but I know I can't turn back.

I can hear Dad yelling inside the house. "Why isn't the ambulance here yet? They should be here!"

"Calm down, Dell," my mom says as I push open the door and rush inside. "I heard the sirens. They'll be here."

"Yeah, Dad, chill," whispers Ann. Her voice is weak. She looks worse than she did before. "It'll be here in a second."

"No," I tell them softly. "It might take a little longer . . ."

Fifteen minutes later I wipe a flood of tears from my eyes so I can see the ambulance pull away with *both* of my sisters in the back. There is no room for the rest of us, and nothing we can do to help anyway. All we can do is watch them go, and pray for a miracle.

As soon as we've gathered a few things, we climb into Dad's car so we can hurry off to the emergency room.

"It isn't fair," I tell myself over and over while staring blankly out the car window on the drive to the Seaside hospital.

"Life is many wondrous things," mumbles my dad, "but fair isn't one of them."

# CHAPTER 39
## ANN

I know my life depends on me being in the ambulance right now, but every last ounce of me wants to be somewhere else. Just seeing Bree lying there — barely alive — hurts more than any physical pain I've ever endured.

*Why did you have to run across the road? Please don't die, Bree! We still have a game to play . . .*

Though it's hard talking through the oxygen mask they have over my face, the whole way to the hospital I keep telling her to hang in there, that it's going to be OK. She doesn't respond. Bree has an oxygen mask too, but even though it's covering part of her face, I can tell that she's in a bad way, because her cheeks and forehead are all swollen and bloody.

*Please wake up, Bree! Please!*

I keep feeling the biting sensation inside my chest as we're screaming along the highway, but it doesn't bother me much. The only thing that matters right now is Bree, and getting her safely to the hospital.

Once we arrive, we're taken immediately in different directions — her to a trauma unit, and me to a cardiologist.

By the time my parents arrive, both sets of doctors have come to separate conclusions that the tiny coastal hospital lacks the expertise to properly treat either of us.

"What exactly is wrong with Bree?" I overhear my dad ask the doctor.

"Well . . . everything," comes the sobering reply. "Spleen, lung, bones, and internal bleeding. But mostly what we're worried about — and what we're just not staffed to handle — is the brain. She's taken quite a hit, and the swelling is extensive. We've treated the pressure, but she'll be better off at a hospital in Portland."

He glances over at me. "And Ann?"

"We've already contacted her doctors at Saint Vincent's. They're expecting her. We're sending both girls there just as soon as the Life Flight crew is ready."

It doesn't take long before Bree and I are wheeled, side by side, to a red-and-white helicopter and are on our way back to Portland. It's my first-ever helicopter ride, but I hate it. I want to enjoy it, but I can't stop crying.

Bree still isn't moving.

She won't talk to me.

Doesn't even make a sound.

The medics tell me I need to calm down, that my crying is only making things worse on my heart, but I can't stop.

*That's my sister lying there!*

My dad is with us in the helicopter, and he, too, keeps telling me not to worry, that everything is going to work out, but how can he know?

The butterflies in my stomach say not to trust him.

To help calm me — and my butterflies — they eventually inject something into my IV, and then the world fades . . .

The next day I wake up in a tiny room in a Portland hospital. My vision is fuzzy at first, but my ears work fine, which is probably why the first thing I recognize is the sound of my mom crying.

She stops when she realizes I'm awake.

When I ask her what's wrong, she says, "Nothing," but I know it's a lie.

When I ask her how I'm doing, she says, "You've been better, but you were a lot worse yesterday afternoon. The doctors aren't quite sure how your heart kept going, but it did, and you're stable now."

My eyes are focusing fine now. I look down to find all sorts of wires and gizmos running in and out of me. "So . . . I'm going to make it?"

"You still need a transplant," she says carefully, "but for now, they think you're OK. At least, you're in no more imminent danger than you were before. But just to be sure, they're hoping to keep you in their sights until they find a heart. You're number one on the list now, so that's good. Just need to find a match."

Mom was choking up as she spoke, but now, all of sudden, she's sobbing.

"What's wrong?"

There is a box of tissues next to her chair. She grabs a handful and dabs at her eyes. "Well," she starts, trying hard to hold it together, "it turns out there's another girl in the hospital right now . . . who's a very good match for you." A flood of giant tears flow from her eyes. She dabs again and continues, keeping her gaze on the floor. "The girl is alive, but she's . . . not doing well. There's a good chance she won't make it. And so if she dies, well . . . it means you'll have your new heart."

Now Mom finally looks up at me, and I see something in her eyes that makes my stomach turn. I've never seen anyone so broken in all my life. Suddenly it hits me. "You mean . . . *Bree* is a match?"

Now I'm bawling too. Mom is so stricken that she just buries her face in her hands.

As the enormity of the situation overcomes me, I have to lie back on my pillow. I can't look at my mother right now, all broken and torn. I close my eyes, squeezing out the last remaining tears, and lie there for what feels like forever, drowning in the thoughts that fill my head.

I've dreamed of finding a donor for months, but not like this. This is all wrong. I'd honestly rather die than live with my sister's heart beating in my chest.

*Any heart but hers! God, do you hear me? Any heart but Bree's! If you take her, you have to take me too!*

What good would a new heart do me anyway if I can't enjoy my new lease on life with my little sister? I need a heart to be able to swim and run again, but why bother if I can't swim circles around Bree in the pool, or run her out of my room when she gets into my stuff?

*No, this is all wrong.*

"I don't want it," I tell my mom eventually. "If she doesn't make it, give her heart to someone else."

"You know she'd want you to have it, right? Just like she wanted you to have that date with Tanner."

I can't respond. I can't entertain the thought right now. I know Mom is right, but it hurts too much to admit, because then I might also have to admit that the only reason Bree is in this condition is . . .

*Because she loves me.*

There is a quiet rapping on the door. A second later my dad pokes his head in and then enters all the way. Cade isn't far behind.

Dad comes straight for my bed and gives me a hug. I can tell he's been crying too.

After he lets go of me, he bends down next to Mom and wraps his arms around her, as though he's somehow shielding her from the awfulness of the situation.

"How is she?" asks Mom.

"The same."

"One of us should be upstairs with her. In case she wakes up."

*Or in case she doesn't.*

"I know," Dad says. "We should all be with her. Which is why I've gotten approval to have Ann moved up to Bree's room. Some nurses should be here shortly to wheel her up."

I lie back down on my pillow and close

my eyes. This is all so surreal; I wish closing my eyes would just make it all go away. I remember when we were in Grandma Grace's room not too long ago, when she nearly died, and I was kind of curious to see what would happen. Well, now I don't feel that way at all. They are taking me to my sister's room, so we can be with her in her darkest hour, but I can't bear the thought of being there should she pass away.

*Please, God, not my sister . . .*

# CHAPTER 40
# CADE

Four days. That's how long we've been at the hospital. Not straight through — we've gone home a couple times to change clothes and stuff — but mostly we've just been here hanging out with Ann and Bree.

I hate hospitals.

I hate hospital food.

I hate seeing wheelchairs in the hallway that I'm not allowed to sit in.

But mostly, I hate seeing my sisters the way they are.

They say Ann is stable, but she looks a lot weaker than she did when she was at the beach. I think if she was really as good as she was before, they'd let her go home. But it sounds like they are going to keep her until they can "harvest" an organ from a donor.

A donor like Bree.

*I really hate hospitals.*

Ann looks bad enough, but compared to

Ann, Bree looks *awful.* It's nice that they're in the same room and stuff, so we can all be together, but I kinda don't like to look at Bree, because her face is all messed up. They've shaved several spots on her head where they had to drill into her skull to release the pressure.

*Gross.*

Every time I look at her injuries, I remember how sick I felt when I saw that speeding car. I can't get the image out of my head — watching her shoes fly and seeing her body bounce.

"Can I go for a walk?" I ask my parents early in the evening of day four. "I need some fresh air."

"You won't get lost?" asks Mom.

I roll my eyes and drop my chin. "I could give tours of this place."

"Just . . . be careful," says Dad. "And don't be gone too long."

While I'm wandering the halls, I stop by a vending machine and drop three quarters in for a pack of gum. Then I continue my journey. I know where I want to go, but it's on the other end of the hospital and down several floors. Along the way, I am reminded over and over again how life isn't fair. Each room I pass has some other sorry soul who is right in the middle of lots of unfairness.

In one room there is an old man with tubes hanging out his nose who looks like he's already dead. The most unfair part is that there's nobody there with him.

In the next room there's a baby in an incubator with thick scars down her chest like Ann's, only newer. Two young parents are crying over her.

A couple rooms farther, a priest is saying a prayer beside a bed, with family members gathered around.

In a waiting room, I hear a crying husband asking for news about his wife. His two teenage daughters are clinging to him. All of their faces are wet from tears.

The elevator is superslow. On my way down, my thoughts return to Bree and Ann. Everyone wants Bree to live, and yet . . . if she dies, it's good news for Ann. Everyone wants Ann to live too, which she will, for sure, if Bree dies.

*Talk about unfair!*

When the elevator opens, I'm in the lobby of the emergency room. I've been itching to get down here for a couple of days now, but my parents made me stay with them. I take a seat near a window, open up my pack of gum, and start to chew.

After a little while I build up the nerve to ask one of the nurses at the desk about something that's been on my mind. "Excuse me. Um . . . can you tell me, like . . . how many people die here each day?"

She looks horrified. "What? That's an awful thing to ask, young man. Go find your parents. You shouldn't be up here at the desk."

Is it such an awful thing to ask? I just want to know what the odds are of a new heart coming in for my sister. Someone's heart other than Bree's, I mean.

I take a seat again near the window. Maybe thirty minutes later, the nurse behind the desk stands up all excited and makes a call for assistance. A minute later several people in medical scrubs begin gathering by the ambulance entrance. A minute after that I see the lights of an ambulance zooming up the road. It pulls right past me and stops at the door. A teenage girl is pulled from the back of the ambulance and wheeled into the hospital, where she is quickly carted off, surrounded by the blue scrubs.

Five minutes later, another ambulance pulls up, only this one doesn't have its lights on. Only one person from the hospital goes outside to help the medics. The gurney is covered up with a thick white sheet. Nobody is hurrying. Then the nurse asks, "Is that

Mr. Donor?"

The medics look at each other, confused for a moment, and then they get what she's asking. "Yeah, his license says he's a full organ donor. He's all yours."

*A donor?*

This is what I came downstairs for, what I hoped to see, only now I don't want to see it.

*A dead body.*

Staring at the sheet as it passes by, I suddenly wish I hadn't come to the ER, or wanted to know how many people die here each day. It really doesn't matter to me anymore. As far as I'm concerned, one is too many.

*Especially if that one is my sister.*

*Or my other sister.*

# CHAPTER 41
## EMILY

"Where have you been?" I ask Cade as soon as he comes into the room. I am reminded that Ann is asleep on her bed, so in a quieter — but firm — voice, I add, "Your father is out looking for you right now. You're in big trouble when he gets back. You've been gone over an hour."

"I was looking for . . . something." The way he says it tells me there's definitely more to this story.

"What 'something'?"

"You'll be mad."

"I promise I won't."

"Can I ask a question first?"

I wave him over to sit next to me. "Anything."

"OK. Does God pick and choose?"

"Pick and choose what?"

"*People.* You know . . . who lives and dies."

"Well . . . yes, I suppose he does. Why do you ask?"

" 'Cuz you're always saying that life's not fair, and people dying is like the unfairest thing of all. But you also say that whatever happens, we have to trust God, because he has a plan that we don't always understand. So . . . maybe life's not really unfair at all. Maybe *God* is unfair."

His comment hits me like a load of bricks. I pull him closer, wishing he didn't have to witness all of this *unfairness* in our lives right now. There's so much I want to say to him, but as I look at my daughters lying peacefully on what could very well be their deathbeds, the words are slow coming.

Like a flash before my eyes, I am reminded of the story I told the kids about the train engineer who had to choose between saving his own son and saving a whole trainload of strangers. With unbelievable grace, he chose to save the strangers on the train, sacrificing his only son in the process. As the image dissipates in my mind, a strange sense of peace courses through me. Before, when I first told the kids about it, I was so sure that I could never do that — never pull the lever that would send a train plowing into my own little child while I stood helpless and watched. But now, seeing both of my daughters side-by-side on their beds, is this so much different? What if instead of lying in bed, one of my daughters was on the train and one was on the tracks, and I knew that either Ann or Bree *had* to die so the other could live? Could I make that call? How on earth could I choose which one should live?

Or what if that trainload of people weren't strangers to me at all? What if they were my family? What if Dell and Cade and Ann were on the train, and it was Bree alone on the tracks?

*It would still be unbelievably hard . . . but the choice would be clear.*

Through a fresh round of tears, I tell my son, "I was wrong, Cade. I've been wrong all along. Life *is* fair, it just doesn't always seem so in the moment. And God is fair too, though I'll admit he has to make some very tough choices every single day." I squeeze a little harder, until he finally resists.

"Maybe you're right," he says at length, "Because he did finally find a donor for Ann." He pauses and sighs. "But I doubt that guy's family is going to think it's very fair."

Now I sit straight up and square his face to mine. "What are you talking about?"

"I went down to watch for ambulances in the emergency room. I saw them bring in a dead body, and they said he was a donor."

"You sure they said 'donor' and not

'goner'?"

"Uh-huh."

My anxiety is shooting through the roof! "Well, that doesn't mean — Cade, just because someone is an organ donor doesn't mean their genetic makeup will be a good match for Ann."

"But it would be cool, right?"

I glance at Ann, then at Bree. "Yeah. The coolest. But don't get your hopes up, kiddo."

"Yeah, I know. But I'm kinda pretty sure, Mom. After they took the dead guy away, I came back upstairs, and I was passing the nurses down by their little station and I overheard them talking. Someone mentioned Ann's name and she said they just got a heart in that'll work."

I can't breathe.

*If my pirate-child is playing some sort of a joke, I may never forgive him.*

"Cade, are you sure?"

He nods. "I bet they'll be here any minute."

My own heart leaps when the door flies open thirty seconds later. Only it isn't the nurses or a doctor. It's Dell. "Oh good, he's back," he says, sounding at once relieved and excited. Then his eyes light up as bright as they will go. "You guys are never going to believe this . . ."

My face is suddenly dripping with the happiest tears I've ever cried. "They found a heart," I tell him.

"How did you know?"

I squeeze Cade as hard as I possibly can. "I have my sources."

My eyes bounce from Dell to Ann and finally land on Bree — sweet, precious, broken Bree.

*Now we just need one more miracle . . .*

# Chapter 42
## Ann

I remember my doctor sitting on the chair beside my bed, way back before summer started, when he first told me I would need a transplant. He said it was natural to be scared, and that I might even feel uncomfortable with the thought of having someone else's heart beating inside me. But he promised me, in no uncertain terms, that once I had a new heart, I would not feel any different.

My doctor was wrong.

When I came out of surgery three days ago, the first thing I felt was the weight. Not the weight of the heart, exactly. Physically it feels the same. It's more like a weight on my soul, reminding me with every pulse that someone else's life is over, and mine just sort of rebooted.

So yes, I feel different now. I feel lucky and humbled, and at times a little sad and guilty.

I found out just today that the guy who "donated" his heart was in his twenties. No wife or kids, so that's good . . . I guess. He was riding his motorcycle on some country road when a teenager drifted lanes and hit him head on. Apparently Cade saw both of them when they arrived at the hospital. The girl is still in bad shape, but word is that she's probably going to make it.

Bree, on the other hand, remains a question mark. We're still sharing a room in the ICU, so at least I can be close to her, but she still hasn't woken up. The doctors claim the swelling in her brain has gone down a lot. If Bree's still "there," we should start to see progress soon.

Mom and Dad seem a little torn at the moment, and I can't blame them. They're superhappy that I'm on the mend, but nervous to death about my sister. Laughter and tears — that pretty much sums up every moment that they're here in our room.

After dinner Mom takes Cade home for a good night's sleep. Dad wants to stick around a little longer.

"How you holding up?" he asks after they're gone.

"Ah . . . you know. I'm OK."

"I want the truth, Ann. What's on your

mind? You've been kind of up and down today."

"Not just me," I point out.

He smiles and nods, then glances at Bree and all of her machines and monitors. "True. I suppose we all have."

I watch for a moment as Bree's chest rises, then falls. Then rises again, and falls. "Actually . . . there is something."

He scoots closer to my bed. "I'm all ears."

"I was wondering about the Winner's Game. Are you and Mom still playing?"

With a grin, he pulls his little notepad from his back pocket. "We've been focused on other things this week, so we've stopped scoring — or at least I have. But after we get through this stuff with you girls, I really want to start up again."

"But what if Bree doesn't make it?"

"She will."

"But what if?"

"Then we'll still play. I don't want anything to ever come between your mother and me again."

I gently run a finger down the outside of my chest, feeling the bandages beneath. "You mean like last time, when me and my heart came between you?"

He gives me a puzzled look. "Why would you say that? What happened to your heart was out of your control. Your mother and I didn't need to drift apart like we did just because of that. Our problems were our problems, not yours, Ann."

I nod that I understand, though part of me is reluctant to believe it.

"Anything else?" he asks.

I look at Bree again. There's a scar on her forehead that may never go away. If she ever wakes up, she'll have that as a constant reminder that when she tried doing something nice for me, it backfired. I've had so many questions since she got hurt, I don't even know where to begin.

*If she lives, will she resent me?*

*Will she regret what she did?*

*Will she still love me?*

*Will she want to finish our game?*

*If she dies, does that mean our Winner's Game has no winner?*

"Ann? You're kind of zoning out."

*Yeah, I guess I am.* My gaze moves from Bree's face to her heart monitor. It's a graph I am all too familiar with from past and present experience. "Sorry. I was just thinking."

"About . . . ?"

I shrug. "About *why*? When it was me whose life was at risk, I thought I understood. I'd already died once anyway, so I

461

was kind of OK with the fact that I might die again. But now that it's Bree? It just doesn't make any sense anymore. Why does it have to be like this? Why did I have to have a heart problem in the first place? And why didn't my earlier surgeries fix me? If they had, Bree would be fine. We would never have gone to the beach for the summer, I wouldn't have met Tanner, and Bree wouldn't have gone running off looking for him." I place my hand over my new and improved heart. "Just . . . lots of whys."

He nods. "Is that it?"

"Well . . . no. I've been thinking a lot about my new heart. I'm struggling to understand why that guy had to crash on his motorcycle. Why did the girl have to hit him? Why am I the lucky one who is sitting here with a beating heart, while he's having a funeral?" I pause to take a breath, then finish with one last question. "Why does one person have to die for another one to live? I used to think I knew the answer, but now that it's more real — now that someone is actually dead and I'm still breathing — I'm having a hard time remembering what I thought the answer was."

Dad is smiling patiently. He reaches up and takes my hand. "Perfectly reasonable questions, Ann. I guess I don't know the answers to all of them, but I will say this. *Life is tenuous at best.* It's fragile. And it's impossibly short, no matter how long you live. The thing that's easy to forget is that nobody was meant to live forever — not in this life anyway. We're here, and then we move on, some of us faster than others. But once in a while, those who are leaving are able to give a wonderful gift of life to someone else, like you getting the heart. But that doesn't change the fact that everyone — you, me, your mother, Grandma Grace, and yes, the guy on the motorcycle — we're all going to die sometime."

"And Bree," I moan, getting choked up.

"Yes," he whispers. "And Bree."

I can feel my cheeks getting hot. And wet. "I think that's what's been bothering me the most. I wouldn't mind if it was me dying — Heck, I thought for sure I was going to die when I went out in the ocean after Cade. But every time I look over at Bree, I worry that maybe it's her turn instead of mine, and I'm just not sure I'm ready for that."

"Me neither," he says, as much to himself as to me.

Dad hangs out until the nurses come around for their nine-o'clock checks on me and Bree. I think he's thinking — or wishing — that their assessment will show that Bree has improved, but no such luck.

"Status quo," says the chief nurse with a grimace after she's taken all of Bree's vitals. "Sorry, Mr. Bennett. You probably hoped to hear something else, but hang in there. You never know what tomorrow brings."

*So true.*

Heck, you never even know what today brings, let alone tomorrow! Like, one day you wake up hoping to set state swimming records, and later the same day you end up drowning at the bottom of a pool.

Or one day you go in for a routine checkup, just to see if your medicines and therapies are working, and you find out you're going to need a transplant.

Or one day you're riding your motorcycle down the road, enjoying the sun and the wind, and the next thing you're lending your spare parts to the sick girl on the sixth floor with the bum heart.

Or in Bree's case, one day you wake up with some brilliant plan for how you're going to win a game, and you don't even realize it but you've easily done the best job truly loving your siblings and making them feel special, but you wind up broken and bent in the back of an ambulance, then lying in the ICU beside your sister, just waiting to die.

*So, yeah . . . you never know what tomorrow brings . . .*

Usually I feel like the nurses wake me up every hour throughout the night and by the time morning comes I'm more tired than when I fell asleep. But not this time! Somehow I manage to sleep though their overnight checks, which is a miracle. For the first time since Cannon Beach, I wake up feeling completely rested.

These past few days I've gotten used to wishing Bree a good morning as soon as I wake up, even though she never responds. So first thing I do is rub the tired out of my eyes and roll over to face her. "Hey, Breezy, good —"

*She's gone. Her bed. Her monitors. Everything . . . gone.*

In a panic, I hit the red button next to my bed.

A minute later, I'm still alone in my room.

I can't take it. I climb out of my bed, exit the room in pajamas and bare feet, and rush down the hall.

Toward the end, before the hallway turns, I see Mom and Dad talking to a doctor outside the waiting area.

*What are they doing here so early? This*

*can't be good . . .*

As I pick up my pace, the doctor turns and leaves in the opposite direction. Mom is breaking down in tears. Dad is crying too. He wraps his arms around her in a tight embrace.

"Where is she?" I ask tentatively as I approach. "Where is Bree? Why did they take her?"

My questions catch my parents by surprise. Mom unwraps herself from Dad's arms and opens hers up for me. "It's OK," she whispers in my ear while we're hugging. "It's going to be OK."

# CHAPTER 43
## CADE

The summer is almost over, which totally blows. It feels like I've lived at the hospital all summer long. I wish we'd stayed longer in Cannon Beach, but oh well.

With only one weekend left before school starts, Mom and Dad decided they need to finally take their date for the winner of their first week of the Winner's Game — apparently Dad gave Mom more than a hundred kisses on the cheek right before they counted the scores, so he's the winner, though Mom says she secretly won.

"What sounds good to you?" Dad asks my mom as they put on their jackets.

"Chinese."

"Mexican it is," he jokes. "Kids, don't wait up. We might be very late."

"Oh, one more thing," says Mom. "Ann, a little bird told me that a guest might stop by later. So if the doorbell rings, I suggest you answer it."

They aren't gone thirty minutes when a car pulls into the driveway.

I'm dying to know who it is, but Mom said Ann should answer it, so I stay parked in front of the TV. When I see who is standing on the front porch, I quickly turn down the volume.

"Look at you," says Tanner. "As good as new." He pauses, focusing on her head. "Did you color your hair?"

"Yeah," she says, grinning from ear to ear. "Just a few highlights. It was on my bucket list. But what are you doing here?"

He smiles. "I have two very important things for you." He holds out a familiar notebook. Its tiny pen is still tucked inside the spiral binding. "It was Bree's. It was next to her on the street, and it got left there when they took her away."

Now I turn the TV completely off.

"Wow," she says softly, as though she's holding something sacred. "I can't believe it. We all thought this was lost." She flips to the first page, smiles, and then asks, "What's the other thing?"

Without waiting, or asking, or anything, he leans in and gives her a kiss. Not on the cheek. I'm talking *a kiss*.

Ann is totally blushing by the time it is over. Heck, I'm probably blushing too.

*Don't they know I'm right here watching?*

A second later her head snaps around and we stare at each other for several moments, both of us feeling a little embarrassed. Then she turns back to Tanner. "What was that for?"

"For Bree. Right before the accident she made me promise that I would give you your first kiss."

Ann places her hands on her hips. "Well, it's been over a month. What makes you think somebody else didn't beat you to it?"

His face drops instantly. "Did they?"

"No," she says with a giggle. "You got the first. And if you're lucky, you might get the second."

This time she reaches up and kisses him!

This time I have to close my eyes.

When I open them, Bree is crossing the room in her wheelchair with a giant smile on her face. "Ha!" she says. "B-t-dubs, I'm totally going to win now. That was way more than a one-point kiss. I should get like a bazillion."

"*Two* bazillion," says Ann, "because that was our second kiss."

"Oh man, I missed the first one? Why didn't someone tell me? I was stuck in the bathroom trying to get my sweats up over this stupid cast."

"It's probably better that you didn't see," Ann tells her. "This way you'll have more to look forward to with your own first kiss . . . in, like, six or seven years."

"*Six or —* ? Try, like, one year. Or less." That earns a good laugh from everyone.

Tanner can't stay long, but he does come in and hang out for a bit. One of the first things he comments on is Bree's fuzzy pink slippers. "Those are nice," he says, pointing at her feet on the wheelchair. "Are they new?"

"Yeah," says Bree. "I just got them the other day when I finally came home from the hospital. My best friend has a pair just like them, and she picked them out for me." She glances at Ann and smiles.

Bree doesn't bother telling Tanner that not only did Ann pick out the slippers but she paid for them herself.

When I see my sisters smiling at each other, it's hard to believe that our family is still, like, . . . complete. One night we left the hospital not knowing what was going to happen to Bree, and the next morning, very early, my parents got a call that she was starting to wake up. They yanked me out of bed, and off we went to be with her. Because she still needed a lot of medical attention, they took her out of Ann's room and moved her to a place where they could have lots of doctors and stuff without bothering Ann.

That was almost three weeks ago.

Ann's recovery from surgery is going much quicker than I would have thought. She can't run or anything yet, but even within a few days at the hospital she was already getting up and around, and now she's able to do light chores at home. And apparently she's well enough to kiss!

*Yuck.*

Bree still has a long way to go. She'll need lots of physical therapy after she's out of the wheelchair, but I don't expect any of that to really slow her down. Heck, I wouldn't bc at all surprised if she's not already thinking about how she can get her wheelchair to the top of the hill at the park for a quick ride down.

No, I take that back. She's probably thinking about how she can get *me* to ride down the hill in her wheelchair. And honestly . . . it sounds like a lot of fun.

Dad and Mom don't get home until almost midnight. Ann and I are asleep on the couch in front of the television when they come in. Bree is in her wheelchair on the other side of Ann.

"Kids," Dad says. "Wake up. We want to

show you something."

We all exchange confused looks as we make our way to the front door to look out at the driveway. There, parked behind Mom's minivan, is the Walrus.

"We had dinner at the Stephanie Inn," Mom explains, "and picked this up on the way home."

"Once you have your license, it's yours to use," Dad tells Ann. "At least until Bree is old enough to drive. And then eventually it'll be Cade's turn."

All I can say is, "Whoa."

"Totes awesome!" adds Bree.

Ann is kinda stunned. "For real?"

"For real," says Mom. "With one stipulation."

"Anything."

Mom smiles. "Every new driver needs to give it a new name."

Ann nods. Then she touches her chest with one hand. "That's easy," she whispers. "I'll call it Stan."

"Stan?" I ask. I've never known anyone named Stan. "What kind of a dumb name is that? I thought maybe you'd call it Tanner."

She takes a deep breath and sighs. "Tanner has my heart, Cade. At least for now. But Stan . . . Stan was my donor. I never asked for it, yet he gave me his heart freely."

The next Friday, after the first week of school, Mom picks me up right at the final bell so we can take a quick trip out to the coast. Ann and Bree want to go too, but they aren't up for the drive. Our first stop in Cannon Beach is at Grandma Grace's nursing facility.

As usual, Grandma isn't doing well, so it's not much of a conversation.

"Grandma, it's me, Emily."

She blinks that she understands. Then she says, "You came."

"Yes, we came." Mom scoots closer. "I have some news. Ann got her new heart."

Grandma's eyes light up for a moment, but then they fizzle, like she senses that there's more news.

"Bree, however, was in an accident. We probably should have sent word, but I didn't want to worry you. She was hit by a car right here in Cannon Beach, but had to be taken to Portland for treatment, which is why we haven't been around lately. But . . . she's doing a lot better. She's lucky, Grandma. Really lucky to be alive. It was touch and go for a while."

"Not luck," Grandma mumbles. Then she looks right at me, and clear as day she says,

"It's always in God's hands."

"That's right, Grandma," I tell her. "And God has very big hands."

Grandma's tired eyes are dropping, like they always do when she's had enough. She takes a deep breath through her oxygen tube, then closes her eyes all the way.

Mom needs a few things from the beach house before we leave town, so that's our second stop. While she's inside gathering them, I sneak outside to the beach. The tide is way out, so I run down to the base of Haystack Rock and begin digging in the sand. A minute later I find another Christmas tin, this one decorated with Santa. It could easily hold a dozen sugar cookies, but the weight of it feels like there's nothing in it.

When I open the lid, there is a piece of Bree's art-stock paper inside. It's rolled into a scroll and bound in the middle with a rubber band. I dry my wet hands on my shirt and brush off all the extra sand, just to make sure I don't ruin whatever it is, and then I gently roll the rubber band to one end.

On the inside of the paper is a beautiful sketch of our family, mostly done in pencil. Bree, with her short hair, is at the center. To her left are my parents, hand in hand. Bree has her arm around Ann's shoulder, and

Ann has ahold of me. The only splashes of color on the entire page are the vibrant red hearts on everyone's chests.

At the top of the page, centered above our heads, are the words, *"For where your treasure is, there will your heart be also."*

Beneath the sketch, in smaller letters, it says, *"My heart is with my family."*

Maybe it's silly or dumb, and I probably wouldn't tell my friends this, but seeing what Bree made for me — and the fact that she hid this treasure in the sand for me to find — makes me smile on the inside.

I'm superlucky to have older sisters.

I have a treasure.

*I'm rich!*

# EPILOGUE:
## EMILY

It's been a long six months . . . but we have survived. And that's saying something!

Ann's heart is better than ever — she's even started swimming again, though not competitively. We're trying to ease her back into a normal life — not pushing too hard, but neither are we pulling back on the reins so much that she feels stymied.

Last weekend was her winter formal at school. She invited Tanner to go with her, and she described the evening as "magical." I was surprised when she chose a gown that revealed part of the scar on her chest. "It's who I am," she said. "It's part of me, so why should I hide it?"

I guess she has a point . . . and I couldn't be prouder. She's a beautiful young woman, and I'm glad she's starting to recognize that.

Bree moved from wheelchair to crutches to a walking boot in record time. At the end of the month she'll get the boot off, and then it's back to normal. Part of her recent therapy has been swimming with Ann, which has been great for both of them. Now Bree swears that not only is she going to get a first kiss at an earlier age than Ann did but she's also going to break all of her swimming records.

Ah . . . sibling rivalry.

Then there's Cade, who continues to be a little pirate. Not in a bad way, though . . . *in a movie*! The director of the film in Astoria — the same one who kicked us off the set for Cade's treachery — tracked us down about six weeks ago through information we filled out on the liability forms back in June. He said they weren't happy with the way some of the pirate scenes turned out, and he wondered if Cade would be interested in being in the retakes. "On one condition," Cade told him. "That my sisters can come watch."

"Do you want them to be in it with you?" the director asked.

"Nah, I just want them to see how good I am at it. They'll be totally jealous."

*Such a little pirate.*

While Bree was still on crutches, Grandma Grace finally passed away. It was a sad day, but not unexpected. Surprisingly, she went very peacefully. We were all there with her over a long weekend. The last thing she said was, "It goes by so fast."

I assumed she was talking about life, which is funny because she lived longer than most. "Yeah, Grandma," I told her as I squeezed her hand. "It does."

*Whether you're a baby or a grandmother — or anywhere in between — it goes by so fast . . . and then it's time to move on.*

"Welcome to God's hands," I whispered as she closed her eyes for the final time.

It's the middle of December; today is my and Dell's twentieth anniversary. I'd hoped to be spending the day in Paris, but with the kids still recovering it just made sense to push back our trip by a couple of months. Of course, we still don't know where we're going. As of last week our Winner's Game was tied, so tonight's score will be the one that decides it all.

"You ready?" Dell asks as he slides into bed next to me with his notebook in hand.

"Ready to win, yes."

He chuckles. "I still don't get why you'd choose Paris in the middle of winter, when we could be lying on a beach in Cabo."

"Hey, a girl can dream, can't she? And this has been my dream for twenty years."

"Keep dreaming," he says with a wry

smile. Then he props a pillow behind his back and says, "OK, let's do this. The suspense is killing me." He quickly tallies up his points and proclaims, "Seventy-one. Not bad, considering the late nights I had to work this week." He pauses, and zeroes in on me. "But is it enough?"

With a long sigh, I look at the number at the bottom of my page. "I only got *sixty.*"

Dell immediately stretches his arms in triumph. "Cabo, baby! Here we come!" He leans in and gives me a little peck on the cheek. "Sorry, dear, you'll just have to try harder next year." He hops off the bed and heads for the computer. "I'm going to book plane tickets right away. The closer it gets, the more it'll cost."

I watch him as he walks away. I love watching him. He's so cute when he's happy! Once he's far enough away, I glance down at my notebook again. The number I wrote down and circled at the bottom of the page may say, *"Sixty,"* but I know my actual score is somewhere in the eighties.

*Good thing we don't count each other's tally marks!*

He's been so good to me lately, so willing to help out and do things for me — like bringing me flowers for no reason at all, or staying up late to do the dishes so I don't have to face them in the morning — that I just didn't have the heart to tell him that his effort wasn't enough to win.

*Because it was! He won ME! We won together!*

And if he wants to go to Cabo San Lucas so badly, then that's what I want too, because I know it'll make him happy.

Twenty minutes later, while I'm downloading a new e-book to read, I hear the inkjet printing our tickets to Cabo.

Dell brings them over to show me. "We got pretty decent seats," he says as he hands me the papers. "Now the only question is, do you want the window seat or not?"

I glance only briefly at our seat assignments and then give the papers back. "You choose, dear. I'm fine with whatever."

He hands the papers back to me. "No, you need to take a look at our tickets and make a decision."

To pacify him, I pick the papers up, stare once more at the seat assignments — 19E and 19F — and then set them down again. "Middle is fine, Dell. You take the window."

He chuckles lightly and says, "Suit yourself, but don't blame me if I have the best view of the Eiffel Tower when we land."

I quickly pick up the tickets again and read the details a little more closely: *"Port-*

*land to New York. Then New York to Paris*"!

"Why?" I ask, now wiping at a couple of stray tears. "You won!"

"I know."

"So *why*?"

"Because, I love you, Emily Bennett. Not like the noun. Like the verb." He pauses. "I didn't fully figure out how to play the game until we went out for Grace's funeral. While we were at the house one night, I went back and counted up your grandparents' scores from the year they went to Paris, just to see. It turns out your grandfather won too, and yet they still ended up going where Grace wanted."

"Really?"

"Yep. And that's when it hit me. The Winner's Game — or life, marriage, whatever — isn't about winning at all. If you're focused on winning the game, you're still more focused on yourself. It's ironic, right? To win the game, you have to lose, because then you know that the other person is happy, which is what really makes you happy."

I have to giggle at his logic. "So maybe we should rename it the Loser's Game, because if you win, you lose."

Dell smiles affectionately, then leans in and gives me a heartfelt kiss.

*Oh, how I've loved our kisses in recent months!*

"No, dear. Your grandparents gave it the right name. Because when you finally play it right, no one can lose." He kisses me once more, this time on the cheek, then slides up closer and wraps an arm around me. "*Je t'aime,* Emily."

His pronunciation is terrible, but probably no worse than mine. No matter how he says it, I know it's true . . . because he shows me every day. "*Je t'aime* you too."

# ACKNOWLEDGMENTS

In chronological-ish order, I wish to personally thank the following people for their contributions and support in the creation of this book, prior books, or my career in general:

Robert & Diana Milne — Not just with my books, but with *everything,* you are always there to help, support, cheer . . . whatever is needed at the time. Specific to writing, you once made an investment in your son, and I hope you feel it has paid dividends. I love you, appreciate you, and thank you for everything.

Nancy McCusker — As my high school English teacher, you once said I should consider pursuing writing as a career. You also said I should spend less time sleeping in class, but that's beside the point. The key thing is that you believed in me and you encouraged me to do better. I've never forgotten . . . and I'm still trying to do better.

Jeffrey Lambson — Thanks, man. You read a book, liked a book, published a book, and distributed a book . . . and I can't thank you enough.

Richard Paul Evans — Little known fact, but when I was first getting started I modeled everything I did after you! Is it a coincidence that both of our first published works were Christmas novellas? Nope. I'm sure you don't remember, but at my first-ever book signing (in Sandy, UT) I was randomly paired at a table with you, and I couldn't have been more excited. Thanks for writing books that inspire readers and writers alike.

Joyce Hart — As agents go, you were a peach! Thanks for the hours you spent on my behalf, especially early on. Thanks for getting me in the door with such a fantastic publishing company. Thanks for your guidance and tutelage. And finally, thanks for your understanding.

Christina Boys — With each new book my appreciation for you grows! You are a master at your craft, taking my so-so ideas and seeing their potential. If only I could execute to the level of your vision. [Sigh.] Thank you for your patience, and thanks for buying into the idea that a good novel need not be bad to be good.

Jason Wright — How many blurbs have you given me now? And how much advice have you offered over the years? You've gone above and beyond to be a mentor and friend. Heck, you even put me in one of your novels, which is an honor I will forever cherish! Thank you, thank you, and thank you. I could say thank you till I'm blue in the face, and it still wouldn't be enough.

Rolf Zettersten — You add such a personal touch to leadership, and it has been appreciated for as long as I have been with Hachette Book Group. Thanks for your encouragement and support, and for going to bat for me through six novels!

Mikayla, Kamry, Mary, Emma, and Kyler — You're all growing up way too fast. Stop it! Thanks for joining me on this roller-coaster ride for the past handful of years. I know, sometimes on roller coasters we all just want to throw our hands up and scream, and that's OK. It's still been fun! I love each of you. You're all so talented and awesome in your own ways. Thanks for being the best kids a parent could hope to have.

Rebecca — What else can I say that I haven't told you before? I love you, and that's all there is to it! As this book comes to a close, hopefully I can spend a little more time on the verb and less on the noun, but I love you all the same. You, alone, have made it possible for me to do what I do. I couldn't ask for a better spouse or a truer friend. *Je t'aime* forever and ever . . .

# READING GROUP GUIDE

1. At the very beginning of the book, Ann is given a diary and encouraged to document her thoughts, feelings, and experiences while battling for her life. The attending nurse labels this activity "expressive therapy." In your experience, how does keeping a journal or diary help you sort through your troubles?
2. At the end of Chapter 9, Ann discusses her physical scars. She also reflects on the unseen scars within her family. What are the most obvious Bennett-family scars? Which are the deepest? In your opinion, what sort of scars are the hardest to heal?
3. In Chapter 13, Emily asserts that, "We shouldn't measure lives by their length. There's nothing that says eighty years is better than fifty years is better than fifteen. It's how we live that counts." Do you agree or disagree with this? Why?
4. Would you live your life differently if you

knew you only had a short time to live?

5. Chicken or egg question: What comes first, the noun of love, or the verb?

6. While lamenting the thought of losing her daughter, Emily tells her children the story of a train engineer who knowingly let his child die so that all of the people on a train could live. How do you feel about this story? Emily initially says she couldn't do it; she couldn't stand by and watch her child die when she could prevent it, even at the peril of others. If you were the engineer, what would you do?

7. One line from Chapter 17 poses an interesting question: "We, as a family, treat complete strangers better than we do each other. Why is that? Why are we so hostile to those we're supposed to love, yet kind and courteous to people we don't even know?" Have you ever witnessed or experienced this phenomenon? How do you explain it?

8. Given the circumstances, are Emily and Dell too protective of Ann? If you had a child with serious health risks like Ann, how would you respond?

9. The members of the Bennett family are certainly not without flaws, but they also have some strong points. How would you describe each of their various individual

strengths and weaknesses?

10. Discuss your thoughts on the idea that we can all be "God's hands" in doing good for others. Have there been times in your life where your immediate needs or prayers have been met through the generosity or sacrifice of others?

11. Of all of the characters in the book, who do you think learned the most from playing The Winner's Game? Discuss how this character grew and evolved from the beginning of the story to the end.